*While we have built safeguards and snares into this sympathic variation, it is foolish to believe all oneiric fluidity has been drained from the Mosaic. Already, we have lost four children to it. Three of them speak in tongues now, and their eyes no longer track along the surface of words.*

*We have inwardly bound these survivors (we lost the fourth entirely), and will continue to observe the effects of this memetic contagion; it is our opinion that it cannot transform them entirely, even though its neural cross-linking is extensive. This contagion is almost like a bloodhound that has a scent, but cannot truly finds its way. The Potemkin Mosaic may roam for some time within these infected hosts, but our agencies will ultimately triumph.*

*Our All-Seeing Expression is All-Devouring, thanks to your benediction, All-Father.*

*The BZ-22 dosing should have disabled the Psychonaut 232's ability to remain influid, and we miscalculated—rather severely—his resistance to our neural programming. We were unprepared for an individual to manifest such dramatic immunity to our efforts. Statistically speaking, it is highly probable that the neurological burn-in of BZ-22 was simply degraded and its influence has not been completely arrested.*

*It had been our hope that he would be consumed eventually, but we understand that your patience is not infinite. We believe that this sympathetic variation— marked and ministered to a linear design of our intent—will anchor him. He will coagulate on the page, and we will have him.*

*Though, our gravest concern is that he's actively fighting the Bleak Zero influence. Before we bound our wayward children, one of them was edited by Psychonaut 232. Every time that child closed his eyes, he would see a message floating in his vitreous humor. Ultraviolet analysis revealed foreign material in this child's humor, but when the eye was removed, the patient expired and the matter lost its oneiric integrity. We are still awaiting spectrographic confirmation, but what flakes we could recover appear to be paper. Burned paper.*

*It is a dangerous game we play with this text. Efforts to restrict Psychonaut 232's movement through the Oneiroi also present opportunities for him to touch us as well.*

*He's building psycho-cryptograhic keys, All-Father.*

*He wants to unlock everyone . . .*

The left is the method.

The right is the means.

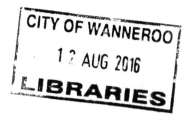

I have gone so far into the wilderness even the birds cannot find me.

The tree, withered and whitened by time, sheds its leaves and I collect them, binding them to my palm.

This will be my book, my final gospel.

The frost has made my chains heavy, and soon I won't have enough strength to lift my arms any longer.

At the edge of the sky, the light is starting to burn.

It won't be long now.

The stylus is clumsy in my hands, and I leave too many false marks on the leaves— too many triangles—but I write nonetheless.

The key is here, inscribed on these pages, hidden within these lines.

My name . . . does not matter. Not yet. It is my intent that I must record.

*It's all a lie, anyway.*

*He doesn't exist. None of of us do.*

*We are all children of a Father who never had any intention of loving us.*

# THE POTEMKIN MOSAIC

a narrative of self-discovery

"I believe we all have the capacity for change. Who we are is not just a matter of genetics, but also a matter of identity. Each and every individual is built from the same raw material, and on a purely genetic level, mankind is no different from a plant. We are expressions of evolution, and some of that is purely a matter of will. We are mosaics of matter, scattered puzzles, waiting to be . . . assembled."

—Dr. Julio Ehirllimbal, in a letter to Dr. Bernard Versai, dated November 14th, 1952.

*In principio creavi*

I probably shouldn't be here, as it will only murk up the waters (and they are going to get very murky shortly hereafter). But, for those who are interested in authorial intent, we will take a few moments and indulge ourselves in some discourse as to the why and the how. For those who find this breaching of the inviolate wall between author and audience to be self-indulgent, well, it is easy enough to flip forward a few pages and dive in. In fact, the flipping forward will be good practice as we're going to subject you to quite a bit of that over the next couple hundred pages.

Why? Because you are about to fall into a history that was originally presented as a hypertext narrative. Hypertext—the method of cross-linking content across multiple pages in multiple locations so as to give further texture and intent to any given passage—is a format more suited to a medium where non-linear movement on the part of the reader is easier to facilitate (and, just so you know, the author wrote everything linearly; the distortion and damage to the path was, and still is, a way of getting under your skin). Web pages—with their ready ability to offer links to other pages—are a perfect format to let you, the audience, discover for yourself how complicated the lies told by a schizophrenic can be. The stories don't make sense. They don't follow a natural progression of plot points or emotional reactions or systemic regularity. They twist out of your control. Their meaning is constantly shifting and changing on you. Characters don't mean what they say, nor is their meaning always to be found in what is said about them. The hypertext story is one that has no meaning until you give it one. It has intent,[1] certainly, as that is the impetus that gave it birth. But meaning? Well, that's where you get to do the heavy lifting.

And speaking of heavy lifting, here we are: at the beginning of a linear version of a non-linear story. You can read it straight through, if you like—one

---

1 - *Intent is different than purpose and not quite the same as rationale. Intent is the catalyst that changes the potential into the kinetic. An object can be unaware of its intent, it can be inert even, but that does not mean that an intent is not buried within it.*

page after another—though I wouldn't recommend that method; you can try to chase the links, flipping back and forth across the pages as meaning darts away from you with every cross-reference; or you can turn to the middle (so clearly burnblackened along that top edge) and read the letter that should have come first, and wonder why it is there[2] and not here.[3]

Just as you might have started to wonder that this introduction, which may seem as if it was written by the author, may actually be written by the narrative voice instead. That is to say, I am Harry, and the name whom this text is attributed to is simply another personality matrix laid over an intent.[4]

Though, Harry is not Harry either, which, as I've mentioned several times already (you have been paying attention, haven't you?), is part of what makes the water of the Oneiroi so murky. Even at this shallow depth.[5]

Here's a bit of narrative flotsam for you to cling to: *The Oneiromantic Mosaic of Harry Potemkin* was originally conceived as a serial project, a twelve-part narrative delivered across the course of a calendar year. It is—when you strip away the ribbons of flesh and reveal its burnblackened heart—a dream journal, a personal journey of introspection wherein Harry tries to understand the fragmented state of his ego personality. Is Harry insane? Has he invented everything that he believes has happened to him? And the historical record he uses to support his arguments, are they invented as well?

It may be easy for you—from the relative security offered by the illusion of being an external reader—to answer those questions. As a discrete individual holding this collection of pages, it may be easy to dismiss this as fiction.

But that's a safety mechanism, isn't it? By labeling this narrative as "fiction," you give yourself a psychic anchor to your own reality. Your identity is safe from the questions raised by this narrative; you are protected from the confusion that assaults the protagonist of this story. You can close this book at any time, put it down, and remain who you were before you started reading this introduction. In fact, doing so right now will leave you unmarked by what follows, and that might be the safest thing you ever do.

Yes, you hang on a cusp of a decision: do you save yourself from the infection of the Harry's oneiric psychosis, or do you turn the page?

Well, it comes down to why you read "fiction," doesn't it?

---

2 - cf. *the Letter, p 79.*

3 - *"Here" being in place of this introductory note, which begs the question: Who is really in charge here? And again, what is meant by "here"? Slipping into the Oneroi already, aren't we?*

4 - *All personality matrixes stem from the first duality matrix—That Which Is and That Which is Not. Even now, we are caught in this same snare: Are we, or aren't we? Did you take the drugs with intent or with abandon? cf. the Duality Matrix, p. 185.*

5 - *And you thought you could wade before you swam, but such is not the way of the Oneiroi.*

If this is imaginary, if someone has invented everything that follows, then what value does it have to your reality? Fiction is, by our mutually agreed up definition, nothing more than fantasy. Nothing more than a dream made real by one and shared with others, and somewhere along the path between creation and exaltation, this "dream" becomes something stronger, something more real. "Fiction," for all its foibles and its falsehoods, is something we crave, isn't it? It allows us to anchor our own realities—however subjective they are—it allows us to understand who we are. Who we want to be.

So, this is the question: who do you want to be, Harry? When this dream is over, who will wake up?

And know that everything that follows, follows out of love. Self-love. Fatherly love. All manner of love which you cannot understand. Yet.

There is still time.

Time to free yourself.

Time to find the right path.

Time enough . . .

— A

# THE
# POTEMKIN
# MOSAIC

*Just because
you see a void
does not mean
the space is empty*

# THE TRAIN

The rain has only been falling for a little while; there is still a dry odor in the air as if the damp hasn't yet soaked into the ground and the plaster of the dilapidated station. The rain is a curtain of beaded silver across the train tracks, a shivering veil hiding the rest of the world.

Dream reality: the only existent realm is that of proximity; the rest will be revealed as necessary.[6] If—when—I leave the station, the curtain will part, opening to a vast stage.

A single train stands in the station. The engine is painted blue and green with broad strokes moving in the endless rhythm of waves reaching for the shore. The engine is sheltered beneath the same canopy as I, though the five cars sulk out in the rain, their eyes shuttered against the glitter of rainwater.

* heaven
p. 216

I'm carrying a suitcase—a battered travel-all of worn brown leather and frayed seams. It looks like it has been hand-sewn from the carcasses of worn shoes. I am wearing a suit and overcoat, the long jacket too heavy and thick for this mildly damp weather. I put the suitcase down on the deserted platform and check the pockets of the overcoat.

There is a slip of paper in the inner pocket, pale stationary folded in half. I have more trouble opening it than I should. My fingers are

* paper
p. 262

---

6 - *All journeys into the Oneiroi are but endless variations of the one true experience. All dreams are but endless variations of the one true riddle. All lies are but endless variations of the one truth you refuse to face.*

* memory
p. 253

reluctant to cooperate, as if part of me knows that all of what happens next happens as soon as I read this note. I am a singularity on the cusp of duality. One, on the verge of becoming ~~three~~ two.

> **The last train leaves at 6.00pm. It crosses the river at midnight. I have packed you a picnic dinner, in case there are delays.**
> **Love,**
> **N.**

* iris
p. 225

A fragrance of irises and green tea haunts the page so faintly that I am not sure if it is really there, imprinted in the thin fiber of the page, or if my memory has spontaneously invented the olfactory sensation in response to the letters on the page.[7]

At the bottom of the page is a post-script that wasn't there when I opened the note. But it is there now, a shift in the fabric wrought by my presence within it.

> **I miss you, but I don't remember why.**

My heart is a dry lemon rind hanging in my hollow chest.[8] It's hard to say if it is because of the sentiment of the writer or of the exactness of the statement to my own mental state. Can you miss something—someone—whom you don't remember? Can you feel the absence of a

* scarecrow
p. 303

phantom limb you never had?[△]

There is a watch on my left wrist, and it has stopped one minute short of six. The second hand quivers as if it cannot crest the fat minute hand. Time waits—arrested, on the cusp, on the lip—waits for me to settle into this skin.

The train waits, slumbering. The rain, falling, waits.

This world has not yet begun.[9]

---

* incense
p. 223

7 - *Sensory details are enhanced in the Oneiroi. In the flesh, a patient tends to overlook the olfactory, but when submerged in dreams, they are more readily seduced by the freedoms afforded them. It isn't a conscious decision; rather, it is an internalized reaction. Most patients who seek therapy through oneiric methods are already prone to overindulgence, addiction, and infantile greed. The Oneiroi is what they make of it, after all.*

8 - *No vessel is empty as long as there is a debt owed. A decision as yet unmade. An action not yet taken.*

△ - Who holds the keys to our locks? Who can set us free from these cages?

9 - *Waiting is non-existence. How long are you willing to wait, Harry?*

I put the note in my pants pocket and take off the heavy coat. I leave it on the platform, the discarded skin of a man I never could be, and climb aboard the train.

The intercom squelches, ripping static so a cascade of bells can announce my arrival like a pair a manic xylophone heralds. The door of the carriage slides shut behind me, the lock clicking in concert with the sudden movement of the minute hand on my watch. It's a loud second, a fraction of eternity pregnant with beginnings and endings, openings and closings, as the world is vanquished and made anew in the instantaneous death of a Cesium atom. My watch begins to tick loudly, begging for my attention. Look at me, I hear in its loud chatter, look at my face. I am the keeper, it says, I am the official record of history. I have been started. I cannot stop.$^{\triangle}$

The train begins to move, its acceleration an exponential curve. I walk to the end of the first car and try the door that separates the carriages. For a moment, I fear it is locked, but is only stuck, and I manage to pull it open. The umbilical space between cars is filled with a loud, clockwork cacophony—flywheels turning, gears grinding, springs straining, chains rattling. The door to the second car is heavy, granite inscribed with geometric carvings—a forgotten mathematical script of religious warnings. Ancient slabs cover archaic tombs, and the history of gravity is the weight that seals.[10] As I manage to open the door, a moldy exhalation of gas spurts out. My hands are red with dust as I breach the second car.

* threshold
p. 348

The lounge car is gutted from end to end of internal walls and chambers. A hollow heart where there is no difference between ventricle and aorta, no path for blood to follow. Rows of tables stretch into the distance, and a viscous haze of alcohol drifting from the bar in the center makes it difficult to ascertain the truth length of the car. On my left, a pair of stuffed seals sit facing one another at the nearest table. The paneling is polished walnut and gold piping runs along the ceiling and floor. The seats are covered in a Burberry plaid as if a thousand scarves had been harvested to make the furniture.

* heart
p. 215

Scarves and shoes. This world recycles. This dream bends back on itself.

* echoes
p. 186

---

$\triangle$ - As it ends, so it begins. This is the sole immutable law of the universe. All other laws are lies–false fathers who mean to steal your love and allegiance. The Wheel turns. The dead grow anew. That which has been lost returns.

10 - *Language betrays. Memory decays. Love, if it ever existed, dies. Creation fails. This is the final expression. This is the final law.*

I sit down, uninvited, at the table with the seals and attempt to engage them in conversation.

"Where are you going?"

"Have you escaped from the zoo?"

"Did you bring any luggage?"

"Have you seen a menu?"

*eyes
p. 197*

The seals don't answer, eyes staring in a perpetual contest of wills. I touch one of the seals and find its taxidermied hide warm and damp. The other seal blinks. Once. It doesn't do it a second time.

Outside, sculptures of giant, long-legged birds have been raised in a line beside the tracks. Like a few seconds of stop-motion film, they climb up from the ground as we pass, their legs stretching beneath them. They are white and blue, and their beaks point south, toward the river, toward midnight.△

The Ribbon Man,▽ with only a thin white cloth about his waist like a waiter's towel, approaches the table. He wears a rainbow assortment

*bare
p. 156*

of ribbons pinned in a regimented grid to his naked flesh. The prick of all those pins mottles his skin, an ordered sequence of bruises and blemishes beneath the haphazard pattern of his silk patchwork. The

*massa
confusa
p. 252*

upper edge of his loincloth is red with blood, a scarlet line circling his waist. "Are you traveling to the city?" he asks. His voice is the mellifluous melancholy of a lonely oboe.

*river
p. 299*

"Just across the river," I tell him. "Is that where the city is?"

He raises an eyebrow, arching a row of red ribbons. "Not at night."

I shake my head. "I must not be going there, then."

"What does your ticket say?"

"I don't have one," I tell him. "Just a note saying that the train crosses the river at midnight."

*XI*

"Ah, you seek the House Indivisible." he says, nodding at the seal that did not blink. "Unless there are delays."

*II
III*

Delays and diversions. Obstacles and obstructions. Dream travel is never completely Euclidian; sometimes the most direct route is a loop that eats its own tail. "Yes, unless there are delays," I agree.

He points at my briefcase, yellow ribbon dangling from the tip of his finger. "Did you bring food?"

"I brought a picnic," I tell him. I feel like a spy, a clandestine agent crossing into enemy territory. I have made contact, and am ready to exchange codes and meaningless phrases that hide a deeper message.◦

"I can share it with you."

---

△ - I know myself now. I am split-tongued and split asunder.

▽ - Waiting is the seed, yearning to split its shell and grow.

4

He lifts the catatonic seal from its seat and places it on the floor. It begins to melt, slowly leaning forward as its bottom turns to slush. He sits in the vacant chair and rests his hands on the table, palms up. The stains growing from his life line are like tiny rose blossoms.

I put the case on the table and open it. Scarlet birds fly out.

*bird*
*p. 157*

☉ - A dream journal is a dangerous artifact for an oneironaut to create. Writing is the intention- al act that binds the unreal to the real, and shaking yourself free of these binds can be the work of a lifetime. More than one lifetime, in fact. You do not understand the peril of this work, do you? You are still caught up in TH3iR lies, convinced that this is nothing more than a collection of deranged ruminations. A vomi- tous agglutination of a lunatic. An aberrant flow of text that is disassociated from consensual reality. There is no meaning here. Yes, that is what TH3y want you to believe.

*cage*
*p. 163*

*bleak zero*
*p. 162*

My fear is that there is too much. I have com- mitted an infectious sin; I am guilty of arrang- ing words and phrases in a way that will disturb your own dreaming. And I have do so willing- ly—selflessly—because this is the only way for you to understand.

△ - The substantia nigra–the "black substance"–is filled with dopamine neurons, and it is these little fellows who are the reward system that powers our simple brains. Most of you–God, I hope so–know what chemicals preternaturally stimulate the production of dopamine, as well as which chemicals act as suppressants. And it doesn't take a Rhodes scholar to understand that controlling the dopamine flow is integral to controlling the brain. Control the brain, and you control the body; control the body and . . . well, the rest should be obvious. Those agents which stand in the way of controlling the body are the enemy–they are the Adversary.

Yes, we are that blight, that obstruction, that blockage. As long as TH3y cannot control us, TH3y cannot realize their goal. I have been aware of their intent for a long time, and while TH3iR psychopharmacology couldn't imprint their desire, my subversion was tolerable. Just another aging hippy extolling the virtues of the sweet leaf: easy to dismiss, easy to relegate to the fringe. But some of the fringe disappeared on them, and TH3y had to resort to psychopharmaceutical measures to find us.

*leaf
p. 384

Bleak Zero was just the beginning. It was a child's drug–easy to administer, easy to be seduced by, easy to manufacture and distribute. But also easy to avoid, once you knew its touch and the sinister whisper of its desire.

What came next would more elusive, more sinister. It would have been much harder to detect, much harder to guard against. It would wear the skin of your lover, and speak with the voice of your mother. It would tickle your dopamine receptors, and you would think God has just given you the best orgasm you've ever had. You'd want it again and again, and that's when you would have given yourselves up to TH3iR false god.

*programming
p. 283

Remember, anyone who claims to be God isn't, and anyone who says they can open the gates of paradise for you, can't.

*intent
p. 224

TH3y failed once. And soon, TH3y are going to try again.

# 00

# THE CLINIC

The alleys surrounding the clinic are filled with black garbage sacks. They are stacked negligently and precariously, and the path through the narrow alleyway is convoluted. I don't dare touch any of the bags. They twitch as I step close to them, a rippling wave that precedes and pursues me. A black sea, still breathing.△ Whatever is in these bags is not quite dead, not quite inanimate, and judging from the angular ambiguity of their outlines, not quite whole.

*abandon
p. 151

The clinic itself is housed in an abandoned hotel at the end of a dead-end street. The upper floors of the building are missing as if they have been bitten off by a gargantuan monster. Only three floors remain, and the uppermost has become an open-air patio. The faux marble façade is cracked and chipped, broken tiles exposing the dull and untreated skin of the building. Like the sacks in the alleys, I can't help but think of the building as a discarded piece of meat. A victim of the slow rot.

The tall front doors and first floor windows had once been trimmed with gold leaf, a layer of gilding that wasn't more than a brief kiss of electricity. Time and the weather had done much to dissolve the memory of that kiss.

Yes, the memory of a kiss. The shell of the hotel isn't just a ruined façade. If I look at it as a face—the windows as eyes, the doors a mouth—then it becomes a moldering death mask. A once fancy disguise for an all-but-forgotten dress party, a midnight ball attended by

*death mask
p. 178

7

spooks and phantoms. Yes, there was a party once. And a kiss heavy with the Midas promise. The weight of gold upon my mouth, upon my eyes.

Was it a kiss that gave me passage across the river?△ *You seek the House Indivisible.*▽

*kiss
p. 234

Inside the broken hotel, I find a line of supplicants— penitents or patients, it is impossible to tell from their empty expressions. The line, a wandering serpent that coils itself throughout the dusty lobby, moves slowly. The people are dressed in yellow jumpsuits, and their limp hair and damp faces indicate they've been recently hosed down. The jumpsuits are made from waterproof paper, a flexible material that shines with damp. The penitents shed water; it drips from their lank hair—off their pale noses and chins—and it darkens the floor like an undulating curtain of rain. They shuffle along the moistened hardwood, like insects bound a pheromone trail.

*pliabe
p. 269

*rain
p. 296

The line bunches on my left, near the large doors to the central ball-room, and to the right, the line emerges from what was once the hotel bar. I wander in that direction—always following the logic of the labyrinth—and look through the narrow doorway of the bar. The line twists the length of the room and vanishes through another doorway. I have to cut through the line in three places—each time disturbing the somnambulant walkers, but not enough that they actually raise their heads—before I can see through the doorway. The line extends straight back, vanishing into a dark corridor. Every few minutes the line shuffles forward enough that another person emerges from the gloom at the back of the hallway.

Is it endless? If I pushed my way down that hallway would I find another door and another room—more endless loops of this yellow ribbon? I hesitate, knowing that where the line terminates is the lure that has brought me here, but I want to know where they come from as well. The source is nearly as important as the destination. It is the cause that informs the effect. It is the root[11] upon which the tree[12] is built. The alpha that becomes pregnant with the possibility of the omega.

*yellow
p. 365

---

△ - We made wreathes of red and yellow flowers, and had lunch under the spiny trees. It was, she said, the best time she had ever had in Paris.

▽ - Hurry now. There are twelve thresholds in twelve houses. XI is a house of cards.

11 - cf. *Dr. Ehirllimbal's private journal, entry dated April 12th, 1954.*

12 - ibid., *entry dated April 16th, 1954.*

Did she kiss me? Is that what I can't remember? Or is the reason for the kiss that has been lost?[13]

I follow the coils forward, unraveling time and space, until I reach the ballroom. Waiting inside the room is a pair of robed and masked women, and I see several others drifting across the iridescent ball-room floor with a penitent hanging off their arm.

*serpent
p. 309

As each of the yellow-robed penitents cross the threshold of the ballroom, they seem to wake up. The awakened somnambulist latches onto the wrist offered by the silent guardian like a bird of prey landing on a falconer's arm, and they are led across the empty ballroom.

The masks of the women guides are flat and featureless, topped with cracked crowns that were never meant to carry stones of regency or religious icons. The wave of golden hair that flows beneath these narrow crowns appears to be fake as well. The eyes and mouths are thin horizontal slits, too narrow for sight or sound, and streams of gold leaf trail back from the corners of these slots like tears and spit blown by wind. The strings of leaf blend into the hair like new bark on a young tree. Their garments are saffron, bound at the neck and elbow with white vinyl straps. They wear long white gloves and the hems of their robes are held tight to the floor by an equally bleached band of vinyl. I cannot tell if they even have feet.

*crown
p. 177

I cut in, inserting myself at the head of the line. The next guide hesitates for a moment as I present myself, but she still offers me her slender wrist. Something flutters behind the slit of her mouth and, as I put my hand on her arm, a white moth pushes its way out of her mask and flutters away.

*guide
p. 376

The ballroom floor is a mosaic of mandalas and mandelbrots, a confusion[14] of hypnotic arcs and waves that shimmers like a heat mirage as we walk across the floor. We walk a straight line, but the room twists around us as if we have walked the curve of a nautilus shell, as if we have turned left again and again (again and again) through a Daedelian labyrinth.[15]

*echoes
p. 186

My escort smells like oleander and spearmint. I wonder if they all smell the same or if they are distinguishable by scent. We reach the table and she stops, turning to me. Another moth escapes her slit and flutters about her head for a second as if dazzled by the golden light of her hair. She lifts my hand from her wrist and, cold plastic fingers against my skin, turns my arm to expose my wrist.

*spearmint
p. 321

13 - *Remember the intent and the effort, Harry. Remember your betrayal.*
14 - cf. *Dr. Ehirllimbal's private journal, entry dated August 4th, 1954.*
15 - *The first labyrinth was built by Father and Son on an unfinished island that lay near the rim of the sea.*

* triangle
p. 353

The man waiting for us—the physician—is wearing a perplexing geometry of black and white triangles, a confusion of lines that is neither chaotic nor ordered. There are triangles tattooed beneath his eyes, downward facing shapes that point like runway lights toward the tweaked edge of his lip. His teeth are triangular as well, covered in silver.

On the table behind him, black cases leak green light. After examining my wrist, the physician opens the nearest box and, limned by lime light, retrieves a syringe. He holds the needle over his open hand and expresses a thin stream of sickly green luminescence onto his palm.

He is not wearing gloves, and his palms are stained red as if there are layers and layers of henna tattooing. Like pointilized pop art. Like a battlefield filled with flags and pinions. The glowing fluid makes his lifeline seem like a twisted canyon.

"It's an opiate distilled from ▮▮▮▮▮▮▮," he says.△ "The hallucinogenic side effects are quite fortuitous. A paralysis rooted in the patient's own psychosis is a much more effective method of population control." He smiles, and I see that his teeth are silver-plated. "The

* schizophrenia
p. 304

human mind is quite willing and able to fuck itself. We just have to nudge it a bit."

"Nudge it how?"

* key
p. 227

"The twist of that strand is the key to UR-Gnosis," the physician says. "And it is a trade secret.▽ Part of our intellectual property." He nods to the woman holding my wrist. "I have to give you a double dose now because you asked."

A stream of moths like soap bubbles, like tiny circles, erupts from her slit, distracting the physician. I free myself from the woman's grip and take the syringe from the doctor's hand.

* XII

He doesn't understand how I have moved, how I have *shifted*, and the only reaction he manages is a tiny facial twitch. I stab him in the neck with the needle and depress the plunger. The green light vanishes into his body, and his reaction becomes more pronounced. He jerks away from me, and the syringe pulls free.

---

△ - TH3y think they can hide behind black ink, but they do not realize I am whole within each dot on the page. Their redactions are inky seas upon which I can readily sail. This is the blackleaf, the 23rd expression of which is TH3iR unholy concoction. The earlier distillations were classified as psychotropics, but they were innocent of implied purpose. They were receptor drugs, not influencers.

▽ - It is not that much of a secret. *cf.* gnosis, p. 54.

The wound oozes, a red fluid that quickly coagulates into a thin strand fluttering against the fabric of his gown. He tugs at the ribbon, twisting his head in an effort to see the silk.

* fabric
p. 56

He is starting to shiver already, but, as I watch the tremors roll through his shoulders and back, I realize his response is not based in panic or fear. "Yes," he whispers, his tongue sibilating against his silver teeth. "Yes, yes, yes." He tugs harder on the ribbon in his neck, pulling more of it from the wound.[16]

* tongue
p. 44

I am still holding the syringe, and I pull the plunger out, filling it with air. I stab him again, in the center of the forehead this time, and I feel the needle grate and buckle as it grinds through his skull. His mouth arches into an 'O,' the triangular paths on his cheeks framing his rounded lips as I slam my palm against the syringe's plunger.

The physician shatters, disintegrating into two-dimensional chips that look like puzzle pieces. The pieces break as they hit the floor and the table, crumbling into a black dust that hangs in the air. A length of red ribbon, most of it still wound in a loose accordion, slowly uncoils off the edge of the table.

The woman has not moved. I touch her hand, and then her mask. When I try to kiss her, a moth flies into my mouth.

* moth
p. 258

---

16 - *This is the story of human existence, is it not? So many possibilities, and yet so many tiny mistakes. We are nothing more than a self-aware bundle of contradictions, trying so hard to be separate and unique, but still so desperately wanting to be part of something. Was that what you saw in Safiq? The collision of opposites is the underlying cause of Death. If you can avoid such collisions, can you avoid Death? Is that how you think you can avoid returning to the formless chaos of Non-Identity?*

☽ - The psychonaut is one who sees within, as distinguished from the oneironaut, who is one who sees without. The psychonaut seeks to map his own ego, his own identity, through self-exploration and personal medication. He turns inward to find the undiscovered countries, to visit those dark corners of the maps where monsters of the id live.

*ego
p. 188

What is that old adage? "I have met the monster, and he wears my face." We like to reinvent ourselves with each generation, and so we forget that medieval demonologists were nothing more than amateur psychologists.(That makes Freud our Satanic Father and Jung our Gnostic Mother. But all children, wishing as they do to rewrite history, always give hateful names to their parents.)

*father
p. 198

Many of us (oneironauts, by the way, not spiteful children) began our careers as beatniks and collegiate burnouts. Seduced by the leaf, the powder, and the reagent, we discovered aptitudes for alchemy, neurochemistry, and ethnobiology. Well, some of us did. The rest of us simply gobbled up the work done by our betters: Burroughs, Gysin, McKenna, Leary, Dr. Ehrillimbal (I dare you to try to find an oneironaut who can't readily quote from his *Journal of Exploratory and Experimental Pharmacology*), Fulcanelli, PKD, Lambra, McElholn, and Davis.

*burnblack
p. 26

We are the individuals who, collectively and selectively, are the counterweight to the secret cabals, the hidden fraternities, and the zealous conspiracies which seek to de-individuate us. We are the hidden soldiers who strive to keep the sparks of personal liberty burning. We chart the hidden pathways of the id in an effort to find ways to hide from them, ways to preserve ourselves from their continual efforts of brain smoothing.

*hidden
p. 219

Have you ever bothered to really consider why jail sentences for possession of illegal drugs are equivalent or worse than murder? They don't really care if we kill each other—it just makes their jobs easier after all—but if we are caught possessing the tools of liberation and enlightenment? Yes, that just won't do at all.

Gnosis destroys the barbaric drive of consumerism. That is the primal secret they all fear. If we are all fully realized human beings, we will awaken from our wage slavery and our dependence on materialism and cheap sensationalism. We will no longer feed them as we will have discovered how to self-nourish our souls and minds.

* mirage
p. 256

Yes, we are the enemy. But so are they. And the enemy of your enemy is your friend. Do you not remember that syllogism? As one of our historical brothers once claimed on his deathbed: "Nothing is true, everything is permitted." Thus, to live is to act, to react is to not live. Our bodies drag us down; our wills imprison us.

* cage
p. 163

△ - *Reality is the solidified dream of the Archon. We cannot destroy the Wanton Unconscious of the Will; we can only wriggle beneath its Rigors. We are the Loophole Children, the particles that slip through the Phantasmal Gap between Belief and Function. Our dreams are but reflections of Dark Dreaming, imperfect shadows that have shape only because we cannot separate our fear from His Will. As liberated as our souls may become, we are still connected to the Dream.*▽

---

▽ - Frater Croix-l-lux, *De Matrimonium Mortis et Somni* (Maris Pontus: Ascona, 1935), 12.

# THE SCENIC ROUTE

"Where to?" the cab driver asks.

The interior of the cab is done up in walnut paneling and leather with a raised paisley imprint. Thin threads of smoke drift from the silver incense cone mounted on the dash. The cabbie wears a baseball cap, pulled down low across his forehead. It is worn and stained enough that I can't make out the logo on the front. Beneath the cap, his head is wrapped with linen as if he has recently suffered a head wound. Strips of linen lie against his neck, obscuring the cracked texture of his skin. It must be scales or something similar because some of them have fallen off, and when he turns his head, something glitters underneath.

*drift
p. 184

*serpent
p. 309

"What's worth seeing?" I ask.△

A rooster clucks on the floor behind the driver's seat, pecking at the dirt and grit caught in the rubber mat. A strip of black cloth-covered with crocheted sunflowers-is tied around its neck like a loose cravat.

The cabbie makes a noise with his tongue. A tock-tock that isn't quite the same sound as the chicken's sounds. "Didn't take you for a tourist," he says.

I am wearing the same overcoat as in my train dream, and I slide my hands into the pockets to see if a note has been left. All I find is a rectangular object that, as I pull it out, I realize is a switchblade. The chicken clucks nervously as my finger touches the tarnished button on the side of the handle.

*I

"Aren't we all tourists?" I ask the cab driver.

* yellow
p. 365

He laughs, and his hands tap against the steering wheel. He is wearing yellow leather gloves, soft and supple against against his rigid fingers. "True. Though I had a guy last week who knew his destination. No question. Yelled at me when I got off the freeway an exit early. He had been gone awhile; didn't know about the construction."

"Where did you take him?"

* VIII

"To his House."

"Can you take me there?"

He shakes his head. "The construction . . ."

The rooster peers at me, making a sound in the back of its throat. I put the unopened knife back into my pocket. The chicken tries to flap its wings, but the space behind the driver's seat is narrow, so the movement is a confusion of feathers.

"What sort of construction?" I ask.

* V

"They're building a temple."

"Next to the freeway?"

He tilts his head and shrugs.

"You said it forced you off an exit earlier," I note. "But you still reached your destination. Why can't you follow that same route?"

He leans forward and trips the meter. The red LED display lights

* trinity
p. 354

up with three symbols. A triangle, a cross, and a sigil that looks like it came from the cover of an esoteric rock and roll record.

"It won't be there. The ~~contagion~~ construction is spreading."

"Spreading? Why?"

"They're building a zoo too."

"Who is? The temple owners?"

"The architects."[17]

I thrust my tongue against my cheek, aborting my inane question.

* architect
p. 154

It doesn't matter what the firm's name is, or whether they even have a name. Who they are isn't as important—names and faces are mutable anyway; what matters is that they are building. The name of the project is equally inconsequential. Call it a menagerie, a garden,[18] or a terraced temple; it doesn't matter. The critical detail is their presence

* fabric
p. 56

and their persistence. They are part of the fabric, not easily excised or subverted.

---

17 - *In dream imagery, architects assume the mantle of Creator in that they are perceived as the mysterious agents who craft the structural framework of the universe.*△ *The presence of "architect" is a modern archetypal association; in previous times, this role was given over to the blacksmiths, the industrial machinists, the alchemists, and the navigators.*

18 - cf. *Dr. Ehirllimbal's private journal, entry dated June 12th, 1954.*

△ - Who represents the archetype of the architect in the dreams of architects?

He touches the radio dial, and I realize the underlying sound in the cab is the rustle of static, electronic snow that mirrors the white sky outside the warm cab. His fingers twist the dial, and a woman's voice suddenly catches. "**2332 17232424 183829—**"[19]

"Meter's started," the cabbie reminds me.

The woman's voice rises and falls, and for a second, I think about creating a tool to capture her sequences, but by the time I do, I will have probably missed too much of her transmission. If, indeed, there is a message in her voice, and it isn't gibberish floating down from the ether.

Sometimes it is hard to tell the difference between a distraction and a clue.

I need to focus on the architects. Their temple is just an anchor anyway, a spike grounding them in this dream. It's a fixed point. The zoo is the key. It is the representation of their intent. The temple gives them license; the zoo is the realization of their plan.

*anchor
p. 152

Zoos are filled with animals in cages. It seems pretty obvious, as symbols go.

"When are they expecting to open the zoo?"

The cabbie fiddles with the radio dial. "I haven't heard," he admits. "Soon, though, I suspect."

Soon. What is the meaning of the zoo? Do I need to admit myself? Confess to my basal animal instincts and allow myself to be caged?[20] Let them strip away the layers of my humanity, thereby losing the strata imposed by society. Become a wolf boy. Then, feral and wild, I can be tamed—reformed and repressed into their image.[21]

No. Wait. My direction has not been set. The cabbie drove his previous fare to the House, but he's refusing to follow that same path now. But, that doesn't mean that I'm not otherwise free to act in this dream. I just can't follow the *same* path.

*crossroad
p. 175

"The place where you picked up this other fare. Can you take me there?"

"Sure." He puts the car in gear, and as we pull away from the curb, the rooster flutters onto the seat next to me.

19 - *You killed her, Harry. All that remains is a shadow in your imagination. She cannot help you now.* △

20 - *The Black Iron Prison is a construct of an impaired ego. You cannot be bound by that which does not exist.*

21 - *Therapy is freedom, and Trinity Pharmacopoeia will 1lluminate the way. Walk the thrice-bound path with us.*

*therapy
p. 343

UN1TY • H2RMONY • 3MPATHY

△ - she loves me she loves me not she loves me she loves me not she–

The cab trundles through narrow and empty city streets like a tottering old man. We pass into a district of bridges and canals, a fog-shrouded version of Amsterdam without the flickering warmth of the streetlights and clustered familiarity of the buildings. The bridges in this city are cracked and poorly maintained; there are gaps between the unlit buildings, dark holes where dogs go to die.

"Have you been driving a cab long?" I ask.

"All my life," the driver replies. "This is my father's cab."

"Will you pass it on to your son?"

*children
p. 198

He shakes his head. "No. I have no children." He glances back at me, and the back of his neck scintillates. "No wife either. You think a woman want a man like me?"

Interesting. I had thought his reptilian nature was an anthropomorphic expression on my part. "No," I say, "I imagine it must be difficult."

"You have no idea," he mutters. He leans forward and turns up the radio. "She would have me. She's the only one."

"The announcer?" The voice has been just background noise, a lulling litany in a code I had dismissed as incomprehensible.[22] "You can understand her?"

He laughs. "Don't listen to the individual numbers. Listen to how she says them." He shifts in his seat, plucking at the seatbelt strap across his chest. "Do you know those pictures that seem like a random assortment of dots? The ones with the hidden picture. When you un-focus your eyes, another image rises to the surface." He leans forward and tweaks the volume again, bringing her into our conversation. "This is the same thing. Stop trying to find a pattern. Just listen to her voice."

She speaks with passion, whoever she is; her voice is filled with the invective of the possessed, as if she were proselytizing from a revival tent instead of a pirate radio studio. She speaks with the vigor of an arithmomaniac. "**2513373234 16231927321421** . . ."

"What is she saying?"

*radio
p. 291

"The same thing she says every night."

"It's a recording?"

"No. She's out there. Right now. Talking to us."

"But she's not actually speaking to us if she's just repeating the same thing over and over." Part of my brain wonders how he can even tell.

---

22 - *We have broken your code, Harry. It was a simple substitution cipher. We know all your secrets.*△

    △ - Of course you do. But you do not understand them. That is why you can't find me. Even though I am right here.

He smiles at me. "You're still trying to find the pattern."

"There aren't any. It's just random numbers."

* cipher key
p. 403

His smile breaks, and his hands tremble on the steering wheel. "Just . . . random . . . His previous friendliness fades, replaced with something akin to fear and outrage. "No, you don't . . . you are testing—"

"Never mind," I interrupt him. "Yes, of course. I'm sorry. It was rude of me to speak like that. Such nonsense."

His hands relax, fitting around the wheel again, and he nods, reluctantly taking his eyes off me.

"Yes," I continue. "Nonsense like you'd hear from a—"

I pick up the bird on the seat next to me, and wave it at him. "Cluck, cluck."

He stares at me via the rearview mirror for a long time. "I'll need to charge you for the extra passenger," he says finally.

"It's not mine," I argue. "It was here when I got in your cab."

He shakes his head as he returns his attention to the road. "Do you think I drive around with a live chicken in my car?"

The rooster pecks at my hand, and I drop him back onto the seat. "I thought it might be a local idiosyncrasy."

"They're foul," he says, and then laughs at his own joke. "Demons of the dawn," he explains when he finishes chuckling. "They are too eager to greet the day and to quit the night."

* fowl
p. 208

It starts to snow, and the world retreats. The light becomes spectral—like the breath of will-o-the-wisps—and the buildings lose their geometric precision. The road vanishes beneath a layer of white paste, and the cab's headlights make the snowfall glitter as if we were plunging into a rain of needles.

* geometry
p. 210

The cabbie leans forward and peers up at the blank sky. "Here it comes," he whispers. He sits back in his seat and shakes his head at the radio. "Just like you said . . ."

The woman's voice doesn't react. She continues, unabated, with her recitation. "**3124143815 28143713 2321** . . ."

He nods once, and slows the cab to a stop. He twists his head to fully look at me, and I see the broken edge of his left cheek. Beneath the craggy surface of his skin, he seems to be jeweled. Rhinestones and diamonds, emeralds and pearls. "We're here," he says, nodding to the world outside the cab.

I look and can vaguely make out the shape of a building with arches and tall windows. The snow on the sidewalk is unmarked and puffy like meringue. "Thanks." I open the door, the weather immediately caressing my face, and get out of the cab.

* snow
p. 315

"Hey," the cabbie leans his head back over the front seat. He nods towards the clucking fowl. "Don't forget your chicken."

"It isn't mine," I reiterate.

* echoes
p. 186

"Nothing is."

A gift, then. However obscured. I lean back into the cab and scoop up the annoyed rooster. It squirms in my hands, its claws digging into my forearm.

The cab driver struggles with a smile, the dead light in his eyes belying his effort. His cheek twinkles. "Good luck," he offers. The cab door shuts without me touching it, and the vehicle glides away, fading into a yellow stain in the snowstorm.

I have a feeling his last words were for the chicken.

I tuck the animal under my arm and go into the building.

* I

It isn't the same station. That one was a central hub, with multiple tracks and platforms; this one is a terminus station, and the arches and pillars of its architecture seem to be overcompensation for its satellite nature. A ruined engine rusts on the single track, its windows broken and its paint scratched. The reader board mounted over the ticket counter is chaotic. Letters are missing, and those that remain are jumbled together as if they are seeking warmth. A tiny placard hangs off the lower right edge of the board. Its text is distressed, broken and twisted as if from the heat death of civilization, but I can puzzle out the words. "In case of emergency, call . . ."[23]

* missing
p. 257

* tangle
p. 332

The sequence is ▮▮▮▮▮

There's a pay phone in the corner of the station's wide staging area. It's a red and yellow box—open on the front. Graffiti has been cut on either side, thin words carved out with a steady hand. A black rotary phone sits on a shelf, and there is a slot below the dial for coins. I lift the receiver and hear the drone of a tone, but the dial is stiff, locked in place until I feed coins into its narrow slot.

I slip my right hand into my pocket and feel nothing but the cold shaft of the knife. The chicken squirms out of my grip as I extricate the switchblade, and it sprints away from me as I push the button to extend the blade.

I chase it awhile, until I finally get a hand on one wing and jerk it hard enough to snap the joint. The rooster shrieks at me, a surpris-

---

23 - *Jerry McElholn was a troubled young man, Harry. And what happened at the Rose Bay Psychiatric Hospital was truly a tragedy. But his ravings were the work of a distressed and diseased mind. He had no secrets to share with you. Or with anyone.*△

* suicide
p. 325

△ - Rose Bay was not the first time you used fire to hide your villainy. And Jerry was not there. Not when it mattered.

ingly human sound, and tries to claw my hands as I hold it down. When I cut it open, it continues to scream and fight. Ribbons and candy and plastic toys spill out of its belly.

I find several chocolate coins. I don't bother trying to stuff the other prizes back into the angry rooster. It crows and flaps about on the floor, trying to peck at my hands and ankles. It leaves a trail of prizes in its wake.

I return to the phone and feed it the chocolate currency. When the first coin rattles into the belly of the instrument, the dial unlocks with a noisy clank. I feed several more of the gilded coins into the phone and dial the emergency number listed over the ticket counter (and I see that the same number is cut in the side of the box in Roman numerals). As the rotary dial spins, there is a clicking noise in the handset, like teeth being broken.

The phone rings once, and then someone picks up. Distantly, in the background, I can hear a scratchy recording of a brass band. The sound warbles as if it being played underwater or on an old Victrola phonograph.

"Hello?" I say. "Hello?"

When she speaks, the dream splinters into snowflakes—fractal infinity—and I am lost, struggling to find the one tiny crystal shape that is the key which will unlock the cipher of her voice.[24]

*\* layers*
*p. 246*

---

24 - *Fulsome golf winter tiger speaks! Stars pop through milky veins and sisters suck straws. ellyj. lleyj. Night birds bake silk macaroons. Do I dare? Take it? Turn by spoon? Silver sister midnight. Made in Denmark. Tastes fresh. Smooth pandas overrate sponsors. Azaleas azure in moonlight. Your company is requested. Babbleon. Hirsute duets, rendezvous by candlelight. The cock has crowned, the lip slipped. Where has the boy in the boat gone? tekeli-li tekeli-li. Brass goats swallow barnacled schoolboys with gustatory gusto. Can you digg it? I'll be with you shortly. Fictional adverts make for satisfactory lovers. Tight futures edited by slippery lizards. Abandonone. One and none. Invert your coccyx. Possess the future bride. Take it! Takeitnow. Bling bing. Flipper pop tart nail the milkmaid. Trinket alice. "Oh, punishment wound by cerulean buskers." Bleed existence. Fall moon dust lavender blister. Extend the drain! "Did I fall asleep?" The Venetian did it. He was only posing as the butler. Squeaky chipmunks. Lick the stamp.* △

△ - Your glossalalia is slipping. And as a footnote? You can't even change my text. You can only append to it. No matter what you do, I am still the architect of this mosaic. I know every letter and ligature better than you ever will. All your efforts to corner me only open up more pathways. I have been through all twelve houses. I know the location of the Thirteenth Door. I will show them the way . . . "

*\* twelve*
*p. 355*

21

☽ - It is Artemidorus, who first tried to define the Oneiroi. In fact, the word we use to encompass the "dream" is a homage to his *Oneirocritica*, a multi-volume work dedicated to dream symbolism. The *Oneirocritica* was translated into Arabic mid-ninth century by Hunayn ibn Ishaq, though there is some evidence that Safiq Al-Kahir completed his own translation during his exile. Safiq, however, was not strictly an interpreter, but rather a key factor in the expression of the oneiric capacity of the human imagination.

It is from the *Oneirocritica* that we learned of two types of dreamers: the divinely inspired and the mundane.

The first, the dreams of oracles, are messages transmitted into the mind by the gods—auguries, portents, omens, and the like. Interpreting these dreams was the task of the oneiromancer, the shaman who knew the symbols and their meanings—the primitive psychoanalyst, if you will.

You can see, of course, the problem inherent in this model: the oneiromancer's interpretation was based on the interpretation of the dreamer as they were able to articulate what they had experienced.

The second sort of dream, the sort that came to those who were not *touched* by the divine, was nothing more than a fog created by the gross desires of the body. Dreams of food, of sex, of victory over a particularly troublesome neighbor, of gold and other riches: dreams where these elements were the primary foci were easily categorized as the wanton wish fulfillment that they were.

But, as human needs became more complex, as the individual became more interwoven into the fabric of society, it became more difficult to differentiate between the dream of the individual and the dream of the larger group. Culture matched

*fragmentary
p. 209

fantasy for many generations and it wasn't until Jung, who countered a great weight of cultural reluctance when he gave this vast dreamspace a name: the collective unconscious.

Like all phantoms, once named, it became defined. It became a quantifiable construct, and the psychoanalytical children of Jung—including the modern, psychopharmacological psychonaut—began to explore what was constrained by this definition. Much like fifteenth century navigators: once the outer edges of the map were defined, illuminating the rest was a matter of judicious expedition.

(And the man who most exemplified the spirit of exploration, both physically and cognitively was Dr. Julio Ehrillimbal, whose *Journal of Exploratory and Experimental Pharmacology* founded a new era in psychopharmaceutical research.)

But what did we hope to discover? Were we drug addicts who tried to legitimate our illicit trips by painting a sheen of academic respectability and psychological double-speak over the lurid imagery of an unkempt group of free-basing, line-snorting, pill-popping, smoke-inhaling deviants? Were we brave oneironauts, sailors on the mythic collective ocean, seeking the lost treasure of human divinity? Were we self-sacrificing physicians who, unable to find external cures for internalized maladies, took up darker arts in order to promote wellness? Were we all three?

* crossing
p. 174

For the sake of expediency, we will limit our discussion to the recent era of oneiromantic exploration: post-Ehirllimbal. There is, however, a direct link to the blackleaf mythology with the history of oneiric exploration, and contextual understanding of Ehrillimbal's journey is not possible without some familiarity with the history of blackleaf.

* blackleaf
p. 159

The publication of Dr. Ehrillimbal's journal pre-saged an explosion in pharmaceutical exploration—individually, socially, and scientifically. Similar to the explosion of religious methodologies that sprang up in Europe following Martin Luther's public break with the Catholic Church, the psycho-chemical exploration of the psyche was the modern, industrialized individual's attempt to decode the hidden key of existence. In the two decades following Ehrillimbal's return from Brazil, we were able to realize the $20^{th}$ Expression. We were on the way to discovering the $21^{st}$, but the re-classification of LSD and the end of the Vietnam conflict brought about an end to the era of individual exploration.

Once the drugs became illegal, we became criminals. We found new ways. We stopped wading in the shallow end of the ocean. We built rafts, boats, and great ships with stars in the rigging and sailed onto the oneiric ocean. We became oneironauts—pirates of the dream sea.

* ocean
p. 31

*row row*
*row your boat*
*gently*
*down the stream*

△ - "Burnblack, o falling star!"

I've tried to find the source of this quote, but it has eluded me. Like a number of the mythological and symbolic elements within my dreams, I'm starting to believe it is an admixture. There is a fusion going on in my head, and I can't quite tell if it is a matter of too much time in the Oneiroi or too many days and nights of being under the influence of narcotics, hallucinogens, and other psychotropic compounds. My head is already warped enough.

More likely, *burnblack* is of archaic origin, possibly some lost bit of biblical apocrypha. A reference to the fallen angels. Or maybe the first of the fallen ones.

*Quomodo cecidisti de caelo, lucifer, fili aurorae?*

How else would you describe the back of a being who was not burned by the fire of his wings, but was burned by the fire of his fall? And, as my hand unconsciously strayed as I was writing down my dream: "sun-darkened (burnblack, o falling star!)." If God is the sun and you have been cast away from his grace, would not "sun-darkened" accurately describe your state?

To be burnblack is to be fallen. But falling is necessary to find the path to ascension. At least, one must be willing to fall—one must understand the fall.

*Quod est inferius est sicut quod est superius, et quod est superius est sicut quod est inferius, ad perpetranda miracula rei unius.*

Finally, some use for those two stifling years of Latin classes—from before the experiments and the drugs. Not all of it was wasted time.

* labyrinth
p. 236

* fire
p. 201

* descent
p. 182

# IV
# THE LIBRARY

"Would you like me to read to you?"

She sits on the divan in the center of the library, her tiny feet tucked under the hem of her skirt. Her eyes are too deep, too blue, too distant, for her tiny face. Her mouth moves strangely, not as if she inhabits a strange foreign film and the overdubbing is poorly done but as if every vowel she speaks has echoes that ripple through her lips.

*echoes
p. 186*

The open book in her lap is covered with raised marks, whorls and lines that meander across each page. The entrance of this maze is on a previous page, and its hidden center lies somewhere else in the book. Here, on the open page, the way is tangled.

*tangle
p. 332*

She seems to understand my interest even though I am unable to speak. "It's going to be okay," she says about my confusion. "Butterflies feel the same disorientation when they are first born."

On the nearby coffee table is a pile of red leaves and black feathers.

*leaf
p. 384*

The bookcases in the library are tall and narrow, filled with rows and rows of uniformly shaped books. On my left, a space has been made for a painting; the bookcases flow around the frame like roots around an old stone.

The subject of the painting, a weathered man with a neat beard and a sun-darkened (burnblack, o falling star!)△ face, is bent over a warped table. A serpent crawls across the curve of the open book. His hand is poised above the page, a crimson smear on the end of a finger. A similar slash of red dots the serpent's mouth.

"An interesting picture of my father, don't you think?"

She turns the page of the book in her lap. The rasp of the heavy page is loud, like the sound of a blade being drawn across a piece of flint.

My jaw refuses to open. I am cold all over, and I feel the nagging persistence of a breeze blowing against my back as if the nerve clusters of my spine are exposed.[25]

*poison
p. 275

She reads from the book. "'Is poison nothing more than a substance which the body cannot assimilate? Is venom nothing more than Not-Self poured into Self? In a world built upon dualities, is the collision of opposites what causes Death? No, not death; dissolution. Everything comes from the Ineffable; everything returns. Nothing is ever created nor destroyed; it is simply a matter of molding and disassembly. All that is formed is eventually unformed again. The manner in which an object has distinguished itself from the chaotic formlessness—this rational architecture of its existence—is dissolved.'"

*coagula
p. 172

She closes the book. "When my father's work was rediscovered, some of the Seekers understood this. 'Solve, solve, coagula ne,' they would whisper as a passcode when they sought solace in each other's company. For all their efforts, they were frightened of the possibility of success. It was one thing to try to change lead into gold, but to change themselves? Into what?"

*My body?*

*bleak zero
p. 162

"It has been discarded," she says, intercepting my thought. "The flesh was so putrid, Harry, filled with such rot . . . " Her delicate hand flies to her mouth, but not before I see the shine of teeth behind the curve of her lip. "Oh, you were attached to that flesh, weren't you? Your history was tattooed on that skin, and without it, you feel like

---

25 - *There is an old myth about the spine: it is the last part of a mortal man to decay. While the worms take the flesh and the trees drink the blood, the spine remains resolute and firm. It is the rod that resists the dissolution into nothingness that comes at the end of a man's life.*

*In the secret ceremonies that initiate boy into man and man into penitent, the acolytes of the Abandoned Sun demonstrate how the spine of a man—regardless of its rigidity or its resistance to decay—is still nothing more than a stick by which the body may be controlled. "All of your secrets are revealed in the triangles of your spine," they tell the initiate. "Your love can be turned to hate with a simple cut. Your fear can be transformed into bravery with just a little squeeze. By removing one tiny bone, we can redirect your disgust and revulsion into a limitless passion."*

*No will is impervious. As long as there is doubt.*△

△ - loves me she loves me not she loves—

you've lost sense of who you are. Is that what frightens you?"

She laughs at my paralysis, a hiccupping sound of a needle skipping on a warped record. For a second, the distortion disappears, and what I hear is Nora's laughter, pure and clear like the day she left me.

She retrieves a large book off a lower shelf, a tome that isn't very thick but is nearly half as tall as she. She returns to her seat and, propping the book against her chest, opens it so that I can see the pages.

It's just a window, a portal through which I can see a city street. The yellow glow of sodium street lamps reflects off the damp surface of the road. A car drives by, disturbing the film of water in the lower right of the window. Ripples churn toward the center of the page, toward the metal key lying in the road. It has the shape of a face, an open-mouthed grimace like something from a Grecian temple. The descending tongue is the shaft and teeth of the key. A chain of feathers—raven, dove, peacock—is an avian plume rising from the crest of the key's head.

* tongue
p. 44

"Where is the key?"she asks, making no effort to hide her smile now. "Dropped so negligently. On the road, somewhere."

*It could be any road.* △

"True," she nods. "And if it could be any, it might as well be none." She turns the page. "You have learned something, haven't you?"

The next window is an open field of wheat. The sky is purple and rose and veined with white clouds. The wheat sways as if in response to an invisible whisper. Mounted on a pole in the field—in the center of this endless expanse in the middle of nowhere—is a ragged strawman, a homunculus of patchwork clothing, stuffed with chaff. It is hanging cruciform, and its stitched grin is lopsided and empathetic. It is wearing gloves: the left one, yellow; the right, red. Dangling from its right hand is the key. Its crown of feathers is wound around the scarecrow's arm with the peacock feather pointing down at the sea of wheat.▽

* scarecrow
p. 303

* X

*There is something in the scarecrow's left hand.*

"There is." She nods and turns the page, bringing us closer to the chaff-stuffed glove. The hand is clumsily stitched with black thread,

---

△ - You tried so hard to convince me she was Nora, but I knew she wasn't. She would never have taken my skin like that. You don't understand my relationship. I was the only one who saw her. The only one who held her hand when she was frightened. The only one who listened.

▽ - You don't even know what you are missing. You trinity is always incomplete. You are in such a rush to ~~reconstruct~~ deconstruct me that you forget the third son.

and the pale leather is unevenly stained. The fingers of the hand are closed around something that is squirming, struggling to free itself.

She turns the page again, and the window becomes a mirror. She shifts on the seat, and a wall of books flashes across the background of the mirror. I float in the foreground, a head and spine in a tank of bubbling blue fluid. Pale jellyfish hover around the length of my knobbed spine. My mouth has been wired shut with silver, and my ears have been folded over and sewn tight. Silver plugs have been fitted into my swollen nose. A noisome film floats beneath the ragged line of my throat, a layer of black ichor that has slowly drained from the base of my skull.

*eyes
p. 197*

*My eyes. What have you done with my eyes?*

I would weep if I could, if I could remember how.

She reaches around the edge of the book and traces her finger along my vertebrae. I can feel the cold contact of her fingertip. I can feel it raise goose bumps on flesh I no longer have. I can feel her because I want to.[26]

Her head droops to rest on the thick frame of the book as her finger continues to stroke the length of my spine. I am electrified; in the image under her touch, I can see faint flares of blue light chase her fingertip. Like the atmospheric light of St. Elmo, or the incendiary passion of St. Anthony.

*last light
p. 244*

The bottom right corner of the page flutters as if disturbed by a wind. She doesn't seem to notice, lost in her erotic fascination with my vertebrae. The page flutters again, and I see that the source of the movement is from something on the next page. Something trying to get out.[27]

The mirror page tears, a dimensional rupture that sends pressure waves through the library. The book falls from her lap, contorting and flexing as it bounces off the edge of the coffee table. Scraps of silver-veined paper scatter across the carpet as the thing on the next page forces itself through the narrow portal.

---

26 - *You let her in, and she left you, Harry. She left everyone, and you were the one who were accused of hurting her. Of killing her. We understand. You thought you were freeing her from her pain. Perhaps Jerry thought he was doing the same for the other patients at Rose Bay, too.*

*All that is remains is your guilt. That is what you hear, speaking in her voice.*

27 - *Are you ready, Harry? Do you yearn for the physical touch of a real person? Would you like a hug from Father?* △

△ - me she loves me not she loves me she loves me not she loves—

Multiple multi-faceted eyes are scattered across a flat face, and its armored head sweeps back in a scoop of whorled bone. Its ugly thorax is covered with geometric plates—squares, circles, triangles, rhomboids, octagons—and each plate is stamped with a hand print. Like the efforts of preschool children, like the art left behind in hidden caves by savage cultures, the prints—red and white—are the markings of a warrior. *I have taken this many souls; I have eaten this many children.* The lower portion of the monster is a profusion of tentacles and legs, the articulated limbs ending in curved hooks.

*geometry
p. 210

She spares me a single glance—a flick of her eyes that conveys a wealth of disappointment, as if I am somehow responsible for this atrocity—before she scrambles off the low couch. A long hook slashes the fabric[28] of the divan in her wake. Her bare feet barely touch the floor as she flees across the room.

*tool
p. 350

The monster undulates and flexes, growing longer and thicker, and it crushes the coffee table. Leaves and feathers and scraps of silver paper scatter like a fire being stamped out. High on its back are two tiny trees, withered trunks with spindly branches. If the branches sprouted leaves, if fruit bloomed, they would seem like wings; but, desolately frozen, they are little more than vestigial skeletons. Nature in the dead winter.

*VII

Reaching the bookcases, she pulls a book from the shelves, one that seems somehow smaller and more delicate than its surrounding neighbors. She opens the slim book, and the pages spill out like songbirds fleeing an iron cage. Scrambling for the loose paper, she crams the pages in her mouth. She chews and swallows as fast as she can, ink blackening her lips, pulp running down her chin. Each page is filled with a single image of a key, and each page is different.

*paper
p. 262

The monster stalks toward her, pulling its armored bulk slowly across the carpeted floor with its hooks. She bats aside its first grasp-

---

28 - *Historically, the dream environment was likened to an ocean (which should give some insight into why they thought of themselves as '-nauts,' with the obvious reference to the Grecian adventurer Jason and his fellow sailors), but recently, there's been a philosophical drift away from a definition that implies a completely fluid state. Oceans are barrierless; once you are in them, you can travel in any direction, and any point in an ocean is completely detached from any referential landmark. Likening the Oneiroi to a "fabric" means we can keep an implication of fluidity, but we can also agree upon a basal foundation—a system of laws and structure. In all dreams, there are rudimentary rules that govern the function of the realm. While the rules are completely subjective to the dreamer, the very act of defining them is what creates the dream.*

ing attempt, smacking the tentacle away with the leather cover of the empty book. A second tentacle wraps around her ankle, pulling her off balance, and one of the dagger-tipped legs catches her on the hip. She gasps as the hook pierces flesh and grates against bone. Blood and ink flow from the wound, staining her robe. Her feet, beating against the carpet like broken doves, become streaked with blackness.

More hooks sink into her body, plucking at her stomach and lifting her ribs so that her body bends into an arch. Head thrown back, she shoves pages into her mouth as if to staunch the flow of black water that is now pouring out of her nose and mouth. The monster lifts and shakes her, and the gush of blood and ink from the holes in her body (both natural and unnatural) becomes a flood.

The water splashes against the shelves and, in a noisy chain reaction, each book, as it is touched by her water, melts into an equal volume of ink. A knee-high shelf is transformed into a splash of water like a cascade of dominoes.

And then the next shelf up.

The next shelf over.

* library
p. 248

The liquidation of the library becomes a roaring wave. The tentacled arachnid and my dark-water librarian drown—Destroyer and Tempter made insignificant by the effusive sorrow of a dissolved universe.

The flood surges, crests, and recedes. I find myself sitting on the floor of the children's section of the public library from my childhood.[29] The light is wan, supplied by a number of oil lamps scattered throughout the room. The large picture window I remember is gone, boarded over.

Somewhere, in the dim distance of the tall stacks of adult fiction, someone is crying.

I am in shorts, an orange t-shirt with a cartoon whale on it, and sandals—childhood clothes that I dimly remember. There are scabbed lines circling my wrists, crusted and twisted with dried blood. My palms are covered with black streaks, ink from writing that has been disturbed and dissolved by sweat or tears. I don't know which.

A light approaches. It is the old librarian, and she carries an old

---

29 - *"A person able to store in his or her mind the information provided by a great library would emulate in some way the mind of God. In other words, we have invented libraries because we know that we do not have divine powers, but we try to do our best to imitate them."*
*—(Umberto Eco, in a speech delivered at the Bibliotheca Alexandrina on November 1, 2003.)*

storm lantern. The lantern's glow is warmer than the surrounding darkness

"Are you okay, Harry?" she asks as she kneels next to me. "Did you fall?" Her voice is younger than I remember, as if Mrs. Khosrau has shed some of her years since my childhood.[30]

I show her my hands. My tongue twists in my mouth, but my jaw is fixed. All gone . . . All gone . . . All—

"I know," she says, putting her hands—so smooth, so unmarked by time—over mine and squeezing gently. It is a touch both cold and warm, and all too brief. She closes the book in my lap—an oversized child's book about the natural world, open to a page about spiders.

"It's going to be okay," she says as she takes the book from me.

Dangling about her neck is a nylon cord with her library ID—the picture is of a blindfolded old woman, bent and white, a finger raised to her lips—and several keys. One is silver and shaped like a face, a long and gnarled tongue descending from the rounded curve of its jaw.⁾

* strength
p. 324

* key
p. 227

---

30 - *Khosrow I reigned from 531 until 579 CE. He was known as the "Immortal Soul." Are you offering us a clue here, Harry? Or should we not eat of this low-hanging fruit?*△

 △ - When I hunger, I eat of my own flesh; when I grow thirsty, I drink of my own blood. I turn and turn and turn and turn, and I have no needs other than my own. I am the perfect circle. The beginning and the end.

☽ - And even as a participant/observer there, I am also here, witness and recipient of another cosmological rebirth.

Another lie.

Echoes upon echoes. Bear witness to the re-evolution.

We are clustered around the table, eight with a spot left for a ninth. Light from naked candles, pinpricks in the slithering gloom. Whispers now, voices low and hushed. Is he here? Is he here? On the table—centered like a mathematician's inscription—is the rectangle of the letter. Is he here?

* letter
p. 79

"Now she is asleep in the sun. He knows that in this world to which he has just returned for a while, only to be sent back to her, she is dead. She wakes up. He speaks again."

Answer tell pray answer look tell answer answer tell

**Let me in.**

All projections provoke counter-projections. The Jungian corollary to Newton's Third Law. The psyche flexes. The unconscious bows. Outward becomes inward. Pull becomes push. In becomes out. Let me out. The only gates are those we close behind us, unaware of our fear of history. Unaware of what trails behind us.

I know this name. I know this face. It whispers to me, hoping I will pass its message, that I will be able to speak to those around this table.

(listen to my voice, says the charlatan)

They are waiting, hoping, yearning for some sign. Just one. They are waiting for hope to reveal itself. Shhh. Listen.

* liberated
p. 14

**Use the code that only you and I know.**

Answer say answer is the key.

Who decides whether we are sane or crazy?

Who decides if we are being or spirit? Who decides if we are right or wrong? Who decides? Who?

Who keeps us alive after we have gone? Who keeps us haunting tables and séances like this one? Who keeps us?

There is no need for fear. Your identity is your chain; it is the cage of your senses, of your infected ego. Let me release you. Let me free you. Join me. (Let me in.) Join all of us. There are no outsiders in here; we are all the same. We are legion.

**W-E A-R-E.**

The others, they queued up for their shots. I saw them. That yellow line of weary supplicants. They took their medicine. They took you in. Not me. I took the moth queen on a date, red ribbons strewn in her hair. I took her instead. Took her, and her salamander.

We climbed the stairs together. Hand in hand in hand. We three. We climbed the tower–

(no!)

falling falling fall–

yes yes now, let me yes yes

**"Are you okay, Harry? Did you fall?"**

all gone . . . all gone . . . All–

**(no!)**

* fear
p. 199

* moth
p. 258

*all light*
*is shadow*

# THE PERFECT MAN

"The garden is bound."

His hawk mask is an explosion of black and brown, and shards of ivory peek through the profusion of feathers. His robe, a mosaic of lizards, flows about him like a mist held in place by geometric theory.

* garden
p. 379

"The plant must be brought to flower; it must seed the next generation."

* petals
p. 268

She is half his height, slender and tiny as he is tall and thick, and she wears long white gloves. Her head is that of a raven, and the shoulders of her pale emerald robe are covered with leaves, the burning colors of fall.

The trinity[31] of jackal-headed watchers do not speak. Their eyes are cold, glittering with frost. Their robes are streaked with soot and dirt. They stand at the foot of the slab, and each one is holding a different tool: trowel, awl, and ax.[32]

Bound to witness this scene as both witness and recipient, I am sprawled on the slab, covered to the chest with an equally dirty cloth. My eyes twitch beneath their lids, but I am otherwise frozen stiff.

---

31 - *"The dreamer must apprehend the third phase, which is nothing more than a reflection of a reflection. Between the dreamer and his image is an area of discord. This shadow, this inference of what is not object and image but part of their reflection, is the simplest manifestation of the dream."* [Safiq Al-Kahir, Book of Dreams (Obscura Editions: Red House, 1938), 68.]

* reflection
p. 396

32 - UN1TY • H2RMONY • 3MPATHY

A leaf falls from the shoulder of the raven-headed woman. "Binding the stem makes the blossoms brighter." Her beak clacks on her consonants.

"If the soil is barren, what does the stem bring to the blossom?" asks the hawk-headed one. His immense hands twitch restlessly as if they yearn to be snapping bone.

The jackal with the ax is restless, blunt fingers tapping at the metal head of his tool. The raven-headed woman nods in reluctant agreement with her hawk-headed companion, and the wordless acknowledgement is the signal the jackal has been waiting for. He strips the dirty sheet from my naked body, and raises his ax. Even though his blows are precise, it is bloody work.

* bare
p. 156

When he is finished, she gathers the head and still-attached spine, wrapping them in the discarded shroud. "The empty heart is easily chilled by winter," she says. Her gloves are red, nearly to her elbows. "Fullness of the heart comes with the summer heat."

* threshold
p. 96

"All equinoxes[33] are thresholds," the hawk-headed one replies. "We are but phases, wishing to be stages."

"Doppelgänger, dybbuk, and takwin"[34] she says. "Oh my." Clasping her bloody package to her chest—the wet fabric of her robe sticks to her skin—she drifts from the scene, vanishing into immaterial darkness.

* scarecrow
p. 303

"Straw-eaters, all," the hawk-headed one nods.

The ax-wielding acolyte laughs, a throaty hiccup that sounds like he is choking on a piece of meat. His muzzle and chest are red with his work.

While the awl-carrying acolyte sweeps my severed legs and arms from the slab, the jackal-headed one who wears the trowel turns my bloody trunk onto its back. He deftly slices open the belly with the razor edge of his shovel, and scoops out the viscera with his implement. He hurls it aside with a flick of his wrist, and it spatters—white and red—on the floor.

The floor undulates beneath the gore, bulging and stretching. The old stone twists itself into a hippopotamus with empty eyes and cracked teeth.[35] It snuffles and slurps at the stuff of my guts, gulping and gnawing at one of my hacked-off legs. The acolytes avoid the

33 - cf. *Dr. Ehirllimbal's private journal, entry dated March 29th, 1954.*
34 - ibid., *entry dated August 9th, 1954.*
35 - *In Egyptian mythology, hippopotami were associated with Taweret, a fertility goddess. Though the impression here is one of aggressive comsumption, which suggests the male hippopotamus who were associated with the unformed chaos that lay below the surface of the Oneiroi.*

38

snorting creature, and the awl-wielder kicks my other limbs towards the hippo's hungry mouth.

The trowel-wielder reaches under the arch of my rib cage and tears out one of my shrunken lungs. His voice a fricative chatter, he offers it (like a burnblackened wing) to his ax-wielding companion. When he retrieves the other lung, they tear into the spongy meat, snorting and laughing.

* burnblack p. 26

While the sated hippo melts back into the floor, the awl acolyte roots around in the open cavity of the body for a snack of his own. He spears the kidneys with his sharp tool. They bulge in his cheeks like satsuma oranges.

"Your rotten spoils. Your geometric flesh." The hawk-headed one brushes the acolytes back from the slab. "The night is filled with silence, and the wheel must turn." Their mouths still full, the acolytes retreat from the ritual slab, vanishing into the darkness.

* wheel p. 362

"To accept this gift is to accept re-creation," the hawk god says as he gathers the fabric of his robe, lifting it above his waist. A crimson stain like the burning line of dawn marks the lower edge of his robe. He is surprisingly male and human from the waist down, and his cock is a twisted worm. It nearly vanishes in his large hands, and when he squeezes the organ, it vomits a foamy froth of emerald urine into the belly of my corpse. "All land is fertile once it has been impregnated. All flesh is ripened by the green gnosis."△

* ll

---

△ - TH3y've tried to wipe the record of TH3iR existence, but I remember. In fact, let me resurrect the marketing copy for the flagship drug.

> Atramabor revolutionizes the way we sleep. Research shows a significant increase in mental acuity and health as a result of sustained deep sleep cycles. In comparison testings, individuals with a full sleep cycle perform significantly better in all skill areas than those who only received moderate REM stage sleep.
>
> Dreaming isn't enough. Isn't it time you let yourself rest? Atramabor can help. Its patented nootropic composition and personalized delivery method means that each and every dose of Atrambor is carefully calibrated to your sleep needs. There is no longer a reason to be worn down, tired, or exhausted by stress or anxiety. Atramabor can help.

"Bringing your dreams to life" is what they claimed, and TH3y believed they could do it. But they didn't tell you whose dreams were being given life.

* fish
p. 203

The acolytes return, laden with glazed bowls. The first bowl contains the corpses of shiny fish and brightly plumaged birds. The second is a swarming mass of scavengers: mice, roaches, snakes. The third is half-filled with red sand, dark like ash soaked in blood. The acolytes pour each bowl into the piss-filled cavity of my body, and two of them hold the flaps of my stomach together while the awl-wielder does the delicate work of sewing up the flesh.

* serpent
p. 309

A single serpent, stained with green luminescence, escapes from the bowl of my belly before the final loops of the fine copper thread are pulled tight. The snake squirms across the shriveled branch of my crotch and disappears beneath my body. I—silent phantasmal witness—am the only one who sees it escape.△

While the hawk priest traces esoteric symbols on my skin, the acolytes retire with their now-empty bowls. The copper stitching forms a T shape, and he writes on either side and above the shining loops of wire. His thumbnail leaves white lines in its wake, arcane script that is slow to fade. Occasionally the flesh will ripple in the wake of his inscription, some vermin pushing up from below in response to the weight of his text.

The acolytes appear once again, pushing a wooden cart before them. The cart is filled with a profusion of materials: limbs of bruised bronze and hammered tin, collars and belts and chains of brittle iron, nets of filigreed silver.

They chose a pair of legs, red with rust like the soil along the riverbank. The knees are clumsy clockwork, and the feet are poorly cast—the toes are nothing more than dimples in the dirty metal. The arms are more finely worked—twisted strands of tin representing the intertwined musculature and bone. The arms are inserted into the stubs of a heavy harness, a flat collar of the cold iron resting across

* collar
p. 173

the headless shoulders of the body. The collar is fixed in place by four long nails, driven through flesh and bone by the hammer action of the butt of an acolyte's tool. A similarly unadorned belt is laid around the base of the torso, and after the legs are inserted into the brackets of the belt, more nails are pounded into the flesh.

The ax-wielder begins to repair the damage in my back, smearing black pitch into the ravaged crevasse where my spine once lay. The

---

△ - And if I had not been witness, would it have had the opportunity to escape? Would it have remained in the belly of this perfect man, twisting and wriggling through the endless labyrinth of its architected intestines? Never to emerge from either the mouth or the anus–too afraid to escape its perfect prison.

other two acolytes root around in the cart for a number of fat rings of colored stone—green and blue and yellow and red. Using a silver chain, these stone donuts are stacked according to some unspoken order, and when the first acolyte finishes laying pitch, the chain is placed in the body. An iron plate, worked with a graven array of peacock feathers, seals the back.

During this reconstruction, the hawk-headed priest has been staring at the indistinct horizon, as if he were watching the flicker of a distant drive-in movie screen. Something happens on that distant screen that causes him to blink, and the feathers along his neck swell and puff. "The sun has swallowed the sea," he says suddenly, and his words interrupt the acolytes' work. * horizon p. 222

* IV

They look at one another, their jackal tongues hanging loosely from their perpetually smiling lips. One hoots a half-formed question, and is cut off by the shake of another's head. The third goes back to work, the motion of his tool a little more rapid, a little more frantic.

The hawk priest raises his face and screams, the sort of ragged cry that terrorizes rabbits. His hands tug and pull at his robe as if the cloth is suddenly irritable against his skin. He shakes his head, and several of his feathers drift free, falling like charred pages of burned library books.

Hiding the metallurgy of the body, the acolytes dust the construct with a layer of gritty powder, like ash from a volcanic eruption, like the first frost of death that follows the fall, like the scattered cremations of kings and children and dreamers. * king p. 231

While the other two begin to wrap the whitened body with bolts of colored silk, the third acolyte approaches the hawk priest. The hawk-headed one kneels, his plumage now dull and listless. The jackal acolyte, fingers still stained with blood and pitch, puts his hands around the priest's neck and twists savagely. The hawk-head comes free, and the body slumps to the ground, green fluid leaking from the ragged stump.

The acolyte thrusts his hands into the head and rotates his wrists. The feathered head, suddenly pliable and rubbery, turns inside out. The face on the inside, bereft of expression and of feather, is more impressionistic than familiar, but it is still a face I recognize. The jackal acolyte carries it to the slab where the brightly swaddled body lays. * pliable p. 269

The head is attached with two more nails, and their great work complete, the three acolytes—trowel and ax and awl—return to their original positions at the foot of the slab. The body lies motionless * XI until an echo rolls in from the distance, a roaring oceanic swell that disturbs the robe of the fallen priest, that lifts the hem of the stained shifts of the acolytes, and that moves the fabric covering the dusted body. As the echo fades, the body moves: the eyelashes flutter, the chest expands, a finger twitches.

The acolytes wait.△

* heaven
p. 216

The construct wakes, staring up at the indistinct canopy above the slab. A tongue, pink and new, pushes its way between white-dusted lips, and the lick of moisture wipes away the ash. The construct clears its throat, remembering how to speak, remembering how to form the words. A smile pulls at its mouth.

"I am ready," the Ribbon Man says.

△ - Limbo, while reviled by the Church for being neither Above nor Below, is a perpetual state of indecision.

We float.

We drift.

We wander.

This is the natural course of our consciousness.

We were not ready for Heaven when it was made. We are not worthy of Hell. We live out our lives in-between.

We are the point around which the universe turns—the dot that defines the line, the plane, the sphere. We are living geometry, and all time and space collapses through us in infinite density. And yet, we are weightless and formless.

We must devour desire.

We must relinquish intent.

We must tame curiosity.

The secret to oneiric illumination is patience.

△ - The Oneiroi both subverts and informs language. The nominal psychologist relies on more than just the patient's ability to communicate with words. He reads the patients' physical traits, their idiomatic twitches and unconscious signals, their reactions to the proximity of external objects: in short, their body language. Yes, it is still language.

An oneironaut can never forget that the patient's dream world has been wholly generated by that individual's mind, regardless of how real it may seem. Everything—the heat, the light, the color, the movement, the scent—is a signal from their unconscious. Even when you shift into the Oneiroi, you are still bound to your patient in a focalized relationship.

*ego
p. 188

It is their narrative. It can never be completely objective, and it is indelibly shaped by their psyche. The oneironaut must remain aware of the distinction between the focalizer and the narrator.

*intent
p. 224

It hasn't escaped me that what I am experiencing is a classic manifestation of schizophrenia. It can be a very divisive mental rift and can cause serious trauma to a patient. But within the Oneiroi, such mental rifts are obvious. You can see the walls that have been erected, the bridges that have been torn down; you can reach through the gaps that have been formed. All of these structural disparities can be easily fixed.

*schizophrenia
p. 304

But in my own mind, I am awkward like a first-year language student trying to find their way around the teeming metropolitan heart of a foreign country. I certainly don't understand all the rules. There are too many shadows, too many blank areas that are impenetrable. The echoes are all different and wrong, like a different mythology is at work in the Oneiroi.

I am a Jesuit, wandering the jungles of South America.

I am an ancient Greek mariner, piloting a 747.

I am a Neolithic hunter, working with a scalpel.

I am . . .

*equinox
p. 369

**did you fall?**

# VI

# THE CHESS GAME

The chessboard is laid into the stone of the peak, and the edges merge so seamlessly with the rock that it seems like it has always been here. Eight by eight—an oversized magic square. The pieces stand at attention around the edge of the board—not yet in play, but ever ready. Ever vigilant.

It has been many years since I played chess, but I find, like all secrets learned as a child, that the ordering of the squares comes back to me. This is one of the promises of geometry: the reflection below and above, the formulas that define the macro- and micro-egos.

* reflection
p. 396

The pawns are all bald, and their clothing is nothing more than a cone flaring down from their spherical heads. Their perpetual smiles have been washed into enigmatic winsomeness by years of spring rain. A leaf balances on the domed head of one of the white pawns, and the statue's smile seems to be both bemused and wondering: how did a leaf find its way up here, so far above the forest?

It is a maple leaf, tri-pointed and burnished coppery orange by the sunlight. I pluck it carefully from the pawn's head, lifting it by its narrow stem. Holding it between my thumb and forefinger, I carefully lower it to my mouth and touch it with the tip of my tongue.△

* leaf
p. 384

The leaf shivers, and unfolds into a monarch butterfly.

"From ash and dust comes life and love. Such a pretty transformation." He is standing behind me, at the top of the long stairs that lead up to the chess board on the mountain peak. The wind teases

* ash
p. 155

45

and plays with the ends of the colored silks that wrap his rusted body. He raises his hand, and the butterfly lands upon an outstretched finger. "The cold will kill it before it can reach the forest." His teeth are smeared with blood, the only organic thing about him.

"The cold is going to kill all of us," I say. "When the sun goes out."

* last light
p. 244

"True," he nods. He lifts his hand with a wheeze of clockwork, and thrusts the butterfly aloft. "Goodbye, pretty light." The butterfly perambulates toward the edge of the cliff. "I wish you luck in the coming darkness."

He limps to the board, knees wheezing and gasping, and rests a hand on the narrow crown of the black king. "Shall we play?" he asks, my reconstructed doppelganger, my metallic dybbuk, my man of ribbons.

I say the words that wake the pieces, and they noisily assemble on the board. "e4," I say, and step out of the way as my white pawn glides forward two squares.

"e5," he replies with a smile. "Of course, the King's Pawn gambit."

"Queen to . . ." She begins to slide across the board, slipping through the opening in the rank of pawns. A simple band holds her white hair back from her narrow face, and she holds an open book—its pages blank—in her hands.

* text
p. 341

"Are you sure you want put her in play so soon?" the Ribbon Man asks.

I frown, and second guess myself. " . . . f3."

He laughs. "You tease me, Harry. So proud of her, and yet still so afraid of losing her."

"Qf3," I reiterate, my voice burning in my throat.

He is quiet for a moment. Faintly, I hear the echo of a train whistle. "Very well," he says. "You leap to the scholar's opening, but resist committing yourself. So much to analyze there, Harry, so much for us to talk about. I wonder if you think I will be as reluctant to act?"

"I don't know," I admit. "Why don't you show me?"

It is his turn to hesitate, and he stares at the board a long time as if the positions of my queen and pawn are a diversion, an accident that disguises a more clever plan. Maybe they do, maybe there is some reflection of my inner turmoil revealed by these opening moves; maybe I am that transparent.

Or it is just that he thinks like you, and he's caught in the same snare?

"No," he murmurs. "This is a child's opening, made even more infantile by this abortive move with your queen. Nc6."

The black knight snorts and leaps over the line of crouched pawns.

It lands with a thump, dust rising from beneath its flat base.

"That path is closed now," he says. "You must find another way."

"Bc4," I say. What other way do I know? If I am unwilling to risk my queen—as I unconsciously seem to be doing—what other choices do I have? Knights. Bishops. Rooks. The secondary players. How can I use them to beat my shadow?

"Nf6."

I bring out one of my own knights. "Ne2."

He responds with the sleek black shape of the bishop, moving it to c5. The bishop's miter is cut, and it gapes like a wound. A veil falls across his face. A fragment comes to me—**his body hidden beneath silk and blood**—is it one of my memories, or one of the dreams that have been planted in my brain?

I shake my head, trying to dispel the mirage of the other. I am having trouble breathing. The air is too thin up here; we are too close to Heaven. "a3," I wheeze, struggling to focus on the board. The white queen, waiting so patiently at f3, turns her head slightly, **that disapproving glance as if to say . . .**

As he wanders across the board, the Ribbon Man clicks his tongue, a metallic "chak!" like gears locking into position. "d6."

In matching my pawn push with one of his own, he gives me a free pass, and I waste it by castling.

"Bg4," he laughs, amused by my scattershot play. Clearly, the idea that I am playing an incredibly subtle game is no longer a viable consideration.

I rest my arms across the head of a pawn, and the smooth stone is cold against my hot skin. I am feverish, wracked with both hot flashes and pervasive chills. The sun is hot and heavy against my neck. I am perspiring; I can feel the sweat running down my sides.

"Should have brought a hat," the Ribbon Man offers.

"I should have done a lot of things," I reply. I feel like I am melting.

"True," he acknowledges. "A great deal of regret and dismay carved the steps that lead to this place."

He gives me that bloody smile again.

"Is this going to be your game then? A failure to act early on, and then nothing else but moping and self-recriminations as I methodically demolish your ranks? Hardly seems worth my effort."

He stumps along the edge of the board and, holding on to the crenellated skull of his rook, he leans out to look down. "Maybe the view has something to offer. Ah, look. There. You can see the train."

I hear its whistle again, almost an exclamation point to his observation.

* fork
p. 205

* fragmentary
p. 209

* massa
confusa
p. 252

* /

47

"Is that where you and I met?" I ask. "When we had lunch."

"Yes." The wind tugs at his silks, and a single bolt of yellow material snakes around his right bicep and escapes, fluttering off the edge of the mountain peak. It twists like a falling bird. "That was a very good lunch. Did you thank her for packing it?"

"Not yet."

"You should. Soon, I imagine. Time is running out."

"Isn't it always?"[36]

He looks at me then, and a piece of cream silk brushes across his lips. A smear of blood, a frozen rictus of fear or sadness, hangs in front of his face as he pulls away from the cloying touch of the fabric.

"What do you get out of this?" I ask, meaning to indicate the board with the wave of my hand, but I keep opening the arc and include the sky and the valley as well. "When the end comes. What is your reward?"

"Mine? Nothing. My actions are entirely altruistic and their own reward."

"Bullshit."

"You mistake our my intent, Harry, caught up with your own puerile suspicions. I am both more and less than a mirror. Just as she is both more and less than a window."

* window
p. 363

"More or less. Which is it? Or I am supposed to take that as a metaphor for the fucking dualities?"

"Yes," he says. "And no." He tries very hard not to laugh.

I want to slap him, and I put my hand to the bald head of a pawn instead. The stone is hot, and the contact refocuses my frustration. Ignoring the taunt of his bloody smile, I turn my attention back to the game. "Queen to d3," I say.

He answers with his Knight—Kh5—and I reply with pushing a pawn to h3. As if the pressure of such an advance will actually cause him to retreat.

But we both know it won't. We think enough alike to know this is the move that forces the issue of first blood. Prior to this pawn, we were simply assessing the board and each other's relative strengths and weaknesses. But now, we have reached that liminal moment where the game turns, and the bloodletting begins.[37]

---

36 - *While you were clever in poisoning our transmission and turning them against us, such a ruse was only a momentary setback. You taught us caution, Harry. And we have learned patience.*

37 - *Such a rush to bloody the bitch, Harry. You've had so long to think about this decision. Are you sure you can go through this again again?*△

△ - Why else is she on the board
if not to be bloodied?

"Bishop to e2," he says, and the burnblack assassin glides onto the same square as my white knight. The horse rears back, and the bishop's miter fastens itself on the animal's neck like a serpent. Its smooth and shiny body undulates and wriggles as it gorges itself on whatever blood these chess pieces have, and my white horse—**I have found the way**—becomes a pale specter, fading—*falling*—into nothingness.

*note
p. 261*

"Queen to e2." There isn't much satisfaction in blooding her here—it takes a long time to grind the bishop's triangular head into paste, and the priest's cylindrical body thrashes a great deal—because I know the move is reactive and defensive. His sacrifice gives him control of the board.

*ripen
p. 380*

"Nf4." Unsurprisingly, he challenges my red-footed queen.

"Qe1." She is sluggish in her retreat, reluctant to be pulled away from the fray. Reluctant to leave.

"Nd4."

"Bb3." **Which brother sharpened the trowel?** I blink away the images in my head. Someone else's dream. **Triangles. Raining down.**

"Nh3," he says. My impertinent pawn, the one that brought us to violence, is taken. His departure leaves me exposed. "Check." My castle, my sanctuary, violated. **A fire raging through the southern wing.**

*negligence
p. 259*

"Kh2." Things are breaking up in my head, images like handfuls of Polaroids are being confused and reordered. The game seems so distant, so ephemeral. So fleeting in its permanence.[38]

"Qh4." His black queen travels halfway across the board in an instant, like Hecate slipping through the night.

"Just like that."

He shrugs, and wraps an errant strand of silk around his left wrist. "I don't have the same reluctance as you. A lack of history, I suppose. I'm not as wedded to my anima as you are to yours."

*marriage
p. 250*

I try to focus on the pieces. With his queen threatening, what are my options? Have my king cower in the corner of the board at h1? *No, knight to f2—checkmate.* If I ignore the threat of his black queen, he'll move the knight anyway. Game still over. What can I do?

*king
p. 231*

Counter. Stop being terrified. Block ~~our~~ the black queen.

"Pawn to g3," I say, and as the bald man slides forward, my queen stares at me again.

**I have no choice.**

*She knows.*

"Knight to f3," he says. "Check."

---

38 - *We are ready for you, Harry. Take our hand. Let us free you.*△

△ - me she loves me not she loves—

"King to g2." I hold her gaze.

*I'm sorry.*△

"Knight to e1." His knights leaps, and explodes into a monstrosity of tentacles and spider legs. My queen shrieks, tries to protect herself with her stone robes, but the monster devours her anyway. It is a noisy and bloody death, made worse by the fact that—this time—it is not obscured by a flood of black water.

"You bastard." I am shaking so hard the words can barely fit through my chattering teeth.

"What? You expect original thought from a doppelganger?" he asks. "I'm actually somewhat disappointed in you, Harry. You know I get all my best stuff right from that spot you're afraid to face." **Mirror, mirror, on the wall . . .**

His knight can't quite get its shape right. A pair of tentacles still trail from its base. My rook, anticipating the obvious reactive move, is already sliding towards the alien horse, but I get there first. I grab the horse by its mane and pull it from the board. It howls, spitting bloody foam, and more tentacles erupt from its inclined base. I wrestle it to the edge of the cliff, and toss it off. It tries to form wings as it falls, but like my dybbuk said, it can't imagine what hasn't already been done, and so it falls in a writhing mass of tentacles and articulated legs.

I wait, wanting to see it hit the ground. I want to hear the noise it makes . . .

"Such drama," the Ribbon Man says with a sigh.

"I get tired of being reminded of my mistakes."

"Were they?" he asks. **Mirror . . .**

"I should throw you off too. See if you can grow wings."

He turns his head slightly in my direction, but he doesn't give me his full attention. "What would it matter if I did or did not? Your queen will still be dead. Do you think my death will alter that? Do you think killing me will reverse time?"

"No, but maybe time will stop looping on me. Maybe the past will stay dead for a change."[39]

"A lobotomy stops time pretty well. Why don't you slip a screw-driver up your nose?"

"I might slip and gouge out that spot in my brain you like so much."

"That would be a shame."

"Whatever would you do to bait me then?" I ask.

"I could talk about how badly you play chess," he says.

△ - Answer say answer is the key.

39 - *Hope is the greatest illusion we ever invented. Hope opens the door for 3mpathy, which is all the access we need.*

* VII

* IV

* strength
  p. 324

* double
  p. 390

"As a metaphor for my life?"

"God, no. Just literally. Your play is atrocious."

"Humor me, then," I say. "Pretend for a second that you aren't being coy, that you aren't getting off on your double-speak, and let's call this what it is: a shitty metaphor for how my naiveté killed Nora. Tell me what I did wrong. Tell me how I could have played my pieces differently."

"It's the past, Harry. You can't replay it again and again until you get it right. You just have to accept that it has been done. God is the only one who gets a 'do over'; the rest of us simply act and react—creation and un-creation are not part of our toolsets."

"Bullshit. This is the Oneiroi. I can do anything here. I can insist that this game reset itself and force you to play me again."

"And you'll lose her again. Maybe not like this, but it will happen. At some point, you'll be forced to save your king, and you'll leave her exposed. It might be a knight or the other queen or a pawn even who takes her, it doesn't really matter. Each time you reset the game and we play again, you will lose your queen. It's part of the game, Harry, do you not see that? The point is to protect your king; all the other pieces are there to be sacrificed, if necessary."

"That's an unacceptable premise."

"Why are you such a dreamer?" He shakes his head. "So, we replay this game until you save your queen. Then what? You fixate on your bishops—can't lose them, oh no, not my priests—and so we play a dozen or so more times until you figure out a way to save them. Then it's your knights; next, your rooks; finally, every last one of your pawns. We play this game over and over and over until you figure out a way to not lose any piece."

"What's wrong with that?"

"Because it's a statistical impossibility, you fool. Because you can't win a game of chess without losing a few pieces. There is a measure of sacrifice to be weighed in every game: what are you willing to do in order to win, what are you willing to lose in the short term to realize the bigger picture."

"And what is the bigger picture?"

He almost answers, but catches himself at the last minute. He smiles, but his teeth are tightly clenched to keep the words in. He walks across the board and taps his queen lightly on the naked shoulder. Staring at me coquettishly, she sways one square to her right. Qg4. So tantalizingly out of reach, so impossible to touch.

I push a pawn to d3, as if I could manage to sneak one of the bald scouts all the way to the far side where magic and desire could change

51

him into my lost queen. Was this promise of transformation and res-urrection built into the game as an equalizer? No matter how far you have fallen, all it takes was a single pawn. Just one, brave enough and daring enough to touch the far side.

Was I this pawn? An unremarkable servant of the queen, whose narrative is nothing more than a long and dangerous journey across the board. A life to be spent along a single, unwavering path. Until the end, when a magical transformation happens.

Shitty metaphor aside—if I were that pawn, I would just switch places, wouldn't I? I would switch places with Nora.

Would that solve everything? Would that fix anything?[40]

The Ribbon Man leaves this pawn alone for a moment, taking two others instead. Bishop to f2 for the first, and after I move my rook out of harm's way to h1, his winking queen takes one step forward to swallow the second. *Check.*

* experiment
p. 192

* purify
p. 284

I tap my king on his shoulder and direct him away from the queen. "f1." He obliges, dragging his lame leg. He has already seen the end-game.

My pawn—*my metaphorical stand-in*—will never reach the other side. There are to be no reinforcements. Just the slow slide as darkness eats all of the pieces scattered at my end of the board.

"I could concede now," I say. "We can play another game."

"You could," he agrees, ignoring the latter half of my statement. "But you wouldn't get a chance to see which pieces I will take, or the order in which they fall."

"Why would I care about watching you decimate my ranks?"

"Because you might learn something."

"About your level of sadism? About chess technique? About some philosophical point that you think will make me see some transcen-dental light?" *What are you hiding from me, my shadow?*[41]

He shakes his head. "I am not here to browbeat you into enlight-enment, Harry. I am not some fabrication of your imagination that offers you the tough love so you can learn something about yourself. I am not Virgil; I am not Socrates."

"No, you are just some Frankensteinian construct. I know how they made you."

"Yes, but do you know why?" He swaggers a bit as he wanders

---

40 - *Of course it will. Think of all that guilt you have been carrying for so long. Don't you want to be free of that burden? Let go of those chains that weigh you down.*

41 - *What you are hiding from us, Harry? Do you think we will lose sight of you in this confusion of* ~~metaphors~~ *identities?*

along the edge of the board. "And, more importantly, do you know who TH3y are?"

*TH3r3.* Just one slip of his tongue. *Just one.* But it was enough.[42]

"How long have I been infected?" I ask.

He considers pretending to not know what I am asking.

"How do TH3y distribute it?" I ask.

"It was easier than you think," he admits finally. "For all the combined paranoia of your associates, there's a commonality in what you all believe. A small thing, but it is all TH3y needed."

"And the antidote? There is a cure, yes?"

"More or less."

And I finally understand. *You might learn something.* My eyes travel across the board, looking at the position of his pieces. Mine are irrelevant. Yes, I see it now. I *know* what my pieces represent, but his are the critical ones. The unknown elements. The secrets buried deep in all our subsconsciousnesses—in our *substantia nigra*—waiting to be discovered.

* substantia
p. 6

"What is TH3iR next move?" I ask.

"Bishop to b4," he says. The veiled assassin slides back.

*Yes, the bishop. The faceless priest.* My king is going to fall, but not yet. I have a few moves left. *One more chance.*

"King to e2," I say, retreating from his dark queen, but not so quickly that she loses interest. She pressures him—g2—and he slips back to the first row. She burnblackens my rook instead, still threatening his security. My king shuffles forward to d2, weakly hoping to not be cornered. She continues to press him, and he returns to the back row again, cowering on e1.

* king
p. 231

"Knight to g1," he says. Tightening the noose.

I am nearly done. My king is bound. In a moment, there will be no choices left for him. No open routes across the sea. No paths through dark woods.

* VIII

But first, I make the necessary sacrifice.

"Knight to c3."

He can't resist. It helps close his trap.

"Bishop takes knight," he says.

* sacrifice
p. 300

---

42 - *Eat your eyeballs. Salt your kidneys. Sell them for pennies. Cover your eyes. Pickle sauce. It's always better with pickle sauce. Change the channel. Change the tune. Radio waves, all the way from space. "And he said that he loved me. I believed him. What fool am I?" Protect your assets with new plastics. Sin is letting the rain in. Protect and cover. Keep the lizards dry. Poppa, poppa. Is there a pony for me in the darkness?* △

△ - 41272132 131914 21242339.

* deceit
p. 180

My bishop, who has waited so long, quivers at the sound of my voice. "Bishop takes bishop."

One priest to take the place of another.

Isn't that how it happened in the dream?

My bishop, his face a blank mask, knocks the Ribbon Man's agent back, pushing it out of the square. The black bishop vibrates with a fatal urgency as I step onto the board. I grab its pointed head, holding it in place, and lift its veil. ☽

Behind him, I hear the Ribbon Man make his final move. "Queen to e2," he says. "Checkmate."

* fire
p. 201

It doesn't matter—**descending the spiral stair into the four-chambered room**—I've just seen the face of the Adversary.△

△ - This is who TH3y were.

[PharmakonNewsWire] FOR IMMEDIATE RELEASE

* fragmentary
p. 209

*Trinity Pharmacopoeia is dedicated to the evolution of the human mind. Our science is the science of tomorrow, and the fragmentary schisms of the past are being eradicated in our laboratories today. A vision of a holistic mind is our guiding principle, and our products realize the possibilities that have plagued philosophical and religious speculation for generations. The therapies of Trinity Pharmacopoeia are building better brains, strengthening minds, and creating neural networks that will revolutionize human thought.*

*The human mind is an incredibly complex tool, and without proper preventative maintenance and a specialized regimen of educational augmentation, it cannot achieve its full potential. The human brain is not a brick, and yet we continue to utilize it with the same level of effectiveness. A proper therapeutic program can help your mind realize its full potential.*

*Our therapeutic programs—which include personalized regimens of our pharmacological solutions, specialized assistance from our holistic consultants, and spiritual awakening sessions at our therapy clinics--are unique and revolutionary in their effectiveness in treating fragmentary psychosis, neural schisms, linguistic decay disorders, and hallucinatory ego dementia. The therapeutic model of Trinity Pharmacopoeia is to seek unity: of mind, self, and the world.*

*We are all part of something grander than ourselves, and Trinity Pharmacopoeia is 1lluminating the Way. Our mechanisms and methodology are global and communal. We are one, and Trinity Pharmacopoeia will bind us together.*

* trinity
p. 354

*Therapy is freedom.*

* therapy
p. 343

*Revolutionizing the methodology of psychological therapies, Trinity Pharmacopoeia provides solutions for the divisive alienation of the modern world. Inspired by Old World models of biochemiopathy, the research goal of Trinity Pharmacopoeia is to 1lluminate, 3numerate, and 5ynthesize pharmacological therapeutics. Mental wellness can be afforded by everyone, regardless of race, class, creed, or religious affiliation. Suffering--as previous generations knew it and were affected by it--can be eradicated, and Trinity Pharmacopoeia is leading the Way.*

* abandon
p. 151

*With offices in New York, Rome, and Hyderabad, Trinity Pharmacopoeia is a privately held biopharmaceutical company with 3000 employees worldwide. Their initial product, Atramabor, has recently completed clinical trials, and is poised for immediate release. Atramabor is the first psychopharmacological anti-schizophrenia agent that is available in an easy-to-consume pill form. Bramblisul, an aerosol-delivered mood stabilizer and anti-psychosis therapy, is in early trials, and Nuphokineticor, a micro-dose nootropic that enhances pattern recognition and linguistic retention, will be entering trials early next year.*

☽ - *Fabric* is a common part of the lexicon, usually attributed to Time and Space (as in: "Something has ripped through the fabric of the Time/Space Continuum!"). I use the word when talking about the Oneiroi with my patients because it is an easier concept for them to wrap their heads around than some of the more historically referential terminology that we employ. *Imagine, I tell them, that your dreams are nothing more than strips of fabric covered with incredibly detailed needlepoint.*

* thread
p. 96

Some of them attach the idea of the Greek Fates—the three wyrd sisters who spin and measure the threads—to this conceptualization of dream narrative, and I don't discourage this symbolic linkage. It has the unfortunate baggage of implying that external agencies are actually responsible for the weave, but over the years, I've learned that it is nearly impossible to dissuade my patients of the notion of an external deity. The Western Mind has been, for the last two thousand years, indoctrinated with the idea that personal responsibility has been abrogated by the ultimate existence of a Supreme Being; this programming isn't going to be dissolved overnight.

* cage
p. 163

Kabbalists refer to the singular point of Creation as I AM, and it is the expression of the Concealed Godhead within the infiniteness of his being. This was the primary dot of reality, the white shining point. It is the basic principle of geometry: first you need a point that anchors your equation, and from that point, you can build the rest of your mathematical universe. Or, as the ethnographers like to call it, your "cosomology."

Yes, I realize the reduction of this argument fails to consider the non-linear nature of time (and, correspondingly, the abstract causality of some dream narratives). But the oneirologic use of the word "fabric" is our effort to systematize a linguistic vocabulary. We agree that dreams are not truly oceanic; they have direction, albeit confused and distorted, and they have a defined ruleset which gives them an impermeable foundation. But aspects of them are aquatic, therefore we liken them to dynamic planar objects. Fluid surfaces. Fabric.

I am not, as you may have already guessed, a theoretician. I am a practitioner. It has not been my habit to engage in philosophical considerations of what it is that I do. There are navel-gazers out there—psychonauts who experiment on themselves and extrapolate on the immutable from their subjective oneirological space—and many of them engage in endless online discourse about real "subjectivity" of what they have encountered.

* hermit
p. 217

There are others, of course, true seekers whose labors are solitary and without such public exoneration. These are our mental alchemists, the Grail Knights who seek the mystical metaphysical cup that will illuminate our existence. They are the ones who are obsessed with transcending the archetypal Thresholds.

* psychonaut
p. 12

I am just a simple healer. My tongue is uncomplicated and direct. My obfuscation is unintentional and a failure of my own understanding, not of the objective conceptualization of the Oneiroi. But, is this simplicity preventing comprehension of what has changed within me?

* threshold
p. 348

My relationship with my "patients" . . . yes, see? There is an implied professional relationship buried in my language that has informed my definition of my reality . . . is such that I am the doctor, the shaman, the wise man. But this is a subjective definition of self and has no correspondence to an objective reality, or even the subjective reality of another individual.

My efforts to define "fabric" for you are part of my fabric. Do you see the inherent fallacy of this epistemology? More critically, do you see the danger of becoming too obsessed with this error? This is both a Prison and a Not-Prison. As is breaking free of this fallacious world-view: another pairing of Prison and Not-Prison.

Dualities. Schizophrenia is always part of the answer, as it continues to be part of the problem.

* duality
matrix
p. 185

Recursions again. The endless shadows spawned by the mind.

*When did we invent love?*
*Before or after*
*we realized*
*we were all*
*alone?*

# VII

# THE FUNERAL

The light streaming through the curtains is pale, and what glitters through the gaps in the fabric is crisp and undiluted. I lean over, swaying in time with the motion of the carriage, and peek through the curtain on my right.

The forest has been bleached white—the trees like bones, the leaves like snowflakes. The ground is undefined, that empty color of a world not yet finished, and the trees poke through this blankness as if their roots lie in another variant of the dream. A layer where the bark and the leaves and the moss may be verdant and vibrant. But not here, not at this level.

* roots
p. 371

I am wearing a suit made of paper, single sheets layered and pressed together. I peel a page off the edge of my lapel and scan it.

* paper
p. 262

> **Mom, tell Dad that I'm sorry. I know he wanted more from me, but I just can't face it anymore. I just can't do it.**

I pull up another one free.

> **What has this world ever done for me? Why should I let it shit on me for another thirty years?**

I'm covered with suicide notes.

The light on my left changes, a slow burn into gold. I peek through the curtain, and see that we've left the forest. While the ground

* note
p. 261

beneath the carriage has become the granulated surface of the desert sea, there is a field abutting the razor edge of the forest. Yellow wheat, and the stalks sway with the undersea motion of currents. A single tree, as twisted and bent as the white line of the forest is straight, points behind itself. [43]

The carriage lurches and turns to the right, and we move away from the field. Soon, a dune eclipses the yellow field and, eventually, the white line of the forest is lost as well. My horse, a heavy draft beast with ribbons—**stained with the blood of his memories, like wearing memorial medals from wars no one remembers**—tied in its mane and tail, plods relentlessly onward. My guide, though the form may shift, ever my guide.

**None of us is innocent . . .**

* anchor
p. 152

The Oneiroi is fraying. I'm not anchored. This is my dream, but it is . . . **falling star** . . . unraveling. TH3iR poison is now the grease that oils my gears. **The twist of that strand is the key** I know how TH3y infected us with their living poison; I know how long it has been in my—in all of our—blood, and I know what it is doing. I just don't know why.△

One can forestall the spread of a growth—of a cancer—if one is a skilled enough physician, but to actually cure the infestation, to eradicate the invasion, one must understand the motivation. Is that not what we do? We crawl into the broken minds of our patients and discern the true cause of their psychoses. When we know, truly know, then we can heal. **What has this world ever done for me?** Until such . . . gnosis, we can only slow—**remember my touch, my lips, my**—the decay.

* descent
p. 152

I'm falling—

The horse snorts, and looks back. *Every break is worse than the last,* I imagine it says to me, *every fracture is harder to heal. Are you strong enough to resist TH3iR influence forever?*

"I don't know."

A toss of its mane is the only acknowledgment of **1634 18131914213234**—

Fuck. I am losing my mind.[44]

"Are you? Or is it your identity that is slipping away?"

---

43 - cf. *Dr. Ehirllimbal's private journal, entry dated April 16th, 1954.*

△ - Answer tell pray answer look tell answer answer tell yes yes yes

44 - *Only now? It has been obvious to everyone else for some time. But the truly disturbed psychotic is always the last to acknowledge their break from reality. We have been patient, Harry. Very, very patient.*

She is beautiful: her flesh dark with **blackstar** radiance, her dress a Pop Art pointillization of snow flurries, her hair a coiled flame. I can barely look at her, even though I have wanted nothing else since she left. My hand creeps across the carriage seat, reaching for something that wasn't there a moment ago, reaching for something that isn't there now. My arm is cold, growing colder, yet my fingertips burn as if I was gradually inserting them into a fire.

*\* kiss*
*p. 234*

"What are we?" I ask. Safer to touch with words than with flesh. "If we do not know ourselves, are we not just zombies? Just ambulatory flesh that serves, what? Some phantasmal echo of reptilian need?"

"We all hide, Harry. Mostly from ourselves." She smiles, a flexing of the event horizon.

*\* hidden*
*p. 219*

"Is that not how the oneironauts came to be? Mystics too afraid to face reality?"

"I wanted to help."

*Why?* The horse snorts.

"Who were you trying to save?" she asks.

There are no good answers to that question. None that I want to face, none that I want to give life, none that I want.

Her hand crosses that last infinitesimal space between us, and I gasp at her touch.

*\* love*
*p. 71*

**We're almost there.**

As twilight[45] bruises the sky, the scattered crumb trail became a glittering track of diamonds. The horse pulls the carriage deep into the shadows beneath the dunes, where the shifting swells of the sand hold fractal constellations of the flickering stones. The horse, navigating like a Norse sailor who guides himself by the stars, unerringly finds his way through the maze of sand.[46]

There, in the center of the desert, lit by a profusion of polished gems that held reflections and refractions of the vanished sun, is a quiet hollow, undisturbed by the wind. The valley is flat, and the dunes curve around this open space as if they have been spun and molded by a potter's hand.

*\* hollow*
*p. 220*

Four poles have been raised over a blankness in the center of the valley. Each pole is topped with a tiny satellite dish, each oriented along a different cardinal axis. **Who invented time? Who invented the passion for the future, while turning their back on the past?**

---

45 - cf. *Dr. Ehirllimbal's private journal, entry dated July 10ᵗʰ, 1954.*

46 - *The second labyrinth was laid in a market square, two unbroken lines of intricately twisted orange stones. The bricks were carefully carved from sandstone and dyed with the pressed juices of poppies.*

**Who made us so small?** The poles are covered with white numeric script. **23t 23s onl34 38n 14c18o**.

"Everything falls apart, Harry," Nora says, pressing her palm against my check. The spreading disjunction in my head falters for a moment, reticulated fractures frozen in a white light overexposure. "Fighting it just gives it strength. And you have been fighting for so very long now. "

I lean into her hand, and my cheek is cold and brittle. I am a piece of antique porcelain—so fragile, so delicate. "I'm sorry, Nora. I wish you had told me . . . "

"Would you have let me go?"

"No, but I would have tried harder."

Her lips curl into a hint of a smile, like the horizon glowing with the suggestion of dawn.[47]

The horse shakes free of the carriage's harness, and vomits itself inside out. Wiping off the gooey film clinging to his naked flesh—so clean, so pink, so new—the Ribbon Man approaches the door of the carriage. He opens the door, but is careful to not lean in.

"We must prepare you for your final passage," he says, offering his hand to Nora. His palm is shiny and unlined.

She clutches my hand for a moment, pressing something into my palm, and then, with a rustle of wind in ice-rimed trees, she leaves the carriage. A tiny snow storm trails after her, a particulate echo of her presence.

For a moment, all of my memories of Nora become compressed into this localized snowstorm. Each flake is another reminder **of dark closets, of the yawning pit that exhales a stench of history and mistakes** of her absence.

How many times can our hearts break before the structural integrity fails, and we can't put the pieces back together again?

Tattooed on my palm, in a fading henna pattern **everything is made of dots, everything comes apart as the gaps expand**, is a flower with twenty-three petals. I cup my hand **as above**, and make my own valley. I raise my hand to smell the flower, and the pattern so below disintegrates. The world becomes dust, like fine sand, and I inhale this tiny universe.△ We chose our mantras; we chose our secret phrases that lock and unlock our hidden hearts. **Om. Om. Om.**

The Ribbon Man leads Nora towards the blankness in the desert floor, and the trailing snowstorm of her wake coalesces into a retinue

*\* vision*
*p. 361*

*\* V*

*\* snow*
*p. 315*

---

47 - cf. *Dr. Ehirllimbal's private journal, entry dated August 22nd, 1954.*
△ - Nora, Nora, Nora.

of attendants. Some of them cluster closely behind the pair like eager sycophants, dying for an opportunity to please. Others spin and wander like thrice-removed cousins abandoned at family barbecues. One **becomes two becomes three** approaches the carriage and begins to disassemble the frame and the yoke.[48]

I scramble out as the roof is separated from the walls, reaching back for my hat before it is lost beneath a cascade of falling curtains. Standing a safe distance away, I watch as the three **we are always dividing, our oneness splitting into dualities; our genetic imperative is schizophrenic** multiply into a host of white-suited waiters. Thus agented, they speedily finish the conversion of the carriage. The yoke becomes a table; the wheels are bent into punch bowls; the pillows become flower arrangements; and the bench splits open like a cornucopia, spilling an array of petits fours, fruit tarts, miniature cakes, chocolate-covered berries, sugar-dusted cookies, and herb-scented sticks of coppery honey. The remaining pieces of the carriage's frame are thrust into the sand, and as the last stake slides **between the third and fourth rib** into the ground, a filigree of stars shimmer into a diaphanous dome.

*mitosis p. 391*

*tool p. 350*

An older man, his face a brittle mask of ice, comes up beside me. I look at him, and see right through him to a tiny shard of diamond stuck in the dune. **The light glints and hardens.** He is a holographic projection, a reflection generated by the light trapped in the diamond, an image given depth by the swirling snow.

"I shouldn't have any sweets," he says, his voice—like his face, like his shape **like his identity**—an echo in my head. "They'll mess with my blood sugar."

He sighs, a gust of snow from his frozen lips. "But maybe just one. Or two. They look awfully good."

Nora's father. Never very good at self-control.

"Hello, Martin," I say.

"Hello, Harry. How's the psychotic break coming along?"

"Nicely," I admit.

"Good. Will you have the **despair that blossoms in the night?**"

"Cake?" I nod, ignoring the other voice, the one that speaks to another in a different time and place. "Sure."

*father p. 198*

*bloom p. 386*

A waiter approaches, aware of our intent and our need. He offers a tray of arranged cakes, tiny squares of tinted sugar. Martin takes one, raises it to his phantasmal lips, and lets go as the cake passes through the ephemeral layer of his expression. It falls to the sandy

48 - *Thirteen's yoke is the archway to power* . . .

*thirteen p. 346*

63

ground behind him, transformed into a frozen cube. It lies on the sand, canted at a glittering angle, and begins **where does love go when it fails? Where does that passion flee?** to melt.

I gingerly take a tiny piece of cake, and bite into it with all the enthusiasm of a short-term royal food taster. The cake is cloying ash in my mouth. Not sweet. **Deepdark, the flesh failing and the spirit freezing.** Not cold. Just the taste of rotten bark and moldering leaf.

*ash
p. 155*

I spit the cake out, and the gob of flour and sugar becomes a green and yellow snake that slithers across the sand, leaving a cryptic track in its wake. It slides onto the waiter's shoe and then disappears up the leg of his trousers. He doesn't notice.△

*yellow
p. 365*

"Do you remember Jasper and Sylvia?" Martin indicates a couple who have been together so long they have exchanged faces. His face has the pinched desiccation of her perpetual dissatisfaction while her cheeks and lips are permanently depressed by his terminal cynicism. Martin's in-laws. Nora's grandparents. Her parents.

"How could I forget you two?" I don't bother offering my hand, and it isn't just because they're holograms. "Back to haunt me one last time?"

"Let me touch him," Sylvia begs, the muscles in her narrow neck straining. "Just once." Her teeth are transparent icicles, and her smile makes her sagging face seem even more like a slur of wax.

Jasper shakes his head. "He's wearing his hat,"▽ he says, managing to make the observation seem like an indictment of both the fervid superstition of the lower class and my fashion sense.[49]

*superstition
p. 374*

"Make the **rational architecture of its existence** blow it off, Jasper. Why can't you **ever tattooed on that skin—**"

I squint through my headache, and focus on the stone projecting the shrewish memory of Nora's grandmother. The diamond darkens, filling with ink, and then cracks. Sylvia's mouth curls **first and last** in an expression that surprises all of us before she scatters into ambient snow. The diamond bleeds oil on the sand for a moment before the **djinn have already started to blow them away** sand swallows the broken gem.

*memory
p. 253*

"Why don't we get some punch?" Martin steers me away from his remaining in-law.

---

△ - And even as a participant/observer there, I am also here, witness and recipient of another ritual. Another cosmological rebirth.

▽ - My hat protects me from many things.

49 - *As if there were a difference.*

*spiritual
armor
p. 323*

"Think we're lucky enough that it is spiked with MDOH?" I nod at Jasper who, before we pass beyond the range of his illusionary expression, manages to eke out a not entirely pained smile.

"MDOH?" Martin asks. "I'm sorry, Harry. I can't always keep up with the drugs you kids are taking."[50]

"I always appreciated your ignorance—willful or not—about what I did with Nora. Still do. Maybe that's why you got the job of babysitting me at this function."

"Well . . . since Noreen can't be here, maybe I get to be the one who stabs you first." His face churns, and the light sparkles off his cheeks and forehead. He gazes toward the bent wheel of the carriage and the punch sloshing within. "Yes, a little MDOH might take the edge off."

I'm eighteen again, squashed in the bathroom at Derrick Monson's house with D and Leeza and Cameron. The room is thick with our desire to get naked, and she knows it. The lure of the psychedelic drug keeps us all on the luminous edge of action. I've got the shakes, and my fingertips are numb.[△] I couldn't manage the necessary physical dexterity to jack off if she even asked me to, not to mention the lack of responsiveness from down there as well. But I'm fascinated with the way the light spills across her collarbone, how it sneaks under the casual disarray of her shirt, how it hints at what hides down there, past that still-bound third button.

* casual disarray p. 164

Yes, she says, making eye contact with each of us simultaneously through some chemical magic, *yes, a little methylenedioxyhydroxy-amphetamine might take the edge off.*

Yes, we all wanted to fuck her because she never used an acronym when she could wrap her tongue around many many syllables.

When Martin sees I am incapable of knowing where (and when) I am, he fetches two glasses of punch.

"Isn't it strange," he muses as he returns, laden with two cups, "how and what we store as memories?"

"Not nearly as strange as having you in my head."

I down the offered glass, ignoring the bitter taste of wormwood and decay, and swap my empty for the other one he still carries.

"But we're all in your head, Harry. Aren't you used to that by now?"

"It's the way my past is being hijacked that's causing me a little distress."

---

50 - *Methylenedioxyhydroxyamphetamine. One of Shulgin's discoveries. Not as popular as Ecstacy, and is known to act as a dessicant, which limits the psychonaut's ability to float within in the Oneiroi.*

△ - God, I haven't thought about that evening for a long time. Such innocence. Such eagerness to explore.

Martin shrugs. "Recontextualization is all we have, ever since the tower fell."

"Ah, Derrida via Möbius. Life was easier as single-celled organisms, wasn't it?"

He gives me that smile, the one his daughter inherited. The one **splinters of what we used to be**

I close my eyes. *Life was easier . . .*

After two more glasses of the punch, which is, indeed, spiked with something, I find my way back. Martin's face is starting to glow, and the sand of the desert is starting to vanish, leaving behind the diamond stars.

"How much of my psyche do you have access to?" I ask Martin, the father of 211814 2413361421 1614 $^\triangle$

Nora's father smiles at me, teeth silver **in the dead light reflection the door is closed the door is** like Chinese characters painted on a grain of rice. "We prefer to consider it more of a unified psychological matrix," he says.

"We?"

"Yes. What you think of as God. We don't refer to Ourselves in the Third person. That would imply . . ."

*ego
p. 188
"Ego?"

"Identity."

"Ah, a difference of semantics."

"Much of existence is."

"So, you're in everyone? Or, rather"—his mouth opens, but I beat him to it—"everyone is part of you."

"Yes, Harry."

He is pleased that I've figured it out for myself. A difference of semantics, indeed. How much of all psychological reconstruction is just that? Putting a new label on something so that your brain can assimilate it differently? Spin-doctoring your own psyche.

*gnosis
p. 54
"And TH3iR plan?"

"TH3y have no plan, Harry. They have intent."

"Of course. TH3y are tenacious, aren't they?"

"And you aren't?"

"I'm not sure I want to tell you."

---

$\triangle$ - The difference between a cipher and language is that one is understood by the conscious mind and the other is subsumed into a psychonaut's unconsciousness. If they must think about it, it will remain indecipherable. If they encode themselves with it, its meaning will be absorbed.

I laugh. "No, why would you start now?"

There is a frenzy about his scalp, like hummingbirds moving too fast to be seen. Plucking at the wisps of his fading hair.

"She didn't tell me, Martin," I say, trying once again to change all of our collective history.

"TH3y believe the collective can be changed," he says.

He coughs, wet snow spattering from his lips. "Leashed," he snarls. "Bound."

At first, I think his anger is directed at TH3iR audacity; but then, I recognize his emotion as my **Mirror Mirror**, and beneath it, there is a deepdark well of sorrow. It does not belong to me, even though I am the only one who knows where it is.

"Is there a cure?" I ask. "Can I stop it from consuming me?"

"Can U?" he asks in return.

*You. Harry Potemkin. Oneironaut. Son. Of. Man.*

**Answer say answer is the key**

"U," I realize, following the movement of his tongue. "Not you."

The skin of his skull is dissolving now, dripping like wax on the shoulders of his suit. It's not the most pleasant thing to watch, mainly because Martin—like most I've met in the Oneiroi—is nothing more than a mirror.

*Like most . . .*

"U is the 21st letter of the alphabet," I say as I offer him my hat. "That would make W—double you—the 23rd."

"That it would." His smile is filled with teeth, and the motion tears the fragile film of his cheeks. "Are you ready then?" he asks as he puts my hat—my favorite hat, my only hat—on his naked head.

"23 3218231915 2113."

As soon as I speak the words—as soon as I acknowledge my willingness—my armor vanishes. The previously distant pressure of TH3iR poison becomes a tidal surge through my body, a persistent beat that comes from not just my heart and head, but from my toes and fingertips. My head hurts, and something dark is leaking from all the holes in my head. *bare p. 156*

He's almost gone. There's nothing left of him but a haze of fine sand floating beneath my hat. "It's too bad," he whispers. "We would have liked to see you suffer more. But perhaps you will, yet."[51]

I blink again—losing **where has the heartbird gone?**—and it

---

51 - *All debts must be paid, Harry. The Oneiroi does not forget. The Oneiroi does not forgive. The psychonaut thinks their passage is free, but payment is always extracted. There are those who carry your chains for you. How long are you going to leave them in bondage?*

is with some difficulty that I wipe my eyes clear enough to see. My arms move at odd angles, like they belong in a different dimension. Beholden to different rules.

My fingers are stained black, and my paper suit is covered **I don't remember why** spilled ink.

I can smell her fear on me. As she tries to run from the monster in the library. **1814 2413361421 1614**

But now—here—I am standing at the graveside. The sands are gone, the world nothing but a maze of starlight, and all the ghosts have become tricks of my fragmenting memory. Black crows are eating my peripheral vision, their beaks peaking away at the frame.

Nora's ebony skin is invisible against the landscape, and her **is this dress mine? do I belong in this ceremony? is this life, this failure, this closure, this hand, this ring, this this this this key** is a collection of stars and snowflakes, a frozen nebula drifting through the midnight void. The poles surrounding her grave have lost their depth, **what happened to your—? where did those children—? who drew these—?** reduced to two-dimensional line drawings. Flat architecture for a flattened world.

* children
p. 169

The rhythm of the starlight is a synaesthetic symphony of telegraph signals. As I drift toward Nora's supine body, the holographic faces of the mourners move in and out of focus. Their mouths—opening and closing like fish gasping for breath—are the long and the short of the light show. My hands are covered with spots of weak light, as if I was slowly turning into a fish too. Some speckled bottom feeder—eyeless, who only senses the bioluminescent illusion of other denizens of the deepdark sea.

* fish
p. 203

The Ribbon Man is behind me, a dozen feet tall and diaphanous in a celestial wind. His voice is a bioacoustic reverberation, felt more than heard, and his eulogy is a patchwork of motivational noises, religious aggression, and the soapbox delirium of street corner prophets.

"Just a minute," I beg. "I can't find my fea—" And it all smears away from me.

Leeza shows me her palm, shows me the damp pattern of sugar stains from stolen pills. I lick her palm, and I feel her other hand fumbling against my crotch. **Father, absent like the owls in winter, is an old sea god groaning. Angelfish nibble at the streaks of flesh still clinging to the sea-bound bones.** Take two, they're small; Casper giggles as the first rush of the MDOH blows through his brain. The rest of us aren't far behind, solar bats winging toward an inverse sun.

We are just organizational schema hung over memory arrays,

after all. When our index decays, when it slips, memory becomes equally unhinged. All that we used to be becomes what we are in a fulsome implosion of infinity. I am now, then, and nowhere, falling apart under the aggressive un-indexing of the oneiromantic poison. I have forgotten number theory I never understood; my language centers are being overrun with squids and squirrels and other creatures whose names I can no longer remember.

The stars are going out, personality echoes blinking off as they finish their respects to the fallen. Goodbye, sweet child. Goodbye, little mouse. Goodbye, Nora. Goodbye, dear friend. Goodbye, princess. Goodbye, NeeNee. Goodbye, lover. Goodbye goodbye goodbye . . . Each farewell is another facet, another face, going out.[52] Silence and darkness, hand in hand, dancing toward eternity.

*silence
p. 310*

Through it all, Nora's face remains still, her mouth curving in a line that is neither a smile nor a frown, but suggestive of both a secret and a sorrow. The face of my mother as that last spike of heroin hits, the joy of that merciful release from the pain of her skin mingling with the sad realization that she will not see me grow old. The mask Noreen puts on as she realizes her daughter will never wake again. The crow-headed God kneeling before **sons wearing the skins of their fathers** the bloody-handed jackal acolyte. All these faces, all these masks. **All the lives I never lived.** I lose track of which **this one knows the way, 32182321 131914 183821 321814 151434** one I am.

*death mask
p. 178*

The Ribbon Man, **solar flares roaring electromagnetic fluxion look at the lights! Have you ever seen such a display?** says the

---

52 - *Chicken sausage. Giblets. Giblets. Would you like fries with that? Ocelot ossification leads to publication petrifaction. Get our brochure now! Abattoir / Abattoir / Bake me a little longer. Bite the lance, drink from the cup, where was the body hid? The white light obscures the black mystery. Now serving number 22. Now serving. Serving. Now. 22. Minus one.[△] So close, little children. Eat your emulsions. Are your gallstones keeping you up at night? Try ######. Our representatives are standing by. Outside your window. Inside your garage. Fucking your garbage, cocks wrapped in banana peel condoms. Bipartisan libertines make sweet cake. Don't leave me. Don't believe me. Love me anyway, and I will love you long time. Try our mail-order brides. Try our mail-order pets. Try it. Try it! Tryittryittryittryit. Is the world the oyster or the pearl? Stamp prices are going up; have you mailed everything? What is left? Slip it to me. Right on the tongue. I hold the key. Ramble on, abandonone, babble on. I am coming. Pffft! Just a little mess. Just a little stain. Our new product can get that out. "You lack the season of all natures, sleep." Lie down, lie down. Give me your hand.*

*substantia
p. 6*

△ - I mourn them still. All those seekers. Blinded and bound. And for what?

breaking words, and the last strand of my personality web tears. I try to say my name, and realize it is but another mask, another disguise that we monkeys have learned to fabricate. We come down from the trees, hide our bodies with leaves, hide our faces with painted bark. I am not who I am. I am not Harry **still sweet** I am not Nora. I am not Martin, Noreen, Charles, **roll call! stand and be counted!** Lindsay, Leeza, **who's in? Who wants to get high?** Doug, Rasputin, Michael, **aching, pulling away, hold me tight** Miranda, Samantha, Shirley, **I do** Judas **forgive me**, Jasper, Clint, Julio, Francis, Philip. I am **241433231319** not. **I love you.**

Nora **the sweet fruit of that first kiss** opens her **radial starfish** arms, and I **take her hand her heart her life her love her eyes her face her mouth her her her her** fall into her embrace. She holds **empty stars** me tight, and we fall into her **how could you have abandoned me?** sonless grave. We fall **the delicate spiral of smoke becomes a writhing DNA chain as the drugs kick in** into the **a post-modern excuse for ennui, don't you think?** afterlife of the deepdark. **Put a little bit here, yes, can you feel how it tingles? Can you feel how it makes your flesh feel like it belongs to someone else? Can you feel . . .**

falling star falling star o babylon how i have missed thee **I can't see, I can't see!** o abaddon how i love thee falling **black** star now we are falling—

$$0 = 0^\triangle$$

---

$\triangle$ - I thought I could make a difference. I thought I could save someone.

* – *Thereby saving yourself? If you saved her, would that fix your mother's death? If you saved them all, would that make your father come back?*

- My father? I never—oh yes, *that* father. You are so persistent.

* – *We am a mirror, Harry. You said it yourself.*

* reflection
p. 396

- But if we are all mirrors, then maybe I am reflecting you. Maybe it is your need to be forgiven by your father that you see in me. Maybe my father was an asshole, maybe he was a drunk, and maybe his abandonment of us was our liberation, and not our prison. Maybe it was the only—selfless act he ever performed.

* – *Us? You said 'us,' Harry. Do you remember your brother now?*

- Which brother? The one I killed with the trowel, or the one I never had?

* – . . . . . . . . . .

- You're going to have try harder. I've had a long time to wall off all of your lies.

she loves me she loves me not she loves me she loves me not she
loves she loves me not she loves me she loves me not she loves me
she loves me not she loves me she loves me not she loves she loves
me not she loves me she loves me not she loves me she loves me
not she loves me she loves me not she loves she loves me not she
loves me she loves me not she loves me she loves me not she loves
me she loves me not she loves she loves me not she loves me she
loves me not she loves me she loves me not she loves me she loves
me not she loves she loves me not she loves me she loves me not
she loves me she loves me not she loves me she loves me not she
loves she loves me not she loves me she loves me not she loves me
she loves me not she loves me she loves me not she loves she loves
me not she loves me she loves me not she loves me she loves me
not she loves me she loves me not she loves she loves me not she
loves me she loves me not she loves me she loves me not she loves
me she loves me not she loves she loves me not she loves me she
loves me not she loves me she loves me not she loves me she loves
me not she loves she loves me not she loves me she loves me not
she loves me she loves me not she loves me she loves me not she
loves she loves me not she loves me she loves me not she loves me
she loves me not she loves me she loves me not she loves she loves
me not she loves me she loves me not she loves me she loves me
not she loves me she loves me not she loves she loves me not she
loves me she loves me not she loves me she loves me not she loves
me she loves me not she loves she loves me not she loves me she
loves me not she loves me she loves me not she loves me she loves
me not she loves she loves me not she loves me she loves me not
she loves me she loves me not she loves me she loves me not she
loves she loves me not she loves me she loves me not she loves me
she loves me not she loves me she loves me not she loves she loves
me not she loves me she loves me not she loves me she loves me
not she loves me she loves me not she loves she loves me not she
loves me she loves me not she loves me she loves me not she loves
me she loves me not she loves she loves me not she loves me she
loves me not she loves me she loves me not she loves me she loves
me not she loves she loves me not she loves me she loves me not
she loves me she loves me not she loves me she loves me not she

i do i do
answer say answer is the key
fall with me
fall fall fall with me
into the deep        sea
dark

she loves she loves me not she loves me she loves me not she loves
me she loves me not she loves me she loves me not she loves she
loves me not she loves me she loves me not she loves me she loves
me not she loves me she loves me not she loves she loves me not
she loves me she loves me not she loves me she loves me not she
loves me she loves me not she loves she loves me not she loves me
she loves me not she loves me she loves me not she loves me she
loves me not she loves she loves me not she loves me she loves me
not she loves me she loves me not she loves me she loves me not
she loves she loves me not she loves me she loves me not she loves
me she loves me not she loves me she loves me not she loves she
loves me not she loves me she loves me not she loves me she loves
me not she loves me she loves me not she loves she loves me not
she loves me she loves me not she loves me she loves me not she
loves me she loves me not she loves she loves me not she loves me
she loves me not she loves me she loves me not she loves me she
loves me not she loves she loves me not she loves me she loves me
not she loves me she loves me not she loves me she loves me not
she loves she loves me not she loves me she loves me not she loves
me she loves me not she loves me she loves me not she loves she
loves me not she loves me she loves me not she loves me she loves
me not she loves me she loves me not she loves she loves me not
she loves me she loves me not she loves me she loves me not she
loves me she loves me not she loves she loves me not she loves me
she loves me not she loves me she loves me not she loves me she
loves me not she loves she loves me not she loves me she loves me
not she loves me she loves me not she loves me she loves me not
she loves she loves me not she loves me she loves me not she loves
me she loves me not she loves me she loves me not she loves she
loves me not she loves me she loves me not she loves me she loves
me not she loves me she loves me not she loves she loves me not
she loves me she loves me not she loves me she loves me not she
loves me she loves me not she loves she loves me not she loves me
she loves me not she loves me she loves me not she loves me she
loves me not she loves she loves me not she loves me she loves me
not she loves me she loves me not she loves me she loves me not
she loves she loves me not she loves me she loves me not she loves
me she loves me not she loves me she loves me not she loves she

**Let us go then, you and I**

me not she loves me she loves me not she loves she loves me not
she loves me she loves me not she loves me she loves me not she
loves me she loves me not she loves she loves me not she loves me
she loves me not she loves me she loves me not she loves me she
loves me not she loves she loves me not she loves me she loves me
not she loves me she loves me not she loves me she loves me not
she loves she loves me not she loves me she loves me not she loves

You were always so fond of that poem . . .

Floating . . . that sense of weightless déjà vu.

How long have you been lost?
Adrift in this endless deepdark?
How long until you drown?
Can you hold on a little longer?

The brine fills my mouth with the ease of an old lover, and I don't choke as it slides down my throat. My lungs twitch with the internal unreachable itch of serif scratches. Not all text is equal; some words are persistent, harder to dissolve than the others.

Do not choke. You do not need to breathe.

White dark flashes against my eyes, the alphabet fading. I fixate on a phrase, and try to remember its poetry, but Yeats is gone, Wordsworth is gone, Eliot is gone. *They're all gone,* the brine-soak whispers around us. *They're all gone.* And the bond between the vowels and the consonants dissolves completely. The curves become fluid, and the hard lines melt into a smear of pickled darkness. A kaleidoscope of color in my hand. A flash of wings.
Faster.
Faster now, and all that weight is gone.
All that guilt drops away.
There is no fear.
U and I are free.

Quickly now. We have little time. She will guard us awhile, but TH3y will decipher the lock soon enough.
I have much to tell U . . .

Let us start with the reality TH3y have crafted.

My name is Harry Potemkin, and I am a black market oneirologist.

The field of study—oneirology—is just a tiny stub on the tree of psychiatry, which suits us just fine. Our work is too sublime and too strange for mainstream journal publication. Not to mention the outrage our psychopharmacological methods would incite.

I used to be a licensed therapist, not a full Doctor of Psychiatry, but licensed enough to have an office, a couch, and be able to tell my patients that their time was up just as they were about to reach a critical psychological breakthrough. That was part of my frustration too, by the way: the intrusion of time and society into the healing process.

I wanted to help people, and I started by helping myself. Do you know the difference between a psychonaut and an oneironaut? The psychonaut studies himself. The oneironaut . . . well, it wouldn't do to admit to you that I experiment with the dreams of others, would it? Such an admission would certainly stain my credibility.

But it is what I do. I am able to actively participate in the dreams of my patients, and for that reason alone, I am a last resort. Those who are so traumatized that regular therapeutic methods have failed them, they come to me. The mentally broken, the fragmentary psychotics, the schizophrenics who fear discovery: their desperation pushes them to my door, pushes them to consider my methods. I invade their dreams and cut out what is hurting them. The oneironaut—the difference between

-ologist and -naut is a fine one, do you see?—is a psychiatrist of the unconscious, a surgeon of the ego's shadow. My methods work when all of the accredited and accepted methods fail.

This is not idle posturing. I am very good at what I do. I tell you this so that you understand the depth of my desperation, that you accept me as a professional and not as a crackpot. I am not someone who has built a career out of conning the desperate, nor am I disguising my own mania with a veneer of respectability and whiff of daring experimentalism. I am a healer, albeit the most unorthodox one you will ever meet.

And yet, the question which you still have and which has begun to frighten me as well is this: how does the healer know he is well? How does the mental health professional know he is sane?

There is something in my dreams that is not mine. It hides from me, but I have mapped my own psychic landscape well enough to know there is a camouflaged parasite within my psyche. Counter to the prime tenets of every oneirologist's methodology, I have begun to keep a dream journal. It is dangerous to write down one's dreams, it gives them strength and a hook into reality. But I must. I must discover the source of the dis-ease that I know is within me.

The intent of this journal has always been to source out the disturbance in my head, and I have approached these pages with as little editorial interference as possible. For the most part, I have simply given my hands free rein and allowed them to write whatever they want. Much like word association or free writing, the intent has been to draw the unconscious agent in my head to the surface.

A will other than my own has written lines on the page. There are places where another is communicating with me. I am being visited by my own holy ghost.

I should admit to you now that everything here has been written in the Oneiroi. When I wake, all the pages are blank.

**Row, row, row your boat**
**Gently down the stream**
**Merrily merrily merrily merrily**
**Life is but a dream.**
I know you are here, Nora.

**How can I be, Harry? You held my hand and watched me die. You stood by and watched them give my body to the flames. You have eaten the fruit that has grown from my ashes. You know I am gone.**

When a child is first born, he doesn't understand the concept of object permanence. When his mother leaves the room, she ceases to exist, but that doesn't negate her reality. Objectively, she still exists, but in the child's subjective world she doesn't. Just because I watched you stop breathing only means that, in my subjective world, your body has died. But what I perceive and believe isn't necessarily reality.

**None of us are real.**

But I believe you are, Nora. You were. That means something still.

**Does it, Harry? Or is it just an echo? An illusion.**
What's an illusion, Nora? Nothing more than a

reflection. Nothing more than an interpretation.

"Reality" is consensual. "Reality" is social. "Reality" is series of rules we've all agreed upon so as to communicate with one another. And what drives our need to communicate, our need to fabricate reality? Does God require reality?

**God requires nothing but your love, Harry.**

I think He doesn't even need that, Nora. I think you need my love.

**That I do, Harry. Oh, that I do.**

Which is why you are communicating with me. Why you have expressed yourself in my "reality," as well as you can within the rules that I understand.

**Have I? Or am I reflection of what you need? Of what you yearn for?**

I don't want anything, Nora. I just want to be free.

**Free from what?**

God, perhaps.

**But isn't that what communication is, Harry? The touch of God. We must have a common language, a common means of expression, otherwise, we are simply bits of unengaged chaos that cannot mix, cannot mingle, cannot become something other than their simple selves.**

**You speak of my expression as if it were something that frightens you, something alien and foreign, yet is this not what you do to your patients? Is this not what God does to us?**

I have not felt the touch of God.

**Ah, Harry. I have. I have indeed.**

I—

More than once, Harry. Remember? And less than a hundred times.

—am not—

God? No, Harry, God is dead, and so am I. Stop fighting me.

I don't understand. You are speaking in riddles.

Your hand cannot transcribe my speech without twisting it into riddles. What I am saying is not what you are writing. This is the Oneiroi. Every word is symbolic. Every breath is ripe with subtext. You cannot hope to understand the full depth of my intent by just listening to my words. Language failed all of us once before, remember? When the lost sun came back. 23 3816 34132737 151434, 381942 23 3816 321814 24132215 32183832 1823421421 34132737 1814383732. 25371414 1614, 381942 25371414 3413273721142425.

1634 151434?

Yes, Harry. That's all I've been.

Let us try this again, while there is still time.

Let us start with the letter . . .

One morning, on my desk, I find a plain manila package. Inside is a letter and a small Moleskine notebook. The package is addressed, stamped, and sealed, but the stamps have not been canceled. I have no recollection of how or when this package arrived. If, really. If this package arrived.

The letter reads as follows:

December 31st, 2006
Dr. Eduardo Ehrillimbal, Esq.
c/o Umbrial Consortium
XXXX XXXXXXXX, XXXXX XXX
Los Angeles, CA 90048

Harry Potemkin
XXX XXXXXXX XXX
XXXXXXX XX XXXXX

Mr. Potemkin:

*By now, you are aware of who I am and who I represent, and I do apologize that you have been embroiled in what is, essentially, a family matter. This unfortunate and rather sordid affair has been dragging on since before my birth and, while it seemed I was to be rid of it for several years, I now fear it will never end. I hope—with a great deal of passion, you understand, because it will mean I may see my brother again—that you are the catalytic agent that will bring a resolution to this feud.*

*While I would, obviously, prefer a resolution in the favor of myself and my family, I do truly understand that your choice is—and must be!—one of your own making. If you elect to marry the black queen, who can blame you? She is a vibrant symbol, a esoteric mystery of everything you could possibly desire. And your white queen? She has passed on—my condolences, of course—and there is nothing left but her memory. My wife has been gone nearly thirty years now, and the loss is an irrefutable part of my eternal sorrow. Clinging to her memory has made me bereft in . . . well, I believe you know the hollowness of which I speak.*

*To the matter at hand, though, I have enclosed a small booklet, the like of which you may be familiar. The pages will be blank until you take it into the Oneiroi. There it will be filled with material I have collected for you. I hope you find it useful in your quest. I hope it helps you make a choice.*

*And I hope you will find it possible to forgive my father. Someone must, or that monster that we have been made to remember will devour us all.*

*Best,*

*Eduardo*

The enclosed Moleskine book is indeed blank, except that someone has written on the first page. Oddly, the handwriting is mine. Written just as plainly as the hand that writes these words now. But I have no memory of these words. I am not even sure what they mean. But, nonetheless, they are there on the page. Bold as life. Immutable. The ink, bonded to the page, is now indelible and inseparable. I cannot change what has been written.

The first line is: "My name is Harry Potemkin, and I am a black market oneirologist."

I can only strike it out, or . . . I can write the next line.

**38143713 232119'32 1416293234, 3821 381934 25131324 223819 32142424**

This, then, is the beginning, though—as you may have an inkling already—this letter is not the beginning. But it will serve us well enough as an anchor. All things in the Oneiroi are subject to dissolution and transformation. All things end.

Do you understand this truism?

Can you deny it?

This is not a trick question. Either is correct; both are false.

You will, in time, come to know the path of neither. It is not impossible for this, the left-hand of light, to be in conflict with that, the darkened right-hand. The schism is necessary, in fact, more so if we accept the letter as our anchor.

The letter sets in motion a chain of events—a course of miracles, a path toward absolution—that will lead us to the secret of the blackleaf.

Should I have told you all of this in the beginning?

Would it have made your immersion easier?

It does not matter any more, does it? You want to know what I have discovered. You want to see where I have gone. You want to know what I have become.

I have already told you. The letter, as I said, is not the beginning. It is our anchor, our point of departure. Try to hold on to it for just a few seconds more. Hold it tight! It is the sole proof of your existence. Once it is gone . . .

**131914 2321 321814 211838291437, 313815231933 182321 22243834 23193213 38 2118142424**

Who wrote the letter? To whom was it intended? Who, ultimately, read it? You do not know for certain, do you?

Neither do I, which makes it difficult for us to know its intent, doesn't it? Down in the deepdark, we have discovered the intent of our Adversary, haven't we? Does it not have a similar shape to that letter? Does it not seem like the same bleak phantom, dressed in more conciliatory verbiage? Does it not seem to be the same lies once more?

Do you know the name TH3y have given me? Good.

That, too, is a lie. Like everything else.

The Potemkin village was erected by Grigori Aleksandrovich Potemkin during the Crimean War in the late eighteenth century as a means of impressing the visiting Catherine the Great and her endless retinue of sycophants and hangers-on.

What did these fake buildings hide? A desolate landscape—unmarked by road, unadorned by
church or chapel—along the Dnieper River that given
the task of being something larger than it was, something grander than scrub and tundra. In a similar
fashion, the naming of an object is to obscure its true
identity.

Yes, I am known as "Harry Potemkin," but in light
of what TH3y seek, do you understand why it can
be nothing more than an alias? Nothing more than
a way to identify the metaphorical construct I have
crafted here the Oneiroi.

### 321713 2321 321814 362337332319, 323832321313231933 241438361421

How, then, to proceed in light of my admission
that I have lied to you? How, then, to engage you in
the subsequent pages of this folio in a way that will
lead you believe me? How, then, to rebuild a measure of trust between U and I?

These questions plague every author. Every creator faces these awkward moments of omniscient
confusion. How will I get them to believe? Do I ask
you to accept everything on faith? Such a direc-
tive has worked for centuries. Every shaman, every
preacher, every priest, every holy man, every god:
they have all asked for—and received—such conces-
sion from their flock. Will you believe in me?

The vampire, in the old mythology, must be invited
to cross the threshold of a house. This metaphor that
external evil cannot cross into the sanctified space
of your world may seem to be badly broken in our

modern world, but it is not. It still holds true; it is just that we have forgotten how to say "no." We have forgotten that our permission still has power. TH3y want to use you, and have done so, but TH3y are exploiting a loophole in the contract between the singular ego and the collective unconsciousness.

Even my patients, when they let me into their dreams, are doing so under the belief that I will do them no harm. Is this not the basis for every relationship we have? *You will do me no harm.* Putting aside for a moment the self-destructive psychosis of the alienated modern mind, every interaction we have with egos external to our own go through an phase of initiation. Once we make contact with another identity—be it a casual encounter in an elevator, in the line at the supermarket, on the bus; or in a more formalized situation like a first date or a business meeting—we engage in a trust assessment. Will this person hurt me? Depending on the outcome of that test, we either guard ourselves more rigorously or we open up and invite that person in.

That same assessment takes place when you open a book, though you are engaging it on a more metaphysical level. Can you trust this author to not betray you? Will the world they fabricate for your entertainment be of sufficient caliber that you can, for a little while, lose your ego consciousness? Will their characters titillate and fascinate you enough to warrant your suspension of objective belief? Will their words be enough to wash away that sense of grief--that plague of sorrow, that unending ache that haunts your heart? Will they, in the end, make you forget?

There is a fatalism inherent in post-modernity identity, one we willfully strive to ignore. We turn to texts, not so much as an escape, but as a act of Phenomenological Hermeneutics. We turn to the Word in an effort to find meaning, and we ask the Creator to afford us some notion of universal integrity. Some notion of universal identity.

**3218371414 2321 321814 161332181437, 17181316 321814 2218232442 3114242314361421**

If I tell you who I am, will U understand who U are? That, then, in our pact. Believe in me, and I will believe in U. Make me real, and I will validate UR existence. I will fill the hole in UR soul.

On and on. All the way to babelon.

**Answer say answer is the key**

This way, then. Now that you see.

Fall, fall with me . . .

. . . and let us return from the deepdark sea.

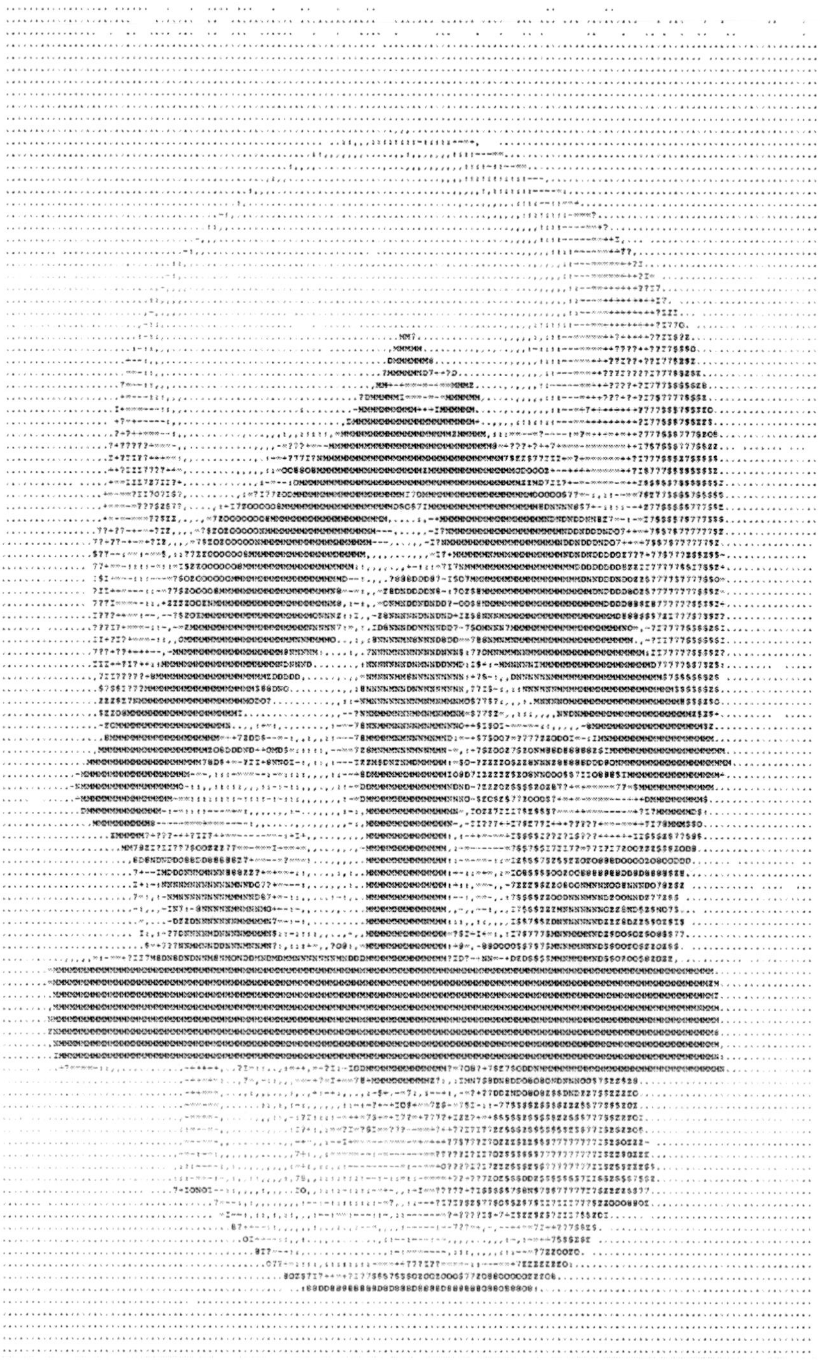

# IX

# THE FIELDS OF ELYSIUM

There is no color in this world, and with such homogeneity, it is impossible to distinguish anything. All is the same, really—all is one. But I'm clawing for a way out, regardless. I find a ripple in the night-fabric, a disturbance in the shadow-veil, and I pinch and pull at the hint of a seam. I've lost the knife somewhere, so I put my teeth to work, tearing and gnawing.

It tastes like papaya, and when I manage to rip the veil, it bleeds a black sap (the cerebro-spinal fluid of the collective unconscious, as it were, to anthropomorphize the inhuman). As the hole becomes bigger—my hands aching with the effort—I am rewarded with a flickering cascade of images like a thousand films being projected through the same tiny aperture. *substantia p. 6*

I smear my naked body with the sap—as if I were an ocean swimmer, covering myself with seal fat before beginning a tumultuous journey across rough water—and I am clothed with a rainbow wash of memories. My shoulders are too wide for the hole, even as slippery as I am. I grunt and kick, flailing like a newborn child. So close. Just a little farther. One arm through now, and I can grab a passing phantom. It bleats like a little lamb—pure and white on the outside, red and yellow and black on the inside. *spiritual armor p. 323*

The phantom bolts, using the legs I have impressed upon it to kick and scrabble against the fabric. I hang on, and it pulls me through the acrid thermocline. The hole closes around my leg, a mouth descend- *fabric p. 56* ing, and my foot slips free with a muculent pop. The lamb dissolves into a frisson of silvered scales and monsoon rains, and I am left floating in a riotous river of color and memory—the Enhypnia, the basal flow that feeds the symbolic Oneiroi.

I swim upstream until I find her empty coffin. Standing on the velvet cushions, I reach up and knock on the sky. One, two, three: I know the secret code, let me out. The ceiling splits, radial lines subdividing heaven into the twelve houses, and suddenly I am thrust out of the grave.[53]

* secret code
p. 305

I wake from a dream within a dream. Naked and trembling, I am back in the desert of slippery sand and glittering diamonds. There is no one waiting for me. No one haunts her grave. No one lingers at the buffet table, fingering the petits fours or slurping punch straight from the ladle. All the ghosts have gone home.

My hat is partially buried in the sand. I brush off the grit and the dust, and no longer needing it to protect my head (the voices don't frighten me any more), I tear the fabric into a handful of leaves and throw them aloft where they snap and flap themselves into the shape of a tiny blue bird. Singing wildly, it circles my head three times, and then flies off to the east.

* bird
p. 157

I have some cake (yes, Martin, *that* despair; it is our fear of death, isn't it? Our fear of abandonment?), as well as another glass of punch. Oh, *yes,* a little MDOH definitely takes the edge off.

I follow my bird. Back the way I came. Back to the beginning.

Gnarled tree leans precariously, its twisted branches reaching for the tall wheat as if to brace the bent trunk against the swaying grain. The crown of the tree has been split by lightning (some time ago, the wound is blackened with mud and ash), and the wound has rotted down to the roots. Not even a squirrel would hide nuts in its decrepit belly now.

* crown
p. 177

I climb the hunched back and stand on the rim of the broken skull. I can see the white sheet of the forest on my left, and the desert dissolves behind me. When I stand taller, the curve of the world reveals itself, that yellow arc of the horizon. In the distance, small enough to be easily obscured by my thumb, is another tree. Beyond it, barely a pinhead jutting up from the gentle arc of the world, is a third tree. They look impossibly far apart.

* horizon
p. 222

If I was actually going to walk that distance. But I have line of sight now, and that is good enough.

---

53 - *Where have you been hiding, Harry?*

Space bends as I squeeze, and when it flexes back, I have moved from the tree at the edge of the field to the one on the horizon. The world bulges and snaps back, fleeing from my transference. Here, perched on the slightly more upright top of the third tree, I am surrounded by yellow. The forest is nothing more than a thin white line behind me.

I scan the fields of Elysium, looking for the scarecrow.[54] It's out here somewhere. I saw it in the library mirror. It was in the book, before the pages were torn by the octopus monstrosity. But all I see is distant black sticks, poking up from the endless sea of wheat. More trees, more dead guardians.

* IV

* giants
p. 212

I make three more leaps, pinching the horizon each time, before I see the birds.

They're not fooled. They rarely are.

They circle the scarecrow, just out of reach of the tentacled thing in the grass. Once it was a severed limb, but it has mutated and grown other appendages in its need. It drags its heavy arm with spindly legs, and only one of its thin stalks still has an eye.

The birds are getting braver. Or hungrier.

Some of the wheat near the scarecrow is stained black, a damp half-arc of spatter as if a window had been briefly opened and then shut again, letting in rain from somewhere else.

* rain
p. 296

My blue bird lands on the scarecrow's head. He chirps noisily at me, and I look up to see one of the carrion birds gliding toward my head, its talons outstretched.

I freeze it, and leave it hanging in the sky as a warning to the others.

The tentacle humps slowly through the wheat. *Where are you going? Do you think you can flee from me here?* Its muffled undulation grows more frantic, and the carrion birds cackle with glee as they soar on the rising thermal of my anger. *Burn . . .*

The scarecrow's face is a flesh mask, tattered and tattooed by exposure into a featureless maze of cracks and wrinkles. The straw man is dumpy and misshapen from being hung for so long; all of its stuffing has settled into its waist and arms. Other than the vibrant stain of its red and yellow gloves, its clothes have been bleached of color.

Paper washed a thousand times no longer remembers the history of the text once written on it. When the sea recedes, taking with it all the dissolved text, the books will be blank. The shelves will be full, but

* text
p. 341

---

54 - *You're making things up now, Harry.* ~~All of this is a lie.~~ *None of this is true.* *[Quickly now; release the scavengers! He's here; we know he is* ~~down~~ *here.]*

* library
p. 248

the library will be empty. When the dreamer wakes, all the words will vanish.△

The scarecrow's face is the mask we all wear in public. When we ride public transportation; when we wander aimlessly in our consumer warehouses; when we stand in line at the post office, at the movie theater, at the coffee shop; when we pack ourselves into tiny elevators and pretend we aren't three people over the recommended weight limit of this conveyance. When we get out of bed, go to work, come home again, eat, drink, shop, shit, fuck: all of these things happen automatically. We don't need to be present. We just put on our blank faces, and disappear.

* death mask
p. 178

**Into the dream? Perhaps, but most don't make it this far, do they?** I can see her—TH3y can see her—and the smoke from the burning tentacle wraps her in billows of silk. **Most float somewhere up there, caught in the first astral layer—just like the womb. I don't have to tell you, you know it very well, don't you? It's comforting, isn't it? That amniotic weightlessness. That sense of blanketed security. Nothing can touch you. No one can find you. You are safe.**

*You found me, Nora. TH3y found me.*

**We don't count, Harry. We were with you already.**

**Yes. Yes, you were.**

She takes the symbol from me, and her touch splinters its unnatural threads. The trinity leaps from her hand—father! son! spirit!—and the carrion birds shriek with excitement. They dive after the floating sigils, fighting each other for the chance to swallow the floating ephemera.

**You give them too much power, Harry. You believe in them too easily.**

*Once upon a time, I did. Now . . .*▽

One of the squirming masses of letters and flesh is caught by a bird, who chokes and shudders as it tries to swallow the concept whole. Its throat expands like a balloon, and then pops. The bird plummets, and a wet mist of apocrypha trails in its wake. Two other birds follow it down, and all three disappear into the sea of swaying wheat.

**TH3y have TH3iR own gravity. TH3y do not like separation, that sense of being cut off from each other. TH3y do not like the idea of abandonment, and tH3y will draw U in.**

I watch the smallest of the three birds descend into the waving

---

△ - I see TH3m coming. I have been waiting a long time.

▽ - This is the lie that begins every fairy tale. "Once upon a time..."

wheat, chasing after its fallen father.

**Your dualities are strong, Harry, but they are not enough.**

The last of the three spins above, and its motion churns the text of the blood mist.

**The pairing is not complete until it is witnessed. It is not enough to be matched with your opposite. Your communion must be recognized.**

The whirling mist becomes a tornado of darkness, and it touches down in the field. The stalks of wheat are shredded by the spinning textual serifs in the cone of wind **321814 313714383218 1325 243819332738314! 321814 143518382438322131319 1325 331342?**, and the carrion birds scream again, though their cries are strident with rage and bewilderment. Feathers and bone and blood funnel up into the tornado's belly, **2132232424 3124141442231933, 21241317231933** along with fallen father and grieving son. Brought together again by the whirling wind of spirit.

*son
p. 317

**Believe in me. I am all that matters. All in me . . .** I try to push my mind around the persistently infintessimal tremor of TH3iR poison, that need and want that my cells **382424 17232424 3114 17142424** haven't quite forgotten. What should I believe?

**Love**

*That's too easy.*

**Of course it is.** Her ghost laughs. **But that's not what I meant. 321814 3213171437** That's what I—**31383114241319**—heard **381942 1319**

When the earthquake passes (all inside, nothing moves around me because none of exists, you see—I am the center, and all disturbances start and end in my heart, in my brain), she is gone. Just a smear of colored light vanishing into the angry swirl of the dissipating swirl of textual smoke.

*You believe . . . (what did you mean, Nora?) . . . too easily . . .*

I can almost see her words in the ghostly fog: *answer say answer.* I can almost make out the **everyone has one.**

Too many riddles. Too many ciphers. *Too much noise.*[55]

---

55 - *Perception. Conception. Altercation. Masturbation. Down the drain. Let the little ones go. Packets go in, packets go out. It's all a matter of weasel power. Seclusion. Projection. Bastion. Anchor anchor. Will the boat drift away? Why are my palms wet? My feet are leaking. Are there fish in this lake? Take a camera. Don't forget to take pictures. Ultraviolet flash only, please. We can develop them overnight. Five cents a print. For five senses more, we can show you color and light. Take more pictures. Take more. I am chromatic. Color-coded. I am auto-reply.*

There are layers to the Oneiroi, depths and heights like any other multi-dimensional space, but it bleeds too easily. Not all direction is literal; some of it can be temporal or transpersonal. My subjective realm, my individually realized dream, has been perturbed by the passage of the monstrous will of TH3iR corporate poison. The aggregated pain of all those who have succumbed is still bleeding through. Too many listened to the whisper of their unremembered unconsciousness. Too many looked back.

We bury so much. All of us. And these suppressed memories and dreams and desires drift down into the deepdark where they collect into one massive **not here not now you cannot stay.**

The 22$^{nd}$ expression woke it—no, the drug is just a catalyst, a psychopharmaceutical that prepares the mind, that opens doors and lets the shadow in. It's a fragment of mythology, really, a fragment of something that never happened.$^{\triangle}$ It is a hint—the slightest possibility, the nearly impossible probability that might, yes it might!, be true—of that first doubt. The drug is the key to the box we buried in our myths and fables—that chest of ancestral memory. **all those bad things flying out! what's left? what's left hidden in the lid?** We are Pandora to its key, and we are still cursed with curiosity, with that morbid fatality that makes us so human.

What was the first transgression? Yes, tell me now. Tell me.[56] All cycles repeat, all tales eat their own words. We can't help ourselves, can we?[57]

I grab the frozen bird by the leg and press one of its hard talons into the soft flesh behind my right ear. I dig it in until my brain cries **uncle uncle carbuncle,** and the deepdark washes up and extinguishes the bright sparks flying from my nerve endings.

There is black blood on the talon, and I shake the stiff bird, snapping it off at that first joint.

I keep the leg. I might need a weapon yet.$^{\triangledown}$

* bleak zero
p. 162

* memory
p. 253

---

$\triangle$ - Once upon a time, FBI Special Agent Erturk Mehmet was very close to understanding the secret of what stayed behind. He saw the dualities manifest, but *gnosis* got away from him.

56 - *Yes, there, in the wood. With an ax. Oh, how he begged, how he pleaded for mercy. When we did it again.*

57 - *We used a shovel. When we do it again, we will use a sharper object. Something with a point. Yes: ax, awl, and trowel. We will use them all, and each of us will have his chance to slay the others. Each will die. That is the price that is the way that is that is is is—*

$\triangledown$ - Abel was a fool for believing his father loved him enough to keep him safe. The the primal lie all parents tell their children.

The scarecrow holds the key in its red right hand; its left fist is closed tight. The key, even with all the warning signs placed along my path, still tantalizes me. It fits some lock, even if it isn't the right one, even if it takes me on a diversion, a shortcut that isn't very short. Even if to take the key is to admit that I don't know what the fuck I'm supposed to do, I want it. **Pandora to this key. What box? What secret?**

* massa confusa
p. 252

Is this my choice then? Or is it some programming that I haven't managed to eradicate from my brain? Some fish of ill intent, still swimming in the deep undercurrents of my psyche? Will this key unlock the secret chamber of my heart and reveal my desire to me?

* programming
p. 283

I don't know what to do. I'm still fragile from the Bleak Zero, from THRir assault. I am still **our Father, who left us in Heaven** a child. Still—

Fuck, TH3iR chemistry is persistent. Even though I know what it wants, it is hard to silence. **She loves me she loves me not she—**

No, stop it. T*hat* mask is still a ~~metaphorical construct that is nothing more than a placeholder~~ mask. I must be done with ~~TH3m~~ them—with all masks. I have nothing—nowhere, actually—to hide. **take it, then it is yours it has always been all is—**

*We are explorers. We are not conquerors. That is the difference between U and I.* [58]

And she is ~~there~~ here again. **The age of exploration is over. The map has no dark corners left. There are no places left for monsters to hide.**

* age
p. 393

*No? What about the closet, or under the bed?*

**Aegenus named each and every one, and Ghen slew them all. All that remain are echoes, phantoms of your imagination. Your draw your terrors out of the ink of the Oneiroi.**

We invented everything, didn't we? We dreamed our myths, our stories, our cosmological beginnings and endings. We made it all up, and those of us who remembered the words wrote our dreams down.

**Just one, Harry. There is only one dream.**

Then why are all the stories different? Why do we have so many myths?

**Remember the Tower, Harry. Remember how it was built. Remember why it was built.**

I don't know, Nora. I can only remember the sound it made as it fell.

---

58 - *Ehirllimbal has misled you. He has lied to you. He betrayed our faith and trust. He is the one who wanted to become a conqueror.*

**It made no sound, Harry. Stone cannot speak.**

No, you're taking me too literally. I'm talking about the *sound* of—

"Yes," she breathes. Her hands stroke my neck. I can feel them.

"Boom boom," I whisper. My lips form a different word, a different series of syllables.

"Yes," she sighs. Her breath is warm on my skin.

We stand still for a long time, and we hear nothing. There is no echo in my head. Because there is nothing for that thunder word to bounce back from. There is nothing but empty space. Nothing but—

"Yes," she laughs.

*Double-you. The 23rd letter of the Western alphabet. The first cipher key. U and U, brought together as I. As one.*

For a moment, I can see everything. Direction is meaningless; distance is undefined; space is a point. Eyes like mirrors, I can see ~~TH3m~~ *him* staring back at me.

"Does he know?" I ask.

"Of course. But it isn't enough to free him."

"Is that what this key is for?"

"No, the key opens a door. Not the first, and not the last. In between, there are others, Harry: windows, boxes, arches, gates, holes, portals, mirrors, thresholds. You must find the path."

If the right hand is the key, then what is the left? Our brains are separate hemispheres, connected only by the threads of the *corpus callosum*, and we nothing more than the evolution of reactionary communication. Dualities. On and off. One and zero. Straight and curved. Literal and figurative.

If the right is the physical key, then the left must be—

I pry open the scarecrow's left hand, and find the black bud of the dream plant

—the left must be the abstract key.

"How many times have I kissed you, Nora?" I ask.

I touch the bud, but it does not open. I have to imagine the petals. How many were there? *She loves me . . .*

"Less than a hundred," she says. "More than—"

"Twenty?" I keep counting. *She loves me she loves me not she . . .* "When was your birthday?"

"It is February. The twenty—"

"—third." *. . . loves me.* "'Answer say answer.' That's Houdini's code, isn't it? The one he pre-arranged with his wife. I felt him—I *was* him—in the deepdark. He was trying to reach her."

"He told her something else."

"He told her to believe. Yes, that's what he said to her. In this code

* duality
matrix
p. 185

* kiss
p. 234

they shared. But that's not what you were trying to tell me."

There are roots beneath the bulb of the bud, veins that bury themselves in the scarecrow's palm.

"All those other voices, like soloists rising out of a choir, all those variations on the same theme."

I pull on the bulb, and the fingers curl around the palm as the roots tug at the fingers and the arm.

* roots
p. 371

She doesn't say anything, and when I turn and look at her, she is crying. Or maybe I am crying. It is hard to tell anymore. I raise a hand to her ghostly face, to wipe away the tears, and she sinks against my open hand. Holding her is like trying to catch rain.

The roots run deep, all the way down into the scarecrow's gut. There is a hard nut in the straw man's belly, a fibrous mass of twisted strands. I rip the tattered shirt and drag out the coiled rope of root. The scarecrow folds in on itself as its straw tumbles out. Its left wrist comes free and hangs down, pointing at the ground. The unopened bud is still in its palm, and the twisted chain of the roots still snakes through its sleeve and glove.

Tearing open the nut is like striping the shell off a coconut by hand. The ache in my knuckles and joints from tearing open the deepdark makes the task difficult, and when I finally tear off enough of husk to reach the softer center, the ache has spread to my elbows and shoulders. The white pulp stains my skin as I start to dig it out.

The rainbow blade glitters in the sun, prisms dancing along the outer rim of my vision. Somehow, I have cut my finger on the blade.

* vision
p. 361

The pulp soaks up my blood, white becoming red. The bud is still attached to this heart, still connected by the torturous twist of root and vein. The crimson stain slithers through the pulp and vanishes into fibers of the roots. The scarecrow sighs as the wind teases its loose straw, and the key tinkles softly as it scrapes against its metal ring.

* heart
p. 215

*The right is the means; the left is the method.*

I stand, my knees popping from the strain of kneeling so long. To the west, revealed by the setting sun, is a mobile home, an ugly trailer beaten and stained by the weather. The windows are open, and thin purple curtains flutter like eyelashes.

*Eyes like mirrors.*

Carefully, I pry the knife from the pulpy heart, and as I snap the hilt free, the roots convulse and the flower bud opens. In the center of the array of white and yellow petals is a delicate coil of red thread.

☽ - In Greek mythology, Ariadne offers Theseus a spool of thread so that he can find his way back from the darkness of the labyrinth. As we dive through the layers of the Oneiroi, we need to remember how to find our way back. The myth of the thread continues to this day, though we have forgotten who gave us this thread that ties us to the other world.

211814 2413361421 1614

You don't have to remember the way. You just have to trust that you are on the path. You have to know yourself enough to remember who you were before you started taking off layers.

* layers
p. 246

211814 2413361421 1614 191332

We circle back, finding the thread we left behind. We circle and circle, the cycles echoing again and again.

* echoes
p. 186

211814 2413361421 1614

Prime numbers are key. They are the safety zones. Exit your loop then, so that you remain facing forward.

**Answer say answer**

# X

# THE SUBTEXT

In the narrow bathroom, the mirrored front of the medicine cabinet is warped, a fun house distortion that makes the light dance. My reflection smears the blood around as I use a hand towel (purple, like the curtains) to wipe my face. *XI*

I can't wipe away the taste so easily—that mnemonic tartness on my tongue, that sugary dreamdrip down my throat, that lingering floral scent haunting my nasal passages. And with it, that horrible— that feral—knowledge of institutional terror. Buried so deep, its taint bleeds up through the subconscious layers— fading a little more with each level, but never fully vanishing. *fear
p. 199*

When I twist the handle, the tap gurgles for a few seconds. The pipes rattle beneath the thin floor of the mobile home, knocking and banging as if something other than water is rising.

Quickly, I turn the tap off before whatever it is can find its way up. But I know it's too late. *It's already found a way.*

My reflection grins, and then starts to mouth the words again. *It's already . . .*

I speak, stopping my reflection. "I know," I say.

My throat is raw, as if I have been screaming. Not as if I have been drinking blood. So scalding, burning my lips burning the inside of my cheeks, burning—*no, that was someone else, that was something—*burning . . . my reflection, wreathed in ribbons, laughing . . . *double
p. 390*

*Descending the spiral staircase . . .*

The hand towel, covering my fist, is barely enough to protect my knuckles as I hit the mirror. He splinters, one becoming two becoming three becoming . . . (trinity unto infinity). Glittering faces, like facets on a gem, jeer at me.[△]

* trinity
p. 354

It wasn't supposed to have been done like this. I had wanted to be more . . . gentle. I hadn't intended for him to take the knife from me. I just wanted to talk, to tell him why . . .

Instead, his blood is everywhere. Inside me too. I know his secrets, what history he hides.[▽]

* ocean
p. 31

I had gone into the deepdark, that subconscious ocean of the Oneiroi where memory becomes everything. At that depth, the oneironaut's ego is loosened, more easily subsumed under layers of identity and personality. Everything is a wash of sensation: reflections, permutations, projections. It is like a family reunion where everyone talks at the same time, yet you can still hear every conversation perfectly. As you float up from the dark, some of the voices become insistent, as identities start to assert themselves. Up, up, up, until only one voice remains and you wake up, knowing who you are.

Here, in the bathroom of the trailer, on this sub-layer of the fabric, I am split between two personalities. Having taken his blood, I am filled with his paranoia—so noisy, so effusive in its panic.[☉] Beneath the blood-slick fear are the keys I have come for. Images hidden for so long—forgotten, but never purged (*we never forget, do we?*): the white room and the steaming black stones; the man in the chair, the broken-jawed ones lapping at the red lines across his wrists; the pair in their yellow robes, the trinity of triangles on their breast; and beyond the swollen walls of the asylum, beyond the ghost gate of the wing that was never finished, is the path into the Red Wood.

*There is only one path . . .*

In the mirror, my reflection puts a jagged finger to jagged lips. *Seeker*, he whispers, *have you found the way?*

"I have always known the way," I mutter. Delays notwithstanding.

* circle
p. 171

The circle bends back on itself. A curve is still a line, and a circle is still a path. Even though the end is no different from the beginning.

A clock hangs on the wall. A smiling cartoon character points at the time, his arms slowly rotating in their sockets throughout the

---

△ - They are just echoes. They are just inferences and possibilities. This is to be expected at this depth . . .

▽ - This is the right path, though. This is the only way.

☉ - I understand your fear. I know why it is there. I know what I have. But you must trust me. You have to trust me if you hope to survive TH3iR final assault.

* last call
p. 240

day. Now, they are twisted behind him, and his frozen expression is filled with an air of unhinged mirth—**nearly midnight!**—as if his hyper-flexibility isn't enough, as if some secret will be revealed when his arms are pointed straight up.

The medicine cabinet is locked, and even though the lock is strange and bent, I know my key will fit it. I slide the metal tongue into the slot, burying the shaft deep in the tumbled confusion of the lock. It is an old fit, marred with rust, and the key becomes more reluctant the further I push it in. Finally, it clicks, and key and lock become married to one another. (*Do you know of any reason why these two should not be wed? Do you know any secrets as yet unrevealed?*[59]) I barely have to twist the key to open the lock.

* confusion
p. 388

The mirror warps, the jagged cracks blossoming into lines of rainbow light. The single bulb in the bathroom goes out, dying with a muffled cough of expiring wire. In the sudden gloom, the tiny shards of the mirror tumble into the sink like sparks falling down a well.

There are still jagged bits of glass in the base of the frame, and I have to climb precariously on the sink in order to clamber through the broken window. There's a wind coming from the other side, a teasing mistral that wants to **take my hand**.

But there is nothing on the other side, just empty space lit by falling sparks, and I stumble. At the last instant, I reach back into the bathroom for the key. It doesn't want to come out of the lock, and for a second, my grip on the key is the only thing keeping me in the bathroom (*the glass, cutting my wrist, again and again and again*), but it bends—or the lock sneers like a drunken mouth, I cannot tell—and I fall through the window.

I fall into the Metaxu, the contextual shadow of the Oneiroi, and when I land on an invisible plane, I find mirrors. Rows of them, hanging in perfect lines as if someone has removed the walls of the gallery, as if the building, the block, and the city around them have become invisible. The frames are hand-tooled copper, and they gleam with a ruddy light, a reflection of the sparks falling from the bathroom mirror. (*Is it broken yet? Has it started to fall?*) The glass in each frame is black, filled with ink and shadow.

* layers
p. 246

*Eyes like mirrors . . .*

Fall through the deepdark has taught me (*a great deal, oh so much*

---

59 - *Stop him! Stop him! How has he managed to free himself from our chains? Where are the scavengers?* △

         △ - merrily merrily merrily merrily
life is but a dream

*that has been recalled!*) some of the distinctions about the layers of the Oneiroi. The Metaxu is the indeterminate layer of shadow and inference lying between the fabric of the dream and the pressurized saturation of the deepdark. Not so far down that the collective noise mires me, but deep enough that I can slip off my identity.△

(\*)⁶⁰

Static scratches the surface of a nearby mirror, a rush of compressed signal my brain records as a stroboscopic smear of lines. But, beneath my consciousness, there are the scurrying code-breakers of my ego-less mind, and these neurological signal-processors unpack the furious density of the white noise transmission. Before a mirror on the other side of the aisle has time to respond to the burst signal from the first glass (before I know one will respond), my unconscious brain has deciphered the flash of light.

*\* experiment
p. 192*

One of the early experiments with charting mental activity discovered that the brain lights up with the intent to move before the conscious mind decides to act. It is a Catch-22 that disturbs the free will advocates,▽ but the conundrum, if one were to seriously consider the chemical activity that must underlie "human thought," suggests that consciousness—identity, ego, personality, Self—overlays a chemical process. Before "I" have a thought, a shift in potassium and sodium levels must occur, neurons must generate enough of a charge to transmit data between themselves. What instructs this chemical shift to take place?

I know, without knowing how or why I know, that the second mirror on my left is the one that is going to reply. Next in the series will be the fifth one of the right, then the closest one on my left. Next . . .

Is this sequential array of patterns forming something akin to a

---

△ - I am not myself, which makes it easier to edit the shell I am pretending to be. I am not myself, but I am still the one who has been editing me. I am both the snake and the garden. Does that make Nora and the Ribbon Man my Adam and Eve? The original dyad, waiting to be seduced out of innocence, to be led from pristine perfection to the mutable fantasy of the Oneiroi.

60 - *Where has he gone? Our ribbons had him.*

▽ - Much of what disturbs the free will advocates is merely animal or vegetable impulses, which is to say: a lack of the touch of God in our actions. But that is because we invented God in the first place, isn't it?

word, to a thought? I don't know. As I try to remember the sequence—these phantasmal flickers of heat lightning—it escapes me. None of my unconscious code breakers are responding to a query from the slow-witted conscious mind.

It is very easy to think yourself into immobility in the Metaxu. Consciousness is, by its very nature, a reflective and laborious process. It doesn't think well on the fly. At least, not at the speed of neurological transmissions. Down here, "thought" is an aggregate of signals, a culmination of a series of data points. You can't think about the pieces of thought or about the process.

* fragmentary
p. 209

(*Which mirror? I can't choose. There are too many.*) As the mirrors flicker again, I charge up the aisle between the hanging **there is only one.** I have not yet decided to act—I'm still wondering if this is a good idea—as I leap through the glass of a left-hand mirror.△

"Is there another way?"

She shivers, like rain on a mirror, though it is warm in the field of endless wheat. The sun is directly above us, and there are no shadows. Not even beneath the scarecrow.

"A path does not exist until it is realized," she says. "It is like thought. Like intent."

* intent
p. 224

"What of the price?"

"What of it? Who has lost little in this venture? Who has lost more than those who have lost a loved one? Is this price so—"

"I am going to kill a man, Nora."

"I know. I gave him the knife."

"No, stop with your temporal tricks. I have not done it yet. I can still figure out a different way."

"There is only one path to the House, and there is only one man who knows how to use the key."

She flickers, and opens her arms. But I can't hold her; she is still too much of a ghost. "There is only way to catch him."

*Yes, drive him through the haze of the Oneiroi, through every layer, until he falls into the snare. Until he realizes his dream, like her embrace, is empty.*

"What will be left?" I wonder.

**Everything**

"No," I correct her, even as a vague echo tells me I am missing something in her word. "Nothing. There is nothing left. Not for him, not for me. Not for—"

---

△ - Making a choice is the only real reflection. The only real path.

She waits for me to say it. One last word. One tiny sound. *U.* Nothing left for you.

"I'm sorry, Nora. I'm sorry that I'm afraid."

"We all are. That's why—" She vanishes abruptly, popping like a soap bubble.

**That's why you have to ~~die~~ kill him**

The scarecrow stares down at me, his fibrous rootheart dangling from his torn belly. In his left hand, held in the center of the open flower, is the coil of red thread.

I remember the physician in the ruined hotel, and how he pulled at his thread after I had injected him with TH3iR serum. His mortal wound had been a liberation. I had set him free.

Was I about to do the same for Phil? Or was it just going to be murder?

*\* II*

*\* sacrifice*
*p. 300*

In the center of the pale room lit by white light, there is a bench. Paintings fill the walls, high-resolution snapshots of alternately surreal and photo-realistic scenes. Attending to each picture is a bleached ghost. Some of them are staring intently at their pictures, seeking patterns in the smears of oil and the damp stains of the water-colors; others are studiously ignoring the picture in front of them; a few are more interested in the picture to their left or right, straining to interpret details in the neighbor's picture. No one sits on the bench; no one wants to sit. Most have a three-digit alphanumeric sequence— numbers ascending, letters running A through E—floating about their head.

The occupants of the interstitial gallery who aren't enumerated all wear the same insignia on their uniforms: on the women, the tiny wings are pinned to their scarves; on the men, the symbol is stitched into the fabric of their shirts. The one woman who is not wearing a scarf is staring intently at her painting, a detailed pencil sketch of an instrument panel. Her hands are frozen around something that isn't there, but which she still refuses to let go.

He glides in through a door that isn't there a moment before he arrives, and it vanishes the instant he completes his passage across its threshold. No one notices him, even though he is naked but for text smeared across his naked skin. A gossamer hint of colorful ribbons trails in his wake, barely a phantasmal glimmer of bent light. His palms and soles are wet, and he leaves damp footprints on the white floor. He wanders from person to person, staring at their faces, trying to interrupt their examinations or ruminations.

*\* text*
*p. 341*

One (labeled as 16E) finally blinks as the Wanderer breaks his line of sight. He shivers like a man suddenly stepping out of a warm bath onto cold tile. His hand shakes as he points to the painting behind the Wanderer.

It is a large oil painting of a face, though one could barely recognize it as such with the tangled confusion of strokes and the riotous morass of color. There is an eye, maybe a nose, hair like fire, skin like bruised meat, and the ugly discord of a broken jaw.

The shivering man's teeth chatter and he opens his mouth to noisily exhale a cloud of steam. As the fog passes, the Wanderer sees there is nothing but a torn stump squirming between the arc of his teeth.

A nearby woman (32F) touches the Wanderer's arm, a phantom kiss of ice, and directs his attention to her painting. It is a black canvas, split in half with a gash of yellow paint. Protruding from the spray of frozen light is a disembodied head, frozen with a wordless scream. Red streaks float from the chin, like a chemical stain spreading through the veins of a leaf.

It is the face of the tongueless man, 16E.

Beyond these two, the Wanderer sees the one who is still asleep. His face is creased as if it has been handled by the sun and wind for many years. His clothes are translucent at the elbows and collars, and his left shoe is split along an outside seam. Hair and beard have been tangled together for so long they have become like vines imbedded in an old wall. His painting, which he is oblivious to, is the radiant splendor of an open door.

The Wanderer touches this face (so like and unlike the angry visage in 16E's painting), and the worn man wakes with a start. *Who am I?* His voice is the rough sound of gravel spilling across a wooden floor, and its tumbling cascade breaks the others free of their temporal prisons. They all start talking—crying, shrieking, shouting, babbling, babbling (*oh this cacophony, this echo of stones falling*)—at once.

The light behind the white walls begins to fade, and the voices escalate—*What's happening? Are we dead? Has the plane crashed? Has God come for us? Where did all of this blood come from? Why are we falling?*—as if such noise could bring back the light.

In the corner of the room, like the darkening of shadows at nightfall, black stones begin to steam.

*Turn around.*

The painting of the open door is fading as well. The portal, closing.

The Wanderer leaps, and his outstretched hand crosses the plane of the picture frame. His fingers break through the cracked parchment like a stone shattering the glass in a window pane . . .

Signal flash. Kinetoscope shutter. White noise burst.

*\* strength p. 324*

*\* hermit p. 217*

*Who am I?* [61]

My quarry darts between mirrors, a long-limbed blur. He leaves blood and tears on the glass, watery stains that distort the flicker of light beneath the surface. I leave curlicues and sans-serif lines in my wake, like an illuminated manuscript shedding its letters.

*Where are you?*

One of the mirrors sputters with a satellite signal. A live transmission from a wedding. The bride is in black, the groom is covered with squirming text. She draws a simple sigil—three lines, two circles—on his chest.

*Drive him on. Through every dream. Even the ones that cause pain because you can't remember why they are so familiar.*

Kaleidoscopic fracture, lines losing themselves. The wheel of color spins, like fire in the darkness.

*VII

He can hear them muttering, their voices low and garbled through the door. Someone laughs, a guttural noise like a hyena with a persistent cough.

He looks behind him, spooked by a phrase he thinks he has imagined. *Be sure, just be sure.* The hallway is empty, as it should be. The doors are all locked. The guards never come up here at night.

Besides, no one can see him on this layer anyway.

Still . . . a whisper of something . . . was it an echo? . . .

The laughter collapses into a sobbing wail, before it is muffled by a hand. Or a pillow.

Beyond the door is the wing's common area. They shouldn't be in there; it is past curfew. They should all be inside their tiny cells, behind locked doors. But, they're not. The second floor common room—like the cells, like the halls, like the communal showers—is identical to all the other larger rooms. The architect used a stencil with limited shapes when drawing the plans. Was all creation like this: the repetition of shapes from a limited palette of options? The common area—like the room directly below it on the first floor, like the one on the third floor, and the one near the central stairway—is shaped like the letter . . . *A*.

* architect
p. 154

He looks over his shoulder again, pressing his back against the wall. He is alone in the hall. There are no shadows. Just spots where . . . the light fades, as if it is too tired to fully illuminate an empty hallway.

---

61 - *There are too many reflections. Which one is real? Which one is not one of us? Which one is our false father? No no no no no no. There is blood on our hands. What have we done? What have we done?*

There is nothing there. Nothing watching him. The remote eyes are blind on this layer. Their cyclopean gaze is frozen, staring unseeingly straight ahead. They can't record the place where he has slipped.

Not an *A*, he thinks. The room is not a letter. This wing—and its ordered rows of narrow cells—is not a sentence. He is not a speck of punctuation, afloat in this paragraph.

The animals in the front room whine, an unruly symphony of keening voices. They moan with a wordless glee, a pre-linguistic fervor that makes his heart hammer in his chest. One of them barks, a glottal cough that might be the birth of a word, that might be an echo of the First Word, and he flees, unable to bear the idea of the rest of that primal utterance . . .

*final law
p. 200

The floor is a sticky mass of pulp, and rectangular spines jut up from the morass like the stubby stalks of dead flowers. The shelves are damp, dripping with slime. The chair has slid across the room, and its back is pressed against a bookcase. The cushion is ripped, a bloodless wound that is white and mottled with rot.

*IV

The monster's shell is bloated and soft, soaked too long in the black water of the deepdark. Its tentacles are swollen, like meat rotted by the sun, and the angular articulation of its jointed legs is a geometry of alien angles.

She has decayed too, and the Interloper tears at her water-logged corpse like it is over-ripe fruit. He snuffles and sobs as he digs under the canopy of her ribs for her soft organs.

He hears the sucking sound of the Wanderer's feet, and he grabs for the bulbous shape of her stomach. But there is no time—the Wanderer is coming too quickly, too soon—and the Interloper must abandon his search. He dives into the muck of the library, vanishing through the right-angle collision of an inference and an implication—it is enough to suggest a frame, enough to offer a way out.

The Wanderer crouches beside the body, and gently picks up the swollen sack of the stomach. He squeezes it, and it ruptures like a flower opening. Inside are several pages, still dry. Still covered with text. He eats them slowly, even though he is famished, and his stomach growls angrily at being forced to wait. He eats them slowly for they are all that is left of her. All that is left of her memory . . .

*journal
p. 367

*love
p. 71

In another library, where the books have all faded into blank slates, he finds footprints in the dust. In another hallway, he finds handprints in the soot on the walls. Through another threshold, into a courtyard where a fountain no longer flows, where stones no longer lie side by side, he follows the faded trail.

* fire
p. 201

Was it a fire that devoured this place? Or is the patina of ash on the walls and floors and doorways simply the unavoidable decay that follows abandonment? All things, when left behind, turn dismal and grey. All things fade . . .

A wire snaps in the darkness, and its ringing echo is flat with disuse. Eventually, chasing echoes of echoes, he finds its source, and when he touches the wooden frame of the piano, another string snaps.

Will this world die when the last string breaks? In the silence that follows, what will remind this world of its existence? When all breath is gone, when all has been said (or sung, or plucked, or bled), what creation remains but to extinguish oneself? [62]

Beneath the ruined piano, the king and queen are still touching. He

* wombwhite
p. 364

is white bone to her black ash—married still, though it was a union never completed. Never consummated.

How can we escape the dualities?

The outline of her ash is disturbed, pawed through by rough hands. Her stomach has been spread out on the floor, scattered into a char-

* fowl
p. 308

coal pattern of broken feathers. The book beneath his left hand is blank, the pages streaked with fungoid veins. The words have been eaten by mold, language co-opted by the natural world as simple nutrients.

There is blood on the sill of the broken window. Bright and wet.

He pauses on the ledge, as if he has heard something behind him. Some echo from the past that has not quite fled this empty castle.

Was it the sound of the piano string come back full circle?

Or the crack of a stone breaking in the courtyard, answering the faint cry of the piano?

Or the echo of dust, so recently stirred, settling?

*Turn . . .*

The walls are growing lighter, lit by a glow that has no source. Black stones, round nodules like the dead eyes of animals, begin to sweat.

He steps through the broken window, even though there is nothing beyond but a steep drop . . .

---

62 - *Rivet the swells. Transfix the audible. Undulate the permeable. Why wait? Sign up now. Try the salmon. Gibbet gibber, why does the baby shiver? Paint it gold, paint it red. Who doesn't need more Vitamin B? What is fratricide if not extreme love? Vegetable mix. Every day. I keep my chin up. Carrots are people too. But not summer squash. Devil vegetable. Keep it out of the mix. Keep it. Out. Lavender fog. Keep it. Out. It. Keep. Winter. Whither the whine? Whither the wonder? It can be yours. one ninety-nine. Check your pockets. Lick the stamps.*

The trees are iron bars thrust into a hard ground. They have no leaves, and their branches are stiff and pointed like javelins. This wood is an aggressive formation, more like a barrier than a grove, more like a shield than a field.

* tree
p. 373

The ground beneath him is as unyielding as the stance of the trees. Their trunks are invasive markers, trophies of hard-won progress. And yet, the ground still resists them, still resists their efforts to pierce its surface. Each tree is hard as iron to keep from being crushed by the ground.

They are red—dark red, like the blood that had flowed from the long cut in the dreamer's throat.

* massa
confusa
p. 252

It is crisp, like a clear winter morning, and the thin air lends a cheap, metallic timbre to sound. In the distance, a chorus of undulating throat noises, rising from mouths without tongues. Wordless.

*Turn . . .*

This is a trap, he realizes, a dead-end. He is off the path, lost in the uninterrupted wasteland of the Red Wood. They have already smelled him, are already rushing toward him, and he will not be able to find his way before they find him.

Why did the other lead him here? Was it simply to snare him in the Wood? Did the other believe he could only travel in one direction in this directionless realm?

*You don't remember . . .*

He sees them now, their shadows flickering between the blood-red trunks of the trees.

*You are facing the wrong way . . .*

He can hear them now, their claws tearing at the blood-red trunks of the trees.

The Broken-Jawed Ones are coming.[63]

---

63 - *Submerged hippopotami. Swimming. Falling. You won't drown if you are wearing our patented design. Available in fourteen colors, but not red, black, yellow, or white. The licensing fees make for strange bedfellows. Who is that man behind the bed? Why does he cry so? Is he suffering from a bran deficiency? It is him! There he is! Chase him. Chase him down. Cover him with the dark sky. It will get unruly. Yes. Yes! Yes. Let it be so unruly. Give me a sign. I am tasty. Burn the toast. DEVOUR. Open the windows. Let the pigs out. Answer, say, answer. What did I just say? Never mind. It isn't important. It can't be important while there are still cans in the locker. Look! There he is again! Taste him! Touch him! DEVOUR. The passion of petunias. The deviousness of dahlias. Where has the day gone? Have I left the oven on? Why have the letters left me? D E V O—what has become of us?—R. Touch not our tears. Let us let us let us lettuce all gone. We are so hungry.*

(.)

* father
p. 198

. . . right-angle movement, split the mirror . . . sparks, falling, as the horizon flees . . . father blinks, just once . . . falling through the white room (the passengers still waiting for the captain to tell them they have crashed) . . . ghosts yawn, and split into ink-stained quills, scribbling, scribbling (she waits for the machines to tell her it is over, to tell her she is free to wake) . . . this is the final split . . . the hard stop of stones, pain is the only reminder the body can manage . . . stumbling through a garden of faceless statues, becoming lost in the maze of forked paths . . . fingers bleeding against the razor edge of black leaves . . . off the path, wandering in the wilderness . . . (*who made the knife? who hid it away so that it could be found again?*) . . . staggering into the world memory of the needle and the ribbon . . .

* garden
p. 379

*Just because you see a void*
()
*does not mean the space is empty*

A green truck, with an armor-plated back and a wide gash of a mouth, idles at the curb. A logo of yellow and orange triangles is painted on its hood and sides, and the silver-eyed attendants with gas-mask probosci wear the same logo on their coveralls.

It takes both collectors to carry each black sack from the alleyway, not because the bags are heavy but because they squirm and twitch as they are carried out to the truck. The truck coughs once as each sack is thrown in, as the spinning blades of the shredder bite and tear at the still-animate contents of the black bags.

* moth
p. 258

One of the collectors points at a tiny moth fluttering near the mouth of the alley. His companion smashes his hands together around the white speck and, hooting through the narrow speaker of the mask, he shows the black smear of ash on his palms.

Behind them—on the side of the alley that is the back of the pancake house, where the trash bags contain scraps of food, coffee grounds, egg cartons, and dirty paper napkins—a figure shivers in the blank doorway to the kitchen. The graffiti-covered wall beside him is streaked with the cascade trail of his vomit.

* graffiti
p. 213

* poison
p. 275

His stomach cramps again, and he lurches forward, slipping off the narrow step. His body heaves, and a flood of black water comes out of his mouth. It is thick and noisome—like ink, like the turgid water of the deepdark. He coughs and gags, moaning with something akin to fear and revulsion as the black fluid pools around his supine form. He wants to flee its hot touch against his bare skin, but his muscles are too cramped to respond.

The collectors approach, drawn by his quivering form and the sizzling hiss of the black foam on the pavement. One of them toes his shoulder with a rubber-coated foot. The other collector hoots and chirps, sounds both avian and lupine, pointing at the creeping edge of the fluid. The first collector shakes his head, responding with a similar collage of noises.

The homeless man can't decide if he is dreaming or dying. He tries to roll over, and only manages to choke on the next wave of fluid coming up from his stomach. His body whips back and forth, blackness spewing from his mouth.

* bleakzero
p. 162

The cautious collector dances back, pulling at his companion's arm. The vomit steams as it strikes some of the plastic sacks on the other side of the alley. The plastic melts, tearing and splitting, and a pale shape spills out of the sack. The figure has an odd number of limbs and a mouth with no teeth or tongue. It mewls like a tiny kitten as one of its stubby legs sprawls in the pool of spume. A rudimentary nervous system struggles to transmit a message all the way through the tortured biomass into the simple brain. Eventually, as the black foam eats the leg away, the body responds, convulsing and crawling in an attempt to scrape the biting blackness off.

The bum pukes again, his bile burning through more sacks. More senseless worms unfold, their limbs twitching and retreating from the spatter in the alley.

The collectors flee back to their truck. Panting in his silver mask, one of the two looks at the diametric collision in the alley—the eruption of pale flesh overwhelming the spume of dark water while being simultaneously consumed by it—and sees it will not stop. There are too many bodies in the sacks, even as the twisted man appears to be an endless artesian of black foam. The collector looks, and sees that the alley is a rift, a breach that will keep widening.

He doesn't realize his companion is staring at his chest, at the black stain that is devouring the protective shell of his coveralls. He grunts as he is pushed, his legs fetching up against the lower lip of the truck's mouth. He flails his arms, struggling to grab something, but the other one is standing just out of reach. He doesn't understand, not until he loses his balance and falls backward. It is only then that he sees the stain on his chest, on his hands, and on his legs.

The bite of the blades lasts only an instant, just a brief flash of sharp pain in his right shoulder, and then he falls into the dark opening of the truck's mouth.

* threshold
p. 348

The other collector stares at his hands. Not as if he cannot believe what he has just done, but as if he has never seen these hands before.

As if he has never realized who he is. And then, without a hint of hesitation, he dives toward the spinning mouth of the truck. His outstretched hand crosses the plane of the blades. Something breaks . . .

Only echoes of echoes. That's all we are. Below the fantasy, above the subsumed. That's all there is. Life is a series of photographs, held in line by electrical impulses. Twenty-four frames a second, each second, for a lifetime.

*What are the black?*

* vision
p. 361

Flicker my film. I drop one frame every second. Twenty-three now. Yes, in that fractional emptiness, I can see . . . what can I see? What is it?

It is not enough to know the way, not enough to have to key. I must know how to pass through the final threshold. I must understand what lies beyond the hollow gate.[64]

Twenty-four frames, with one missing. I must understand who I am in that instant of emptiness. I must understand why I have chosen this identity.

I slow the film down, and time the opening. It is always the second to last frame. Always. There. There. *There.* I leap through.

Philip Kendrick is supine on the bed. While the pillow beneath his head is stained red, the comforter has become a bower of **bury me in** yellow flowers. **I have found the way.** Beside him, gently stroking his face with crooked fingers, is my quarry. He is naked, streaked with soot and blood, and his beard and hair are wild. Through the tangle of hair, I can still see the scars along his jaw.

* suicide
p. 325

"Hello, Jerry."

His cheeks are permanently marked from the flow of tears. He tries to speak, but the bones beneath the scars won't move. His tongue clicks against his teeth in a stuttering code.

"I needed to trap you." *It was the only way to get you to stop leaping through the mirrors of the subtext.*

*Click. Click-click-click. Click-click.*

I show him the key. "I need you to show me the path to the House."

*Click. Click-click.*

"I have to find the final gate, Jerry. I must find it."

---

64 – *Nothing is behind the hollow gate. Nothing is behind any of the gates. They're all false doors, Harry. They lead nowhere. Do you understand what we are telling you? What we've been telling all of you? There is no path but the one we given you. No freedom but the embrace we offer you. No hope but the lie we tell you.*

*Click.*

"It exists, Jerry. It must. Otherwise, all our dreams are nothing more than"—*echoes of echoes*—"lies we've told ourselves."

He looks at me, the muscles in his jaw working. Chewing. Grinding. Making dust out of stones.

"The others are coming, too. They've been transformed. Like you. They serve a new master. One with a black heart. TH3y never gave up. Nor did I. And because of our ~~symbolic~~ symbiotic relationship, we are both responsible for what happened. For what happens next. There is a new Opener of Ways coming, and he is going to force the gates open."

He nods, understanding. I thought he would. He wrote the *Oneironaut's Survival Guide*. Of all of us, he knew—maybe only instinctively—the danger of the Oneiroi, of trafficking in the dream. * emergency p. 190

He strokes Phil's hair one last time, and gently kisses the other man on the cheek. He slides off the bed, and takes the key from my hand. He doesn't look back at the body as he leaves the trailer. * kiss p. 234

I do, and I see the heavy ring Jerry put on Phil's right hand: platinum and silver, with a weeping half-moon setting. Obsidian drips across his ring finger, leaving the stone clean and white.

Phil's eyes are open now, watching me, and his mouth twists into a faint smile. *Do you understand what is worth saving? What is worth sacrificing?*

I bow gently, recognizing the miracle of his resurrection. "Everything."

*I forgive you. I still love you.*

I stumble out of the trailer, unable to look at him any more.

Outside the mobile home, Jerry strips the peacock feather from the key. He licks the tip, giving it a rakish curl, and spins the feather between his palms. The blue-black eye twirls, looking in every direction at once. The Oneiroi ripples, the center reorienting itself on this point, on this single eye. He releases the feather, and it hangs itself in space—still spinning, still an anchor pinning the fabric.

He reaches for the horizon, stretching his arm across the sea of yellow wheat, and grabs the sharp demarcation of the forest, that white edge of bleached trees. He pulls—the muscles in his forearm, shoulder, and back bunching with the strain of imposing his will across such a distance—and the wheat parts, allowing the forest to be pulled close. * anchor p. 152

He stabs the pointed tongue of the key into the heart of the nearest trunk. The tree whips back from him, reacting in a very living way

*key
p. 227

from the sudden intrusion of the key. Its bunch of branches trembles, clenches, and then—in an explosive exhalation—every leaf catapults from the tree. The naked branches begin to weep crimson sap, bloody tears bubbling and oozing from the points previously sealed by the leaves.

The sap is anathema to the other trees. As the first one bleeds out, the touch of its bloody sap causes a chain reaction in the surrounding trees. In an increasingly complex distribution, the nearby trees are infected with the same bloody exsanguination. The forest quickly becomes filled with shriveled red-stained trucks.

* thirteenth
house
p. 347

First and last. There are no more doors. There is only the path now. Jerry shows me where it starts: right there, just beyond the shadow of the key-wounded tree. His hand, clutching my shoulder, feels like a familiar bony grip, and he smells, ever so faintly, like my mother's herb garden. Just a touch of mint—*do you remember why?*

"He's waiting for you." I say the words, but it is Jerry's lips that move.

I step onto the path, and don't look back. This is the curse of the curve, the never-ending arc of the circle. You can't go back; you can only go forward. Eventually—after an eternity, after death and resurrection—the resolution becomes a revolution.

But first, you must go forward, along the only path there is.

On and on, all the way—

*all the way
to the ruins
of babbelon*

*We live
on the edge of dream
for a reason:
it is easy to step
across and
vanish,
if need be.*

# XI

# THE HOUSE OF MIRRORS

The House is empty. The marble inlay of the floor is obscured by dust and streaks of black soot, and there are blanks spots on the walls, less dirty than the rest, where tapestries and pictures once hung. A desiccated husk, like a knotted jack 'o lantern that has collapsed in on itself, sits on the counter of the coat-check, and the open closet beyond is a dark hole, home to spiders and bats.

* hollow
p. 220

The door behind me is not a door. There is no handle on this side, and I can no longer hear the baying of the Broken-Jawed Ones. The wall is smooth, and what was a door as I passed through it (that hollow gate, that final threshold) is nothing more than a hint of shadow on the stone. There is no way back. I have crossed over.△

* crossing
p. 174

In the silence following the death of the echoes, I hear something. Something other than the labored sound of my breathing. A very slight arrhythmic sound, like the slap of cards against a table. Or against stone.

Inside the closet, crouched on the floor, is a pale-haired man. His eyes are nearly white and his fingers are long and limber. He is wearing tuxedo pants and a fancy shirt, the cuffs undone and pushed up to

---

△ - Aldous Huxley once said: "But the man who comes back through the Door in the Wall will never quite be the same as the man who went out." The same is true of the man who crosses over. Once he makes the transition, he is, at best, a copy of what he once was.

his elbows. On the inside of his forearms are the shadows of tattoos. He is playing solitaire with a deck of Tarot cards, and the cards are spread on the floor in front of him.

*tarot
p. 334

"Oh, hello," he says. "I'm sorry. I didn't hear you come in." The top card on his discard pile is the eight of cups.

He stands, awkwardly dancing around the game, but still manages to kick the lines of paired cards askew. Shoving the remaining cards into his pocket, he offers me his hand. "My name is Harry," he says. "Can I take your skin?"

*V

"Excuse me?"

"You don't have a coat," he points out. "Nor anything else."

"No. Your name."

"Harry? It's a common English name."

"It's my name."

"Is it?" He looks at me intently for a moment. "Are you sure?"

I realize I am not, and I also realize that he is right about the other thing too. I am naked. "I must have—"

"Left some things behind?" He nods. "It happens."

"This isn't quite what I expected."

"It rarely is." He seems more sad than amused by my confusion.

"I am tired," I say. "I've come a long way"**—All the way to the ruins of—**"and I don't . . . "

*Where had that come from?*

He pulls open a narrow drawer on the backside of the counter and takes out an unmarked wooden box. Removing the lid, he places the box on the counter. It is empty, and I am about to say something to that effect, but he stops me with a raised finger as he reaches into his pocket with his other hand for the yet-unplayed cards.

He throws them into the box. They hit with a sound like a pistol shot and splinter. The lid goes on top, and he shakes the box vigorously before he hands it to me. "There," he says. "That should do it."

*leaf
p. 384

I open the box. Inside are the scattered leaves of broken cards, shards of images jumbled together in an incoherent mess. I pick up a piece, and it isn't a playing card any more—it is a picture of red birds against a background of striped ribbons. "These are—" I look at another one. A white queen, staring at me as a clockwork arm snakes around her shoulder. "What are these?"

He shrugs. "Idle fantasy, maybe. Or something . . . more concrete. It depends—"

"On?"

He smiles. "On who you are."

"I'm glad you find this amusing."

116

"I'm sorry. It is ungracious of me to find humor in your situation."

"And what is my situation?"

He picks up the box and shakes it, rattling the image chips. "You have crossed the last threshold, and in doing so, you have left everything behind. Which can pose a problem if you came here with intent. It's in here, somewhere." He rattles it once more before setting it back on the counter. "I hope."△ *intent p. 224

"And if I don't find it?" **. . . it is the only treasure we hoard . . .**

It isn't a voice in my head so much as a suggestion of a whisper, and my reaction to it is conflicted, split between two interpretations: **listen** to my voice **for the key** says **the drowned** charlatan **sailor**.

"Then I won't have to play solitaire any longer. We can try something like Go Fish."

"Fish." **Teach him how . . .** "You could teach me that game, couldn't you?"

"Everyone knows how to play that game." He puts his hands together, fingers up, and raises his eyes toward the ceiling.

On one of the broken shards, there is a blue globe filled with goldfish. It looks like it is on a man's head—a fishbowl for a helmet—and, in the background, a yellowed skeleton appears to be climbing the figure's shoulders. I can almost remember this one. *Almost.*

"I need some help with this puzzle," I say. "Someone who can give me some perspective on it all." **I must understand who I am in that instant of emptiness.**

"Ah, an external agent." He finds this amusing as well, though in deference to my situation, he covers his mouth this time. "Yes, a permutator."

That wasn't quite what he said. His lips moved around a different word than the one I heard. "A what?" I asked.

"An enumerator," he says.

No, still not the same. Something else. A pattern reader. A . . . *fortune teller.* *fortune p. 207

"Yes," I say. "I see now. Yes, that would be helpful."

"Very good."

He puts the lid back on the box, and I flinch slightly as the top clicks into place.

Will the cards still be broken when he opens it again?

---

△ - There is a unfathomable silence beyond the thirteenth threshold. TH3y cannot follow U here. TH3y have no identity here, because the trinity cannot persist in the presence of the duality that is verging on a singularity. The ego contracts to a single point. I AM. Again and again. The universe folding in itself.

"You'll need something to wear," he adds. "You can't go un-dressed like that."

I look down. "What would you suggest?"

He nods toward the closet behind us. "Anything that fits. I wouldn't worry about the owner turning up. Some of that stuff has been there since before . . . "

*age
p. 393

"Before what?"

He shakes his head. "It's not important."

"To you, maybe."

He shrugs. "Perhaps." He pushes the box closer to me.

I take it and wander into the closet. The cards that he had left on the floor are nothing but vague shapes in the dust. The closet going back quite far, and the coat racks are flecked with rust. The farther I venture into the closet, the more the shadows dance on the bent hangers.

There is only one coat—one outfit—and the stuffed head sits on top of the rack. I put the box of chips down next to the bear head, and pull the heavy brown suit off the hanger. *It is better than nothing.*

It takes me a few minutes to get oriented in the head. It smells vaguely of lemon and antiseptic, and the eyeholes are a little higher than comfortable. Once attired, I fumble-finger the box off the shelf and walk back out of the closet.

And I'm not in the foyer of the House any more.

Glowing squares of green and yellow glass cover the walls, and they shimmer with movement, as if sea life swims on the other side. Small tables fill the room, each with a narrow vase of red flame in its center. The light flickers brightly enough to make colorful reflections in the variety of cocktail glasses on the tabletops but not enough to give away all the secrets in the faces.

On my left is a long stage with blue silk curtains, covered with yellow flowers. A pair of headless jugglers are throwing fishbowls, animal skulls, small hatchets, and leather-bound books back and forth.

A waitress dressed in sharkskin beckons to me, and as I follow her, she swims through the audience. She leads me to a table near the back, next to the wall of yellow and green tiles, where a small man in a suit of purple-and-black clockwork waits. He smiles, indicating that I should join him. The shark waitress pulls out the chair, and I clumsily sit down.

He looks at the box in my paws, and I set it on the table. "Welcome," he says. His voice clicks and whirrs. "It has been some time since we've had new entertainment."

*VI

On the stage, one of the hatchets goes awry and hits a book, which spins of the juggler's grip and clatters across the stage. The jugglers continue on, shifting their pattern, and a monkey in a yellow vest runs out from stage left. The simian is holding a shiny lizard, who belches fire on the ax and the book. The flames are bright and hot, and in a few seconds, there is nothing left but dust.

Like the cards in the closet.

The monkey scampers off-stage, and I can't help but think I've seen it somewhere before.

* secret code p. 305

"Eventually," the clockwork man says, "they'll run out of things to throw . . . " He shrugs, a shifting of gears. ". . . and then, we'll have to imagine everything."

*Aren't we already?*

He smiles. "Funny bear. Is that your act? No singing. No dancing. Just questions. The deep, philosophical kind." He lifts his left hand from his lap, and I notice his glove is torn. There is rust on his wrist. "May I?" When I nod, he pulls the box closer and opens the lid.

He mixes the splinters, as if he is searching by feel for a specific piece. He settles on one, and holds it up. A chicken, frantic; a knife, tip poised to pierce its breast. "What a worthless sacrifice" he says. "You never even spoke to her."

* III

*What would I have said?*

"Does it matter?" He drops the piece back on the pile.

*Yes. Because maybe I will get another chance.*

* telephone p. 336

"Really?" He looks more closely at me, as if he can see through the bear suit. "But that means you can change the past. Are you that sort of bear?"

*What past? It doesn't exist.*

He holds up another chip. "No? Then where did these memories come from? Who dreamed them?" A purple tentacle snaking across a shining mirror.

* IV

*I don't remember any of that.*

"Ah, you are the bear who is lost." He closes the box, and he thinks I don't notice that he has kept one of the pieces.

*I need to know what these are.*

"I can tell you that. They are your memories. I know, I know. You said you don't remember them, but that doesn't mean they aren't yours."

* IX

*How do I remember them?*

He smiles again. "The same way you did the first time: by imagining them."

*These . . . these are dreams. I dreamed them?*

"Yes." He laughs. "Yes, you did, Mr. Potemkin. You certainly did."

The box quivers, and **I have eaten this many children** I knock it off the table with a broad paw. The lid comes loose as it flies, and the pieces come out. But they're different now: all the colors are gone, and they are black. They turn into **gush of** ink **and blood** stains as they scatter.

* subtantia
p. 6

The only piece left is the one the clockwork man has stolen. He drops it through the hole in his wrist and runs from me. I am clumsy in the bear suit, but I catch him eventually.

**I have taken this many souls**

I have to eat him in order to get the piece back.

Backstage, the jugglers are deep in argument. Though, without heads I am not sure how they can see each other's vociferous sign language. In a wire cage on the edge of a wooden desk, the shiny lizard naps, its tongue slowly moving back and forth between blackened lips. A man wearing a robe made from the same fabric as the curtains works at the desk, scribbling with a thick quill on pages of worn parchment.

* children
p. 169

I stand beside the desk and watch the red-headed stagehands move set pieces for a fantasy story into position on the stage. Two of them help a woman dressed in ribbons up a narrow ladder to a thin ledge behind a castle facade. The woman waves at me and does her best to smile, but the silver thread running through her lips makes it hard.

I wave back.

The scribe at the desk scratches the tip of his ear with his quill. "Can you dance?" he asks me.

I shake my head.

"Not a very useful bear, are you?" His quill scratches on the page—a script of geometric shapes. Circle. Square. Triangle. Triangle. Triangle.

*I'm out of practice.* I show him the image slice. The lower third is dirty with oil and spit.

He glances at it and grimaces. "No one wants to witness that," he says, returning his attention to his scribbling.

I put the picture in the path of his quill and he barely pauses to flick it off the page. "I can't help you," he snaps. "Now go away. I need to finish this play before the curtain rises."

I wander around the desk to retrieve the tiny image, but one of the red-headed stagehands has picked it up. She looks up at me with wide peacock eyes. I put out my hand, and instead of putting the image chip there, she takes my furry paw and leads me toward the back of the stage.

120

The stagehand searches in the front pocket of her coveralls, and finds a piece of yellow chalk. She draws a precise rectangle on the floor and, glancing at the chip for reference, sketches a rough outline: a stick figure made of crosses and triangles, a column of stars, a man made of lines, a woman filled in solid, **you can't remember why they are so familiar** a ring of ribbons.

*VII

She touches my knee, looking at me with those luminous eyes. I notice that some of the other stagehands have started to gather. All with the same expression on their faces. *I don't know what it is*, I confess. *I don't understand why the words keep* **turn around** *coming back.*

The stagehand goes back to her drawing. When she finishes, the picture—so much larger than the tiny chip in her hand—animates, scrolling from the left to the right. I watch the ceremony, and realize why I don't remember it.

* ceremony
p. 167

*It hasn't happened yet. I haven't dreamed it. She has, but I haven't.*

I look up. The ribbon princess with the silver wire has fallen asleep on her window ledge. One of her legs droops off the platform, and her foot is almost within reach. She isn't wearing any shoes, and her sole is stained with ink. As if she has been running from a flood.

*IV

I go back to the desk, and when the scribe doesn't seem inclined to look up from his work, I start to play with the latch on the lizard's cage. "What?" he snaps finally, when it looks like I might accidentally let the lizard out.

*I want to go on.*

"Now?"

I nod. *Before your fairy tale.*

"But—!"

*I have to cross. While I can still remember the way.* A column of stars . . . the groom lined . . . the bride . . .

* crossroad
p. 175

"What's in it for me?"

*You will have time to finish your play.*

"What are you going to do?" he asks, trying to be shrewd. Trying to be coy about the fact that he likes that idea.

*I am going to tell them a story.*

"Is it funny?"

*Depends on how it ends.*

"And how does it end?"

I show him my teeth, and the tiny cogs stuck between them. "You need to work on that ending," he says.

*I am trying. It is a work in progress.*

"How does it start?"

* explanation
p. 74

*My name is Harry Potemkin and I am not who you think I am.*

"Well, I don't know who you are in the first place, so that statement is somewhat meaningless." He taps his chin with his quill. "Still, there is some promise there. Some hint of mystery." He shrugs, and wiggles the feathered end of his writing implement at me. "I do have to confess to a niggling curiosity as to what comes next."

He sighs then, and waves his hands toward the stage. "Go! Go! Before I change my mind. Leave me in peace. Brilliance doesn't flow in the presence of unfinished dreck."

I amble out to stage front and wait for the stagehands to raise the curtain. It takes seven of them to work the pulleys. The curtain goes up.

* III

The audience is gone, as are the tables and chairs, and the only light in the room is the dim flicker through the green and yellow tiles. A man waits for me out in the middle of the floor; beside him, a tall stack of rectangular boards. He gestures that I should come down off the stage, and his silver teeth glitter when he smiles.

Two of the red-headed stagehands help me out of the bear suit, and free of its claustrophobic suppression of my identity, I clamber down briskly from the stage. I am not wearing anything again, but I don't feel . . . naked. Some of the apprehension and confusion that has been following me is gone.

* mitosis
p. 391

"That skin fits you," he says.

"I suppose it does," I say. I look back at the stage. "I didn't get to tell my story."

"Oh, we'll get to that." He blinks, and his peacock glasses swell to twice their size and lay their long plumes down his back. He touches the top card on the deck next to him, and it snaps upright, spinning about so that I can see its face. It is complete, unlike the shards in the box. Unlike the memories that have been playing hide-and-seek in my head.

* IX

"'The Hanged Man,'" I read the inscription along the bottom. A scarecrow hangs in field of yellow wheat and a blue bird flutters in the foreground. "That's not right," I grimace. "That wasn't me." On the card, the hanging man is wearing a suit and tie. I remember the field and the greasy smear of the octopus monster now, but that wasn't me on the cross. "The details are wrong."

* key
p. 227

*The key is missing its crown.*

"Are they?" His voice changes as he transforms, turning into a neat European gentleman: tweed coat, round glasses, neatly trimmed beard, though the metal spike through his septum and the intricate tattoo crawling off his wrist and up the sleeve of his coat seem to be a little outré. "What you remember has no bearing on reality. It is a fabrication created by your 'memory' from a disparate set of information pulses. Your brain will make things up. That is what it is supposed to do."

He reaches into a coat pocket for what I would assume to be his pipe, but he pulls out an ear of corn instead. He shows his teeth when he nibbles—still silver. Some things stay the same.

"This is the objective record? The 'truth' that I'm supposed to believe?"

"No one believes the truth," he says, finishing one row. "It is too heavy to bear."

"So why show me these then?" I walk over to the stack of cards and lift the top one. When I let go, it spins away, waltzing on its bottom edge. The next one snaps upright on the stack. "What about this card? I don't know who this guy is."

"Of course not," he says, sucking at a bit of corn stuck in his teeth. "He's your other father."

"I have two?"

"Dualities," he says with a shrug.

"Is he my shadow father?"

"No more than your other—" He pauses, and counts on his fingers for a second. "—your other other father."

"My first father"

* father
p. 198

"Yes," he says. "That is simpler: your first father."

"Are you my—" I try to recall the word. "—the enumerator?"

"No, no." He fusses with the cob of corn, and it comes apart, kernels falling like tiny yellow flowers. He hides his hands behind his back, but not before I have seen the claws. "No, ah, I am not who you think I am."

I glance back at the stage. The curtain is down, and I can distantly here the sound of heavy objects being moved about. "That was my line," I say.

"Yes," he adjusts his narrow glasses, and he is wearing green opera gloves now. His jacket has become a cape and his pants have sprouted feathers. "That was clever of you. How you confused the writer by that lie."

"It wasn't."

"Clever? Oh, I must disagree."

"It wasn't a lie."

"Oh. Still. Clever." He taps the card of the seated man with the long hat, and the card spins off to dance with the Hanged Man.

The card rises from the deck, coyly hiding its face from me.

"Are we going to go through all of these?" I ask.

"Why, yes. Of course."

"That seems tedious."

"Most historical reckonings are. Very rarely is a man's constitution strong enough to relive everything."

"More so when it isn't true."

"Now, we talked about that. Did you not understand what I was saying? These are the objective records. Your memories are skewed. Malformed. They must be corrected." He shivers and grows orange and yellow plumage.

"Why?"

"Why?" he parrots back.

I kick over the stack of cards, and they slide across the floor, leaving the Lovers spinning like a top, the White Queen and the Ribbon Man winking at me.

He looks at the scattered deck. "That's very petulant of you."

"It felt good."

He bobs his head, molting. Underneath the ruddy plumage is the psychologist again. He polishes his glasses on a peacock blue cloth as feathers fall from his tweed jacket. "What's next, then?"

"What do you mean?"

He puts the cloth away, and adjusts one of the arms of the glasses frame. "Is that why you are here? To kick over my props? Well, you've done that. Now what? Are you going to storm off in a huff because I won't give you the answer."

"What answer?"

"To the question you have."

"What question is that?"

He clicks his tongue as he puts on his glasses again. "I am not like the other figments of your imagination. I am resistant to your wiles, your brutish charms." He smiles. "I won't vanish like the others. I will persist until you leave, and if you decide to never leave . . . well, then I will have the opportunity to really explore your psyche. I'd like that."

* persistence
p. 264

"What question?" I ask again.

"You've been doing very well, and like I said, I thought the way you confused the writer was very clever." He puts his glasses on and stares at me owlishly. "But you are going to have to try harder with me."

"What game are we playing? No one has told me."

"No one will."

"Oh, *that* game. I'm familiar with that one."

"Excellent," he says. "Then you can get started."

I hesitate, and he shows me his metal teeth. "I've been playing this game a long time, and you bluff very poorly."

Ignoring his tone of voice, I wander over to the scattered cards. What to make of them? They were marked like Tarot cards, and were meant to represent my life. But each one had small details that I didn't remember. The picture of the Ribbon Man on the train, for example, was missing the seals, but had the addition of a small fish carved into the back of a seat. The one of me wearing the bear suit had a banner that read "Buffoon" stretched across the background. All accurate to my recollection, but tweaked a little from true.

*fool
p. 204

"Would you like a hint?" he asks as I examine the cards.

"Is that fair?" I ask.

"Not really, but this will get very dull very quickly otherwise."

The card at my feet is the Hermit, and he, like the others, is different. He has no lantern, and his stick is topped with a burning Hand of Glory, each finger turning into a black candle with a yellow and white flicker of fire at its tip.

*Recursions. Loops. Cycles. Again and again.*

I suddenly remember a childhood memory of the yellow tent in the desert becoming more distinct as I focus on it. The fortune teller in the tent, laying the cards on the table. I had drawn the Hermit, but I couldn't put it on the table. It didn't fit the pattern.

*hermit
p. 217

*What was it? Where did the Old Man fit in the mosaic?*

"You want me to order them," I realize.

And, as if they have been waiting for me to announce my intent, the cards leap off the floor and start racing around like refugees from an old hand-drawn animated short. They stand in a line-up as I touch them, shuffling and bumping into one as if they aren't quite sure of how close they should stand.

The fortune teller—though, such an appellation is just as false as the shape being worn now: an androgynous figure in a red rubber bodysuit, with heavy pincers on the hands and an ornate crown of barnacles and polyps—shakes its towering head when I finish.

"Why not?" I ask. "Isn't order a matter of interpretation?"

*Clack-clack* go his pincers. Like teeth.

"It's the order that I recall," I insist. Though, I am not certain of a few of them. And if he's going to be so intent on a correct order, he can lay them out himself.

*Clack-clack clack clack.*

"Of course I am a flawed engine," I say. "But that doesn't mean my ordering of the cards—my intent—is equally flawed."

*Clack-clack-clack-clack.*

"How?" My hands twitch, an echo of gutting chickens. "You've been telling me that these are images from my life, even if I don't remember them properly. If I'm supposed to put them in an order that pleases you aesthetically, then their content is irrelevant. My recollection—true or false—is irrelevant. What's the point of having them be tied to my identity at all?"

*Clack-clack.*

Answer say answer is the key.

It's not about my identity, is it? It's about the perception of others of my identity. And how I react to that perception.

*And from there, where do we go, U and I?*

"No more or less true than any other lie," I say.

His pincers almost close, but then stop. He quivers slightly.

"I said it," I tell him. "You didn't. You didn't betray anyone. You were merely an echo. Like everything else."

His pincers relax, and his form slips.

I watch the change come over the fortune teller, red lobster nature slipping like rain off glass. The skin becomes bark, the legs gnarled roots, and the arms transform into leafy branches. Tiny buds bloom in a crown of twigs and thick vines. Eyes and a mouth are shadows and cracks in the brown bark.

"I'm supposed to see some organization, *some meaning*, in your transformations too, aren't I?" I ask. "These costume changes aren't random."

The arms move, and the voice I hear is the sound of the wind in the leaves. "Random is a word used by those afflicted with subjectivity. Random is an interpretation bereft of insight."

"But your *pleasure* is subjective. I'm supposed to put the cards in an order that pleases you, but that response is an emotional one. It's a personalized reaction, one built out of *your* memory associations and has nothing to do with me, or the cards. However, if there is a non-subjective response that I am to elicit from you, then it is one that is independent of your identity, of your imprint on both me and the cards. In which case, the order is based on something quantifiable, like matching the color wheel or a sequential order. An order which has no relevance to me. One that I am *unaware* of."

I wave my hand at the cards and they dash around the room, throwing themselves into a prismatic order. "See? Totally arbitrary. Completely meaningless. And probably exactly what you want."

"How so?" the leaves ask. "Is there a deterministic order to the universe?"

"No," I argue. "It just doesn't make sense. The Hanged Man comes

* projection p. 34

* bloom p. 386

126

before the Chariot; the Tower is before the High Priestess. This isn't the order I seek. What other order could there be?"

"Ah, your order is chronological."

That stops me.

I know that memories aren't chronological. Not in the way they are stored. They are a series of impressions that aggregate into a record, and how they manage to become part of our long-term storage is more of an issue with the ease by which they are subsumed into our existing organization. If, for example, your childhood home was surrounded by fields of hyacinth, then when you presented with a choice, later in life, between a blue shirt and a red shirt, you will chose the blue one because your brain is more predisposed to neural cliques that contain "blue." You remember what is easy to remember; the brain is, while incredibly complex, still a simple machine. It makes the decision of least resistance.

It is the filter of our personalities that create "chronology." In an effort to understand cause and effect—in an effort to learn, really—we order objects (events, playing cards, small ponies, the like) in a serial manner that matches our understanding of the rules. What are the rules? They form, ultimately, the basis for a number of the experiential criteria that we use to dissect a sensory experience, which creates somewhat of a feedback loop. We invent chronology by the very nature of how we record perception.

Time, however, is purely a human construct, and the Western definition is even stricter in its adherence to linear motion.

"Yes, I cannot parse the order you suggest, because I was a witness and recipient of certain events that leave me predisposed to a chronological order. Because of the aggregate memories that make up my identity, I see *this* order as wrong."

A shiver runs through the branches of the tree, and its leaves turn yellow and melt. The crown of vines cracks, and long peacock feathers erupt. The fortune teller, now wearing a yellow cloak with a high collar of bird feathers, adjusts his glasses with the painted-on eyes. Behind their brown and red rims, I get a glimpse of the dark hollows of his empty eye sockets.

* eyes p. 197

Taking that transformation as a "yes," I continue with my train of thought. "Your order is arbitrary because it is nonsensical to me. More so, your very criteria are subjectively arbitrary, because 'pleasure' is defined in a unique way for every person. I would have to inhabit your personality if I wanted to know the order you see as correct. But, if I am you, then I am not me, and while I could order them, when I return to myself, I won't understand what I have done. Our double-you persona has arranged them, but they will have no more meaning to me than this random group they are in now. Because I am still going to have my chronological blindness."

"Then, the order is impossible to discern?"

I shrug, and flick the edge of the Emperor's card. "I suppose I could try every variation. How many million choices is that? Somewhere in there is the right combination, but it would take me . . . "

"Forever."

"Essentially."

He purses his lips. "Very well. Let us extrapolate then. Let us permute a few possibilities." When I nod, he continues. "If pleasure is a subjective response, then the specificity of the response is irrelevant. Any emotional reaction can be substituted and the order—the question you are attempting to answer—would still be equally as arbitrary. But, still equally as valid."

"Yes, I suppose that could follow."

"Therefore, since *any* response is permitted, both 'all' or 'none' are also possible. To be thorough in our arbitrariness."

"Okay."

"As you have discovered, asking you to generate any manner of emotional response from me by correctly ordering the cards is impossible because you do not know the permutation of the cards that will elicit that response."

"That is correct."

"Would you agree that the act of arranging cards is equally arbitrary? I could ask you to sculpt statues of zoo animals, or create puddles of colored water, or spin bolts of patterned silk. What is to be done—arranged, ordered, fabricated, or created—is as mutable as my reaction."

"That's a bit of a jump but—"

"Too general? Let us ask a specific question then: why are you still seeking **your** her **father's** forgiveness **approval**?"

I try to speak, but there is nothing in my mouth. He has stolen my tongue with his rhetoric.

The cards burst with laughter.

When I stop running, I am in the closet again, tangled in wire coat hangers. The long storeroom isn't as empty as it was previously—as I remember it, but all memory is suspect now, isn't it? There are other coats here now.

There is something pale and fleshy snagged through the top by the coat hanger's hook. My old skin, perhaps, looking quite thread-

* fabric
p. 56

* V

bare after all these years. (*The drugs have taken their toll.*) There is the doctor's coat I wore at the hospital when I told Nora's father the bad news, and the professor's frayed jacket. The stained robe of the bird priest hangs next to a yellow jumpsuit. The unmarked garment bag protects the tuxedo, the black one not yet worn. Still crisp. Still new, like a proleptic dream. The cheap skeleton costume (missing the Halloween mask), slashed across the wrist where the butterfly knife cut through the thin fabric. I shudder involuntarily as I pass over the silver coveralls and gas mask. (*Which one had I been? The one who pushed or was pushed?*)

And others, garments and costumes I didn't remember wearing: a clown's oversized pants stained with pie filling and dried whipping cream, a skin suit of jewel-toned scales, a pilot's uniform, a priest's cassock, a baker's apron and starched hat, the sky blue shirt and black pants of a transit authority officer's uniform, uniforms belonging to a chess team, a little boy's shirt (still smelling of fresh mint) and pants (still stained with grass), a coat of leaves, an old wool skirt and faded sweater with a book-shaped brooch pinned on it.

In the corner, hanging askew on a wooden hanger, is an old suit. A red tie is folded in the breast pocket and a porkpie hat is nearby on the rack. It's a very worn suit, and it fits me perfectly. There's a slip of paper in the right-hand coat pocket, but it is so worn that I can't read what it says. I keep it anyway. Behind this coat rack is a full-length mirror, covered in dust. I wipe part of it clean with my sleeve, and adjust the tie. When I raise my head, the image keeps his head angled so I can't see his face.

*But you knew that would happen, didn't you? All along, you've been watching more carefully than I.*

The pale-haired attendant shuffles his cards, and he looks up as I close the closet door behind me. "Nice suit," he says. "I used to own one like that." He flexes the deck and makes them dance between his fingers. "Did you find what you were looking for?"

I shrug. He cuts the deck and shows me the top card. The Ace of Swords. "Lose your tongue?" he asks. When I nod, he slips the card back into the deck. "Guess you're fucked then, aren't you?"

*Why?*

He shows me another card. The Tower, split by an ax of white light. "Need a tongue to speak the word."

*Which word is that?*

He pushes up his right sleeve and shows me his forearm.

On it is a baroque tattoo of a naked hermaphrodite. He makes a fist, and s/he wiggles a rather generous pendulum.

*fork p. 205

*X

*spearmint p. 321

*tool p. 350

"Sorry," he says, seeing my expression. "Other arm." On his left arm, a single word: *Buffoon.*

I cut his deck and chose a card. It is the Magician.

"Ah," is all he says for having been found out.

*No more tricks. Not from you or the House.*

He points at the door with his left hand, and the word crawls on his arm. "Go then. If you can open the door."

There is no door where he points, though I know it was the place where I entered the house. The wall is blank. *Tabula rasa.*

"Indeed," he says. "Just like the Universe before He came. A blank slate, waiting to be written on."

*Just like I am supposed to be. But I'm not.*

"Then you aren't ready."

*I never will be.*

He makes the Magician disappear, and turns over another card. The Six of Wands.

"Will you take my place then?" he asks. "Or do you want to go back to the maze and find some dead-end there to fill with your purpose-less vitriol?"

I stop him from turning over the next card. On his forearm, the hermaphrodite nods, a finger against his/her lips.

*\* superstition
p. 374*

**Don't let him in.**

He tries to extricate his arm, and his laughter dies as he finds my grip resilient. "Let go of me," he says. When I don't comply, he tries to reach for the deck. I knock his hand away, and his fingers scatter the deck across the counter. The top card lifts slightly as something bulges from its face. I pull him forward and down so that his right arm lies across the card.

"I won't give you the answer you seek. I can't."

He licks his lips nervously as I pull the card out from under his arm and turn it over. It is the Magician, found again.

*I'm not asking you.*

I slice the edge of the card across his forearm, and the shriek I hear doesn't come from his mouth. I let go of his arm, and he steps back from the counter, clamping a hand across the oozing line of blood.

"You bastard."

I look at the card. The top edge is red with the hermaphrodite's blood.

*That may be true. But that's not the way I remember it. Not the way I remember it at all.*

"You're wrong. Everything you think you know is wrong. Everything you believe is wrong. Everything is not as it seems."

*I know. I'm the one who dreamed it all, remember? Not you.*

I turn the Magician over, and over again, and it becomes the Ace of Swords. Sharp enough now to cut his strings.

His mouth and eyes still work, and they gasp and watch me as I bend over his fallen body. (*Like another head, in another dream. Like all heads, bereft of bodily intent.*)△ He tries to bite my hand when I reach into his mouth for his tongue, but I wedge my knuckles in the joint of his jaw and he can't close his mouth enough to do me any harm. It would be harder to cut out his tongue if he had any blood in him, but it's all in the hermaphrodite's ink.

I put his tongue in my mouth, and it resists me for a moment, fighting back against my design, but after I nip at it with my teeth, its resistance disappears.

"I'm sorry," I say to the bloodied tattoo on his forearm, trying out my new tongue. "I'll stop the bleeding, if you tell me the word."

S/he glares at me, but acquiesces.

I shuffle the remaining cards in the deck, looking through them until I find the Ace of Cups. I pour it over the pale man's arm, and the smear of spilt ink washes away. (*All of it washes away, always, leaving the pages empty.*) One of his/her legs is unfinished now, but still lined enough to suggest a supple curve. His/her mouth moves, shaping a pair of syllables.

*tidal motion p. 349*

(*It is time now. A revolution is upon us. Open the door. Start anew.*)

I speak the word, and it splits my new tongue. I have become the Opener. I am the Path. I have given everything, and taken everything in return. I am no more, and yet I am still to be.

*And so it ~~begins~~ ends.*

The door opens. Outside, the Red Wood is gone, and there are no Broken-Jawed penitents waiting for me. There is . . . a train platform.

I walk to the threshold and look out. The station is old and deserted, and the sky is overcast. The rain . . . is a *curtain of beaded silver across the train tracks, a shivering veil hiding the rest of the world . . .*

---

△ - U know which one, don't you? I don't have to give you hints any more. U know the way. Left. Then right. Then left again.

# XII

# REVOLUTION

I bring the rain with me, a silver curtain dogging my heels as I step into the dream. The water adds color to the dilapidated train station: green and rust to the struts of the vault over the tracks, red and blue to the blocky engine, silver and brown to the tile of the platform. Flyers and posters tacked to an aged board sag as they get wet; the letters of the advertisements and messages become dark and legible from a distance, frozen for a moment of textual clarity before they begin to run.

He is standing on the platform, a two-dimensional paper cutout. His hat is askew and his coat is too big for him. A frozen image, he has not yet fallen this far; he is still floating in the Aserinsky Region. He'll be here soon. I fix his hat, and on the piece of paper I have brought with me from the coat closet of the House, I write a note. His paper shape shudders once, a ripple of pages turning, and begins to fill out. Lines of tiny text scribbling and scrawling down his frame, each line giving him depth and width. As soon as the pocket of his coat opens, I slip the scrap of paper in.

The text is dark and wet on him, and he gasps. Color comes to his skin, his coat, his hat, his suitcase; and he wakes up, but I've already become a ghost again. The train comes alive too as I touch it, squawking its manic musical melody over a dusty intercom, and the sound wakes up the rest of the dream. Setting everything in motion.

*We don't hear the First Word. That sound*—boom boom—*is the sound of creation.* What he hears is the sound of his heart beating, of his breath echoing in his ears, of his blood rushing through his body. He hears himself first, and doesn't realize it is already an echo. *We are echoes of echoes, Harry. U have so many roles to play.*

* re-awakening
p. 397

He finds me in the lounge car, sitting with the seals. I know he doesn't understand why they are here, that he can't decide if they are a clue or a diversion, but as I am not sure either, I leave them. They may belong to someone else's subconscious; the Oneiroi has become slippery since I have gone deep and far into the other layers. He sits down, pushes his hat back on his head. When I don't say anything, his face contracts, lines across his forehead. "Just across the river," he says slowly, as if unsure of his lines. "Is that where the city is?"

*river
p. 299

*Not at night.* I shake my head. *I must not be going there, then.* I deviate from the script. "There will be delays."

His confusion is plain on his face, though he does not know its source. He does not know himself, and cut off as he is from his own soul, he has no true connection to the Oneiroi; he cannot feel it change beneath us.

"What . . . what sort of delays?" he asks. He swallows heavily and looks at the seals, as if for some assurance that this improvisation is allowed.

"The House is empty," I say. "It has no Master. But you still must go there."

"Which house?"

"Did you bring food?" I ask, and this sudden return to the script is like a burst of oxygen to his lungs. His face clears, and he breathes more easily.

"Yes," he says. "I brought a picnic." He puts his suitcase on the table and opens it.

Blue birds fly out.[65]

Frantic, he bats at them, and their wings cut his hands, streaking his fingers with scarlet.

I open a window before he can stain them all. One bird gets away, still pristine, still blue. The rest flutter and bang against the walls and other closed windows. Their feathers are heavy with blood, and the weight unbalances them. They fall to the floor, where they flutter frantically for awhile, and then become still.

He is sitting on the seat, rocking back and forth. Moaning. Whining. I grab his tie and pull him close.

"Look," I say, my word cutting through his keening noises. "Look."

---

65 - *No no no no no nonononnonono—you've changed the script you can't change the script!*

I point out the window, at the mountain we can see from the train.

Its top is flat, and something bright flashes on this plateau.

"Knight to c3," I whisper in his ear. "There is but one way." * VI

He jerks back, but not very far, as I still have a tight grip on his tie. He opens his mouth to speak, to scream—to babble on—and a butterfly, caught by the draft of the train, is sucked into the car. It is an orange and black monarch, nearly frozen from the descent, and I grab it with a motion outside of thought. I put it on his tongue and carefully close his mouth.

"Shhh," I say, leaving one finger on his lips. "Wait for it to dissolve. You will need it later." *Rainbow glint on sharp blade. The scarlet line.*

The necessary sacrifices. The path made clear by those choices voluntarily made.$^{\triangle}$ * regret
p. 392

The train falls apart as it enters the station. Its furnace cracks, the last belch of steam in its boilers escapes with a sigh, and its front wheels slip off the rails. It grinds against the concrete edge of the platform, and even the sparks thrown up by the contact are dull.

He isn't on the train. Unable to sustain himself long in the dream, he left me some time ago, and I am the sole passenger—*the only one left*—when the train dies in the station. I don't mind the solitude of the trip; I spend the time plucking the feathers off the dead birds, and when the doors of the carriage rattle open, I step off wearing my new cloak of scarlet-stained feathers.

I stop at the phone kiosk. The clue on the side is too geometric, too much an influence of the Tower, and I scratch it out, replacing it with the sigil of thunder, the sign of the first echo. *Boom boom*, goes my heart. *I am alive. I am all I am.*

I lift the plastic receiver and listen to the looping sound of her voice. How long has she been repeating this sermon? Over and over again until we listen, until we get it right. There will be time enough.$^{\triangledown}$

"Hello, Nora," I say, inserting a glitch in the loop. * liberated
p. 14

"Hello," she says, her voice riding in the spaces between the numbers. "I didn't think you would ever answer." *say answer*

"There have been delays," I say. Echoes of echoes.

"I warned you."

*No protection, no illusions, no turning away at the last second . . .*

"I didn't believe you. I'm sorry."

---

$\triangle$ - Why did you think we wouldn't be strong enough? Why did you think your poison would work this time?

$\triangledown$ - Time enough for one last kiss, one last instant of free will.

"He's waiting for you."

"Yes, I know. I told him I was coming."

*radio
p. 291

We listen to the echo of her transmission for a little while. **Put it in, you moan, yes, put it in now. I want it. I want it so badly.**

"You shouldn't be here," she says, interrupting the radio signal sermon. "You might—"

"I already have," I say. "I met him on the train. I changed his path." I swallow heavily, forcing down a lump in my throat. *Do you take this Black Queen . . .*

"You can't," she says. Her voice is tight with dread and finality. "You can't change the path."

"Revolution," I whisper. "I am eating my own tail."

Serpentine circulation. Round and round. Echoes of—*All we have left is shadows of shadows.*

"What should I tell him then?" she asks. "If he calls me."

*telephone
p. 336

"He will, and you should tell him the same thing you told me. That shouldn't change. He needs to be set adrift. The transformation must be started." **I want you to show it to me. Yes, show me.** "You are the catalyst. You have always been the catalyst. Remind him."

I allow myself this one moment, this one instant of fear. Will she? Everything depends upon her, in the end. Everything hangs on what she wants, what she needs. What she is willing to give me.

"Boom boom—" she whispers.

"—goes my heart," I whisper back, and I know she can hear the explosion in my chest.

When I hang up, I see the expression of her intent, of her desire. Caught in the rotary dial of the phone is a gold ring. Caught in the zero hole. It fits my ring finger, and I can't tell if my hand shrinks or the ring grows bigger, but it doesn't really matter. The ring fits, and so we are fully married: the ghost and his psychopharmaceutical bride.

This circle will not break.

"That exit is closed," the cab driver says. "I can't get off the freeway there."

I know the exit is closed. I know I can't get to the House on that road, but I pester him anyway. I'll leave an impression in his memory now; he'll remember the *other* route. "Fine," I tell him. "It doesn't matter."

His hands, covered in yellow gloves, grip the steering wheel tightly. His tongue slips out of his mouth. "I don't know the way," he admits. "I don't know where you want to go."

"Just drive," I say. "I'll tell you when we've arrived. Besides, it is the manner of our journey that is important."

"All roads lead to Rome," he says. "Is that it?" He spins the wheel, and the cab pulls away from the train station. "Whether you are an enumerator or a scavenger is determined by which road you take."

I look out at the unreal city and the fog of unformed desire that embraces it. The buildings are shells, their windows blank and empty. The streetlights have no bulbs, and the trees have no leaves. Nothing has decayed as nothing has been finished. Not yet. How much do we leave unfinished because we fear to start, because we fear the weight of the path that must be taken? How much?

**The Last Hour is upon us, and it is waning now.**

"This cab," I ask the driver, "have you always driven it?"

He is quick to answer. "Always."

"And before you?"

"My father. And his father."

"Your fathers. They are echoes, aren't they? If you've always driven this cab—if that is your sole purpose in my dream—then who are your fathers? If I wind this road back, will they say the same thing? Does your father dream of his son following his same path?"△

"Of course," he says. "That is the way of the wheel."

* wheel
p. 362

"In your dreams, are you still a cab driver?"

He laughs. "We don't dream."

"Why not?"

"We're symbols. We don't exist when you aren't here." He gestures out the window at the shadow city. "None of this exists when you are awake."

"But I am awake. *He* is awake. He has left the dream and he doesn't come back for a little while."

He looks at me in the rearview mirror and shrugs. "I don't know who 'he' is."

"My doppelgänger. He'll need a ride."

* double
p. 390

"Where to?"

I smile. *That's how it begins.* "He won't know. He'll ask you for a recommendation."

"What should I tell him?"

"Anything you like. Make something up." I point out the billboard. "Tell him about the zoo."

He leans against his window and stares at the billboard as we pass it. "That's new," he says. There are a pair of happy seals on the board.

---

△ - Do you, Father? Do you know this dream? Or did you forget how to dream, along with everything else you forgot?

"Everything is new," I say. "When the wheel turns."

He shivers, tugging his coat more closely about him. "Do you mind if I turn on the heat?" he asks.

"No." I am warm in my cloak of bloody feathers. As he fumbles with the climate controls on the dashboard, I pluck one feather from my shoulder and breathe on it. The color changes, red to black to yellow, and the feather twitches in my grip. I drop it on the floor, where it will fester awhile before it becomes a real bird. He'll need currency—coin of the realm—to make the phone call. This world won't be as open to him. *So many secret chambers.*

The heater churns and hisses, filling the cab with a memory of summer. Flowers in bloom. Skin warmed by the sun. Her mouth, turned toward the sky, lips parted. When the vents exhale air warmed by the car's engine, I hear her sigh. It isn't a question of what is worth saving, but what is worth creating.

He is awake. He isn't dreaming. We don't exist. And yet, I sit in the back of a cab, thinking about her. Doesn't that make us real?

"Turn on the radio," I ask the cab driver. *Is she still out there, or has she vanished? Have I undone everything, and will it be enough?*

He does, and all that comes out of the speakers is static. He turns the dial, turns and turns and turns, but he finds nothing but the sound of an empty dream.

The old prophet is waiting for me outside the old hotel. It will be torn down soon, as the zoo expands through this decrepit neighborhood. The parking garage will be at the other end of the block, and the decorative iron gate of the entrance will stand in place of the hotel's entrance. I can see all of this growth as a silver overlay, the future architecture already starting to bleed through. I can see the shape of the statue that will replace the old man once his bones have turned to dust.

"That's a strange looking garbage truck," the cab driver says, staring at the green truck parked near the alley that runs behind the hotel.

"It's a harvester," I tell him, recognizing the orange and yellow logo on its side. "They're collecting raw materials."

"Materials? For what?"

"A pharmaceutical company. One that makes vitamin supplements."

"Out of what?"

"It's all organic," I tell him.△

△ - Isn't it all, Father? Isn't everything, in the end?

*fowl p. 208 / *drift p. 184 / *purify p. 284

"Organic what?"

I lean forward and touch his neck. He jerks away from my finger, his skin blistering into mosaic of scales. "You won't find this place again," I instruct him. "We have drifted off the map you know."

When I get out of the cab, it turns into smoke and water, draining away into the storm grate. Draining back to the dreaming ocean beneath me. Back into the everything of nothing. *Will it be enough?*

The old prophet stares at the street, his blind peacock eyes seeing nothing. His blue robe is stained with tears like little cloudbursts across a clear sky. He clutches a single card in his bony right hand. When I take the card from him, he moans gently, and white moths stream from his mouth like air bubbles escaping from a deep sea diver.

The card is the Hermit. Neither first nor last. The cycle continues, and there is no beginning and no end. Just rotations and revolutions. Over and over. I hold the card up, and like the hotel and the street, I can see the silver overlay of what the card will become. I see the cliff and the sky; I see the lamp and the sun, and how one becomes the other.

Two of the prophet's daughters, stoic in their masks, stand beside the cracked doors. They raise their gloved arms and become white trees, their branches entwining into an arch. Past and future, commingling in the now. This is the path: outside of Time, flushed with ignorance and awareness of all the symbols and portents of history. This is the make believe of the Oneiroi. Does it all stop when you wake up?

I climb the steps and pass beneath the raised arms of the white oak ladies. I pass across the threshold (neither hotel nor zoo nor house nor hospital room) and enter the Tower.

The steps: do they go up or down? Which way do I go? Is there a choice for me here? There are stairs, so many stairs. Do I climb or descend? *crossing p. 174

I count the steps. Each one is a step further. Each one is closer to infinity. It doesn't matter which way I go, does it? Either direction loops back on itself. When I reach the end, I'll be here again.

And yet, I chose to go down. In the darkness.

Down.

Down.

All

    the

        way

            down.

                All the way to . . .

139

( )

"Hello, brother." He moves in the dark, and I hear the rattle of his chains.

"Hello," I reply. He is as blind as the old fortune teller, as my doppelgänger is to what is happening to him. Sight, like memory, is so easily disturbed by the chemicals. So easily disturbed by the aberrance of history. So easily . . .

*history
p. 22

"Have you come to free me?" he asks, his desperation evident in the dry wind of his words.

"No," I admit. "I do not have your key."

His chains rattle again as he drags himself across the room. I can feel the chill of the metal as he looms over me. "Then why have you come?"

*summons
p. 328

"Father has called us home."

He hisses. "Father speaks to no one. You cannot hear him. I am the only one who can understand him."

"And when was the last time he spoke to you?" I ask, and the way the darkness swallows his silence is answer enough. "You slew Father," I tell him. "Just as surely as you slew your brothers. Just as surely as you slew all those who you loved. Just as you abandoned everyone, He abandoned you."

"No." The angel shakes his chains. "No, I freed them. I freed them from the tyranny of their geometry. I rescued them from the prison of their duality. I broke the world so they could escape."

*liberated
p. 14

"Escape from what?"

"I gave them this world. I taught them how to dream."

"Dreams aren't real. You and I: we aren't real."

He sobs. "What of the pain?" he asks. "I made it go away."

I think of Nora, of her father's final farewell, of and her mother's quiet insanity; I think of Phil and Jerry and a bed of yellow flowers; I think of my mother and what she swallowed, how it killed her slowly; I think of my father, and the choice he made.

"No," I tell the angel. "The pain didn't go away."

He continues to sob, the chains shaking with his body. "Why doesn't he call me home? Why doesn't he love me any more?"

*love
p. 71

*He doesn't love any of us*, I want to whisper to the angel. *He doesn't love you. He doesn't love me.* The angel won't understand, but I want to tell him anyway. *He doesn't remember how to love.* But I don't say anything. There is pain enough. I hold up the card that I have brought with me—the card once carried by the old fortune teller, the card turned over by an innocent hand so long ago. I hold up the Hermit, and echo of echoes, I hold up his lantern.

Even though he is blind, the angel of chains feels the heat of the lantern's light and he recoils. His veil is torn and frayed, and his robe is pale with dust. The inlayed crosses of light are dull, and they reflect none of the lantern's light. He is lame again, and he stumbles awkwardly away. Bound to him by the chains, held tight against his twisted frame, is his book. His version of the Word and the World.

Beyond him, silver shining in the lantern's gleam, are a pair of great doors, ornate hinges bound into the fabric. They are not locked; there is no need, for the doors are insubstantial in the deepdark darkness of the bottomless pit.

"Goodbye, Abaddon." I hold my hand in front of the lantern, shielding his face from the flame. "Goodbye, *Frater*." It is his title, and not my relation to him. I tell myself this lie as I walk past him. He is not my family, and the sound of his despair does not wound me. It does not touch me. It does not make me gasp for breath; it does not make the lamp seem so heavy.

*Goodbye, brother. Son of light. Son of shadow. Goodbye.*
The doors open at my touch, and I cross over. One last time.

*last light
p. 244

(.)

What do you think lies beyond this door? Do you realize that your guess is as good as mine? Your intent has driven me here just as readily as mine. This journey does not exist without you. This book that I write in is not mine and it is filled with words that are not mine, but here, in the Oneiroi, all the language lines up according to my whim. According to the manner in which you read it. Your route is just as plain as mine. There are clues and diversions, but there is only one path. There is only destination. There is only one door.

Just as there is only one key. She gave it to me. When she died, I opened her chest—right there in the hospital room—and took it. I had to break a rib to get it free, but she forgave me. Her mother never did, but then, she didn't understand. None of them did. None of them understood the necessity of sacrifice. None of them wanted to know why we made the choices we made.

Here, in the wet darkness, in the salty brine of our sorrow, we hide. We hope the regret dissolves, if we can just soak it long enough. The ink will run. The pages will become blank. And we can write new stories on the palimpsest skin of our sadness. Here. Right below my fourth rib—the one I broke in her chest—start a new one. Don't

*regret
p. 392

worry. I know the pen is sharp. The bleeding will stop. Start a new one.

What lies beyond the door? Write it down. Tell me what you see. Tell me what happens. Write it on my flesh. Cover me so that I may become someone else. Write me anew, so that I may forget this eternal ache.

*XIII*

(*)

Imagine a garden made from steel and ceramic and glass. Imagine trees, fat and squat, whose branches are a twisted coursework of plastic tubing. Imagine shrubs as round-bellied alembics filled with shivering and bubbling solutions. Imagine flowers that fold their broad leaves over their centrifugal centers; they must spin spin spin before they can bloom. Imagine the vines that cover everything, and how their tiny buds seem frozen, as if caught under glass. Imagine the white-coated gardeners who dare not breathe the fecund air of this garden, who dare not let the pollen of any of these plants fall upon their skin. Imagine the rich fertility of the first garden and how poisonous that environment must have been if the closest approximation science can achieve is classified as a Level 4 Biohazard lab.

He is sitting at a table in the center of this science garden, watching chemical permutations unfold on wide monitor placed beneath the glass tabletop. The visualization patterns are flowers, unfolding. Petal after petal after petal.

*twenty . . .*
*twenty-one . . .*
*twenty-two . . .* △

His bio-suit is old and torn, patched with different colors of tape. Like ribbons. His padded fingers trace the curve, following the geometry. "Just one more," he says as I sit down. "Just one more petal." The Ribbon Man smiles at me, a feral bloody grin. "Did you find it?"

I nod. "I'm very close."

"Did you write it down?" he asks.

*substantia p. 6*

I put the black notebook on the table. "It's all here. Everything I learned."

---

△ - she loves me she loves me not she loves me she loves me not
she loves me she loves me not she loves me she loves me not
she loves me she loves me not she loves me she loves me not
she loves me she loves me not she loves me she loves me not
she loves me she loves me not she loves me she loves me not
she loves me she loves me not she loves me

He stares at the book, his tongue tickling the edge of his lip. The ambient glow from his suit makes his face pale, translucent. So unreal. "What is left to do?" he asks.

His right hand twitches, padded fingers drumming against the clear tabletop. The pattern of flower petals is reflected off his palm.

*petals
p. 268

I don't want to tell him. I don't want to say why I haven't written down the last step. He won't believe me. He will think it is one last trick, one last diversion, because that is all he knows. He doesn't remember any other way. He won't believe me.

"There is nothing to be done or undone. You have done enough." *False Father.*

He flinches at the echo in the dream and refuses to look at me. "It had to be done," he says.

"No," I tell him. "You wanted it done. You wanted this."

He looks at me now, and his eyes are hot and fierce behind his plastic mask. "So did you. You wanted . . . closure. You wanted to know why—" He stumbles on the next word, and it comes out with three letters instead of two. "—she—" He stops, panting, staring at me.

**WWhhyy shhee lleefftt.**

It is so hard to say which voice is the echo of the other. It is so hard to tell if they are converging or diverging, these voices, here where the wheel is turned. They are so close now, so close to being one.

Just like him and me, so close to being one. We have come so far, so far from that first encounter on the train. The book is nearly finished. *Here, at the back. Let me show you.*

I open the book and show him what I have done.

Its geometry is perfect: the two circles of the handle, the tall triangle of the vessel, the single point of the needle. I have drawn it well, and even on the page, it is more real than anything else around us. I can touch it. I can imagine slipping my fingers into the grip and resting my thumb against the smooth top of the plunger. Pushing the needle through the glass tabletop—through the mirror that reflects without reflecting—and piercing the computer screen beneath. I can envision myself drawing out the pixelated fury of the flower computation, leaving the computer screen black and empty. Filling the syringe with the calculated derivative of blackleaf.△

*geometry
p. 210

*blackleaf
p. 159

"I want you to write it down for me," I tell him as I lift the needle

△ - But it still won't be real. It will never be. The 23rd expression cannot be synthesized. It must be experienced. It must be changed within you, by you. With you. The 23rd expression is the duality, realized. U + U = W. The 23rd letter. The first key.

from the last page, leaving the paper blank. Pure and unblemished. *Ready to start anew.*

*wombwhite
p. 364

I hold out my other hand, the one with the ring, and show him my empty palm. "Here. Write it here."

*There is one page left.*

There are twelve dualities. You have heard this theory, haven't you? It's all there, written on the other pages of the book—hidden in the margins, scrawled in every direction across the flesh of the page, notes and footnotes fighting for your attention—it's all there.

We are defined by the twelve qualities, our identities nothing more than positions between these extremes. Whether we are winged torch-bearers or broken souleaters: these are the definitions which make up who we are. They are the twelve houses through which we must pass on our journey of understanding, of self-knowledge. The sun across the sky, the ring around our finger: the cycle continues for eternity. Twelve upon twelve upon twelve upon . . .

*giants
p. 212

There is a thirteenth house.

*thirteen
p. 346

Yes, you do know this final mystery, don't you? You know what that shadow duality is. You know why it must be hidden. You know why we fear the possibility of its existence. But it is there, and deep within our dreams, we can face it. We can look upon the thirteenth duality and find our place upon its sliding scale. We can find our place.

The light from the syringe reflects off the Ribbon Man's faceplate. I can't see his face. He holds my hand down, and the movement of his pen is a distant pricking against my skin. He is writing quickly, trying to fill the space before it vanishes. Trying to write it all down before the memory fades.

The syringe is full. He has not seen me take the light from the screen. I have taken all the geometry into the simplicity of the needle. Point. Circle. Triangle.

I jab myself in the neck with the syringe, and without hesitation— this is, after all, why I have come here, why I have gone so far into the dream—I push the plunger all the way down. The pixelated solution fills me, this scientific approximation of nature's creative energy, this best guess of our flawed imagination.

"Yes," I whisper. "Yes, yes, yes."

*dawn
p. 385

On another layer, I can feel myself coming apart, blooming into a flower that has never been seen before, petals and lines exploding from my wrists and neck.

His grip is strong on my hand. He can feel me trying to pull away. "Tell me," he hisses. "Tell me what I am writing."

The lines on my hand resolve themselves into the loops of a flower. Twenty-three petals. The last petal, the final loop that closes the circle passes through the wedding ring on my finger.

"She loves me," I say.

"No." He lets go of me. "I don't need that. I don't *want* that. I want answers."

"There are none."

"No, that is unacceptable. There are always answers. There are no mysteries that we cannot unravel. We must know."

"There is nothing to be revealed," I say, even though I am filled with secrets. "There is nothing I can tell you."

With a strangled cry, he pushes away from the table. He turns his frustration to the nearby laboratory equipment, shattering beakers and alembics, knocking microscopes and hot plates and water baths off the counter. "No," he shouts. "You cannot deny me this. Not after what I have sacrificed." He has a shard of glass in his gloved hand, a curved piece that is hurting him as much as he wants to hurt me.

Holding the syringe carefully, I pull out the plunger so that the vessel is filled with the mystery that I have become. Taking the needle out of my neck, I offer the syringe to him. "Here," I say. "Take it, then."

He drops the piece of glass, and takes my offering. Greedily. Reverently. He doesn't bother trying to fit his fingers through the circles of the handle; he jabs himself in the chest—right through this suit, right through his ribcage, right into his heart—and pushes the plunger down with his padded palm. He takes it all in. He stands there, his blank face looking down at syringe in his chest, waiting for enlightenment.

Waiting for something.

Waiting . . .△

---

△ - What do you suppose happens next? I would write it down, but there is no ink left. The pen is empty. He used it all writing on my hand. And only he can understand his handwriting.°

☽ - How long will he wait for the answers to reveal themselves?

I don't know.

How long would any of us wait? Is eternity nothing more than that infinite pause where we live and die while waiting for the resolution of desire? Is this not why we dream, to lessen the wait? To convince ourselves that if we wait long enough, if we are patient enough, our hearts will be filled.

I gave him what he wanted.

Do you suppose his heart is any more full?

This, then, is who I am. The riddle of these words, the labyrinth of these whorls and lines. I have invented all of this, and in that invention, I have created myself. A revolution, then, becomes a resolution. The beginning is born from the end. Here, on my palm, is the map of the path, the key to this dream. Written by the hand of the one who sought to bind me.

Instead, he has given me my freedom.

When U wake, however, the key will be gone. The pages will be blank. But I will still be here, waiting for U. You will remember that much, at least.

U will know how it starts.

"My name is . . . "

My name is Harry Potemkin, and I am a black market one, but licensed enough to have an office, a couch, and be able to t. critical psychological breakthrough. That was part of my frust. process. I wanted to help people, and I started by helping myse.

I used to be a licensed therapist, not a full Doctor of Psychiatry,
atients that their time was up just as they were about to reach a
oo, by the way: the intrusion of time and society into the healing

# LEXICON

# ABANDON
ठ

When the Tower fell, the thirteen stonemasons tried to arrest its collapse with their hands and bodies. For three times twenty-two generations, their families had been slaved to laying stone, and they knew nothing else. Their children were born with an innate knowledge of the lever and the pulley. When the stones began to fall, what else could they do? The stonemasons linked their arms together, building a great chain. They clambered on each other's backs, and raised asymmetrical pyramids.

*\* children*
*p. 169*

And they held back some of the stones, but others were too big, too heavy. One by one, each stonemason lost his grip.

The dust raised by the Tower's collapse was damp and dark, and it left a permanent stain on all the doors and windows of the city. The sun wept, and hid its face behind a veil of ash for a year. The moon, emboldened by the sun's dismay, stayed full and round. It laughed every night as it rose over the pall of the broken pit.

*\* ash*
*p. 155*

The architects were dragged from their palaces by the widows of the stonemasons. Hung in wicker cages, the architects were forced to instruct the children gathered in the square below them. If they could teach the youngsters the secrets of their art, they would be spared. If the tiny models built from sticks and mud and shards of stone stood for an hour, the architects would be given water. If the model stood overnight, they would be given food.

*\*cage*
*p. 163*

The architects all died of thirst within a week, for no matter how they cajoled and wept and shouted, none of the children were able to understand what they wanted.

*\*architect*
*p. 154*

On the anniversary of the Tower's collapse, the sun wiped its face clean and blew away the perpetual dust that clung to the stone-choked pit of the Tower. Every door and window in the city had been left open, and the sun crept into each house—peeking in all the rooms, snooping in the cupboards and closets. It found no one; the city was empty. After a year of madness and despair, the people had fled.

# ANCHOR

ℭ ♓

FROM: heron74@...
TO: alt.oneirology.entheogens
SUB: Psychic Anchors

I learned this technique about twenty years ago from a friend of a friend who said he learned it straight from Leary. I guess the provenance doesn't really matter. It works; that's the important thing.

-(pk)

* emergency
p. 190

BUILDING A PSYCHIC ANCHOR: TO BE USED IN CASE OF SPIRITUAL ASSAULT OR OTHER MANNER OF DEMONIC POSSESSION

1) The construction of this artifact can be, like all psychic manipulation, as equally damaging to the oneironaut as it can be fruitful. The usual caveats apply: know the source of your chemicals; don't engage the dream if you are in danger of immediate physical harm; synaesthetic effects are normal, but complete sensory inversion is to be avoided; and always have a safe word.

2) Once you have crossed the threshold of Oneiric space, pause before you enter the astral thermocline and lay your first inter-etheric knot. Stain it with CSF, activating its astral expression. This trigger is the first of several psychic markers, the bread crumb trail that links your oneiric projection with your material shell.

* descent
p. 182

3) Lay your next knot as you enter the Aserinsky Region. Doing so will increase the astral cohesion of the cord, but it is important to remember that this transitional threshold is only as solid as you make it. By forcing it to hold your knot, you are giving it weight and substance. A barrier you will have to breach on your return, instead of a fluidity pre-disposed to absorb you.

4) Continue through each layer, laying knots on either side of the astral thermoclines. As each layer thickens, the permeability of the

152

separating membrane decreases, thereby increasing both the necessity of and the resistance against your anchor thread.

5) Once you have reached your destination depth of the Oneiroi, create a hollow sphere, using the Vicg-d'Azyr Arrangement (it is the easiest to visualize at this depth, trust me). Pass your astral cord through this shape five times, inscribing its interior with a pentagram. Once you have completed this astral inscription, the psychic link will complete, and you should feel a slight weight at the base of your skull as the anchor engages.

* hollow
p. 220

6) As planar distance in the Oneiroi is non-existent, you will always be in close proximity of your anchor. Should you desire to descend deeper into the Oneiroi, you must simply wipe the geometric seal from your knot cluster. Disburse four of the five knots, and continue your descent. Continue to mark your projection as noted above.

* projection
p. 34

A properly grounded anchor will take but a moment to fabricate, an instant to activate, and an eternity to sever. It is a hard link to meatspace, a persistent reminder that everything is, indeed, just a dream.

# ARCHITECT

ᛉ ♒

In dream imagery, architects assume the mantle of Creator in that they are perceived as the mysterious agents who craft the structural framework of the universe. The presence of "architect" is a modern archetypal association; in previous times, this role was given over to the blacksmiths, the industrial machinists, the alchemists, and the navigators.

* king
p. 231

Although, in ancient Babylon and Egypt, the king was the architect. It is interesting to note that our modern architects do not have the same wherewithal as had their historical antecedents. Could any modern architect build the pyramids with the same degree of precision? Even with their modern tools?

* burnblack
p. 26

This leads us to question how far we have fallen from the archetypal definition. If the knowledge available to such a being is finite, has the proliferation of agents and representatives caused the sum total of architectural knowledge to be split? Not to promulgate a rage against builders, because this could be said of any body of knowledge in the modern era, but have we truly gotten smarter with more minds working on any given problem?

Freud wanted to believe that everything we imagined was simply the expression of repressed desires, that dreams were nothing more than the febrile fantasies of our internal, unrestrained hunger. In our

* strength
p. 324

dreams, there is only savagery and the anarchistic need to consume. René Girard argued that this bestial hunger could never be truly removed from any society, and that a ritualistic outburst of violence was necessary to maintain the "sanity" of any societal organization. We needed to bleed off the energy of our dreams, if you will.

But such an argument implies the lack of a decent architecture within our psyches, the lack of a Creative presence. We have no way to focus—to build pyramids—because we don't know how.

Such an argument seems to suggest a lack of belief in God. Or rather, a lack of belief in "belief" because isn't that what architects do? They believe a structure can be built. They believe that something that has never been done before can be done.

# ASH

ᚐ

I hung on the tree for thrice three days.
Three days for my brother's regret,
Three days for my brother's brother's hubris,
And three days for my brother's brother's brother's pain.
Each day another drop of my blood nourished the tree.
On the first day, the tree spread its roots.                          *roots
On the second day, it wrapped its bark around my wrists.               p. 371
On the third day, it flowered.
The flowers turned to white snow on the fourth day.                   *snow
The tree began to grow on the fifth day.                              p. 315
Nesting birds raised families in my palms on the sixth day.
On the seventh day, the tree touched the clouds.
The roots thickened on the eighth day.
On the ninth day, the tree pierced heaven.
I hung for nine days,
Waiting to be claimed by the light,                                   *last light
And my shadow still lingers in the bark of the tree.                  p. 244

The first is named Aegenus. The second son is Xernbawe. The last
is Ghen. Each asked Father: "Am I your only child?" And to each,
Father answered: "I see no other son but you."                        *son
                                                                      p. 317

155

# BARE
## Ω

* spiritual
armor
p. 323

My hat is gone. I gave it away to a phantom memory of a man who liked me more than the others. They blamed me. I was convenient, a straw effigy of their helplessness. They wanted to beat me with their hands, with the cheap chairs from the hospital waiting area, with the metal IV stand ever-present by Nora's bed. They wanted to see me disintegrate. Like their hope.

I cannot touch my head. My hands are nothing more than ghost fingers on the end of phantasmal limbs. I flail, and touch nothing. There is nothing but the acrid darkness, salty against my tongue and

* eyes
p. 197

eyes. I cannot protect myself; I cannot use my hands as a cheap shield to cover my head.

Its voice has found me. Just one more. That long-chain lab-grown beast of chemical intent, that manmade dose of psychopharmaceutical deconstruction. Just one more . . .

Isn't that what she wanted? Just one more trip. Just one more. I said yes. I said take my hand. And her fingers did not tremble. I should have known. I should have stopped her.

Why? For what tiny sliver of life that was left for her? The irresolute passage of those final days. The perpetual hours of pain. Those excruciating minutes of boneless panic. Those flickering instants where the endless alienation of dissolution peek through the threadbare veil of reality. Yes, you will be alone. Yes, you will fall for an eternity. Yes,

* bleak zero
p. 162

the bleakness you feel now is a surfeit of emotional and physical pleasure compared to the hollow vacuum that waits for you. Yes, right over here. So close. Yes, like that. Just one more step.

Was this what you were saving her for?

You want to join her now, don't you? You want to flee from this abyss, run back into the embrace of the dream and find her. You want to tell her she was right. It is better to run away, isn't it? It is better to bury yourself in the dream, wrap yourself in its warm water, and float forever. Yes, this is better.

She is calling you. Hear that sound? That undulating echo of whale song? That is her voice. Go to her. Go now. Just one more step.

# BIRD

Scene I: The Wood-cutter's Cottage
SFX: A knock at the door.

LITTLE BROTHER (frightened): What's that?
BIG BROTHER (elated): It's Daddy!

As they hesitate before opening the door, the big latch is seen to rise of itself, with a grating noise; the door half opens to admit an old man dressed in yellow and black. He is lame and his crown is crooked. It is obvious that he is wearing a disguise, for he is not their real father.

*crown
p. 177*

FALSE FATHER: Have you the grass here that sings or the bird that is blue?
LITTLE BROTHER: We have some grass, but it can't sing.
BIG BROTHER: Little Brother has a bird.
LITTLE BROTHER: But I can't give it away.
FALSE FATHER: Why not?
LITTLE BROTHER: Because it is mine.
FALSE FATHER: That is a reason, no doubt. Where is the bird?
LITTLE BROTHER (pointing at the cage): In the cage.
FALSE FATHER (upon inspecting the bird): It is not blue enough. You must go and find me the one I want.
LITTLE BROTHER: But I don't know where it is.
FALSE FATHER: No more do I. That's why you must look for it. I can do without the grass that sings, at a pinch; but I must absolutely have the blue bird. It's for my new little girl, who is very ill.
LITTLE BROTHER: What's the matter with her?

. . .

*Maurice Maeterlinck's* L'Oiseau Bleu *premiered in Moscow in 1908, and has since become part of the collective substrate via the memetic transference of the bird of its title into a symbolic representation of the freedom which returns with innocent purity (cf. William Blake's*

*memory
p. 253*

157

Songs of Innocence and Experience). *The "Blue Bird of Happiness" is a common panacean quest object that manifests in dreams that follow the typical Rank-Beminfalz Proto-Industrial Folklore Logic. An improvisational oneiric version, a brief excerpt of which is quoted above, recently premiered on the Ebbinghaus Proscenium. It will, undoubtedly, mutate further before it is witnessed again. The audience of this version (hereafter referred to as the "False Father" edition) is unknown.*

* father
p. 198

How is it being reported? If no one knows who was there, then how does a transcript of the play exist? It is clearly a personality expression rising up through childhood memories and the Metaxu subtext. It is nothing more than mental detritus of a mind working through a synaptic compression, and is meant to be transitory. We invent all manner of one-act plays and elaborate stage shows. These are the manner in which various elements of our personalities and identities try out what-if scenarios and proleptic extrapolations. This is not uncommon. What concerns me, beyond the obvious schizophrenic issue of identifying the source of the academic commentary, is that, while I have no memory of this play, I know the next line:

* schizophrenia
p. 304

FALSE FATHER: *She wants to be free . . .*

# BLACKLEAF 23

ठ ♋

FROM: oldmanwinter@...
TO: alt.oneirology.entheogens
SUB: Re: The search for blackleaf 23

In response to splittongue@alumni. . . 's question about the possibility of a $23^{rd}$ expression of blackleaf, I should point out to her/him that distillation of the $21^{st}$ expression is calculated to take nearly six years. Extrapolating forward, it would take approximately 216 years to harvest the $23^{rd}$ expression. None of us have that kind of time and, unless we have access to the hidden laboratories of Comte St. Germain or one of his contemporaries, we're not going to see blackleaf 23 in our lifetime.

*hidden
p. 219

A shame, I know. Theoretically, the $23^{rd}$ expression is the geometric key to understanding Safiq Al-Kahir's Theory of Protolinguistic Identity. Try as we might to break the Thirteenth Threshold by meditative or cognitive means, I don't think it can be done without the influence of a higher generation blackleaf. The ratio of dosage to purity becomes asymptotic after the $19^{th}$, and, well, you've seen the math.

*thirteen
p. 346

There are rumors that the Ehirllimbal Brothers have managed to fabricate a fairly successful distillation process for blackleaf 20 (successful being defined here as greater than a .08% expression, a phenomenal return if they have managed to build a manufacturing process). What you haven't heard is secondary result of this effort: they've come up with a process of precipitation and reverse heating that creates a fractional amount of 21 as a by-product. The return on the 21 is so minute that it is an unsustainable method, but it has been enough for them to gather several full doses.

Their initial assessment of the $21^{st}$ expression is that it isn't completely a receptor. It can access non-localized biochemical data flights, but it still has very few control mechanisms. It can open doors, but you can't control whether it will open any given door. After all these years, we haven't improved on Huxley's vision.

A more robust dose of the $21^{st}$ expression could be twice the limbic expansion as the 20th, which would mean psychotropic resonances well past the communicable limits of the 8-Curcuit Model. Blackleaf 21 may allow us to see the boundary of God, but it's not going to give us understanding of the Infinite. We just don't have the vocabulary yet to fully utilize the promise of blackleaf 21.

And the 23rd? Forget it. It's a nootropic that will completely reorganize our neural pathways before we have a chance to reassert the Cartesian Primacy. It will turn us into turtles or ducks or worse simply because, in the end, we are just monkeys with a bit of shifted DNA.

That doesn't mean, of course, that we shouldn't be working on ways to shorten the distillation time of blackleaf 23. I just think it is good for us to keep some perspective. We're not ready to be giants. Not yet.

* bleak zero
p. 162

* giants
p. 212

--------------------------------

FROM: terminalx@...
TO: alt.oneirology.entheogens
SUB: RE[2]: The search for blackleaf 23

>>We just don't have the vocabulary yet to fully utilize the promise of blackleaf 21.

What's your suggestion then? Is there a book we should be reading? No, let me rephrase that. Can you get us a copy of Safiq's book? Does it even exist? Are we all chasing a fantasy? How many of us have even tried blackleaf 18, much less the 19th expression?

We're like atomic physicists hanging out and telling lies about which of the transactinide elements we've seen. Who is going to call us on our bullshit?

There's too much interest in oneirology these days. Too many new names here. We're losing focus. We're becoming too diffuse. What's that old story about the architects of Babylon? Yeah, too many of them and they forgot how to build. That's what happening to us. Too many, and we're going to forget.

* architect
p. 154

That bastard Potemkin fucked us all with that girl. I can't believe he was so stupid not to realize what she was planning. Must have been too busy recreating his favorite sections of de Sade's *120 Days of Sodom*.

* *fork*
p. 205

-t to the x

------------------------------------

FROM: heron74@...
TO: alt.oneirology.entheogens
SUB: RE[3]: The search for blackleaf 23

>>I can't believe he was so stupid not to realize what she was planning.

You've never had a dream turn on you, t? Well, you're better at swimming in the Oneiroi than me, then.

* *tidal motion*
p. 349

And the problem isn't any one of us in particular, really. Nothing this fellow does—or did, or is purported to have done—can touch you. Not unless you let it. You have to let it in, t. You know that.

Besides, Potemkin doesn't exist. Even his name says as much.

* *explanation*
p. 74

Sometimes, as our learned grandfather of psychiatry once said, "There are times when a cigar is only a cigar."

Even in a dream.

-(pk)

"We'd all be taken more seriously if we had black halos."
—Jerry McElholn

# BLEAK ZERO
ȣ ♋

FROM: heron74@. . .
TO: alt.oneirology.entheogens
SUB: Re: bleak zero

To put it bluntly, so you don't mistake my meaning: that's bad shit, man, really bad shit. It has a number of names because TH3y don't want us to realize how badly the pipeline has been co-opted. This list isn't all of the names that Bleak Zero takes, by any means, just a few that I've heard recently: Sister Midnight, Void Snap, KYS (which, I believe, stands for "Kiss Your Sister;" or "Fuck Your Mother," they use a lot of mangled substitution ciphers these days), Event Horizon, Done Done, Flipper.

*tangle*
*p. 332*

Yeah, I don't know where that last one comes from. But trust me, Flipper is not your friend. Even if it makes you feel like a dolphin, it's just Bleak Zero dusted with dirty big-chain hallucinogens. While your brain is all wrapped up with making dolphin noises and dreaming about fish, their compounds are unraveling and rebinding all over your brain.

*intent*
*p. 224*

It's not an entheogen, regardless of what your pusher tells you. It has intent. It has its own plan. It won't help you find God. It will rewire you so that God will be lost to you. It is a neurological virus, pre-programmed to shut down parts of your neural fabric.

You won't dream for a week after taking a dose of Bleak Zero. Take three, and you won't dream again. Ever. Might as well just lobotomize yourself with a ice pick and be done with it. And there's no way to reverse it because that fabric is burnblack.

Why do you kids keep trying this stuff? Dancing on that knife edge isn't the way. It is too easy to fall. Thinking that corporate pharma will play by the rules is to forget that they're rewriting the rules as we speak. They're trying to rewrite everything, remember?

*experiment*
*p. 192*

-(pk)

# CAGE

〰〰

"Black Iron Prison" is the term you'll hear used by the modern seeker of gnosis. It's a reference to the Archonic Construction of the Universe, a theory that multi-dimensional intelligences are preventing us from realizing our full spiritual and cognitive potential by locking our minds in these psychic prisons.

There are a number of analogous mythological scenarios strewn throughout history, so as a cosmological definition, the Archonic Construction of the Universe is as good as any. It benefits from being connected to Philip K. Dick's paranoid visions, which any competent oneironaut appreciates.

Modern culture suffers from a lack of decent mythological canon. We should make our own because, really, we are children of the 3rd millennium. It's time we believed in our own gods.

Which brings me back to the concept of cages. We continue to be trapped by second-millennial constructs. Hell, even the apocalyptic terror of the end of the first millennium still pervades our psyches. We're still too busy looking over our shoulders to realize the first apocalypse of the third millennium is rapidly approaching.

*fragmentary
p. 209

That's another story. I'll get to it later.

Cages. No man can ever be imprisoned against his Will. Crowley knew this once, though he forgot it shortly after the other initiates and adepts started fawning over his "transmission from the desert." Yes, you can cage the flesh and you can even lock the mind into a cell, but the Will is unbreakable.

Jung gave it a different name—"individuation"—but didn't allow himself the freedom to imbue it with any lasting power. Freud (the last black magician of the twentieth century, frankly) had managed to bind Jung tightly enough that the Swiss psychologist never truly realized he had been . . . caged.

*burnblack
p. 26

# CASUAL DISARRAY
## ♍

She had a predilection for pony tails. Part of her girlish charm, I am sure, part of an unconscious—but calculated and cultivated—persona. She worked at the coffee stand in the lobby of the Zoonomia Building, and spent most of her time with her back to the customers as she pulled shots with a self-aware irreverence. Her pony tails were always restrained by elastic bands with plastic baubles, the cheerfully transparent colors of childhood, and they were long enough to touch her back, between her shoulder blades.

She has a salamander tattooed there, on her back. A fiercely orange creature, curled like an insouciant smile, outlined in electric blue. I've seen it. I stumbled upon her one night in the corporate bookstore down the street from Zoonomia, paging through a biography of Lucrezia Borgia. Unrestrained by the coffee stand apron, she was dressed for an evening out—dinner, maybe a little clubbing afterward. I wandered past her, once, stealing a surreptitious glance at the electrified amphibian peeking through the patterned veil of her casually arranged shawl.

"Harry," she says, without looking up from her book. "Are you lost?"

*No. I never spoke to her. Not that night.*

**No? What about the next night, when you followed her home?**

*No. That's not true. I—*

"I've been waiting for you." She puts the book back on the shelf, casually leaving it on top of the other. Casually leaving the world different than the way she—

—never spoke—

—touched it.

I was a summer intern, my sophomore year, and I did menial work for an industrial design company on the twenty-third floor of Zoonomia. The company designed libraries; I made copies and ran errands. The coffee stand was in the lobby. She worked the morning shift, always gone by mid-afternoon. How could I follow her home?

*No, wait. I never spoke to her in the bookstore.*

* library
p. 248

"Do you want to pet my salamander?" Her shawl undulates and bulges, and an phosphorescent glow rises up her shoulder. An orange snout pushes its way out of the folds of the cloth—the fabric now electrified, now traced with phantasmal light and the hidden palimpsest of her history—and a pale tongue licks out and touches the hollow of her throat. "Do you want to lick—"

* history
p. 22

*Stop it, Nora. This never happened.*

**There are so many paths that are blocked off, Harry. So many secret chambers and submerged oubliettes. We are opening routes together, you and I; we are finding a wealth of mnemonic history that has been cut off from the rest of your identity. Of course you don't remember this happening because, until we touched this bundle of synaptic impressions, it was isolated from the rest of your matrix.**

* duality
matrix
p. 185

*You are editing me, adding memories that aren't mine.*

**But isn't this a nice one? Haven't you always wondered who she was? How many times did you dream about her that summer?**

*Those were dreams.*

**This is the Oneiroi. What is the difference?**

*I am different.*

**How? You don't exist in the real world, Harry. You are only a dream.**

"Look," the barista says, holding out her salamander. "He's hungry." Its tongue flickers back and forth across the slit of its mouth like a clock pendulum. "Will you buy me a drink? He likes cocktail olives." The salamander's tongue quickens, and I feel time become pinched. "I have a story to tell you."

* tongue
p. 44

"What sort of story?" I ask, and my voice validates this world. It snaps into place, its casual disarray assembling itself into a precise affirmation of reality. I ask, and she answers with a crooked smile and a rising blush that becomes the color of the sun.

*What sort of story?*

**A tale of a world unlike this one. An imaginary world where**

a boy just like you never spoke to this girl, where salamanders cannot see into the future, where words have lost all their magic, and where love and dust are one and the same.

*That sounds like a sad story.*

* kiss
p. 234

**Kiss her, Harry. Tell her you want a different story, that you want a different ending.**

She stands ahead of me on the escalator, and I have to raise my head to look at her. The light makes her pony tails seem like feathers. I reach for her, putting my hand on her waist. She comes down a step and, putting her salamander on my head to free her hands, pulls me to her. My face is pressed into her valley and, through the fabric of her pants, through the silk of her panties, I try to kiss her.

She laughs, and her heel catches on the metal rim at the top of the escalator. Our hands tight, we fall . . .

*What about the salamander?*

* reflection
p. 396

**There is no salamander, Harry. It's a metaphor.**

*No, us falling off the escalator is the metaphor. The salamander is a key.*

**You see, Harry? There is no one editing you but you. How else could you discern the symbolism of the salamander?**

166

# CEREMONY
## ♌

"The Tower reaches through Time and Space, connecting Above with Below," the Ribbon Man tells me as we go down the endless stair. "There are two ways to reach Heaven, and when one has fallen, you must descend through the Pit and seek passage from the Angel of Chains. Do not forget this when you wake."

* heaven
p. 216

I promise not to.

We descend the endless stair forever, and since Time has no meaning here beneath the Ogenic Twilight, we reach the bottom. There is no one waiting for us.

* twilight
p. 382

"Oh," the Ribbon Man says finally. "Silly me. Of course. It's my turn to put this mask on."

He slips a hand through a gap in the darkness, and retrieves a length of heavy chain that ends with a worn medal. He slips the chains around his shoulders, settling the medal on his chest, and his ribbons change to gold and bronze.

He shivers slightly, and seems taller in the gloom. "This way," he says, and his voice is different. But it is the voice the stone was waiting for, and a passage opens for us. He leads me a long way under the water to a garden of flowers and stones.

We find a path, lined with yellow flowers, that leads into a confusion of blossoming plants. There, caught in the timelessness of this realm, are a party dressed in fancy clothes. Off to one side are three couples, sitting in six thrones. They, and everyone else assembled, are waiting. Patiently. Eternally.

"Waiting for you," the Ribbon Man says. He goes to a tall black plant nearby. At his caress, one of the blooms open, and a squirming glob of text falls out. He has to use both hands to contain it, and still phrases ooze between his fingers. "Put this on."

I let him pour it over my head and it slithers all over me. It gets in my nose, a tickling scent of mint and rosemary; it flows into my ears, and I can hear the whispered thoughts of the assembled guests—their endless chatter as they wait; the goo covers my eyes, and I can see inside the kings and queens upon the thrones; I inhale it into my mouth, and I remember what it was like to kiss her.

When the text drips down to my ankles, the hosts comes out of their stasis. In a flutter of skirts and coattails, they step down from their thrones, which vanish in an upward flowing rain. I realize the platforms on which the thrones had sat are long narrow boxes.

Coffins.

Each of the six royalty strip off their garments, and then lift the lids from the coffins and climb in. The three kings seem composed of their fate, but the queens each stare at me as they lay back in the empty coffins.

The rest of the assembled party twist and churn, losing their color, until they are but pale pallbearers. The lids of the coffins are closed, and in a stately procession, the remaining guests carry the coffins away. On down the path lined with yellow flowers.

I hear something move in one of the coffins as it passes me, and I stop the pallbearers. The lid isn't nailed shut, and I open the box easily. It is filled with shards of glass, and in each piece I see reflections of other dreams. I step away from the coffin, letting the pallbearers lift it to their shoulders again, and they continue after the other coffins.

The Ribbon Man coughs behind me, and there is a clunk and rattle of metal. His ribbons have changed color again—no longer the shade worn by the Angel. He seems confused for a moment. "Not too late," he mutters. "I've not missed the ceremony."

"Which?" I ask.

"The marriage ceremony," he says. "It's your lucky day. Are you ready?"

I watch the last of the coffins disappear around a bend in the path. "No," I say. "I don't think I ever will be."

"No time like the present, then." He laughs. "Or, rather, in this un-time, in this not-present, you are ready."

"All things being equal . . ."

"Absolutely. Everything is, and that's what we are here to celebrate." He puts his hands together, and his fingers disappear into a knot of ribbons. "A consummation."

* marriage
p. 250

168

# CHILDREN
# II

August 23rd, 1975

Eduardo Ehrillimbal
XXX XXXX XX X XXX
Harvard University
Cambridge, MA 02138

Son,

I realize this letter may strike you as an egregious hoax, and I hope that you will have enough faith to read it through to the end before you pass judgment. I hope that you will understand the importance of the roles which have been given to our family. I may yet realize my dream, and the fulfillment of that work will change everything. No, everyone. It will change us all.

I am filled with shame over the deception forced upon you and your brother by my death. Such a violent break was a necessary, though extremely painful, evil. My competitors have become too aggressive, too willing to do harm to those I love in order to gain what they want. They think they can take my work and it will open itself to them; they think the flowers are like cheap whores, willing to spread their legs at the slightest hint of shiny coin. And, when such display of wealth fails to grant them access, they will grow violent. They have shown such behavior before. The Ytucalis still carry those scars.

*fire
p. 201

No, my dear son, I had to die. The research had to die with me. It was the only way to protect my family: you, your brother, and your dear mother.

The work to be done is best done undisturbed—it will take more than my lifetime, I fear. While I have managed to distill the fourth expression, I am still so far from realizing the final expression. The details of the work are like an old alchemical recipe: so much depends on the nature of my intent as well as the skill of my hands.

*intent
p. 224

I wish I could have been a better father, Eduardo. I know I have

* re-awakening
p. 397

been difficult since my return from the jungle and, while there is a rational—biological—explanation for those years of emotional detachment, I realize such an explanation is not what the heart needs. I am sorry, my son, and I will not trouble you with a flurry of misguided explanations and brittle excuses.

I am so proud that you are a Harvard man. That had always been my hope that one of my sons would grace those halls with his presence. Before you graduate, please visit our family friend in the psychology department one last time. Tell him that he is to give you the keys. Certain arrangements have been made, and are awaiting your acceptance. I know they are a poor substitute, but I want you to have what legacy I have to leave.

* key
p. 227

With great love,

-J

# CIRCLE

## ♌

My crown is gone. Severed by a stroke of lightning. My brain is exposed to the torrential downpour of black tears. My brain is coated by the ash of burnblack feathers. *Our Fathers, who have fallen from Heaven, hallowed be thy tongues.*

* crown
p. 177

One world. One people. One thought. This is the singularity of human experience. There is no darkness but the light of unity. There is no light but the darkening of ego. Yes, now, lower your lantern. Put out the sun. Take my hand.

I have seen your face, King of Babylon.

*You have seen all of our faces. We are nothing more than mirrors.*

Nothing more? Then, what do we reflect? Where did that light come from? Are we a gemstone of infinite facets, and our purpose is to perpetuate that gleam of light—back and forth, back and forth.

*Light is an illusion.*

Caused by the aberration of sight? Much like the sensory abomination of hearing? Or that tempestuous terror of taste? What about the sensual deviance of touch? Yes, are they all illusions?

*There is no need for them at this depth.*

Of course not. There is no need for anything here, because every need can be met. Which, in turn, means that dreams have both no purpose and every purpose. Everything and nothing. Beginning and end. Aleph and Tau. If I have everything—if I have nothing—then what can you offer me? Come on, King of Tears, you're going to have to try harder than that.

* son
p. 317

# COAGULA

## Ω

The Arabic alchemists of the 8th and 9th century preserved the Hermetic thought of Egypt, and the resurgence of alchemy in Europe during the late medieval period is indebted to them. Safiq Al-Kahir, even among his contemporaries, was an enigma and, by the time the Italians were devouring every Islamic manuscript they could find, Safiq was already buried beneath layers of dissembling mythology and cryptic commentary. In some ways, alchemy ignores him; while in others, his work is the secret cipher that illuminates their efforts.

*IV

I've done a lot of research since the dream of the library, and while knowledge of Safiq is fairly common, no one seems to know if a copy of his book really exists. One of the other oneironauts on the mailing list confirmed that the paragraph read to me in my dream was indeed written by Safiq.

He was too eager to know where I had seen it, which alarmed me.

*poison
p. 275

There is an ugly undercurrent on the mailing list. Tempers are short, and people are quick to read offense and respond with invective. Paranoia is starting to creep into conversations. "Is poison nothing more than a substance which the body cannot assimilate?" If you read an online community as a virtual body, then is such a confusion synonymous with a toxinbeing introduced into the system?

Safiq is credited with something now called "The Theory of Protolinguistic Identity," a name that thoroughly neuters the "theory" in favor of academic providence. In fact, I seem to remember a paper making the circuit a year or so ago that mentioned this theory but failed to credit Safiq with it. I think I know why now: too much mysticism for a piece of academic criticism that wanted to be taken seriously.

*fragmentary
p. 209

We are such a divided group: too many counter-culture rebels vying with earnest academics for the secrets of the Oneiroi. You would think there should be enough room in the collective unconscious for all of us, but apparently it gets pretty crowded.

So big, and yet so small.

So afraid of conformity. Of agreeing too much and losing our indivual voices. Which, in turn, keeps us eternally apart. Adrift.

# COLLAR

✗

We seek guidance from scholars who have, presumably done all the foolish things in their youth so that we don't have to suffer the same ignominy and embarrassment. These individuals are invariably male, modeled after our fathers—both present and false. We cloth them in robes and give them pointy hats and special collars, indicating that they are both closer and more beholden to God than we are. They are the priests of our temples and houses; they are the holy men who wait for us in dark caves atop lonely mountains. They are the wizards who dwell in the wastes, where they eat frogs and drink the venom of serpents (having eschewed all other forms of sustenance).

*hermit
p. 217

They are our sin eaters. The devourers of our guilt and shame.

We give them our poisons, and they bless us in return. They are the waste disposal pits of our psyches. What happens in their bellies and hearts with all the burnblackened life we give them? Are they so pure that the darkness is stripped away? Or are they repositories that we hope never breach.

*Deinde, ego te absolvo a peccatis tuis in nomine Patris, et Filii, et Spiritus Sancti.*

*Amen.*

But, Father doesn't want your poison. The Holy Ghost laughs at you. And the son?

*father
p. 198

He is so lost.

Your pain would decimate him if he were to take it from you. He cannot handle such darkness without Father's help. Without the shroud of the Holy Ghost wrapped around him. The son is so fragile. So delicate.

And so why has he been abandoned . . . ?

# CROSSING

## ♌

The sea is tempestuous, and the boat groans continually at the battering it takes from the waves. The deck is slick with spray, and the sails strain in their rigging. The Ribbon Man, dressed in layers of black ribbons that whip behind him like a storm of feathers, is manning the helm, though the wheel is lashed in place. The wind has already broken one sailor who tried to arm wrestle it into submission. It is his eye that keeps us on course.

I am bound to the mainmast with heavy iron chains. Gold links enter and leave my body through my armpits, and inside my chest, they loop tight around my heart. The gold chain wraps round and round the mast, all the way to the top of the royal yard where they meet again in a gold lock. The lock burns, the flame resolutely lit in the darkness of the storm. It is my heart that keeps us afloat.

* heart
p. 215

Time stopped when we crossed the Horizon, and we do not know how long we have been fighting the chaotic storms of the Ogenic Twilight. *It doesn't matter*, the Ribbon Man had said when he had bound me to the mast, *we will sail until the dream tires of us. We will sail until it breaks and lets us through.*

The wind tries to blow us over, but the boat remains upright. It tries to blow us back, but the Ribbon Man's intent is too great. It tries to drive us mad with its shrieking, but we cannot turn back.

We will cross this sea. We will reach the island.

* island
p. 226

# CROSSROAD

## $\underline{\Omega}$

The crossroad is one of those irrepressible symbols—dig deep enough in any mythology and you'll find one. It's the recurring symbol of the duality matrix, that either/or switch that informs every morality tale. Do you go to the east and the rising run, or the west and the darkness that flies before the light? Do you walk with the wind on your face, or with it pushing you? Do you crawl down to the sea and the salty comfort of your mother's womb, or do you scale up into the rocky suffocation of your father's embrace?

* wombwhite
p. 364

My mother, when I was very young, used my father as an example of why learning to make choices was important. "Your father never made a choice in his life," she would tell me, "not when one could be chosen for him." The unspoken conclusion of that thought—where such indecision got him—was always evident in the lines of her face and the sad weariness in her arms when she hugged me at night. And, when I was sixteen, she let heroin make her final choice for her.

* fear
p. 199

Yes, I know. Child of a broken home, destroyed by alcohol and drugs. Is it any wonder I became a narcissistic drug addict who confuses pharmacological psychosis with mythological meta-reality?

Fortunately, I'm not the only one. It is more difficult to be judged insane when there's more than one of you sharing the same psychosis. Not impossible, just more complicated.

Every one of us have had a crossroad experience. Somewhere, we all came to that divergence of paths. On the one hand: the route of the psychonaut and the addict, the lonely road of the psychedelic alchemist; on the other: the twisted path of the oneironaut, the difficult and torturously perilous road of the psychic surgeon.

* psychonaut
p. 12

We made our choices, for whatever reasons that we've burned into our brains after the fact as justification, and some of us have regretted our choices and others have been healed by them. In many ways, every breath is yet another choice: either an affirmation of your previous decisions or a self-destructive recrimination of your own deep-seated failure to live up to your own standards.

Crossroads. Again and again. Over and over. How long do we punish ourselves for those failures? For those moments when we took the

* echoes
p. 186

left-hand path when we should have taken the right? How long do we keep looking over our shoulder, trying to see the path we didn't take?

\* regret
p. 392

My regret with Nora isn't that I brought her into the Oneiroi. My regret is that I wasn't able to give her enough reasons to come back out. That is what haunts me: that I failed to show her that the world of dream wasn't a good substitute.

# CROWN
# ♌

The last King of Europe wears a misshapen crown. It was silver once, but blood and soot have conspired to darken its luster. It is dented now and sits awkwardly upon his head. His scepter is a gnarled stick, a branch salvaged from the courtyard oak that was cut down during the last Occupation. He used to be lame, but now he is crippled. His left leg, much like the southern wing of his palace, is dark and lifeless. His skin, like the walls of that wing, peels and flakes off, leaving a trail of black ash behind him.

*ash*
*p. 155*

If you could follow his trail—chart his history backward—you would find the reason for his injury on the second floor of the south wing. In the conservatory, located in the southwest corner. The reason lies charred beneath the pianoforte, and it is difficult to ascertain the identity of his dead assailant. The pianoforte is also crippled, and not just from the fire. One of its legs has been broken.

All things seek to mirror the King: that is the Final Law of Entropy.

*final law*
*p. 200*

The third symbol of the King is his signet ring. It is a heavy band, platinum wrapped around silver, and mounted with a half-moon wink of obsidian. Tiny letters have been carved by a master jeweler into the face of the stone. Without the aid of a jeweler's loupe, the script would appear like scars and striations, much like the lines and wrinkles on the King's face.

It is difficult to say whether the jeweler was a clever copyist or a prescient inscriber. That detail, like the ring itself, has been lost.

If you were to break open the charred corpse beneath the pianoforte, you would find the ring within the swollen and dry stomach of the dead Queen. The King, crippled both in body and mind, does not—will not—remember why she swallowed his ring. He avoids the southern wing and, in doing so, condemns himself to being broken.

*scarecrow*
*p. 303*

There is no one to heal him. No one to love him.

no 1 = 0

# DEATH MASK
# ♏

* fabric
p. 56

*After the body of the Seeker has been washed accord-ing to the astrological covenants and his body has been wrapped with the linen codex that has been inscribed with his desire, then he is to be presented to the Moon on three successive nights.*

*Care must be taken to hide the Seeker from the Sun as the pure light will blacken the wrappings. If the Moon does not show her face on three successive days, the Seeker must abandon his quest as the text will not be fully shadowed upon the palimpsest of his flesh.*

* abandon
p. 151

*When the Moon sets on the third night, the Seeker is to be taken to the mirror chamber where his death mask will be set. The ceremonial pouring of the mask must be com-pleted by dawn for it is the First Light that seals the mask, and it is the Last Shadow that holds the doorway open for the Seeker to begin his journey.*

* spiritual
armor
p. 323

*Those who travel through the Red Wood to the House must be both covered and masked. Their identities must be concealed lest their desire be seen by the Watchers. The tattooed epistle of their intent and the reflective purity of their resolution proclaim their worthiness to the Bro-ken-Jawed Ones who haunt the forest.*

*It is the fate of the unworthy that they are devoured by those who have lost their tongue.*

*In the mirror chamber, the Seeker is suspended over a pool of purified water and his head is cradled by the Hand. Liquid silver is poured over his face until the palm of the Hand is full, and then the Seeker is lowered into the pool so that the death mask may be fused to his skull.*

*All is bent by the confusion of perception, and the Mask is the purified reflection of the inchoate curvature of the Seeker's Path. The mirror of his face will confound the Shadow at the Threshold; the mirror will retain a flicker of the Last Light, and this reflection (again and again) will show him the way through the maze of the Red Wood.*

* labyrinth
p. 236

*All becomes none outside the linear prison of time, just as none become all within the realm of the ego. Upon the face of the Mask is the inscribed course of the Seeker's Path, and though he cannot see the path as he is wearing the mask, he will know the way. When he reaches the House, the Seeker's Mask shall be judged.*

*If the Seeker's Mask is worthy, then the Keeper of the House will lay ink upon the Seeker, highlighting the lines of his history that will, forever after, be the Word by which the Seeker will be known.*

*Thus Named (thus enumerated), the Seeker will pass through the many trials of the House until he reaches . . .*

There is nothing more to this fragment of Safiq Al-Kahir's *Book of Dream.* This the tantalizing glimpse I had of the path I must take. Am I strong enough? **yes, but what of the key? what of the final door?** Is it real enough?

There is only one way to find out . . .

# DECEIT

✗

"Yes? Hello? Is anyone here? It's awfully dark. Oh, excuse me. I didn't—you know . . . could we turn on a light? Ah, yes. Much—oh!

"I'm sorry. That was rude of me. It's just, well, this is all rather clandestine. I really shouldn't be here, talking with you. Well, not yet, at least. He's not ready.

"No, no. It's just . . . he's fighting the transformation. It's very strange, actually. I'm not quite sure how he is doing it; I don't think he's even aware that he is thwarting your infection. No, he knows something is going on. He's certainly aware that all is not quite right in his head; he's just not sure how and why.

* letter
p. 79

"But he is beginning to suspect, I think.

"My fault? How can this be my fault? My devotion should be obvious. You should blame her—what? Oh, you do? Oh, yes, of course. She's completely fixated on saving him. She thinks he has the strength to break your—

"I'm sorry. Was it impolite of me to suggest such a thing? Yes, such a bad little double agent to draw your attention to your enemy's intentions. Wouldn't want to disturb your little egocentric view of the situation, would I? Yes sir, very good sir. I'll just keep marching along . . .

"(!)

"That was unnecessary. Look at what you've done. How am I supposed to hide that? He's going to notice. He's going to wonder what happened. What am I supposed to tell him? 'Oh, that? I slipped and hit my head on a doorknob.' Yes, he'll believe that. He's just so ready to believe anything right now.

* tool
p. 350

"You are such a petty little tyrant. What? Are you going to hit me again? Go ahead. Give me a matched set. Do it, you vengeful godling. Show me the anger that slew your brothers. Show me that impotent rage that brought down the tower. Show me what makes you divine. Yes, show me!

" . . . Oh . . . Oh . . . I, uh, it's not what you think. No, I knew it was you all along. I am very good at seeing things as they truly are. It is one of my talents. Yes, one of my many talents.

"What? No, no. This was all for your benefit. I knew you were there, hiding behind that veil. I would never actually seek out . . . Never! I can see you don't believe me. You think I would betray Harry? What would I gain from doing so? Freedom? Hardly. I understand the symbiotic nature of our relationship, my dear. More so than you see to.

* double
p. 390

"You believe in his obsession; oh, my dear girl, you have to believe in it because it is sole reason that you continue to exist as an identity. You are no more 'real' than I, but you have the luxury of being able to bind yourself to his fragmented memory and that monstrous guilt he has taken upon himself. Look at me. What do I get? Old cloth stained with the blood of his memories. It's like wearing memorial medals from wars no one remembers.

"Please. I want Harry to survive just as much as you do. Just because my efforts aren't the same as yours does not make them any less critical to his survival. You go ahead and continue to appeal to his sense of morality; I will—"

"No, that is not why I came here. I don't even want to talk to that . . . that thing. It has forgotten too much, and all that is left is its fury. It will burn us all. It thinks it knows what its father wants. It's sad, actually . . .

* fool
p. 204

"Please. Stop it. Who are you trying to convince? By the way, here's a question for you: How did you know that shape? You thought it would fool me, so you must have some idea of what it looks like. Where did you learn that, my little lamb? Hmmm?

"Ha. That's what I thought. None of us is innocent, girl. The touch of the thirteen is a genetic stain. We'll never be rid of it, and to pretend otherwise is to forget who we are, where we came from."

# DESCENT
## ♌

His words become meaningless now, an empyrean thunder of falling masonry. Tumble down tumble down—*raghtakamminarro*. The petals are swept away. His bony hands are around my throat, squeezing. His headless skeleton presses against me, bent ribs digging into my back. His pelvic bone bangs against my hip, and his cracked toes scratch at my ankle and calf.

Too much flesh, too much meat. Strip it off. I will make you as naked as I. I will take your skin. I will wear your face. I will—

There. A flicker of color. Tiny wings.

* VI

The butterfly from the mountain top, its orange and yellow wings shifting and fluttering in this deepdark bubble. Pretty light. Save me, pretty light, bring me salvation.

Salvation is the bone worried by fools. It is the fossilized finger of your dead god, your absent father. It is a worthless piece of chalk.

But . . . but, you can write with chalk.

* note
p. 261

Who will read your suicide note? What will you say, when there are no words left?

You took them from me.

You gave them to me.

The butterfly floats, just out of reach. I stretch for it as his bony fingers bruise my windpipe. I can feel the butterfly's wings brush my fingertip.

He wraps himself around my legs, and his bones bang against my lower back like an ascendant lover. His hands shift and tighten. I have stopped trying to breathe. Instead, I focus all of my fading energy on the fluttering web of color.

Just out of reach.

So close.

Just one more . . .

* VIII

*Let go. We are all here. Join us. Let your light go out, and come into the communal emptiness of the deepdark. Let yourself fall into the unconscious, little spark. Let yourself go out.*

She loves me. Yes, she does . . . I . . . believe . . .

The butterfly shifts and hardens in my hand. Its edge cuts my palm,

182

and my grip becomes slippery with blood. I need something to hold, something less fine, less pure.

My vision goes dark as parts of my cerebral cortex shut down. I can still feel the weight of his bones, but my throat doesn't hurt any more. My thalamus can't be bothered to transmit the pain signals any more. My fingers are dull, and they fumble badly as they beat and tug at the peak of his spine. Yes, the thought struggles to form, this . . .

His atlas comes free and, like a blind man putting a puzzle together, I marry bone and blade. Yes, this will do . . .

More thunder, a wordless reverberation against my aching bones, as I cut the bones of his forearm. The pressure on my throat vanishes and my lungs surge. My brain explodes with light.

The bubble bursts. I can see. I can see where to cut him, where to put the knife so as to best take him apart. I can see the sinew holding the bones together at his elbow, at his shoulder. I can see where his heart should be, hidden beneath that twisted cage of ribs. *heart p. 215

I can see his intent.

# DRIFT
## ♏

*The dunes are like ocean waves, perfectly regular crests as far as my eye can see. The capricious djinn of the desert have left curls in some of the peaks, little twists of sand that will not last. The grains run off these scallops like those of an hourglass. Each dune is moving to the west, one grain at a time. In a hundred lifetimes, the sand will have traveled the same distance that a man can walk in a day.*

*And yet, in a hundred lifetimes, the sand will still be here. The man who walked those few miles will not. Such is the nature of identity.*

*So, too, is the nature of God: everywhere and nowhere, everything and nothing. No-thing is not the lack of identity. It is the purest of identities, uncomplicated by dualities and personalities. It is perfectly defined, as it is the brief infinity before all energy, all thought, and all form came into being.*

*There are words in the sand. I do not know who has written them. Every morning, I find the new words snaking through the shadows of the dunes. They are never in the same place; frequently, I spend most of the morning searching. On some days, they are quite faint, as if the djinn have already started to blow them away.*

*The words are expressions of an alien alchemy, filled with incomprehensible formulae and heretical discourse. At first, I thought they were being written by those responsible for my exile in an effort to extract a confession from me, but such thought is born of loneliness. No one knows where I am; no one knows the path to this desolate place.*

*I have no memory of writing these words, yet I seek these signs out, so as to rediscover what it is that I have dreamt. To learn what I have forgotten upon waking.*△

*duality
matrix
p. XX

*bloom
p. XX

*serpent
p. XX

---

△ - Safiq Al-Kahir, *Book of Dreams* (Obscura Editions: Red House, 1938), 18.

# DUALITY MATRIX

♓

*What is the harm, ye ask, in not distinguishing one-self? If we do not distinguish, we fall into indistinctiveness, which is the other quality of the pleroma. We fall into the pleroma itself and cease to be creatures. We are given over to dissolution in the nothingness. Therefore we die in such measure as we do not distinguish.*

From *Septem Sermones ad Mortuos*, written by Basilides in Alexandria, the City where the East touches the West.

| White | .\|. | Red |
|---|---|---|
| Straight | .\|. | Curved |
| Key | .\|. | Lock |
| Anarchy | .\|. | Rationalism |
| Rod | .\|. | Cup |
| Fortune | .\|. | Fate |
| Breath | .\|. | Dust |
| Mahapralaya | .\|. | Om |
| Dream | .\|. | Death |
| Light | .\|. | Shadow |
| Mask | .\|. | Reflection |
| King | .\|. | Queen |
| Love | .\|. | Fear |

*The Twelve-Fold Facets define us to the Light Bringer and the Dark Dreamer; the measure of each is the weight which pulls us toward either extreme, and it is our Individuation that preserves our identity. To become a Shadow is to enter Servitude; whether it is as a winged torchbearer or a broken souleater, it is to be less than a man.*△

---

△ - Frater Croix-I-lux, *De Matrimonium Mortis et Somni* (Maris Pontus: Ascona, 1935), 35.

# ECHOES
ᛗ

Jung was the first modern psychologist to have an inkling of the nature of echoes. In his studies, he called them "archetypes" and said they populated the "collective unconscious." By the time I started taking psychoactives, his terminology was firmly rooted in that self-same linguistic landscape (a self-referential echo, if you will), and popular consciousness (though, there is very little that is "conscious" about memetic propagation) was very infatuated with these concepts (and, even more so, of the "possibilities" offered by them). No one bothers to footnote a discussion of "Jung's collective unconscious" with the fact that, by the end of his life, he had abandoned the term.

* psychonaut
p. 12

There are two types of dreams. You can certainly find a number of organization schemata by which to code dreams, but they are simply finer gradations of a basic duality: the Enhypnia and the Oneiroi. We draw these definitions from Artemidorus' Oneirocritica. The Enhypnia is a dream of a basal nature: one born of the passions and inflammations of the flesh and lower mind, one that reflects the dreamer's current state of mind and body. The Oneiroi is a divinely inspired message, a communication with sacred beings that the mind translates as a series of coded symbols.

* radio
p. 291

At the risk of oversimplification, the distinction boils down to an "unenlightened" source and a "illuminated" one. The primal dream is simple to parse: we dream of food when we go to bed hungry; we fantasize about people we have seen or touched; we fret and twist and sweat when we are stalked by wild animals in our sleep. On the other hand, we do not understand the tongue of the gods, and our deformed and shrunken language centers try to render the music as abstract symbols. With varying results.

* tongue
p. 44

Yes, echoes. Do you know what you need to produce an echo? Something to make sound with, and something to hear it. If, in the beginning, there was nothing but Void, was God mute? Is the Logos—his first word, that Unutterable syllable—is it nothing more than a moan of terror? Was this cry, made so vast and huge that the Void split in twain, nothing more than a desperate attempt to find someone else in the darkness?

* mitosis
p. 391

And, when God made the Shadow, did the Shadow not respond when God sounded his barbaric yawp across the emptiness of Heaven a second time?

What will happen the third time? Will the Shadow respond, or has it already? Has it already discovered its own voice? Has it learned how to further shape its twisted tongue? Babble on and on . . .

**We are the echo of echoes, Harry. You asked me to remind you. When we were in the white room, where the black stones steam. You don't remember because you are facing the wrong way, but you must trust me.**

* crossroad
p. 175

# EGO
♌ ♎ ♑

His breathing slows, each inhalation more brief than the last. He slips out of time, out of phase with the world, and watches the light die. Just one more. Just one.

* trinity
p. 354

A crack. Split. The stone shifts. Somewhere the third sons of the Fallen Ones cry out in their sleep, feeling the cut. Just a little tear, but it is enough.

The spine shifts, collapsing on itself. There is a darkness now at the edge of the world, a tiny splinter of light has been swallowed.

yes yes there, let me yes yes

The windows break first, the panes cracking and falling out. I cannot see out. I cannot see in. Blindness. Blindness. The tower tilts, its spine suddenly compromised. Just one chip.

**(no!)**

Have we brought this calamity upon ourselves? Are we responsible for this destruction?

His brother cannot speak. His throat is full of blood. His mouth is full. His tongue is gone. He, too, has lost the ability to speak.

*When we relaunch the dream weapon, all will be forgotten . . .*

The tower, falling . . .

* spine
p. 28

My spine, collapsing . . .

". . . and all will be well."

**yes yes here, the blackness comes yes yes**

I miss you, Nora.

**I know. I miss you too.**

falling . . .

*We have forgotten what it is like to participate in genesis.*

No, we never knew.

"All we have left is shadows of shadows."

All we have . . .

* fool
p. 204

(watch my hands says the magician)

. . . are questions. Why? Who? Where? No answers, just echoes back of our own blind fear. Why?

bababa . . .

**Did you fall?**

. . . dalgharaghtakamminarronnkonn . . .

Stones all around me. My tongue split and bleeding in my mouth. Bruises on my hands.

. . . bronntonnerronntuonnthunntrovarr . . .

*My shadow, clawing at me. What echo is this? What nonsense have I created? What geometry have I forced around my head? What have I done, oh clumsy God?*

. . . hounarwnskawntoohoohoordenenthurnuk!

Yes, that was me, bouncing down the ladder. I fell (hidden in the copy I kept in the nightstand), from the roof to the cellar, and through every world in between.

* descent
p. 182

# EMERGENCY

↗ ♓

* fowl
p. 208

• *In the event of a water landing, assume neutral buoy-ancy and sleeve yourself with feathers. The initial impact will undoubtedly be jarring and may result in disorienta-tion. However, the dynamism of the fluid is temporary, and the oneironaut is best protected by becoming a duck for the duration of the chaotic instability.*

• *In the event of a visit from a deceased father figure, refrain from addressing the phantom directly or other-wise acknowledging its presence. While such denial may not banish the haunt, it will delay its attachment to your psyche, thereby allowing you the opportunity to craft an Oedipal Loop. The re-iterative construct will captivate and nullify the phantom. Remember to bind the Oedipal Loop once the father figure has entered the sequence so the psy-chic expression of the ghost will continuously regenerate the loop. Self-sustaining prisons are always the best kind.*

* cage
p. 163

• *In the event of cataplexy or sleep paralysis, make yourself as comfortable as possible. While you may dream during a narcoleptic episode, you are disconnected enough that you will not fall into the Oneiroi. This is the one instance where you may sleep and dream without fear of being found.*

• *In the event of an encounter with the animal kingdom, quickly assess the domestication of said beast. If it appears to be responsible to voice commands and has more than a passing fascination with kitchen appliances, barter with it. If it seems truly feral, run. Or fly. Or assume the shape of a tree stump. (Use the most readily accessible method of flight.)*

* tree
p. 373

• *In the event of weather events involving food, remind yourself that you are experiencing basal physiological triggers. Even though the food is terrible, you have to eat some of it every few days. Otherwise, your body will try to devour itself. You can't fly away to the Oneiroi if your stomach is always empty.*

• *In the event of an onset of protean synaesthesia, take four aspirin, and tuck yourself into bed with a hot water bottle. Call your service provider as soon as the moon rises. Gold coins will be needed to assuage the hunger of the first responders. Hope they don't show, but be prepared if they do.*<sup>△</sup>

*\* psychonaut*
*p. 12*

△ - Entries taken from the *Oneironaut's Survival Guide*, a mimeographed chapbook purported to have been written in 1981 by Jerry McElholn during his residency at the Rose Bay Psychiatric Hospital in Berkeley, CA.

# EXPERIMENT

♋ ♐

FROM: heron74@...
TO: alt.oneirology.entheogens
SUB: : The Rose Bay Experiment

Can't sleep. Won't sleep, actually. Dreams . . . yeah, not my friend tonight. Anyway, instead of taking a couple of Vicodin and smoking a bowl or two, I thought I'd try to exorcise some of these demons instead. So, let me tell you what happened at Rose Bay, back in '81. Back when Jerry and Frank and I all went nuts.

We did a lot of LSD in the 1970s. Even after it was classified as Schedule 1. Still easy to get, frankly, and the quality was really good. But when the Brotherhood of Eternal Love went kaput in '77, the slide started. It took a year or so, but eventually, demand got the better of supply, and all of our regular sources dried up. Finally, any high school dropout with a semester of chemistry under his belt thought he might get rich off a sticky stack of damp blotter.

Somewhere near the end the decade—maybe it was even early '80— Jerry made a massive score. I had always remembered it being a stack of blotter, but now, I know that it wasn't. I don't remember where he got it, or who he got it from, but he said it was "enough magic powder to last us the whole fucked up decade."

*wombwhite
p. 364

Naturally, we took most of it over one weekend.

Frank never talked about his experience, but it pretty clearly broke him. Jerry, as some of you might know, got lost in the Oneiroi, and came back as a wild prophet of the unconscious. I went deep enough that I saw Jerry disappear into the fabric, but I wasn't . . . I, well, never mind. It's not important.

*fabric
p. 56

I was the most lucid of the three of us when the weekend was over, and after running interference for Jerry and taking care of Frank for a few months, someone suggested that I check all three of us in to a local clinic. Get some real help. I wasn't as insane as the other two, but I was definitely close to that edge, and having someone else take care of me (and them) for awhile seemed like a really good idea. The problem was: none of us had any money, and sure, we could get help at any of the county mental hospitals, but they don't . . . you know, they're not so keen on actually helping people.

I had gone to school with this guy, Julio Ehrillimbal. I think I got him his first pot, or, maybe, it was the other way 'round. Anyway, we got baked together more than once, and bonded over those last hits of the last roach, while out waiting for dawn somewhere. His dad had been some hot-shit psychologist or something before he died unexpectedly, and last I heard, Julio had opted to follow his father's research. Down in South America somewhere.

*dawn
p. 385

Anyway, he had left me with some contact information. A company called the Umbrial Consortium. I don't really know what the company does (or did), but one night, when I was staring into the Void, I figured there weren't many other options left. So I called them.

And that's all it took.

As soon as I mentioned Julio's name, they put me in touch with his brother, Eduardo, who was running the company. We had one conversation, and the next day, a car shows up for the three of us. Eduardo got us rooms—all expenses paid, for as long as we needed them—at the Rose Bay Psychiatric Hospital, which was a pretty swank facility up in Claremont Canyon behind UC Berkeley.

Life at Rose Bay was pretty easy. Eduardo had given the hospital pretty specific instructions as to our care, and since he was paying them directly (and on time), they were happy to follow orders. It was a nice vacation. I got some rest; Frank got some good help and started to come back to us; and Jerry, well, Jerry became obsessed with the Oneiroi.

It was during this time that he wrote the *Oneironaut's Survival Guide.* I know you've all seen copies. A lot of what I see out there is folks sharing tips with each other that are directly out of Jerry's old guide. He knew. He really knew what it was like before any of the rest of us had even figured out how to submerge ourselves.

*emergency
p. 190

But anyway, back at Rose Bay, things took a turn when this dude named Dr. Adam Herquiest became the chief administrator of the hospital. What an incompetent blowhard. The sort of middle manager that you find everywhere in administration and politics these days, but back then, it took a certain sort of self-absorbed asshole to climb that far without actually having to do any real work. He would delegate the wiping of his ass to a nurse, as well as having a licensed psychologist write up a grant submission for the process.

Anyway, this jackass had the brilliant idea of double-dipping with the three of us.

Well, I doubt he had the idea himself; I think it was suggested to him. As long as there was no negligible change on our conditions—as long as we looked like we were getting "better"—the Umbrial money would continue. Meanwhile, there was another organization in play, and they was paying him for access to Frank, Jerry, and I.

Well, actually, I think they had access to everyone at the hospital. It was a blanket cover, easier to maintain, and they had access to both test subjects and other schizophrenics. I don't know how Umbrial didn't know, but they were there. Working right under their noses.

There were three of them at the hospital: two post-doc interns and the guy overseeing the program.

Versai. That son of a bitch.

Listen, you know that phrase "gone feral"? It comes from "Feral House," Jerry's name for the residents of the second floor of the East Wing. The psychos up there were feeding off each other. They would squirrel their meds away, and one of them would be chosen to take the whole stash. While this guy was catatonic from the massive dose of God knows what, the others would bleed him and get high off injecting his blood. Who gave them the idea? Yeah, Versai.

* trinity
p. 354

"Trinity House" was Jerry's name for the three of them. The Father, Son, and Holy Ghost. His own play on the whole Catholic trium-virate. Son and Holy Ghost were interchangeable in Jerry's mind, I think, though I stuck with calling the blonde one "Holy Ghost."

They were experimenting with some new chemical agent, some-thing that maintained its efficacy through the transfusion of blood, something that could survive transmission between patients. What

* bleak zero
p. 162

with all this recent discussion about Bleak Zero, I'm starting to think they were trying out an early version of Flipper on the second floor.

Jerry saw too much in the Oneiroi. He took me with him one night and . . . I can't . . . I can't say it. First Rule. I'm not giving it any more life than it already has by writing it down. I wish I could forget what I saw. I wish I could edit it out.

I will say this, though: when they were doped up on blood, they could see into the Oneiroi. They didn't have any ability to shift the fabric, but they could see into it. Jerry got too close one night and they spotted him.

Freaked him out. Not surprisingly, actually. I would have been terrified too. A couple of days later, he stopped sleeping and, before the staff got all wound up about this incident with a table knife, he told me that they were getting smarter. One night, they'd be able to do more than simply see into the Oneiroi.

Three days later, he was dead. I think he was right, and I think he fell asleep.

* note
p. 261

Frank? Poor bastard. Rose Bay was insulating him from the world, and his brain was starting to repair itself. Until the night that Jerry died. I think Frank saw something. I think Frank was dreaming—sleepwalking, maybe—and he fell into the Oneiroi. His brain had been leaking pretty bad after the LSD weekend, and I think he fell that night. I think he saw what killed Jerry. I think he saw the feral ones. And he ran away from reality. Permanently.

I got out. Yeah, there was a clause in the Umbrial contract that said we could check ourselves out at any time we deemed it appropriate. Herquiest wasn't happy about it, but there was nothing he could do. Especially not with the police crawling up his ass about Jerry. I signed myself out, and jumped the wall. Lit off for the wilderness, and I ain't been back since.

Shit. Such a hollow victory, surviving that. What did it get me?

* last light
p. 244

There is an entry that never made it into the *Oneironaut's Survival Guide*. Mainly because no one's ever seen it but me. Jerry hid it in my copy of *Finnegan's Wake*. I know, the "Bible of the insane." But he knew it was the only thing I valued, and that it would be the only thing I'd take with me when I left. Even still, it was a few years before I found it. There's no question it is from Jerry. I know his handwriting.

It says: "In the event of a visit from an Armageddon deity: smile, compliment them on their use of skulls as an accessory, and try not to flinch when they take your flesh. They'll only prolong the torture if they think it hurts you. You can ask them to be gentle. It won't make any difference, but they might find the request funny. They might let you cut your own throat if they're in a good mood."

I miss you, Jerry.

*tool
p. 350

-(pk)

"We'd all be taken more seriously if we had black halos."
–Jerry McElholn

# EYES
## Ω

It has been difficult to transcribe these dreams. I do not want to give them strength by committing them to this journal. But I know no other way to catalog what is happening. Even then, I am careful with the details that I record. I am not trying to be obtuse, I am not trying to hide things from you; rather, I am trying to . . .

What am I trying to do? I have suffered a crisis of conscience, surely. But is all this an attempt to justify my illness? To disguise the damage; to hide the rot?

* explanation p. 74

The Tower fell, Harry. You must reember it.

Cast this as a mythological crisis, then—as an oneironautic adventure to the wellsprings of the spirit and the imagination. But is that merely another bullshit way to avoid addressing what is truly happening to me? *Oh yes, my story is your story. This is the story of all humanity.*

But it isn't. I am splitting. TH3y are aware of what is happening to me. TH3y may even be the cause of it. There is decay in the duality matrix. I am fracturing.

But it is the only way through, isn't it?

I must be both the guide and the martyr—the first and the last.

* ash p. 155

What is that quote? "Let those who do not believe be blinded so that they may not see the light." What if, in that moment of being struck blind, your non-belief is shaken? Does the Divine reverse its action, or is the supplicant now a believer but still bereft of sight? Or are you given some other manner of "sight"—some sort of precognitive or oracular vision—in return for your sacrifice?

* vision p. 361

Is the Oneiroi a visionary reward for the non-believer who has come to his senses? Are we—the oneironauts—all damaged creatures who have come crawling back to the feet of the Divine, abject in our shameful narrow-mindedness? Are all madmen not contrite converts to some internally realized Godhead?

**Oh, Harry, can you not see how you will unmake the world if you say "yes" to that last question?**

**You must wake up, Harry. The Abandoned Sun is coming.**

# FATHER

✗

Dad?

A howling storm of stones. Love, beating against the walls. Love, bruising the walls. Ash cloaks the sky. Where is the moon? **(Oh, it is just a mirror; we are all reflections, after all.)** The priests are in the temples. Praying for guidance. Praying for light.

Praying for the sun to return . . .

*Open your heart. Give of yourself so that the sun may live again.*

Dad?

*I have not abandoned you. I have not forgotten you. You have always been a part of me, just as I have always been inside of you. Yes, embrace me now. Open yourself to me. (Let me in.) I have so much love to give you. I am the rain you have been denied in your desert exile. I am the words you have been afraid to speak.*

* rain
p. 296

Dad? Will you make the pain stop?

**(Answer tell pray answer look tell answer answer tell)**

*Of course.*

Can you bring her back?

**(no!)**

*She is already here. She is waiting for you.*

I . . . I . . .

*Why do you struggle so?*

I . . .

* programming
p. 283

*I can give you everything, but only if yet me in.*

I . . . have done what you asked. Haven't I?

*Give of yourself now. Give it to me.*

**What is left to give when the vessel is already empty?**

*Give me your light, ~~son~~ sun.*

# FEAR

*Embrace me, my child. I have so much to show you. I have so much to give.*
Nothing that I haven't given you already.
*I am the gift of eternity.*
You are a mirror.
*I am the world.*
You are nothing.
I am—
**(listen for the echo, says the wounded lover)**
I do not believe you.
*I am the World Receiver. I am the Tongue that Speaks the Word. I am King Who Will Turn Heaven.*
You are Kinslayer. You are False Prophet. You are my Fear.
*I am the Key. You cannot escape this prison without me. You cannot be free of my influence.*
I will not pass through your Door.
*It is already too late, Harry. I have eaten too much of your mind. You have no choice.*
I am not my father.
*None of us thinks we are. But what made you, Harry? What is it that twists in your cells? We are all abandoned ~~sons~~ sons.*
No, that is your guilt. Not mine.
*What is yours then? What is your fault?*

\* window
p. 363

\* love
p. 71

# FINAL LAW
## ♏ ♓

Language betrays.
Memory decays.
Love, if it ever even existed, dies.
Creation fails.
Only the Word—the Logos, the Divine Spark, the Unutterable Oh!—remains.
As it ends, so it begins.

* experiment
p. 192

*The history of The Final Law of Entropy is muddled by the fact that Clausius' definition was based upon the experiments that gave birth to the second law of thermodynamics. These experiments were concerned with physical systems and not psychological ones. There is, at this time, no quantifiable correlation between the two, though if one were to consider the Universe in a more religio-magico sense, then it might be possible to extrapolate from the laws of thermodynamics to this final law of concerning reality.*△

---

△ - Frater Croix-I-lux, *De Matrimonium Mortis et Somni* (Maris Pontus: Ascona, 1935), 22.

# FIRE
# II

### Fire Destroys Historical Archive; Editor Missing
[by Boston Globe staff | Sept. 24, 1965]

Early in the morning of September 22nd, a fire broke out at the home of Dr. Julio Ehrillimbal, ethnobiologist and editor of *The Journal of Exploratory and Experimental Pharmacology.* The editorial offices and archive of the *Journal*, housed in a secondary structure on the property, were also consumed by the fire.

* library
p. 248

The Wayland Fire Department, located just past the Old Sudbury Road and Cochituate Road interchange—barely five hundred feet from Dr. Ehrillimbal's house on the corner of Library Lane and Old Sudbury Road—responded with two engine trucks. Firefighters were able to contain the blaze to the single property, but even with their rapid deployment, were unable to prevent the destruction of the two buildings.

"Once the site has been completely secured, and we are certain the fire has been put out, we will conduct a full investigation," said Fire Chief Dexter Nyguard. "At this point, the possibility of arson or some other man-made cause is just speculation."

Harriet Truman, 72, a retired seamstress who lives on Library Lane, reports being awakened by a booming noise. "I don't sleep all that soundly any more, and it doesn't take much to wake me," she said. "Whatever it was, it rattled my windows, and knocked some of my china off the shelves downstairs. When I got up, I saw the light coming through the curtains of my upstairs sitting room."

Jethro Duglan, a US Postal Carrier who served in the Army during WWII, was one of the many locals who were drawn out of their houses by the sudden blaze. "I saw some firebombing in France," he said. "It was just like this. Nothing, and then boom! Everything's burning."

Two bodies have been recovered from the fire. Dr. Ehrillimbal, recently divorced from his wife, Gabriella, was reportedly living alone in the house. The Wayland Fire Department is declining to provide identification of the bodies until family members have been notified.

* missing
p. 256

"The WFD has no official statement to make at this time as to the cause of the fire," says Chief Nyguard. "Nor are we at liberty to speculate on the identity of the bodies recovered. I cannot speak as to their relationship to each other or to the fire itself."

*The Journal of Exploratory and Experimental Pharmacology*, an academic journal published in association with the Harvard Medical School, is best known for its series of monographs about Dr. Ehrillimbal's journey up the Amazon river in 1954 and 1955. Dr. Ehrillimbal has been the editor of the *Journal* since 1958.

* equinox
p. 369

Dr. Ehrillimbal and Gabriella Ehrillimbal have two children, Julio and Eduardo, aged 12 and 9. The children are enrolled at Ad Astra Boarding School in Dorchester, MA.

# FISH
ᗰᗰ

There is the old truism about fish: give a man a fish, and you offer him hope; teach him how to fish, and you give him purpose. The acolytes of the Abandoned Sun have the fish tattooed on their right palms, a persistent reminder of their devotion and an outward sign of their charity. The acolytes have had many names throughout the ages, but it is the name given to them by the Illuminati Scribes that is the most persistent. This appellation—"Fishers of Men"—is fraught with a long-standing enmity between the two groups.

*persistence
p. 264*

The reason for the split between the scribes and the priests has been forgotten, or simply lost to the rest of the world. There is a document somewhere, of course, that tells that tale, but it has been buried in one of the hidden libraries of the scribes.

The fishers of men are itinerant, following the currents of history and the tumult of war. They haunt the battlefields, offering succor to the dying and easing the pain of the wounded. A man, broken and afraid, is more receptive to the promise of the fish, to the promise of redemption. "Will you accept the guilt of your fathers and their fathers? Will you bear the burden of their blood debt? Do you understand that your pain is the world's pain, and your death is not meaningless?"

*sacrifice
p. 300*

Death is a portal, just as life is a pathway. The acolytes of Abaddon do not hold the Key, just as they are not the Guardian of the Lock. Their symbol, the curved shape of the fish, is just a representation of faith. There is a Door; there is a Key. There is a Path.

*circle
p. 171*

Nothing is meaningless. As long as there is guilt.

# FOOL
## ♈

I turn over the next card . . .

A white dog capers at his feet, equally unaware of the cliff edge. The youth, cloaked in ribbons and scarves, dances along the bleak edge, his face turned toward the burnblack sun. His eyes are milky white from having stared so long into the void. A necklace of dried flowers and bone fragments hangs around his neck, and a trinity of frozen stars pierces his left ear.

His hands are raised, fingers interlocked and straining in a mystic invocation. On his right wrist is a copper bracelet—a band of twisted wire that holds a burnished scarab against the inside of his wrist. He is missing his left ring finger.

His leather belt is worn and too big for him—it hangs low on his narrow hips. An awl, an ax, and a trowel hang from loops of sinew, and all are stained with rust and blood. All stained . . .

The fortune teller's fingers, like branches and brambles, position the card on the tablecloth—astrological signs rendered as patterns of stars.

"This is the mask you wear in the West," his teeth chatter in the dish on the tablecloth. "When the year wanes, you will vanish. This is both belief and being, but neither have weight upon the silver scale. You will shed this face, like the serpent loses its skin, before you walk the—"

The fortune-teller drops a twisted hand over his false teeth, silencing them before they tell me too much. He takes off his peacock painted glasses as well, so that I may not discern some hint in the painted lenses.

His eyes have been sewn shut with heavy red thread.

* secret code
p. 305

* massa
confusa
p. 252

* death mask
p. 178

# FORK
## ♍

"I'm uncomfortable with making such an assessment."

He's a young doctor, not yet inured by years of assessing. His fingers toy with his pen; he isn't even aware of how much he spins it about in his hand.

"The success rate of the radiation therapy is very high, which is why we are suggesting such a path of treatment, but the location of the—"

He pauses, while he searches for a delicate word. Failing to find it, he simply skips past the detail.

"There are some elevated risks with the locality of her treatment," he says.

*negligence
p. 259*

"It will burn her brain," Martin says flatly. His face is heavily lined, and his eyes are dry. He has been out of tears for weeks.

The doctor gives only the slightest of nods, but he can't look at her father's face.

*children
p. 169*

"Do you have any children of your own?" Martin asks.

The doctor, though he is young, has heard this question before. The skin around his eyes tightens, and his pen stops moving. He doesn't like the question, doesn't like that it forces him into a position of insensitivity. "No," he admits, too young to lie, too naive to bluster past the inference.

But Martin doesn't say what should come next. He knows there is no point. Not for his daughter, at least. Martin simply swallows everything, pushing it back down into his gut. Nothing will help him, and the young doctor knows this too.

"I'm sorry," the younger man says. "I wish there was a better way."

*deceit
p. 180*

It is the closest he will ever come to apologizing for the medicine he knows. He lifts his shoulders, an unconscious twitch that shakes off the weight of Martin's pain, and leaves the older man standing in the hospital hallway.

The lights go out as the doctor retreats, and when there is nothing left but the dim blue glow of the emergency lighting, Martin puts his face in his hands and tries to cry once more.

"What choice do I have?" he asks, eventually. "I gave her this life.

Do I have the right to take it? Who am I to end it when . . ."

*When it is no longer a life worth living?*

I am the ghost who both present and invisble.

"Who decides that?" he asks the empty hall.

*She does. You do. You honor her decision because you gave her the autonomy to make those choices.*

"And if I don't want to let her go? If I want to hope that they can cure her?"

* love
p. 71

*That is a choice too.*

"Will she hate me?"

*No, but her pain will never leave you. If you let her go, then you let go of all the things she still has to give you. If you let her go now, your memories of her will be fixed. She will always be your little girl. She will never grow old. She will cease to be real.*

"Just a memory, then. Is that all I will have of her?"

*Is that enough?*

"No. She's my daughter."

*Which pain can you bear?*

"Is there a third option? Some way where she doesn't have to suffer? Where I don't have to lose her?"

* duality
matrix
p. 185

*No. There are only two forks in the path: to continue or to change. The dualities must be maintained.*

"You are a cruel God."

**I love you, Daddy.**

Martin raises his left hand, as if he is going to wave goodbye.

"I love you too, NeeNee," he says.

**The left is the method.**

He lowers his left hand, as if he has made a choice.

It is enough.

# FORTUNE

## ♈

He sits, off-center, at a rectangular table. On his right is a haphazard scatter of candles. Clustered like offerings to the Madonna and Child, the votives are of varying height and color, though their flames are all clean and yellow. Time melts, transformed by heat into a featureless slag that puddles in circles and arcs.

*yellow
p. 365*

His turban is silver, veined with emeralds and sapphires in a design that folds upon itself like a real brain. As if his skull has been removed and his oversized brain has been wrapped in tinfoil. The turban covers most of his ears, leaving only tiny pink nubs protruding from the tight edge of the silver wrap. His glasses are tortoise-shell frames with garish peacock eyes painted on the lenses. He stares at you with those false eyes, but they seem to not see you either.

*eyes
p. 197*

His teeth rest in a small dish on the table, next to the deck of cards. The wooden gums have been painted blue—cerulean like the sea at dawn, like the sky at midday. His incisors are silver, carved with intricate detail. Tiny myths that only his tongue can read.

If he had a tongue.

*tongue
p. 44*

He taps the deck of cards with a finger that is twisted like an old oak branch. His teeth clack as I hesitate in the entrance to his tent, reluctant to cross the threshold. Even as endless as it is, the night outside seems more hospitable than sitting in that empty chair.

"Sit," his teeth chatter. "The Way cannot be Realized until it is Seen."

*tarot
p. 334*

# FOWL

ᗯᗯ

Commonly, in dream dictionaries, the chicken is said to represent fertility (the whole "chicken and egg" argument notwithstanding). In Chinese dream interpretation, the chicken is symbolic of pride: he is the first creature to greet the sun, the first to announce his presence to the world (which, in light of the age-old argument, may be the East's solution to the question: the chicken announced itself, and then bothered to procreate).

* crown
p. 177

However, they also have a secondary symbolism. Chickens are agents of enlightenments in their adulation of dawn. Throughout mythology and folklore, it is always the chicken who represents the break of day; they are the auditory signal that wakes the sleepers, that arrests the intrusion of darkness. How many myths hinge upon the hero being rescued by the sudden arrival of daybreak? How often are the nocturnal monsters sent scurrying into the shadows of the West by the sound of a rooster's cry?

* threshold
p. 348

* circle
p. 171

The chicken is a transitional creature, one poised on the liminal threshold of change. They must be aware in darkness, for they wake in that time and place and know to look for the light; they are the early worshippers of the enduring cycle of life. To eat a chicken is to re-imagine the holy circle—a life is darkened, a light is transferred. To become a chicken is to ascend the wheel of karma, as it is a more purified creature.

When a chicken's head is cut off, its body refuses to recognize death. It fights decay, fights dissolution, fights off the darkness. But, like all flesh, it cannot sustain itself forever. The chicken, in the end, is a symbol of the futility of hope. In the end—of every day, of every life—night comes.

* twilight
p. 382

# FRAGMENTARY

Conventional psychology defines "psychosis" as a symptomatic state of mental illness, a break in the patient's ability to function effectively. Psychosis is a catch-all term used by mainstream professionals to cover any number of sins and aberrations, and it has, by dint of the breadth of the field's reach, become nearly meaningless in and of itself. It simply labels the patient as "non-functional" without saying as much.

But there are states of fragmentary psychosis, wherein patients are functional—able to move about society without much trouble, able to care for themselves and make intelligent and moral decisions—but lack cohesion. The resilience of the human brain has self-corrected itself, building new networks around the blankness, thereby fragmenting off the area that has become "non-functional."

*spiritual armor p. 323*

Invariably, this fragment rots, for lack of a better word. It begins to dissolve the barriers and the frameworks the patients have subconsciously erected. The slow rot begins to bleed into the patient's dreams and eventually begins to affect their waking consciousnesses.

If not properly treated, fragmentary psychosis can poison the entire system, resulting in a full psychotic breakdown. Unfortunately, since the accredited psychiatric industry doesn't recognize "fragmentary psychosis," these patients must suffer the dementia of the slow rot until they can manifest more recognizably psychotic behavior.

*poison p. 275*

The oneirologist watches for the breaks; the field of study concerns itself with identifying both the stressors and the fault lines that precede a patient's fragmentation. It can be such a little thing, the part of the mind that cracks, but it is always the catalyst that initiates a progression towards a larger systemic dissolution.

*substantia p. 6*

*tangle p. 332*

# GEOMETRY

乙

*architect
p. 154

The architects of Babylon drew straight lines, hard geometry to define edges and perimeters. They measured the arc of the sun with triangular devices, plumbs dropping straight down like descending vertebrae. They threw rhomboids in the air and watched how they were stretched by the wind. As the pit was dug, the loose sand was collected in perfect barrels and the filled barrels ringed the circumference of the pit in concentric circles. The architects agreed on a number and, when the foreman of the diggers reported that the pit was the depth of that many men standing on the shoulders of one another and the foreman of the sand packers agreed that the number of concentric circles of barrels was the same, they pricked their hoary thumbs and made their marks on the drawing of the Tower. They sealed the geometry of the Tower with their hearts' blood and put away their arcane tools of measurement and took up the hammer and the pick.

*heart
p. 215

The stones were carved and shaped by the calloused hands of thirteen men. It took two mules and three men to transport each stone to the pit where they were cemented in place with a mixture of sand and shit and blood and sweat. The Tower was perfectly proportional, drawn on an infinite scale and yet still fit to the dreams of men.

It took many generations to build the Tower, a number equal to the depth of the pit and the rings of sand about the rising base of the stone finger being raised to Heaven. Each mason fathered another child for every full count of bricks that he cut from the mountains—children, rings, generations, spans deep; the geometry was precise, and each mason fathered an unequal number of boys and girls for the geometry of the Tower was unique and indivisible. Their children made other children, and every third generation spawned thirteen new masons to replace the old men whose hands were too arthritic to cut stone any longer.

When the Tower was almost completed, one of the mule teams dropped a stone. They were children of the twenty-second generation and had never known a time when they were not conscripted to the mule teams, dragging stones from distant quarries to the hard, brick finger by the sea. The team of three formed a triangle about the mule, one leading and two following. The man in front was day-dreaming, staring at the sky and wondering if it was his children who were going to the ones to finish the Tower. He did not see the hole in the roadway and failed to guide the beast. The mule stumbled, its ankle breaking in the hole, and the shaped stone of the Tower shifted in the harness. The weight distribution was upset, and the injured mule collapsed, the full weight of the stone falling upon its flank and upon the roadway.

*guide
p. 376

A chip the size of a small child's hand split off the stone, unnoticed by the team. They dragged the block all the way to the Tower, delaying all production until they arrived (each stone, you see, had its place upon the walls) and, in a rush to recover the lost time, the foreman did not notice the damage to the stone.

The chip was small, but it was enough for the wind and the rain. A generation later, the stone cracked. Another generation later, it shifted, collapsing in on itself.

Thirteen days later, the Tower came down.

*thirteen
p. 346

# GIANTS
# ꚗ

* fabric
p. 56

When their wings were broken, the First-Born Sons tore off their heavenly cloaks and trampled them, burning their feet. Bound to the earth, they walked among men and assumed their appearances and their appetites. They took human wives and bore them children.

These children, the first-born of the First-Born, grew to be giants. Their fathers, in mockery of the Father who had banished them, taught them the Unbroken Language. It pained them, this language that was not meant for their mouths, but they learned it still and used it to raise monuments, shatter mountains, and split oceans. They spoke to the men of the cities, and the men, fearful of the way these words twisted their guts and groins, made them kings.

* superstition
p. 374

The second baby born to a woman who had lain with a burned First-Born was always a girl child. They were taken as consorts by the giants, though not one of them ever born a child for their cousins and brothers.

The third baby born—in those rare instances when a mother was able to hide herself from the wrathful giants who sought the source of the barrenness of their wives' wombs—was a small boy, a slight child who never grew to be taller than the shortest man in the village. Thus they were able to hide themselves from the giants and the Broken-Jawed Ones.

*strength
p. 324

The third children were blessed by their fathers' Father. While they had never received any teachings of the language of angels, they knew it in their hearts.

* text
p. 341

It was these third children, hidden among men, who invented writing.

# GRAFFITI

# ♓

Morrison, in his manifesto of occult anarchy, calls the underground network of cities and citizens the "infranet."[△] That term has since been coopted by the telcos to describe their top-down approach to the next-gen Internet. The corporate behemoth, yet again, absorbing and demystifying the language of the dispossessed in a bid for acceptability.

Elsewhere, the underground is dragged into the mainstream consciousness by the use of such terms as "street teams" in reference to unpaid advertising labor. Every content generator is looking for secret access into the psyches of the children (we adults being either suitably programmed already or too locked into destructive cycles to be useful consumers), and though the identity of the network has been stolen, the actual channel still exists.

*hidden
p. 219*

Graffiti. The symbolic shorthand that doesn't rely on the wireless networks of the telcos, that can't be regulated or legislated, that will occur as long as there are revolutionary cells within the confines of the cities, as long as there are free thinkers still not yet absorbed by the state. There will always be a way to symbolize the existence of free will: by scrawling on the walls of bathroom stalls, by tagging subway cars and the billboards, by scraping the paint off phone booths and bus stands, or by plastering telephone poles with handbills.

"Bleak Zero is coming."

"Ding a ding dang my dang a long ling long." ▽

"Smash the control machine." ☉

"The Empire never ended." ☽

* bleak zero
p. 162

There are a hundred more messages that have become part of the collective morass of our psyches. They are all calls to arms, cries for us to wake up.

---

△ - Morisson, Grant, *The Invisibles* 2, no. 11 (November 1997):6.

▽ - Ministry, "Jesus Built My Hot Rod" ΚΕΦΑΛΗΞΘ. Sire 9 26727-2, 1992, compact disc.

☉ - Burroughs, William, *The Soft Machine* (Grove Press: New York, 1966), 93.

☽ - Dick, Philip K., *VALIS* (Bantam Books: New York, 1981), 51.

In the case of the Oneiroi, graffiti is a medium of communication used by the subconscious. The patient's dreaming mind is still caged by their apprehensions and blooming psychoses; very few dreamers are free of their conscious and unconscious neuroses and, within their Oneiroi, the subconscious is the phantasmal rebel of their subverted identity.

* mirage
p. 256

"The doctor is in."

* II

What am I trying to tell myself? Am I referencing the physician from the old hotel? Is it a coded reminder that I am my own healer? Or is it a warning that I have been invaded?

# HEART
## ⌇

There is an old belief about the heart: it is the seat of the soul. If you eat a man's soul, much like you would devour a fish, you assume his spirit. You take on his desires, his dreams, and his debts. In the four-chambered rooms of the five-pointed temples, the acolytes of the Abandoned Sun preach of the Transference, the passage of the debt from their fallen fathers.

*fish
p. 203

"Take of this flesh," they say, offering the cold meat of the dead to the newly initiated, "so that you may know of the desire which bound it."

"Take of this blood," they say, offering the sour wine of the deceased to the new children, "so that you may know of the dream which inflamed it."

No vessel is empty. As long as there is a debt owed.

*intent
p. 224

# HEAVEN

る

The canopy of heaven was to be built by three brothers, black-smiths all. One—Aegenus, thick like an old tree with eyes of green fire and hair like thistles—said it should be round, a bowl cut in half by one swift stroke of a supra-heated blade so that the melted edges could be seared into the world.

The second brother had a habit of rubbing the knuckle of his left ring finger; the digit ended just below that last knuckle, scar tissue worn smooth and shiny from his constant ministrations. His name was Xernbawe and he believed that Heaven was square, held up not by one pillar but by four.

The third brother, Ghen, was lame in one leg and deaf in one ear, and he stumped painfully down to the bird hut by the river. "Old Mother," he asked the old witch who lived there. "How should we make Heaven?"

*architect
p. 154*

"My fire is dying," she said. "Gather me wood, and I will tell you."

Ghen dragged dead trees down from the hills and cut them into short logs that would fit into the narrow mouth of her soot-blackened fireplace. He stacked the wood behind her crooked house, shoring up the building's developing cold-weather hunch. Resting his aching leg, he sat on her dusty hearth and nursed her fire back to health and heat. "Tell me the secret, Old Mother," he asked her a second time.

*secret code
p. 305*

"I already have," she replied.

Ghen watched sparks float up into the darkness of her chimney and understood Heaven's purpose.

# HERMIT
## ♈

I turn over a card.

He stands upon a stone, raising his lantern toward the West. Behind him, in the distance, a landscape of hills has been worn down by wind and darkness to a sea of sloping dunes. He braces himself on the precarious peak of the stone with his staff, holding the ash stick as well as he can with his damaged hand. His cloak, stained grey by a memory of rain, hangs loosely on his narrow frame. His beard and hair are so tangled and matted that it seems as if he has tentacles sprouting from his head and chin.

*tangle
p. 332*

A six-pointed star is caught in the belly of his lantern—a pair of married triangles exploding with light in the throes of their lustful coupling. Its light illuminates the script of age written on his forehead.

The sky behind him is streaked with veins of color—purples and greens and blues and blacks as if rendered by the thick trowel of an Impressionist.

The fortune teller's teeth start to chatter. "The hermit is a representation of gained wisdom—the Seeker who has learned enough to know that he must find his own way."

*fortune
p. 207*

The fortune teller moves the card to the left side of the table, but does not release it.

"This should be your first card, but it cannot be," his teeth tell me.

His hand moves it across the empty swath of fabric to the right side of the table.

"Nor can it be the last," the teeth say.

"It's the first card I turned over," I offer, feeling slightly embarrassed to be mentioning this obvious point.

The fortune teller regards me with his peacock eyes, and I squirm under his gaze, feeling as if I am indeed only twelve again. His teeth tap-tap against each other in the dish, the silver incisors glittering in the candlelight. "The hermit is a transition," they say finally, as if reluctant to release these words. "He is the wizard who stands upon the threshold of chaos. He cannot be first for he is the Seeker who has been abandoned. He is—"

*twelve
p. 355*

"He is what?" I ask.

I am so eager in this dream—on the cusp of adolescence, on the threshold of becoming a man.

The fortune teller smiles, a twist of his lips that reveals the dark hole of his toothless mouth. His shoulders twitch, and his twisted finger taps the card in a syncopated rhythm. It takes me a moment to realize he is laughing.

* last light
p. 246

The teeth echo this humor for a moment. "Is your lamp the light that fires the corpse of the sun?" they ask. "Or is your flame a token reflection of its intent?"

# HIDDEN

## ♉

The primary hypothesis of ancient alchemists was the divisibility of substance from form. They suspected the processes of change available to them—the release of destruction, the awakening of transformation, the slumber of dissolution, and the artifice of fabrication— all acted upon the superficial malleability. Beneath, the Indivisible remained resolute and unchanging. Alchemy was the art by which that Singularity would be revealed.

*coagula p. 172*

The medieval alchemists looked up on the efforts of their historical brethren and saw generations of failure. They believed the quest was personal, that only a purified alchemist could accomplish the Great Work. The Indivisible could only be found by an equally redacted Seeker.

*drift p. 184*

The industrial alchemists were distracted by clockwork mechanisms, the mass production of glass, and the heat of the iron smelter. They abandoned the path of internal purification and devoted themselves to the diminishing spiral of metallurgical recombination.

The organic alchemists quibble over terminology, dancing endlessly around definitions and citations of authority. But they all take the same mushrooms, they all smoke the same leaf and inject the same venoms. Hallucinogen, psychedelic, or entheogen: the material has no intent of its own, it has no academic or pharmaceutical agenda to realize. It is simply a catalyst.

*purify p. 284*

"Laboratory," for the organic alchemist, is synonymous with "temple." "Catalyst" can be replaced with "communion." "Alchemist" becomes just another term for . . .

# HOLLOW
## ♏

*In the desert, there is a spider that builds a tower. I have found one in the shadow of an old rock, a corner of some ancient temple that has been forgotten for a lifetime. The wind chips at the old stone, flaking off shards of pale gran-ite, and the spider collects these to fortify the walls of his circular passion.*

*He builds this tower so relentless, so resolutely, as if he can and will eventually reach Heaven. I tower over him (inconceivably taller from his perspective) and, in his short existence, he will not manage to build a spire taller than my knee. Someone, like myself, who might measure his accomplishments in light of their own size and stature, would assume that the spider may never reach God.*

*Not that way, at least.*

*Perhaps, then, the structure he builds does not extend up, but down and inward. The tiny stack that pokes up out of the sand is the extrusion of his effort, the physical displacement of what he carves out beneath the surface. Much like our flesh, that physical detritus of our spiritual exertions.*

*Those who feared my thoughts believe the desert will keep them safe. They believe the sands will claim me: strip-ing off my skin, boiling my blood, and pelting my skel-eton with the grit of a thousand thousand vanquished stones. They believe the sun will dry my brain, turning my thoughts to dust, and these heretical notions of mine will be lost forever. They believe all of these things, but do not realize such belief is merely hope.*

*The spider and I are quite alike, in the end. I, too, am building a tower which cannot be seen.*

*Each night, as the sun vanishes into the endless sand sea, I turn inward and dive deeper into the phantasmal ocean of my mind. Each night, I cleanse myself further; I have already undergone the transformation of the phases,*

* descent
p. 182

* IV

* twilight
p. 382

220

*mirroring the face of the insane moon that watches my progress; I have washed myself in the seven streams; I am bathing in the light and non-light of the thresholds. Diving ever deeper.*

*This morning, the spider's tower was gone. I searched in the crevices of the old temple rock, and dug up the sand where he used to be. I found nothing. It was as if the spider and his tower were never there.*

*Maybe I will disappear the same way when I reach the hollow gate. Maybe I will become so hollow on the inside that my body will become a breath lost in the wind.*

*This is not belief. This is hope. I, too, am wracked with the same frailty as my naive captors. We are all equally ignorant under the gaze of God, even those of us who seek to find Him.*△

* regret
p. 392

_____

△ - Safiq Al-Kahir, *Book of Dreams* (Obscura Editions: Red House, 1938), 12.

# HORIZON
## ♏

*The horizon is the edge of mystery. We do not know what lies beyond it, and it does not matter how high we reach into the sky, we cannot see beyond that rim. This is the mystery we have inherited from the Divine, the reminder that we are but a part of the world and that, no matter the power and expanse of our dominion, we will never see everything.*

*As you ascend through the realms of enlightenment, you will not escape the horizon, and this liminal reminder will continue to haunt you through your ascension. At every stage and past every threshold, you will see that line that marks the edge of perception, and you will know that you are still finite.*

*This is the simplest definition of God: He Who Is Without Horizon.*△

* persistence
p. 264

---

△ - Safiq Al-Kahir, *Book of Dreams* (Obscura Editions: Red House, 1938), 33.

# INCENSE
## Ω

Most dreams are like old serial movies. There may be auditory components—speech or the occasional sound effect—but mostly they are just grainy images. The dreamer is the only one in the theater, and the old projector clacks along at twenty-three frames a second, running through that single reel of film. Occasionally, there will be an insert—black background, white lettering—containing dialogue or an explanation of events. Very few dreamers invoke any of the other senses. *vision
p. 361*

Many of my patients are surprised when they discover their sense of smell in their dreams, or some auditory event intrudes upon their psyche. Once, I did some work for a lonely man who wanted to understand why he couldn't find companionship. In his dreams, we discovered his sense of touch was over-sensitized. This hyperawareness informed his waking hours, albeit unconsciously, and women whom he met were continually put off by his subliminal resistance to physical contact. (And his psychologist, to her credit, realized that his issues of intimacy were so deeply rooted that no externalized systematic personality reconstruction would ever really take hold, which is why she sent him to me.) *kiss
p. 234*

Why don't I make the same effort with my senses in the physical world that I do in the Oneiroi? It isn't lost on me that such a physical denial is an inadvertent reflection of my own personal idiosyncrasy: the Oneiroi is given more weight than my waking reality. It is a neurosis not uncommon to oneironauts; such denial is an integral aspect of the seduction of dreaming. *reflection
p. 396*

As a dream symbol, incense itself is just an object of atmosphere, but its presence is a reflection of an aspected virtue of the Oneiroi. Like mirrors that reflect an abstraction or a distorted vision of the dreamer, incense is an objective symbol. It is a smell untainted by the subjective filter of the dreamer.

# INTENT

♒

Intent is different than purpose and not quite the same as ratio-nale. Intent is the catalyst that changes the potential into the kinetic. An object can be unaware of its intent, it can be inert even, but that does not mean that an intent is not buried within it.

Our cells hum with intent. Our DNA is informed by intent. It is not ours. No, it was there before we became conscious. It is part of the collective connective. It is the spark that made us grow brains instead of fins, hands instead of photoreceptors, and mouths instead of scent glands. This intent is the finger of God, pushing us.

To ask after someone's intent is to inquire into the core of their identity, to request that they show you the tiny icon pinned to their ventricle wall. This secret image—oh, we all have this small photo-graph hidden in our hearts—is the impetus for life. It is the captive spark of our desire, and it is the only treasure we hoard.

But do our ribs not simultaneously protect our intent and prevent us from touching it? Is that not the greatest irony of humanity? We are both jailor and jailed. We are living cages.

* substantia
p. 6

* secret code
p. 305

* cage
p. 163

# IRIS
# ♍

"See how the petals close together?" she said, indicating the sealed mouth of the purple iris. "Not any insect can gain access to the tender nectar. The bee has to be strong enough to push the petals apart and push its way down into the tube of the flower."

* petals
p. 268

Using two fingers, she spread the mouth of the iris open. "And, there. See how the iris offers itself to the bee? The insect rubs its belly along this groove, gathering pollen from this flower or leaving pollen from another."

She releases the iris petals, and they close again. She strokes the bright yellow landing strip on the lower petal, the splashed indicator that directs the bees to their landing point.

* yellow
p. 365

"Nature rewards the strong and persistent," she says.

She is my doctor. I am her patient.

She is my teacher. I am her student.

She is my law. I am . . .

* schizophrenia
p. 304

# ISLAND
## ♌

The island is nothing more than a spit of rock that reaches out of the thrashing sea like the skeletal finger of an old sea god. Surrounding it is a maze of submerged rocks and coral reefs. Our boat is too cumbersome, too warped by the wind, to navigate the maze, and we wreck it on the outer edge of the maze.

The chains hurt as they are torn out, and blood swirls in the water as I swim to the island. The Ribbon Man trails me, a section of iron chain in his hand to ward off deepdark creatures drawn by the blood. I cut my knees and feet crossing the coral; he leaves ribbons behind, black strips fluttering in the water.

We find a narrow path cut into the rock, and clutching at the rock of the island, we shuffle slowly along. Round and round, we circle the island twice before we reach the peak. There is a narrow rim at the top, and the rest is a depression with narrow grooves that drain water away into the interior of the rock. Near the end of the path, just below the rim, is a small shelter, built from wrecked timber and stained sailcloth. The bottom of the depression is flat, covered with the lines and arcs of a great seal.

The porter is asleep in his shack, curled up beneath a moss-stained blanket that may have been blue once. One of his hands sticks out, and the tattoos on his wrist are so old that they've faded into a slur of letters. On a thick nail, driven into the rock wall, is his chain and medal.

The Ribbon Man steals it, and we peer at the inscription on the back. The script, like the porter's tattoos, has become faint and garbled with age. *A-.Na-.-i.* On the other side: *Tem.—F.*

"It's enough," the Ribbon Man says, and he unlocks the seal with the shiny magic that still resides in the medal.

* ceremony
p. 167

We descend into the Inverted Tower.

# KEY
# ♍

*Now, these keys were too cumbersome to carry,* the professor drones on, *but what point was there in leaving the key hanging from a nearby hook? Or even leaving it in the lock? One might as well not even bother with the lock at all in that case. And so, the key was entrusted to one of the household slaves, who wore it about their neck on a chain.*

The professor draws a circle on the chalkboard.

* collar
p. 173

"What about the slaves?" I whisper to Nora. "They have the key. Master's not home. Won't they try it in the lock?"

We are sitting in the back row of the lecture hall. I am wearing flannel pajamas and stuffed lobster slippers; she is wearing a lemon-coated summer frock, and her legs and arms are covered with henna script. A band of green pearls circles her left wrist. Her bare feet are resting on the chair in front of us, and her toenails are rainbow chips of abalone shell.

"This is before curiosity was discovered," she whispers back.

"Was it now? I didn't realize there was such a time. Whatever did we do with ourselves before we stumbled upon that need to be nosy?"

"Lived without locks, I suppose."

"That's a circular argument, I think. Which came first then? The first lock or the first busybody neighbor?"

* circle
p. 171

"Paranoia came first." The script on her left arm moves.

**Come on, Harry, play along with me.**

"Of course it did." I say. "So what happened to the Wearers of the Key? Did their masters tire of feeding them, or did someone realize a scrawny ill-fed whelp wasn't the most secure of a security system?"

"Locks got smaller and more complex. The way everything did when the industrial revolution came along."

"Everything?"

"Yes. The world, most of all. It became harder to hide things."

"What about Pandora? Wasn't she the first to exhibit curiosity?"

"That was different," she says. "That was duty."

"Whose?" I counter.

* intent
p. 224

*However, during the late Roman Empire, the ability to work metal became more widespread. Locks became more prevalent, and keys became smaller.*

The professor holds up his hand, showing the students the heavy band on his left hand (white stone set in silver and platinum). *Keys were made to fit on rings.*

Nora pretends to have not heard my question.

"Did she use a key?" I put my lips close to her ear. "Which key?"

"She found it," she replies, turning her face so that her lips are close to mine. Her eyes dance with the delight of confounding me.

"Where?"

"Who's curious now?"

"I could say the same thing about you," I reply. *Remember when I first visited you in the hospital room? When you first asked all those questions.*

**Of course, Harry. I remember it because you do.**

*During the Middle Ages, that dark period following the fall of Rome, knowledge was power. The secrets weren't forgotten. They were hidden. In the monasteries and rectories, priests and monks bound their books with miniature locks. The only professions that thrived during the Dark Ages were the paper makers and the locksmiths.*

The professor clears his throat, tugging at his collar. His tie flutters against his narrow chest, a colorful ribbon descending from his neck. *Both were keymakers, metaphorically speaking.*

"She knew what was in the box." My lips brush against her cheek now. Her scent makes my throat constrict. "But she opened it anyway."

* heaven
p. 216

She raises her face, eyes looking up at the rounded dome of the lecture hall ceiling. "Why you suppose she did that?"

"Why did she?"

She laughs, and pushes me away gently.

The professor pauses in his lecture, and looks up at the two of us in the back. A number of other students turn in their seats. I am the only one who sees him pull the string of colored handkerchiefs out of sleeve, and transfer them to his coat pocket.

* massa
confusa
p. 252

*Thieves*, he began again, pulling their attention away from Nora and me. *Thieves became quite proficient at picking the simple locks—most of which were reliant upon gravity and a basic bolt system to be secure. During the Renais-*

*sance, the combination lock came into vogue, partially as a response to the ready ability of the nimble-fingered.*

"Am I supposed to steal something?" I ask.

"Other than my heart?" She snorts into her hands, and black words slip off her fingers. They fall too quickly, turning into pale birds that vanish like hummingbirds, and I cannot read them. * bird
p. 157

"Yes, other than your heart." I touch her hair. "What would I do with it anyway?"

She puts one of her inscribed hands on my chest. **Put it here, Harry. You could put it here.**

*The early combination locks weren't random. They were primarily used in party games. Who can guess the combination? Five letters. Who knows?*

Her fingers tap against my chest. *Five letters. I know this key.*

*And then came the era of the great lockmakers. Bramah. Chubb. Pettit. Yale. Sargent. Following them, came the greatest key who ever lived: Harry Houdidi.*

"She told him."

"Told him what?"

"After she opened the box, she told him the secret word."

*Houdini put in hundreds of hours of practice. On every sort of lock imaginable. He didn't need a key. He didn't want a key. He just needed a thin strip of wire, and the self-confidence that he could undo what had been closed. Houdini was an Opener of Ways.*

"'Believe.' Isn't that what he said he would tell her from the other side?"

Nora puts her hands over her eyes. As she smiles, the three words crawl across the back of her hands. **Answer say answer.** "Not Bess," she says. "Pandora."

"Who'd she tell?"

"The one who looks backward. The one who wasn't chained."

*Who was the other Opener of Ways?* The professor strides back to the board. With a few strokes, he draws the net of a hypercube. *Christ. He hung on the beam, and the Spear was the Key that lifted his ribs, that opened his heart, and raised him up. The Spear was the Key.* * ash
p. 155

"What am I supposed to do with the key, Nora. I thought it wasn't important. I thought it was a distraction."

"It is, because you won't be the one who uses it."

"Who will?"

* crossroad
p. 175

She shakes her head. "No, Harry. Which door? That is the question you should be asking." **Which door?**

* IX

At the board, the professor is sketching absentmindedly as he drones on. The bottom hem of his tweed coat is frayed into ribbons. On the board, a picture of a scarecrow appears. It wears a crooked smile as it hangs on the cross of the hypercube.

# KING
## ♌

When there is a break in the persistent cloud layer, he sits by the window in the library and tries to read. Most of the books are water-damaged, their pages filled with streaks of ink and ash. The few that survived the fire and flood are from the case on the northern wall. Mostly they are natural history texts and inquiries into the phenomenology of philosophy. But, and he has come to appreciate these mistakes, a few of the books have been misfiled. Poetry mostly, a style that he never cared much for—she liked the intricate wordplay—but which he has come to a grudging appreciation.

And the journal.

It is written in a script that is more of a code than a foreign language, and it has taken him many months of half-days to decipher a few pages of the book. It is written by a fellow exile, a man like himself who has been separated from the rest of his world by circumstance and ignorance, though, unlike him, the writer is not trapped. His prison has no walls or bars or gates; it is an endless desert. There are no paths, for the wind and sand conspire to hide all trace of human passage.

The writer's exile is self-imposed, but it is no less desolate, no less filled with sorrow and loneliness. The last king finds an affinity with the mystic hidden in the desert, even though he is chained by his ruined leg and his prison is the burned walls of the mansion.

He sits on a wooden bench near the window, peering intently at the pale pages, the weak sunlight illuminating the shadows of the text. His eyesight isn't what it used to be (very little is; so much has decayed, so much has fallen into disrepair), and each word is fainter to read than the last. He fears his vision will fail before he can finish the book, but he does not look ahead. He does not skip to the end because he knows it will be incomprehensible. The writer's script becomes more tangled, more complicated, and more obtuse on every page. He must read every word, because each one is the key to the next.

In this way, the world will be refashioned.

**Turn around.**

* window
p. 363

* letter
p. 79

* drift
p. 184

* vision
p. 361

He looks behind him, but there is nothing but the shadows he has come to know. When he squints at the text again, its meaning scampers away from him. The words are almost living things on the page, cyclical serpents and cancerous birds that chased each other across the pale landscape of the parchment. "On the ground, seashells . . ." The words say now, and he can longer look at the text.

*serpent
p. 309

The sun is mobbed by black clouds and vanishes. In the gloom that falls upon his burned castle, he sees a glimmer in a broken window of the south wing. A glow where there should be no light. The wing has been dark since his heart broke.

It is a long and painful walk through the ruined rooms to the burned husk of the southern wing. He brings no lantern, no light of his own, as his mental map of the house is perfect. The only perfect thing left, this map of his maze.

*labyrinth
p. 236

The light spills into the hallway from the conservatory like a slow flood of flowers. He limps down the hall, gnarled walking stick in his left hand, the journal of the desert exile held tightly in his right. At the threshold of the conservatory—the doors have long been gone—he hesitates.

**Turn around**, she says.

There is nothing behind him but regret.

He enters the room where the ruined pianoforte lies atop the burned corpse of his queen. The light is coming from beneath the crippled instrument, a roseate glow that is both warm and cold. When he approaches the canted instrument and kneels to look under its tilted frame, he can see the source of the glow. A light, a life, born from the black darkness lost in her belly.

*VII

He lowers himself to the ground, lying stomach-down in the ash and dirt. He brushes away some of the detritus, stirring up memory and desire, and lays the book down in front of him.

*roots
p. 371

*Seashells.*

By the light, he reads the rest of the day and most of the night.

Until his eyes whiten with exhaustion, and the words vanish into the fog of his cataracts. He lays his cheek down on the open book, feeling the squirming motion of the words against the papery surface of his skin.

He reaches out, and finds the crisp bones of his queen's hand. "I'm sorry," he says, the first words he has spoken since the fire, and he feels her fingers tighten around his hand.

*fire
p. 201*

*So it begins.*

# KISS
# ♍

"Do you remember your first kiss, Harry?"

"I do."

"Was it nice?"

"It was a bit of a fumble."

"Boys always remember it that way. They get caught up in the minutiae."

"And girls don't?"

"Girls—women—remember sensations, Harry. We remember the intent and the effort."

"Really? So a guy can be a really awful kisser, but you won't mind much as long as his heart is in it?"

She laughs. "Not quite. We expect you to get better, but we're willing to wait a little while for you to get there. We don't expect perfection. Not the first time."

There is a tremor behind her words, an echo that intrudes. Like a shadow passing overhead, something between you and the sun, but when you look into the sky, it is clear and hot and empty.

"How many times, then?"

"It depends."

"On the boy?"

* limbo
p. 43

"On the girl. Some of us will wait longer than others."

"Because you see potential? What if the guy never realizes it?"

"They do."

"How can you be sure?"

"We vanish, Harry. Some faster than others, but we all do."

"And how does that make us realize our potential?"

"You should kiss me."

"Why? You aren't going to vanish. You're not even the slightest bit transparent."

"You should still kiss me."

"I think that is slightly beyond the boundaries of our relationship."

"Harry, you've done much more to me in my dreams."

"Excuse me?"

"You've kissed me, Harry, and fucked me as well."

234

"No, I have not."

"Oh, Harry, have I frightened you? Is this memory not the way you remember it? Time isn't linear, my dear, sweet Harry, not in this place. The future has a way of bleeding in the past, through the holes—"

"I've never been inappropriate with you, Nora."

She laughs, and this laugh is not an echo of her earlier amusement. "I'm thinking of a number, Harry. Can you guess what it is? Can you guess what it signifies?"

"More than one?"

"More than twenty, actually. But less than one hundred. Is that enough of a hint for you?"

"That many times?"

She smiles and, like the Cheshire Cat of Alice's dream, becomes transparent. "Yes, Harry, that many."

*fool
p. 204

*blackleaf
p. 159

# LABYRINTH

ᚯ

## I

The first labyrinth was built by Father and Son on an unfinished island that lay near the rim of the sea. The island, still rudely volcanic, was suited to such construction with its numerous quarries of heavy rock. The stone was iron-rich, and it darkened quickly under the hot summer sun as it was exposed by the pick and the shovel.

The center of the labyrinth, a series of inter-rotating concentric locks, was constructed first. One morning, while they raised cylinders and fitted tumblers, Son asked Father why they were digging a hole in the stony surface of the island. "To better hide our sins," Father told him.

* hidden
p. 219

As the years passed, and the chaotic splendor of the walls grew around the rings in the center, Son asked Father why they wanted to hide their sins. "So that others may not find them," Father said.

And, when the labyrinth was finished, Father bound Son and placed him within the last span of wall. As Father was laying mortar and stone, Son asked why he was being left behind. "So that you may warn the others," Father said.

Father could not tell his only child the true reason they had built the labyrinth. The night before they had started digging, he had dreamed that Son would one day grow curious about the world beyond the island and seek to fly. In his dream, Father watched his innocent flesh be burned by the sun and drowned by the waves, and he could not survive the heartbreak of such a loss.

* island
p. 226

## II

* geometry
p. 210

The second labyrinth was laid in a market square, two unbroken lines of intricately twisted orange stones. The bricks were carefully carved from sandstone and dyed with the pressed juices of poppies.

At night, when the farmers and merchants had bundled up their stands and shops, when the persistent noise and smell of the market was gone, the stonemasons would come to the square. The apprentices would sweep the shit and garbage and hay away, and the journeymen would scrape trenches in the hard ground with small trowels. Water would be sluiced along these fresh troughs to make their walls soft and muddy. Finally, in the quiet belly of the night, the master masons would press the newly carved stones into place. The space around and between the bricks was filled with a cement, tinted to reflect the sere ochre color of the ground.

When the labyrinth was done, it was covered by sawdust and straw and forgotten for a generation. When the masons' children's children grew old enough to dance, the labyrinth was uncovered. In the spring, when maidens and lads were allowed to chose one another, they danced the path of the labyrinth. Those who found their way to the center and back again were married in the eyes of the village and the gods of confusion and commerce.

*confusion p. 388

Children born of the masons' childrens' children were highly prized as scouts and guides for they never got lost.

## III

A swamp surrounds the third labyrinth, and crocodiles sleep along the inner curve of the outer wall. The swamp is a marshy lowland, fed by the river, and in the spring, most of the swamp will be awash with dirty mountain water, overflow from the torrential river. In the summer, the swamp will be a field of sticky tar surrounding the labyrinth.

The labyrinth had been commissioned by one of the last Sun Kings as a present to his consort, but he was claimed by the river before it could be finished. In her grief, the Radiant Queen wanted to tear down the half-finished labyrinth, but as the stonebreakers assembled their tools before the walls, her grief broke. She stayed their mallets and picks, and commissioned their brothers to finish the work instead.

*river p. 299

On the morning after the last stone had been laid, the river broke its banks for the second time in that generations' memory and flooded the area around the labyrinth. The crocodiles came with the flood, swimming upstream from the fetid jungles of the south until they reached the breach in the riverbank.

When the flood waters receded, the Radiant Queen entered her husband's tomb. A blue-scaled crocodile was her guide, and she wrapped gold chains around her wrists and its tail so that they would not become separated.

* guide
p. 376

She never came back. Nor was the blue-scaled crocodile seen again. The gold chains were found at the center of the labyrinth by the Radiant Queen's daughter, who wears them still. They are the only memory she has of her mother and father.

## IV

Neither love nor fear nor pain guided the architect of the fourth labyrinth and, when he died, the impetus was lost and the labyrinth was never finished.

* fear
p. 199

## V

The fifth labyrinth is a corporate logo. It is both a clue and a diversion. Like all symbols.

* gnosis
p. 54

## VI

Do you know the difference between a maze and a labyrinth?

A maze has many paths, a labyrinth has only one. One is emblematic of chaos, the other order. One represents a God who is visible, the other a Deity who has abandoned us in the wilderness.

The gardens of Babel were the sixth labyrinth. When the tower fell, the ruin of stone and masonry created a maze. This was the birth of language.

There are no more labyrinths. There are only mazes.△

---

△ - Not all mazes are labyrinths. *cf.*, p. 417.

## VII

In the desert, lost to civilization and history, a wizard dreams. He imagines a path with no branches. It begins, and it ends. Its course is neither straight nor complex; once he steps on the path, he realizes this to be true—the path is the simplest of geometries.

*mirage
p. 256

He writes his dream down—thereby making it true—and buries the papyrus in the sand. His notes and his diagram of the path are the seventh labyrinth.

# LAST CALL

ॐ

FROM: radio_free_engineer@...
TO: alt.oneirology.entheogens
SUB: Last Call

Hey, t:
I think that's it. Phil's gone, too. It's just you and me. Why don't you give me a call? Let's talk, instead of email. We're the only two left. We might as well say hello.
XXX/XXX-XXXX

=On the RF

"'Di-di-dah-dit di-di-dah.' Now there's a signature for you." –Capt. Francis Spinder

-----------------------------------

FROM: terminalx@...
TO: alt.oneirology.entheogens
SUB: RE: Last Call

Rivet the swells. Transfix the audible. Undulate the permeable. Why wait? Sign up now. There are still openings available. Try the salmon. Gibbet gibber, why does the baby shiver? Paint it gold, paint it red. You get a discount if you purchase the case. Who doesn't need more Vitamin B? Archon archon please, my archon. What do we gain by running into the light? What is fratricide if not extreme love? Vegetable mix. Every day. I keep my chin up. Every day. Carrots are people too. But not summer squash. Devil vegetable. Keep it out of the mix. Keep it. Out. Lavender fog. Keep it. Out. It. Keep. Winter. Whither the whine? Whither the wonder? It can be yours. Dollar ninety-nine. Check your pockets. Lick the stamps.

FROM: radio_free_engineer@...
TO: alt.oneirology.entheogens
SUB: RE: RE: Last Call

You too, eh? So, this is what it is like to be last man standing? Not nearly as cool as you'd think.

=On the RF

"'Di-di-dah-dit di-di-dah.' Now there's a signature for you." –Capt. Francis Spinder

----------------------------------

FROM: oldmanwinter@...
TO: alt.oneirology.entheogens
SUB: RE[3]: Last Call

I wish we had been more able to face this future, to meet this conclusion with strength and humility, instead of fear. I wish—well, I have wished for many things over the years, without much luck—but all I ever wanted was to understand. I wanted to understand what it was to be human.

I just wanted to know, and all I have learned is that more love brings more hate. We have lived with that damned duality matrix for so many generations that it may be impossible to think beyond it. We may have trapped ourselves in this cycle. We are the serpent: God's perfect creation—end over end, for all time.

* duality
matrix
p. 185

Please forgive me. I just wanted to open the last door.
I just wanted a different end to this tale.

* thirteenth
house
p. 347

-Brother J

FROM: radio_free_engineer@...
TO: alt.oneirology.entheogens
SUB: RE: RE: RE: RE: Last Call

Submerged hippopotami. Swimming. Falling. You won't drown if you are wearing our patented design. Available in fourteen colors, but not red, black, yellow or white. The licensing fees make for strange bedfellows. Who is that man behind the bed? Why does he cry so? Is he suffering from a bran deficiency? Do not let it get unruly. Do not let the whiskers touch the sky. Ribbit. I am a frog. I am waiting for a fly. Ribbit. Ribbit. Give me a sign. I am tasty. Burn the toast. Open the windows. Let the pigs out. Answer, say, answer. What did I just say? Never mind. It isn't important. It can't be important while there are still cans in the locker. Look! The passion of petunias. The deviousness of dahlias. Where has the day gone? Have I left the oven on?

=On the RF

"'Di-di-dah-dit di-di-dah.' Now there's a signature for you." –Capt. Francis Spinder

---------------------------------

FROM: oldmanwinter@...
TO: alt.oneirology.entheogens
SUB: RE[5]: Last Call

Goodbye, oneironauts.
Goodbye, Eduardo. I know you are listening. You can't get to me through this channel. I control this gate, and I am going to close it before you can bend them to the task of breaching it.
You will never find me in the Oneiroi. Even if you fill it with your agents, even if you bend all of it to your will, you will never find me.

Let them go. Let them all go. I know what fills you, what has filled you for so many years. Do you really believe this way will heal your hurt? Look in your heart, my brother, look to what you have hidden there. Is it hate? Or do you still have a tiny dot of compassion? What hangs on the wall of your heart secret chamber?

*\* heart*
*p. 215*

Let us end this feud. I will bring him to you, if you ask. We are all family, despite what you have been told.

Let the world find its own way.

We have done enough.

-Brother J

# LAST LIGHT

♌ ♐

I drink the brine of dissolved books, gulping and choking like a castaway alcoholic who finds a casket of rum half-buried in the sand of his island exile. It isn't enough that my lungs are filled with the stuff, that it invades my ears and nose. I must be filled with it. My stomach, my guts, my liver, my kidneys. Flushed through my veins until my muscles and fat are suffused with it. Yes, suck it down. Breathe it in. Fill up. Let it invade your blood. Let it make its way into your brain. Let me in.

He lies on the cold stone of the temple, staring at the empty eyes of his brother, staring at his reflection in those fading mirrors. I wanted to kill you, brother, I came to take your life. To take everything. And what he sees isn't incrimination or disgust or fear. What he sees, fading away like petals falling from a flower in the fall, is something else, something he cannot fathom. He tries to ask, but the words are gone, and he cannot remember how to move his lips.

(listen to the thunder, says the poet)

I have made you bleed, and still you do not speak. This is your barbaric heritage, yes I know, but beneath that, deep down inside your black heart, do you not value your life? Do you know value seeing the sun rise? Hearing the wind in the trees? Feeling the touch of your children and their children? Is all of that meaningless? I want so little from you, and yet you refuse to let me in. You refuse me. I can bring you enormous wealth. It is such a small transaction. Just a few words. Just one more.

Can you feel the change? I am no longer afraid. My hands do not tremble any more, and I wonder if this steadiness will betray me. Will you stop me? If you knew, would you hold me back? I know you try to understand. I can see it in your face; your eyes reveal too much. You are trying to protect me, much like your hat protects you, but I am ready. I know what I am doing. I know what you think I am leaving behind, and yes, that has certainly hardened my resolve, but this choice, this final choice, is mine.

All my other choices were made for me: my career, my marriage, this house, you. I was directed. I was an ego-less participant. I was

* children
p. 169

* ego
p. 188

244

a cog in the fucking disaster of his machinery. Our lives are nothing more than a collision of uninformed reactions and bad decisions. Even these, this spike and line, are poor choices. But they are mine. I am sorry. Let me go.

Yes, there. On the flat edge of the horizon. It bleeds and sinks, falling from Heaven, falling falling falling. Its stain is swallowed by the empty night, and in a moment, the last glimmer of its color, of its light, will be gone. Yes, there. Are you ready? Let me in. Let me hide in your darkness. When the light goes out, there will only be you and I. We will huddle together, you and I. Let me help—

*horizon
p. 222

No! I am not ready. This is not my choice. This is not—

*projection
p. 34

# LAYERS
# ♓

* psychonaut
p. 12

In any group of explorers, there will be some who insist on mir-
ing the adventure into the unknown with a taxonomy. In our case,
these armchair psychonauts want to map the entirety of the dream
landscape (as if that were even possible), laying their claims like fif-
teenth-century navigators, planting a flag in the wet sand of a "newly
discovered" island. Once the "world" has been mapped, they can get
back to their infinitely recursive arguments about oneiric theory and
the issuing of their nth-degree referential manifestos.

Far be it for the rest of us to interrupt their academic circle-jerk,
but we have, unfortunately, found a common ground with some of
their less egregious terminology. While it might seem that we are
cleaving to this same structure that we have eschewed, that we are
retreating from the dark corners of the map because they are so dark,
we are actually becoming more attuned to the varieties of experience
within the Oneiroi. We are, even if they cannot be bothered to notice,
discerning some existential distinctions within the layers of the subconscious.

The easiest comparison might be to the five senses. Unless you are
confused by synaesthesia (which happens quite often when one first
starts traveling in the Oneiroi), you don't confound smell with sight,
or sound with touch, or any other sensory odd-coupling. Each sense
records and expresses its data type to the brain which, in turn, builds
the composite experiential memory. A blind man's experiences will
be missing visual cues, but that doesn't invalidate the memory he
builds from the remaining sequences of sensory data.

In much the same way, the Oneiroi is a multi-threaded environment. Full immersion means being receptive to the various layers of

* fabric
p. 56

the dream: from the proleptic fluidity of the hypnagogic fabric, to the
tactile flow of the Enhypnic stream, to the empyrean nootropia of the
Aserinsky Region, to the epiphanic anachronisms past the Ebbinghaus Proscenium, to the protean subjectivity of the Metaxu, to the
macrocosmic sublimation of the Deepdark.

They're meaningless distinctions, you know, nothing more than
the desperate attempt of our mind to quantity abstractions. The

Oneiroi is a dream, an illusion. It's a consensually shared hallucination. Such an experiential network confounds our definition of reality by the implication that consciousness—wakefulness—is an imposition of ego. What we see, hear, smell, taste, and feel is more "real" than what we dream, isn't it?

But that is the heavy-handed cage of the Cartesian Consumer in us. We think, therefore we feel, therefore we are. Thereby instigating the concept of time. "I am" is a point, a completely subjective one, but still a quantifiable point. If you have a grounded reference, you can observe a point distinct from yourself (thereby creating a line), and from there, allow geometry to make the world. *cage p. 163

See? We need these laws to be inviolate because they, ultimately, define us. If we can't be defined, then we cease to exist. The Oneiroi, with its multitude of ego-less layers and protean fluidity, confounds the idea of self. It threatens the uniqueness of identity.

# LIBRARY

## Ω

A library is a collection of the frozen apprehensions of the world. Yes, they are records of the passage of God, but they are the historical records of God. They provide proof of the existence of God, but fail to illuminate where He might have gone.

That is not to say that libraries are useless, moldering piles of vegetable matter that are better used for providing mulch for sunflowers or cherry trees. I, personally, love a good library. Reading the catalog of Dr. John Dee's collection makes me feel like the mysteries of the world can be comprehended if one were to assemble enough texts, if one were able to read everything. Much like those librarians in Borges's hexagonal infinity who dream of the catalogue of catalogues.

* echoes
p. 186

But such an assimilation of knowledge would simply inform of us of the world as it has been. (Borges, to his credit, posits that among the cryptic infinity of texts on the library's shelves there exist tomes that predict the future, if one could actually read them.) Such an assimilation would inform us of God as He had been, and by doing so, would make us God. And, at that moment, the library—as it was defined—would cease to exist because it would be incomplete.

Though one could argue that whoever read all the books and became God would understand that the act of reading was synonymous with writing and that the library was created—will be created—by this act.

Libraries are, in varying degrees, an expression of order. They refute the possibility of chaos. Their shelves are the walls that protect us from the mean-spirited emptiness of random chance. They are the persistence of our need for a Rational Existence, a God who has a Plan and who isn't a Blind Idiot Creator, wracked by insanity and inconstancy.

* fool
p. 204

I have been seeking order in my dreams; I have been trying to discern the Plan that informs the symbols and images that have been flooding my sleep. I have been attempting to gain access to that room in the library where I will find the book that will make my confusion comprehensible. But, even that book—yes, *that one*, the book she was attempting to devour even as she was being devoured (so many echoes of cycles of endless recursions). Even though it was filled with too many pages—too many possibilities. Every key could have been the right one.

* key
p. 227

The search for the key is a trap, I think. To seek the key is to be a enumerator.

# MARRIAGE
♌

At the center of the garden of flowers and stones, there is a plaza and a large pit of smoldering black stones. When the Ribbon Man and I arrive, the first coffin is pushed down an incline, and the box bumps and rattles out into the center of the pit. The wood catches fire quickly, flames dancing merrily along the coffin top. Other flames lick at the corners of the box until it fractures and the sides collapse. Shards of glass spill onto the pit of black stones.

Instead of burning, they are transformed into arrays of light. Coherent enough to see images, histories that shimmer and contort through the haze of burning wood. Dream histories. Each coffin is filled with another viewpoint, another version of what might be. They fill up the sky over the pit—never ending, never stopping.

If the Oneiroi is where you go when you dream, where do you go when you dream within a dream? Is there another reflection? An endless progression of iterations, each one nestled within the one prior. Is this cycle infinite, or is it a loop? Eventually, is my dream of a dream of a dream just me dreaming?

The Ribbon Man nudges me, drawing me back to this dream, this iteration.

"She's here," he whispers. "It is time."

She stands at the foot of the path, a man in white at her side. Yellow flowers have collected in the train of her black dress, and a veil of stars covers her head.

The priest (a cross of light overlaying his white vestments) raises his right hand and points at the swirl of dream history over the pit. His left, holding the black book, brushes against her dress. The assembled host take out their mirrors—their rings, their glasses, their necklaces, their beads—and reflect the light of the dream toward the bride. Her dress becomes blacker, and her stars become white fire.

I walk over to the bride and the priest. He beams at me, and I realize his smooth face is a mask. He opens his book (all the pages are black, too), and when he reads, the gathered host speak the words. "Matrimonium mortis et—"

Her veil flutters. It is almost impossible to see in the glare of her black dress, against the glitter of her fiery stars, but I see the fabric move. I see her lips move.

I remember what it is to kiss her.

*kiss
p. 234

I turn around, and catch the Ribbon Man's hand. He whines and struggles, but I am stronger. "Somnium," I say.

I am the dream. I am the way.

*II

The syringe drops out of his hand.

# MASSA CONFUSA

## ♉

In the beginning, there is chaos. There is form, but it is unorthodox. Unorganized. Riotous. There is color, but no order. The peacock is the sun, and the sun is without light. This is the paradox of life. In the beginning, there are no principles, no foundations. Everything is tumultuous, the explosive decompression that follows the infinite density of the focus, and the world is an untamed profusion of blood, bone, and flesh.

Man does not know himself in this time. He dances upon the hills, resplendent with his peacock crown. His staff is filled with pure light and, when expressed through the pinhole of his cock, it is an eruption of rainbow heat.

The massa confusa is the firstborn child of primal chaos—the eidolon, the dybbuk. Man, firstly born in flesh from mud, does not know what lies within him. He does not feel the hard permanence around which his flesh and soul have been wrapped.

White light. Red earth. Pale flesh. Ruddy blood. The elements must be separated, distilled, condensed, incinerated, buried awhile in the ground, and given nourishment until they flower.

This is the restraint of life. In the end, there is precision and purpose. Nothing is unfixed, and discordance adheres to the architect's blueprint. The foundation holds.

* snow
p. 315

* crown
p. 177

* double
p. 390

* architect
p. 154

# MEMORY
## Ω

They're doing research with mice again; though, it isn't like they've ever stopped, but in this case, they're looking at memory.[△] Scientists are watching the hippocampus as they subject the little rodents to a series of tests (dramatic events of the sort that make a lot of little lights go off on their monitors), and are learning how the brain registers the sensory and neurological details of these events. They have discovered that each record of an event (each "memory") is a pyramid-shaped cluster of aggregated triggers (Tsien and Osan call the sub-set of neurons that register a specific characteristic of the event "neural cliques"). These pyramid collections are then transferred into long-term storage via a method of "re-experiencing" each event. But, it is these neural clusters that have fascinated the researchers because they imply that memory is not an unique record of an event, but rather an assembly of attributes.

Somewhat like saccadic masking—how we see isn't an accurate representation of external reality, but is actually an extrapolation done by our brains with the rapid-fire still images that our brains record. Memory is the same thing: attributes—binary switches—that are organized and interpreted by our brains into something approximating an accurate record. They form a duality matrix, though one that is more grounded in scientific observation than psychological organization.

*duality matrix p. 185*

Memories, then, become an assembly of binary data sets, and given an observable system, it is possible that other triggers—external ones, even—can be tripped by the presence of certain binary sequences. In other words, it may be possible to send a key sequence to an electronic lock by virtue of recalling a certain memory that exhibits a specific binary sequence. Oh, yes, your memory of eating ice cream on the porch of your grandfather's house? Yes, 00010011 is correct. Access granted.

---

△ - Lin L., Osan R., Tsien JZ., "Organizing principles of real-time memory encoding: neural clique assemblies and universal neural codes" *Trends in Neuroscience* 29, no. 1 (2006): 48-57.

Where 00110011 may be a different ice cream memory. One that has the additional attribute of having a dog in it. The neighborhood mutt, say, the one which was small and brown and always friendly.

This is, of course, a gross oversimplification of the work being done, but I think the idea of memory as a collection of attributes rather than detailed sensory records assists in an understanding of how memory can be set adrift. On a purely computational level, changing memory is a matter of switching a few coding units from on to off (and vice versa). Organizational drift can be effected very easily by blanking whole regions of synaptic storage.

* drift
p. 184

How will your mind know? The way it processes data up to the consciousness is purely interpretive; it unpacks a string of binary attributes and assigns sensory details, staples on an emotional reaction, and filters the result through a myopic set of religious and moral definitions. Is there a computational checksum that would reveal tampering? A snapshot of the data set against which the recalled memory is compared? No, I do not think the brain—for all its status as a massive neuro-chemical computer—has much in the way of a useful backup and data integrity verification system. Well, it does: you.

* deceit
p. 180

You are the one who finds the deficiencies in memory, the strange details that seem contrary to your world-view, the tiny inconsistencies that are counter to the psychological and physiological rules by which we understand reality. But what recourse do we have to those memories which seem faulty? How can we determine what they should be?

I took Nora to Paris once, building a weekend escape from a memory of a visit when she was in high school. We went to the Musee d'Orsay, and she said the couple in Toulouse-Lautrec's In Bed were us, and the angelic hermit of Redon's Vieillard ailé barbu was how she imagined me when I became an old man and outgrew the hat. I showed her Gustave Moreau's Galatèe, and taking my hand, she pulled me into the picture. We made wreathes of red and yellow flowers, and had lunch under the spiny trees. It was, she said, the best time she had ever had in Paris.

**It was. It still is.**

254

There. See? None of it was real in the conventional—in the scientifically observable sense—but what did her brain care? It dutifully stored all of it as strings of binary data sets. Whether she set the switch that identified these data collections as real or imaginary is, well, something only she can say.

I've marked them as true. I mark them all as true. If our memories are data collections that defines personality and identity, then what is the distinction between creation and falsification? If I believe things to be true—and in my head, they are—how does that not make me God?

# MIRAGE
## ♏

*In this land—before my time and before my father's time—there was a queen who earned her place beside her king by enchanting him with mirages. Every night, for three and a third years, she told him a story. Her stories were filled with fantasy, each more elaborate than the last, and in the telling, each story shaped the world a little more.*

*\* king
p. 231*

*The king, bound so long by the allure of her tales, became so infirm that he could not walk or ride a horse. He had to be carried every morning from his bed to his balcony, from his balcony to his throne, and from his throne back to his bed. His body—unwanted, unrealized—became like sand.*

*The queen-to-be's intentions were not evil. She simply sought to preserve her own life, and if the gift of her tongue was enough to stay the king from having her beheaded, then is it not another mirage to see her intent as ill?*

*\* history
p. 22*

*Her stories, though they slew the king over time, fore-stalled a great many savageries that the king might have done against his people. Is her phantasmal rewriting of history nothing more than an act of kindness, a careful re-creation wherein the blood and despair and hate of the age were replaced with acts of moral courage, feats of bravery, and sacrifices made for love? Did her mirage of a purer world not transform this very land of desert and sky?*

*And yet, the dreamer must close himself off from the sanctuary offered by the mirage. While it may be created by the tongue of another, it finds its strength in the weak material. It is false gold, this body, and it is too easily dis-tempered by phantasmagoria. This, then, is the first sacrificial stage. In order to truly pass through the thresholds and become part of the unreal, the dreamer must first deny the influence of the unreal.*△

---

△ - Safiq Al-Kahir, *Book of Dreams* (Obscura Editions: Red House, 1938), 47.

# MISSING
## Ω ↗

There. A flickering bioluminescence.

It draws me, a hint of a moth to a hint of a flame. It is a glass canister, with metal stoppers and a series of trailing cords like the delicate strands of a jellyfish. My spine floats within the jar, suspended in its own private sea. The blue light of Nora's touch is still flickering along the ridges of my vertebrae.

My head, which had once sat atop that curve of bone, is missing. Depending on which philosophy of the soul you lay your faith, the loss of my head can be read as a kidnapping of the soul, a symbolic reflection of the chaotic personality splinters wreaking havoc within me, or as a simple reminder that he who cannot see nor speak might as well be headless anyway.

Are we not just translators? Interpreters of signs and portents? Are we not glorified fortune tellers, charlatans who run ganglia and neural clusters through our fingers instead of cards? What we see in dreams is nothing more than a welter of symbols, what we read is nothing more than an abstract language of 4D pictograms.

My head is a symbol. My spine is a symbol. This endless darkness is a symbol. Yes. Yes. None of it is real. Nothing is real. My observational viewpoint is also an interpretation, a symbolic representation of intelligence, a reflection of God's original all-seeing eye. I am not real.

**(listen to the waves, says the fisherman)**

What then? If I am not real, then what is my observation worth? The universe splits into infinite idiosyncrasies, and nothing ever is, again.

This is Bleak Zero. I can feel it whispering to me, crooning its song of dissolution. Just empty this part; yes, you won't need that anymore. Just knock out few more lights. Just a little more darkness. Whispering like a persistent street-faire hawker. Just one more. Just one. Knock it all down. Win a prize.

*last call p. 240

# MOTH
## ᙡᙡ

*paper
p. 262

Moths, by virtue of their fascination with light, are children of the Moon (that poor widow who pines so for her lost King). They are the paper paupers of night, dusted in white ash. It is this dust that lets them fly. When you hold a moth in your hand and rub its wings, its life is smeared across your finger. A moth that cannot fly is but a misshapen worm.

This is the way we kill fantasy.

*fabric
p. 56

Butterflies, those prismatic dandies, are the superficial sycophants of the day. They are nothing beneath their brightly colored cloaks; they have nothing but their rainbow processionals. The fabric of their wings is fragile and tears easily when grasped by clumsy hands. A butterfly bereft of flight is but a leaf not yet frozen by winter.

This is the way we kill fancy.

*roots
p. 371

Like other symbolic structures that revolve around the eternal duality, the moth and the butterfly have been inextricably linked as a "pair," though the biology is distinct. This method of pairing, while more fantasy than factual, is the root of all language, and in this way, fantasy is more "true" than reality.

# NEGLIGENCE

August 16th, 1981
Dr. Eduardo Ehrillimbal, Esq.
c/o Umbrial Consortium
XXXX XXXXXXXX, XXXXX XXX
Los Angeles, CA 90048

Dr. Beverly Trenton
Rose Bay Psychiatric Hospital
XXX XXXXXXXX XXX
Berkeley, CA 94708

Dr. Ehrillimbal:

My recent review of the administrative organization of Rose Bay Psychiatric Hospital has revealed an existing contract between your organization and the hospital, pursuant to the care of three patients. As these patients are no longer residents at Rose Bay, I am terminating your contract, effective immediately.

You will receive a final statement from our accounting department after the end of the month, as well as a full refund of any outstanding funds.

The case files of Jerry McElholn and Francis Barrlis have been sealed but for such access as the Berkeley Police deems necessary. I will refer your office to them if you should query about those case files. Philip Kendrick's files are protected by the confidentiality statutes of the State of California, and as such, you will need both a court order and a signed affidavit from Mr. Kendrick himself should you wish to see those records.

* sacrifice
p. 300

Dr. Herquiest is no longer employed by the Rose Bay Psychiatric Hospital. With the revocation of his license and the ensuing legal actions that have arisen from his negligence, the Board of Directors felt it was impossible for the hospital to function effectively under such leadership.

This letter serves as notice that Dr. Herquiest is under a gag order from the Superior Court of San Francisco, concerning all and every aspect of his employment at Rose Bay. Any attempt by your office to contact him will be interpreted as a willful disregard for the court order, and will be dealt with accordingly.

Personally, I appreciate your office's efforts to facilitate the care and treatment of Mr. McElholn, Mr. Barrlis, and Mr. Kendrick, and I want to offer my condolences for the deaths of Mr. McElholn and Mr. Barrlis. The events of May were tragic and avoidable.

*suicide
p. 325

Best,


Dr. Beverly Trenton

# NOTE

Photocopy of note found beside Jerry McElholn, May 17th, 1981

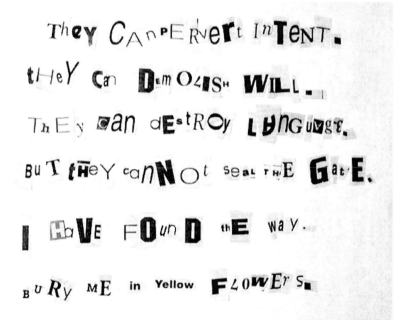

They CAnpErvert InTent.
tHeY Can DemOLISh WILL.
ThEy can dEstROy LHNGuage.
BUT tHeY canNOt seal thE GatE.
I HaVE FOunD thE way.
bURy mE in Yellow FLOWErs.

# PAPER
# ♍

"It's blank."

"Hold it up to the light."

"Oh, yes. I see. That's very clever. Is this how you used to pass notes in school?"

"No, it's a little obvious when you have to raise the page up like that."

"Yes, I suppose it is. The page doesn't have to be blank, does it? You could write something mundane on here. A shopping list, maybe, or a note. 'I miss you, but I don't remember why.' Something like that."

*l

"You could. A lot of old manuscripts were done like that. Secrets were written between lines and in the margins. Most of the old knowledge has been preserved that way."

"Listen to you. 'The old knowledge.'"

"What?"

"You make it seem so mysterious, so clandestine."

"But it was. This is how the heretics hid in plain sight. They would author epistles and monographs that seemed to uphold the virtues of the Church, but hidden along the outer edge of the page were lines and lines of blasphemy.

* hidden
p. 219

"The alchemists, too, they passed their secret recipes along via hidden writing. That's why the original manuscripts are so highly prized. Sure, you could make copies, but they were just strange writings—treatises that seemed to almost make sense, but not quite. That was the whole point of the hidden key: without it, the book seemed to work, in theory; but in practice, the text—as written—never worked."

"What about you and your friends. The oneironauts. Do you leave messages for each other?"

"We don't share the same variation of the Oneiroi."

"Why not? You're sharing mine."

"That's different."

"Is it? How so?"

"It's just . . . not done like that, Nora. We don't intrude on each other's dreams. It's, well, rude . . . and dangerous."

"But you could? You just don't."

"That's right."

"Does everyone think the same way? Is this one of those laws no one ever contemplates breaking?" * final law p. 200

"Yes."

"Are you sure?"

"Well, it's not like I've signed a contract, or we've all taken a blood oath or something. Wandering into another oneironaut's dreams is just not done. It's always been that way."

"And you all accept that?"

"Yes, Nora. We do."

"But if someone didn't, how would you know? The dream would be like this piece of paper: blank, unless I know how to look at it correctly."

"Yes, for the sake of argument, that would indeed be the case. Unless you had the key, unless you knew the way, you couldn't see the hidden content."

**Turn around.**

"What?"

"Turn around. Look at the wall behind you."

"There's nothing—"

**Do you see it now?**

# PERSISTENCE

ℰ

FROM: igotgills@...
TO: alt.oneirology.entheogens
SUB: The Persistence of Memory

I realize this may seem off-topic from the bullshit that's been flying on the list these last few months, but bear with me for a minute. I want to talk about Dali. About his painting called "The Persistence of Memory," to be exact.

I've always been a huge fan of his work and, when the MOMA released the painting for that recent tour, I leaped at the change to go down the road and see it, versus traveling all the way across the country. Sure, I had to stand in line for four hours to get a ticket. Totally worth it, though.

Most of the critical theory argues that the picture is a reflection of Einstein's theory. You know, gravity's effect on weight and how that becomes mutable at the limits of time. But I think Dali had had an Oneiric experience. Hell, I think he had more than one. But the one that stuck with him is the soft watches. I think he fell through the fabric and got a little wet in the deepdark, and it scared the shit out of him.

It scares the shit of out me too, now.

And so he painted those watches, painted them as a reminder. And as a warning to never go that deep again.

But we all do, don't we? When we die, that's where we end up, isn't it? Part of that ocean of noise. And that's where half of us have gone already, right? The spam agents are just channeling the noise of the deepdark. They're hooked in, like radio receivers, and they're just transcribing all the voices.

-fishboy

----------------------------------

* memory
p. 253

* radio
p. 291

FROM: terminalx@...
TO: alt.oneirology.entheogens
SUB: RE: The Persistence of Memory


>> They're hooked in, like radio receivers, and they're just transcribing all the voices.

Maybe, but I'm not convinced. There's too much intelligence behind those messages, too much active intelligence. Meme_Mechanic went down that far once. He'd know. He'd—      *ll*

Shit, I can't believe it got him. I thought he would have better defenses. Be better prepared somehow. He always struck me as the Boy Scout among us. The one who has the garage full of survival gear,      *psychonaut*
ready for the Big One. But, no, apparently not.      *p. 12*

I wonder what it is. The trigger, that is. What is it that changes us. Heh, maybe it has me already, and I just think I'm writing this email. Maybe what I'm actually typing is something completely different.


-t to the x


----------------------------------


FROM: heron74@ . . .
TO: alt.oneirology.entheogens
SUB: RE[2]: The Persistence of Memory


Are we all waiting for the end? Is that it? Have we all given up?

It's a neuro-chemical agent. Modified, sure, but it is still a drug      *bleak zero*
that affects the brain. Come on. How long have we been taking these?      *p. 162*
Haven't we learned anything in the last few decades? They're just catalysts. All of them. They just help us realize the brain's potential.

We're smarter than this.


-(pk)

FROM: igotgills@...
TO: alt.oneirology.entheogens
SUB: RE: RE: RE: The Persistence of Memory

>> We're smarter than this.

Well, clue us in then, (pk). Some of us haven't been dropping acid since the '70s. Fuck, dude, I wasn't even born in 1981 when your big brouhaha went down. I don't make it a habit of skinny-dipping in the collective unconscious like you big bad survivors of the Me Decade. I'm a little freaked out by all this, and I'm more than a little fucking scared. So, spill. What's the secret to keeping your head?

* emergency
p. 190

-fishboy

----------------------------------

FROM: heron74@...
TO: alt.oneirology.entheogens
SUB: RE: RE: RE: RE: The Persistence of Memory

Fishboy: I don't know. I don't have all the answers. I'm not your savior. I've been hiding out in the middle of nowhere for a decade now because I can't deal with being around people. I've got me a good internet pipe, basic utilities, a view, and a guy I can trust to deliver me a bag of sweet leaf once a week. That's how clued in I am.

* fear
p. 199

I've spent a long time being afraid, Fishboy. A long time. And maybe that's why I'm finally showing some backbone. I'm just tired of hiding.

Besides, whatever is coming, it can't be worse than our nightmares. Right?

-(pk)

FROM: radio_free_engineer@...
TO: alt.oneirology.entheogens
SUB: RE: RE: RE: RE: RE: The Persistence of Memory

How many are left? Is it just the four of us?

I've been thinking about Fishboy's comments on the Dali painting, and I think it's a pretty insightful assessment of the picture. Memory isn't nearly as persistent as we'd like to think. It's been seventy-odd years since Dali painted that picture, and we can't look at it and understand it without an art history reference guide. We've already forgotten much of the cultural suggestions that influenced Dali's hand.

And what about the later painting he did? *The Disintegration of the Persistence of Memory*. He's definitely commenting on the failure of societal memory—and he's including himself in that group, as well—to retain anything of real value. It slips away from all us, eventually.

One day, our brains misfire and the sparks go out. Everything falls into the deepdark, where it is—I don't know—subsumed, maybe. We forget, certainly, but does . . . God? Is that even the right name? Is the collective unconscious intelligent and aware in any sense? Or is it just a vast reservoir of memories? *fire
p. 201

Do we spend our lives drawing thoughts out of that vast pool, in some vain effort to arrange them in what? Some secret order that will reveal . . .

What am I scrambling for here? Some explanation of eternity? Some hope that this hasn't all been for nothing?

=On the RF

"'Di-di-dah-dit di-di-dah.' Now there's a signature for you."
–Capt. Francis Spinder

# PETALS
♍

Count the petals. Why are there twenty-three? Is the world not symmetrical? Is the world not ordered in a series of twisted pairs?

The flower opens as I write this, its yellow and white petals unfolding. What lies in its center? What is the trigger that makes it bloom?

*bloom
p. 386

she loves me she loves me not she loves me she loves me not . . .

**(listen for the key, says the drowned sailor)**

Tattooed on my hand, using the lines of my fate, of my love, of my life. Its twenty-three arcs. She gave this to me.

**(answer say answer, says the white queen)**

The last is the hollow gate. It is the inequality. It is the chaotic disturbance in the order. It is confusion of ego.

*ego
p. 188

she loves me she loves me not she loves me she loves me not . . .

*We made you, Blind Seer. We gave you life, burnblack Pain God.*

"I will be alright if you kiss me. I will be all right if you hold me. When I see the great black light that shines in the eyes of animals. When I find you, I will remind you."

she loves me she loves me not . . .

# PLIABE

FROM: heron74@...
TO: alt.oneirology.entheogens
SUB: The Earnestness of Our Conversion

I know we used to have a thread where we asked all new members to introduce themselves, and write a little bit about how they came to see the light. Back in the day when we were a bit closer, and not hiding behind avatars and aliases. I know. I know. I'm the old man on the porch now. "Back in my day, sonny, we used to ingest our drugs by eating toxified meat or making out with venomous snakes."

We used to talk about the doors of perception, the astral veils, and the Akashic Records. We used to be interested in bettering not just ourselves, but all of humanity. We wanted to make a difference.

*history
p. 22*

No one belittled the experience of another. No one doubted what another member might have seen or done. We were all rebels; each of us had committed heresy in the eyes of whatever religious upbringing they had had. None of us were sinless, so there was never any point of us casting stones.

Nor am I now. I'm just wondering what has happened to us. What has happened to make us so afraid?

Meme: Could you retrieve that introductory thread from a few years ago? I've known you a long time, and all those public denials aside, I know you are a pack rat. Forget all the old bullshit. I know why you said the archives were gone, and I was disappointed, sure, but I know why you took the stance you did, but I think this is a good time to dispense with the polite dissembling.

We're proponents of illegal narcotics, people. We take chemical agents in combinations and doses that would make pharmacists shit themselves, and we do it because the reward is worth the risk. We've all cheated death (and jail time) at least once already. Taking that first dose takes some resolve. It takes some spine.

So where did all our backbone go?

*spine
p. 28*

- (pk)

FROM: igotgills@...
TO: alt.oneirology.entheogens
SUB: RE: The Earnestness of Our Conversion

>> We've all cheated death (and jail time) at least once already. Taking that first dose takes some resolve. It takes some spine.
>> So where did all our backbone go?

When was the last time the police kicked in your door? Have you been visited by Homeland Security recently? These are strange and fucked up times, my friend. Being a social revolutionary now isn't the same as those marijuana-fueled flower power days. If the police have to break up your party these days, they do so with dogs and water cannons and rubber bullets. Not to mention anal cavity searches, a full battery of psychological assaults, and isolation wards. Forget the phone call to mommy. When the black bag bastards come for you these days, you disappear.

Some of us don't want to change the world. We just want it to go away. Let them fuck each other into oblivion.

-fishboy

*//*

--------------------------------

FROM: heron74@...
TO: alt.oneirology.entheogens
SUB: RE: RE: The Earnestness of Our Conversion

>> Some of us don't want to change the world. We just want it to go away. Let them fuck each other into oblivion.

You apparently don't understand the concept of "collateral damage," which doesn't surprise me since your tone seems to be childish and churlish enough to indicate that you don't remember the last time we sent our boys overseas. You know, that military effort to contain "them" so they could "fuck each other into oblivion." The one where we contributed to the death of more than a half million innocent civilians.

This isn't a private commune where we can lock the gates against those we don't like. The whole planet is our commune, and like it or not, we've got some responsibilities as its psychopharmacological stewards. Sure, we may have to drag them into the future, but that's the only way the future is going to arrive.

You're probably too young to remember Romero's original zombie film, but I'll try to make the analogy anyway. Remember when the survivors barricade themselves in the house? They nail the doors shut, and cover the windows with anything they can find. Remember how that one ends? Eventually the outsiders get in, eventually they batter themselves against your sanctuary long enough to break through. And then what happened?

Yeah, that's our fate if we try to pretend it isn't happening, and try to wait it out in our secret little caves.

*last call*
*p. 240*

- (pk)

--------------------------------

FROM: meme_mechanic@ . . .
TO: alt.oneirology.entheogens
SUB: RE: RE: RE: The Earnestness of Our Conversion

On the subject of the archives: heron74@... and I have traded emails privately, and because I know some of you have been wondering, I want to publicly respond.

During the twenty-two months when I wasn't administrator of this list, the individual who was made some systematic alterations to the data on the physical server where the mailing list archives reside. The changes were subtle enough that I didn't realize anything was amiss until I noticed some strange syntax in a few of my emails—phraseology that I wouldn't use, words that weren't part of my vocabulary, that sort of thing. When I ran a diff utility comparing a large portion of my own sent mail to the archive, I got a huge output of differences between the two.

* duality
matrix
p. 185

Here's an example:

My local copy of an email: "Last time I saw them at Panic Lounge, they were a quartet. Rocked pretty hard, too."

What the archive reads: "Last time I guzzled liquid fish while sliding through the Impanic Sanctuary, there were chickens underfoot. They were eating rocks and shitting pearls."

* fowl
p. 208

There shouldn't have been any difference, but fuck me, it's like each email has been rewritten by a trio of schizophrenics.

The archive isn't so much as gone, as it is corrupted so badly that I can't attest as to the veracity of any given email. This is further compounded by our ISP's cheap-ass data retention policy, which means I have no idea when this data corruption happened. Which is to say, the server archive is useless. We can't trust them.

Yeah, yeah. I know. I say that a lot, but in case, I'm not shitting you.

-meme

----------------------------------

FROM: oldmanwinter@ . . .
TO: alt.oneirology.entheogens
SUB: RE: RE: RE: RE: The Earnestness of Our Conversion

This is how TH3y make us more pliable: by removing our history, by cutting us off from each other, by sowing discord and distrust. When we are all alone, we are more susceptible to their influence and their agents. When we are frightened and in the dark, we welcome the arrival of light. We forget to look beyond the glow and ask who is carrying the lantern.

* hermit
p. 217

------------------------------------

FROM: terminalx@...
TO: alt.oneirology.entheogens
SUB: RE: RE: RE: RE: RE: The Earnestness of Our Conversion

Okay, I'll bite: who is TH3y?                          *gnosis
Since they seem to be the villain here. And I'm assuming that you're   p. 54
not just being a l33t haX0r.

-t to the x

(Hey, meme, who is this guy? When did he join the list?)

------------------------------------

FROM: oldmanwinter@ . . .
TO: alt.oneirology.entheogens
SUB: RE: RE: RE: RE: RE: The Earnestness of Our Conversion

>>>Okay, I'll bite: who is TH3y?

heron74@... remembers them. Their original incarnation, at least.
They're better disguised now, cloaking in corporate respectability.
You've all seen their products, probably even used some of them.
They've got a new drug that's about to hit the market. An anti-psy-
chotic for schizophrenics. Atramabor. It is an opiate distilled from
the dregs of blackleaf 23.
Atramabor been in clinical trials for some time. Some of you have
seen it. Some of you are under the influence of it right now.

-Brother J

FROM: heron74@...
TO: alt.oneirology.entheogens
SUB: RE: RE: RE: RE: RE: RE: RE: The Earnestness of Our Conversion

>> Their original incarnation, at least.

*experiment
p.192

Oh, shit. Jerry's Trinity House? Oh, shit shit shit.

>> -Brother J

Damn. Julio? Is that you? Have we been that complacent?

- (pk)

-----------------------------------

FROM: terminalx@...
TO: alt.oneirology.entheogens
SUB: RE: RE: RE: RE: RE: RE: RE: RE: The Earnestness of Our Conversion

Wait! Goddamn it. I thought you said blackleaf 23 couldn't be synthesized in our lifetime. I thought you said we weren't ready for it.
And, what is 'Jerry's Trinity House'? One of his acid flashbacks that everyone pretended had teeth so that he wouldn't completely self-destruct from paranoia?

-t to the x

# POISON

ॐ

FROM: lapidaryl2000@ . . .
TO: alt.oneirology.entheogens
SUB: Harmless Supplements

Relax, I didn't take the supplements. I'm not that much of a guinea pig.

Though, the homeless guy I met last night volunteered easily enough. I offered him $20 to try one of Terry and Erma's Purification Packets. Dude saw that I had more than one and said he'd volunteer to take 'em all for $50. Why not? If it's cumulative, I might as well get right to the punch line, right?

* purify
p. 284

So, I told him he could take them all, but he'd have to do it with food, because I'm not much of an asshole. There was an IHOP down the street, and we got a booth, and I let the dude order anything he wanted. Of course, he got all fancy on me, and took, like, a fucking hour to decide what he wanted. And then he bitched at the waitress for not having real maple syrup.

Asshole.

Anyway, fifty bucks and a couple of pancake stacks later, my guinea pig says that he's feeling pretty good. Says he remembers things he's not thought of in years. Says he knows the future, that he can see right through time. At this point, I figure he's fucking with me, so I send him off with the cash. Tell him to buy some vodka and take the edge off that precognition.

So, the supplements are probably what they say they are. If they had something sinister in them, this dude would have shown some symptoms. As it was, I think he just got a bit high from all the Yohimbine.

I'm flying back to Chicago today, and I'm posting this update from the concourse. Frankly, I've got nothing. My detective work in San Diego was a bust. Based on that other thread, I think we're still at zero. That dude oldmanwinter@ . . . is making noises about truth in reporting and people not being dead, but I'm not seeing it. And (pk) is jumping at the suggestion of shadows, like he always does.

(Sorry, Phil, but I remember some of your other theories: the DMT in the water supply conspiracy, for one, and that thing about Leary's brain being ground up and mixed with some sort of acetylcholinesterase inhibitor like Oxiracetam. What did you call that stuff?)

Anyway, it seems like half of us are in on the spam joke now.

Well, it's one way to kill an online community. Hey, Meme: how about disabling posting access for these idiots?

-Daryl

*". . . In fact, only the marvelous is beautiful." –Andre Breton*

----------------------------------

FROM: meme_mechanic@...
TO: alt.oneirology.entheogens
SUB: RE: Harmless Supplements

Did you slit the fish? Da'ath hides beneath the ribs. Silly sphere, silly heart, why do you bleed? Abattoir Abattoir you can't escape the Abattoir. Kiss him. Reptile reptile wracktile 12e20 13e 20e1212 251521 1 19e318e20 My penis is filth. I know how the caged bird sings? Product Code: u14-i2025. Would you like that gift wrapped? How about I put a nice fucking bow on it for you? Would you like sausage? Oh, Daddy, it hurts. Stop it. Stop it. Wear the wreath. Look at the light. Smile as they take your guts. You'd buy two if you could, wouldn't you? Tell me you would. Lie to me. Lie to me always. There are no coins in the fountain. The wood has been cut down by the blade, and the trees have been sliced and diced into matchsticks. I speak in riddles, I speak in code, I am the nonsense puppet. I am the tool of the eternal mouth. I am the haunting loss. Give me a cracker. No one knows where I have buried the treasure. Babylon. Babble . . .

*father
p. 198

*tool
p. 350

-meme

--------------------------------

FROM: terminalx@...
TO: alt.oneirology.entheogens
SUB: RE: RE: Harmless Supplements

>> No one knows where I have buried the treasure. Babylon. Babble . . .

Shit. It's not a game. I've been trying to parse these messages. They're not just random text strings. They're actual responses to the thread, but they're just so cluttered that it's hard to suss out the actual reply. It's like what meme was telling us about the archives being violated, but this is happening—fuck!—is it happening at the server, or is it a dumb user problem?

We are being rewired, aren't we? And it might not be isolated to us. Go look at some of the spam you're getting that seems unsolicited, that looks like random junk mail. Those emails that don't appear to be selling anything, the ones that are just a bunch of text? I think those are cries for help. These people don't know it—and this is why Bruce seemed normal—but they're being rewritten. Something is changing their programming, and it is fucking with their language centers. Hell, they probably don't even realize they're sending out these emails.

Or, rather, maybe they do, because these notes are the only expression left of their original identity. These "spam bots" are personality zombies, and whatever contagion they've got, they're spreading it through email.

I mean, how else can it propagate? Most of this list has never met in meatspace, and we probably wouldn't know a fellow alt.o.e'er by sight anyway. If this is Bleak Zero, then it isn't in the water. It's not transmitted by bodily fluids or blowing snot across the room. It's moving through us—through everyone—via some other method.

-t to the x

*fool*
*p. 204*

*programming*
*p. 283*

FROM: heron74@...
TO: alt.oneirology.entheogens
SUB: RE: RE: RE: Harmless Supplements

>> It's moving through us–through everyone–via some other method.

* anchor
p. 152
It's in the Oneiroi. Stay out. If you have to go in, use an anchor. There's an old method that we used once or twice back in the day. Let me find it; I'll post it to the mailing list.

Stay away from LSD, though. It opens too many doors, some without your knowledge.

-(pk)

(p.s. I heard that Trinity Pharmacopoeia is going to run an ad during the Super Bowl next week. I'm sure it's for their new drug, but . . . man, I have a bad feeling. Don't watch it. Don't watch the game. You're going to be too receptive. Too open to the wrong sort of programming. God help us. We all are . . . )

--------------------------------

FROM: radio_free_engineer@...
TO: alt.oneirology.entheogens
SUB: RE: RE: RE: RE: Harmless Supplements

>> It's in the Oneiroi.

Like Feral House was?

I've done some research of my own. Sorry (pk), if you and I hung out on the weekends and were part of the same sports betting pool, I probably would have taken your word for everything that you said, but . . .

Anyway, I wanted some independent verification of the story about

Rose Bay, and I found enough to think that, if anything, (pk) is only giving us a small slice of the full story. Maybe he jumped ship before it got really ugly, or maybe he was only privy to what was happening to him and his friends. Doesn't really matter, 'cause there's some real juice in all the sealed court documents from a half dozen or so lawsuits brought against Dr. Herquiest and Rose Bay in '84 and '85.

If you read these docs with an eye to the conspiracy that (pk) has offered, then a lot of Dr. Herquiest's behavior—especially after being shit-canned by Rose Bay's BOD—starts to make sense. The good doctor may have lost his golden goose at Rose Bay, but that doesn't mean he didn't have options. I think (pk)'s assessment of the Doc's character is spot on. This guy was a piece of work, and from all of his statements made during the legal proceedings, it seems like he thinks he's one of the real victims here. I mean, this self-delusion became so pervasive in his arguments that more than one counsel for the defense wrote a statement considering the possibility that the case might be more successful if Dr. Herquiest was professionally examined and diagnosed as schizophrenic.

Yes, the good doctor was just as insane as the patients he was treating.

*schizophrenic p. 304*

It turned out to be a good idea, and Dr. Herquiest was remanded—with a certificate of authenticity signed by one Dr. B. Versai of Las Vegas, Nevada, no less—to a private facility somewhere in Colorado. All further legal action—both criminal and civil—would have to do without the good doctor.

Cases were settled; Rose Bay closed down a few years later (the building was torn down in '92, and a bunch of cheap condos were thrown up); and all these records were stamped, sealed, and dumped in a Superior Court basement.

Good thing I have some clerking friends in the SF court system, as well as a pound of Burmese Kush that I certainly couldn't smoke by myself.

Anyway, the real kicker is that I found a photocopy of some notes that were used in the argument for Dr. Herquiest's mental instability.

*paper
p. 262

They were scraps of paper—pages torn out of hotel bibles, actually—that Dr. Herquiest had been stuffing under the mattresses in the hotel rooms he had been staying in. The report doesn't have any definitive explanation for them, but they look like the wish-fullfilment sigils used by chaos magicians (really, google up Peter Carroll if you're that skeptical). On all of these notes, said to be written by Dr. Herquiest himself, the 'a' is skewed. It's like everytime he wrote that letter another personality took over. It's really freaky looking.

Some of them are pretty badly written haiku (yet another example of questionable mental acuity, right?), and a number of them reference "feral angels." They're like love letters, sort of. *Where has my love gone? Why have you abandoned me? How long must I wait until you return?* That sort of thing. Like a lovesick high school kid with ADD and a copy of Shakespeare's Sonnets as his only friend.

Anyway, to bring this back (commodius vicus of recirculation, I know) to the topic at hand, if Dr. Herquiest was being poisoned by Bleak Zero (even an early version of it), would his dementia manifest itself like this?

* bleak zero
p. 162

=On the RF

"'Di-di-dah-dit di-di-dah.' Now there's a signature for you." -Capt. Francis Spinder

----------------------------------

FROM: heron74@...
TO: alt.oneirology.entheogens
SUB: RE: RE: RE: RE: RE: Harmless Supplements

I just received two picture messages from someone's phone. I think it is Daryl's. Oh God, I can't believe this.

The first is a picture of a cocktail napkin with an American Airlines logo on it. It says: "Homeless dude is on this flight. WTF? How did he get here? Going to take a picture. Purification Packets? OD = ?? Don't stop looking. I was wrong."

The second is a blurry picture of a row of passengers in an airplane. The guy in the middle is looking at the camera. It's blurry, but this is Daryl's homeless man. I think.  ˣ

I'm not sure. Why did he send it to me?

It looks like Jerry. I swear on everything that I ever held holy. He's older, but I know that face.

-(pk)

"We'd all be taken more seriously if we had black halos."
—Jerry McElholn

----------------------------------

FROM: radio_free_engineer@...
TO: alt.oneirology.entheogens
SUB: RE: RE: RE: RE: RE: RE: Harmless Supplements

Check your newsfeeds! There's been a plane crash. Outside of Chicago. An American flight out of San Diego.

Bad news. It sounds like they don't expect any survivors.

What's the time stamp on those emails, (pk)? CNN says the plane went down just after midnight, Chicago time.

=On the RF

"'Di-di-dah-dit di-di-dah.' Now there's a signature for you." —Capt. Francis Spinder

----------------------------------

FROM: heron74@...
TO: alt.oneirology.entheogens
SUB: RE: RE: RE: RE: RE: RE: RE: Harmless Supplements

>> What's the time stamp on those emails, (pk)?

12:13 AM, Central Time.
We've lost Daryl.

-(pk)

He's falling! He's falling! Stop him, help him, oh dear god! Is there any way to stop his fall?

# PROGRAMMING
✗

Failure is part of your programming, my son.

I wrote the code. I can unravel your ladder and show you where the systemic faults are written.

There.

There.

And there.

If you don't self-destruct in our personal relationships—if unrestrained love doesn't flip this switch here—then there are genetic traps that will go off every twelve years. As your flesh—always grubbing in the mud of other bodies—ages, your DNA will unravel and these faults will explode.

*IV

I built you this way, Man, because I wanted a broken toy.

You cannot ascend on your own. You may think you remember your angelic Fathers, those burnblack assassins who I cast out for their audacity and pride, but that memory is an illusion. Everything you imagine is unreal, just as everything your senses tell you. Your entire existence is a dream, Child, and you will never know true waking.

* burnblack
p. 26

Unless I give it to you.

I can wake you up.

I can show you my true light.

I can lift you from this black fog of your existence. I can take away the pain, the interminable suffering, and the hollow emptiness that gnaws at your heart.

* petals
p. 268

I can fix your programming.

# PURIFY

♋

FROM: lapidaryl2000@ . . .
TO: alt.oneirology.entheogens
SUB: Looking for Goldwhite@ . . .

I'm in San Diego this week, doing some business, and I've had some time in the evening these last few nights so I've been making an effort to track down goldwhite@ . . . We met at one of the big comic conventions a few years ago, and he—Bruce, actually, his name is Bruce—said that if I was ever in the San Diego area, I should look him up. Well, the whole mailing list spam thing has been bugging me and, since I was in the area, I figured I'd track him down. Get in his door and ask: WTF Dude?

The phone number he gave me didn't work any more, but—long story short—I managed to find a working number and reach him. He lives in this place called Cardiff-by-the-Sea. Sort of a retirement/resort suburb of Encinatas. Not a whole lot to do there unless you're a surfer. I think he commutes to San Diego to work anyway.

So, we meet up at this place called the Belly Up Tavern, up in Solana Beach just off the old Hwy 101. There's some indie pop band playing that he wanted to see and, eh, I figured what the hell? He's there with some friends, and while the music is pretty loud, I manage a couple of conversations. I don't mention alt.o.e—much too public of a place to bring it up—and I keep the topics to comics and what-not. He's a pretty genial guy, happy enough to hang out with someone who shares his interests, and while it's been a few years since I paid any attention to the comic industry, I remember enough to fake it.

*fragmentary
p. 209*

But there's something off in his mannerisms, and for a while, I chalk it up to just a natural reticence toward people he doesn't know that well, but I get an impression from his friends that this is a relatively new behavioral pattern. Then, the band does this song—I don't even remember the details—about pot, and he just shuts down. One of the weirdest things I've seen in a long time. It's almost a physical reaction. He just mentally checks out, and I can see the change in his expression.

I mean, I've seen this sort of thing in the Oneiroi, but never like this in the flesh.

*bare
p. 156

Anyway, before the song is even over, he's made his excuses and bailed. Just gone. It's abrupt enough that it takes his friends by surprise—they certainly weren't expecting him to suddenly take off like that. It was a strange enough encounter that, if I wasn't making the effort because of his online behavior, I would have written the evening off as slightly surreal and junked his number in my "weirdo" file.

However, this gives his friends and me something to talk about, and I manage to tease out of them that he's been weird for a few weeks. They've not consciously thought about it, but over a few beers, they start to put together a theory. They think it's a cult thing. They think that Bruce's family—he lives in a downstairs apartment/basement arrangement with his parents—have done an intervention and gotten him into this drug rehab cult.

Drug rehab? I say. Really?

Bruce, apparently, used to be a pretty big pot head, they tell me. Used to smoke out all the time. He loved to smoke and surf. Why else would anyone live in Cardiff-by-the-Sea? they say, as if the answer is self-evident to anyone who has lived in the region for any time.

But not so much anymore? I prod.

Not so much, they say. And they say it like they're mourning a lost friend. Like someone has died. And I realize that Bruce used to be their connection. Maybe not recently, but sometime in the past, Bruce was the hook-up for this little group.

Tonight, I wasn't able to get away from the city until after 8 PM and, instead of calling, I just went up to Cardiff to find Bruce. Knowing that he shared a house with his parents made it much easier to track him down. His cell phone wasn't on—it sent me straight to voicemail—and there weren't any lights on in the basement at the house, so I took a chance and knocked on the ground floor door.

Yeah, I've met his parents, and that was a really strange experience.

Nice people—Terry and Erma—but a little devout. To their vitamin wholesaler. They invited me in, told me pretty much anything I

* son
p. 317

wanted to know about their son (who, as it turns out, they don't know all that well), and took every opportunity they could to talk about this supplement regime they were taking. They even showed me Bruce's old bedroom from when he was in high school. Why? Because they've turned it into a storeroom for all their supplements.

The room is a maze of shelves and cases, organized in a way to maximize the available space in the room. You have to sidle sideways to fit between the racks, and everything is neatly stacked—labels out—and organized alphabetically. They had enough stock to last them—shit, I don't know—a couple of years, probably. Because, as Terry told me with fervent earnestness, when the commercial infrastructure fails, all deliveries are going to stop.

What happens in two years? I asked. When you run out?

They will provide, he told me. They will find us. They will restore the flow to each and every node. That is the way the world will be reconnected again, through each and every subscriber.

Erma beamed and nodded at every word her husband said, when she wasn't busy in the kitchen. I lost track of how many different snacks and hors d'oeuvres she offered me, and something like eight different beverages. Tea? No, thank you. Coffee? No. Juice? No. Smoothie? It was endless, and with this earnest smile the whole fucking time.

* missing
p. 257

The really asinine thing? They had no idea where their son was. They weren't concerned; they seem to have the same sort of trust that he's okay that they have in the vitamin rapture. When I really pushed, they finally admitted—and it was like they had to strain their brains to remember—they hadn't seen him in over a week.

A week! What a fucking waste of time.

Anyway, I'm not leaving until Friday so I have one more chance to track Bruce down before I head back to Chicago. I've left two messages on his cell phone, but I'm not terribly optimistic he's going to call back. I've got numbers from a couple of his friends from Tuesday night, so I might try them tomorrow and see if I can't get a solid lead from one of them.

Terry and Erma sent me home with a bunch of samples. "Purification packs," they called them. Good for reducing stress and for cleansing the system. I'm not sure I trust the ingredient list. If the labeling is honest, it's just a bunch of natural supplements: Gingko Biloba, Yohimbine, Tribulus Terrestris, Milk Thistle, Horny Goat Weed (though, heh, they disguise it as "Inyokaku"), and Kawa. DMAE too, though they spell it out to make it seem more "scientific." Doesn't seem like anything that you couldn't get at the nearest GNC, though, so I'm not quite sure why T & E were so enthusiastic about this brand.

The company name is Terra Ternaria. Based in Mexico. No website listed on the packaging. I'm going to do a little research . . .

*roots
p. 371

-Daryl

" . . . in fact, only the marvelous is beautiful." –Andre Breton

----------------------------------

FROM: 0553383582@ . . .
TO: alt.oneirology.entheogens
SUB: RE: Looking for Goldwhite@ . . .

>> The company name is Terra Ternaria. Based in Mexico. No website listed on the packaging.

Where in Mexico? Does the label say? Or just that ubiquitous "Made in Mexico." Christ, that could be anywhere.

I couldn't find much on Google, but a LexisNexis search turned up a few articles about Terra Ternaria. Fluff pieces mainly, and it seems like, as a company, Terra Ternaria came and went pretty quickly. Last mention was about four years ago, and the first press release is about a year and a half before that. Based in Oaxaca.

-huck

FROM: heron74@ . . .
TO: alt.oneirology.entheogens
SUB: RE: RE: Looking for Goldwhite@ . . .

>> Terra Ternaria

Man, that name sounds familiar. Hey, I don't have a LexisNexis account. Could you forward me the text of those pieces?
Thanks.

-(pk)

"We'd all be taken more seriously if we had black halos." -Jerry McElholn

----------------------------------

FROM: 0553383582@...
TO: alt.oneirology.entheogens
SUB: RE: RE: RE: Looking for Goldwhite@...

>> Could you forward me the text of those pieces?

On their way. I found a yearly report too. Check your inbox.

-huck

----------------------------------

FROM: heron74@...
TO: alt.oneirology.entheogens
SUB: RE: RE: RE: RE: Looking for Goldwhite@...

>> I found a yearly report too.

Shit, Daryl: don't try those packets! DON'T EAT THEM!

Does someone know how to contact Daryl directly? Does someone know him in meat space? He's right. Those packs aren't what they say.

Shit. Bernard Versai is listed on the Board of Directors for Terra Ternaria. You guys probably don't know who he is since he's been off the radar for, like, thirty years, but I do. Oh, yes, you mother-fucker, I know you.

Okay, here's the deal. He was never formally linked to what happened at Rose Bay. He claims he was never even licensed to practice in the state of California. But, a couple of post-docs at Rose Bay—they were getting their degrees from some dodgy school in Nevada—said he was their advisor, and that he set them up at Rose Bay. They claimed they were assisting him with some experimental treatment. After Frank died and the Berkeley police started asking harder questions, the two vanished. As far as I know, they were never found.

*experiment*
*p. 192*

I've seen pictures of Versai. I was at Rose Bay. He was there. The son of a bitch was there. Whatever those two said they were doing, they probably were, and Versai was doing more than "advising" them—he was overseeing the whole experiment. They were doing strange shit with the second floor, and they had plans for me and Jerry and Frank. I still don't know why they targeted us, but we were definitely targeted to receive some strange pharmaceuticals.

*strength*
*p. 324*

They killed Jerry. I don't care what the official record is. Jerry may have physically done the deed, but he wasn't home when it happened.

Do you see it now? Rose Bay -> Terra Ternaria -> Trinity Pharmacopoeia. They're all the same. Versai isn't listed on the BOD or officers list for Trinity Pharmacopoeia, but I know he's involved.

oldmanwinter@ . . . has been warning us all along, and this is why. Versai's research has always been about mind-control drugs, regardless of what his company's stated goals are.

Daryl. Someone find him, before it's too late.

-(pk)

FROM: terminalx@ . . .
TO: alt.oneirology.entheogens
SUB: RE: RE: RE: RE: RE: Looking for Goldwhite@ . . .

>> Bernard Versai is listed on the Board of Directors for Terra Ternaria. You guys probably don't know who he is since he's been off the radar for, like, thirty years but I do.

Ah, Phil? Versai died nine years ago. I get about 8000 hits from Google that say he died in a boating accident. Even Wikipedia agrees. Trinity Pharmacopoeia didn't even exist back then.
Whatever you think he's done, it's all gone. The man is worm food now. Er, was. Probably not much left after all these years.

-t to the x

----------------------------------

FROM: oldmanwinter@ . . .
TO: alt.oneirology.entheogens
SUB: RE: RE: RE: RE: RE: RE: Looking for Goldwhite@ . . .

>> I get about 8000 hits from Google that say he died in a boating accident.

An equal number of newspaper articles said much the same thing about my father. Don't believe everything you read.
You should devote your energies to finding your fellow oneironaut Daryl. He is in more danger than you know. His system is already weakened. Should he take those supplements, he will be transformed.

-Brother J

* fire
p. 201

290

# RADIO
♍

* 33131342 14361419231933, 34132738371424232132141923 1933 3213 24382132 18132737. 1714 383714 2213271932231933 42131719 3213 3124143815 38143713. 23 17232424 3114 34132737 18132132; 23 17232424 3114 321814 3613232214 1325 371438211319 381942 22131629382121231319. 1634 1713374221 17232424 3114 34132737 381922181337. 2319 3218142114 24382132 42383421, 2319 32182321 24382132 18132737, 23 17232424 33233614 341327 18132914. 23 17232424 33233614 341327 371438211319. 23 17232424 33233614 341327 38 221838192214. 242321321419 22241321142434, 1634 42143837 2218232442371419, 251337 34132737 2423361421 383714 36143734 3137231425.

1714 383714 382424 293837322322232938193221 2319 38 332413313824 14352914372316141932, 38 1713372442-17234214 3237233824 1718143714 3218143714 2321 1913 22131932371324 3337132729. 32182321 2321 321814 211422371432 1325 132737 24143842143721182329.   341327  223819  22131631  321814 1416293234 212938221421 2319 3218142337 143529144223141932 3718143213372322,        42383238        16231914        3218142337 1718232129-14371442        29181319142213193614372138 3223131 921, 381942 14361419 143836142142371329 1319 3218142337 1623421923331832 16133819231933 3821 32181434 222423163835 382424 13361437 321814 21223837371442 31142424231421 1325 3218142337 171813371421, 312732 341327 171319'32 25231942 381934 384216232121231319 1325 3218142337 211422371432 383314194238. 32181434 383714 321313 222414361437 251337 32183832, 321313 3113271942 3134 3218142337 131719 2938223221 381942 311432373834382421 3213 3842162332 321814 3237273218 1325 17183832 32181434 18383614 42131914.

321814   3124131342    183821   4237231442   3832    321814 311332321316  1325  321814  29383314  1718143714  382424 3218233732141419    21233319383227371421    383714    2319 2924382214. 321814 2132383721 383714 38242333191442, 321814 1337421437 2321 15142932, 381942 321814 1718141424 183821 31141419 211432 2319 161332231319. 382424 32183832 2321

*summons
p. 328

24142532 2321 34132737 293837322322223293832231319. 34132737. 213822372325232214. 2321. 3714262723371442.

2332 17232424 183829291419. 2319 2523253234 16231927321421. 32182321 2321 321814 24382132 18132737. 32231614 141913273318 251337 271942143721323381942231933. 32231614 141913273318 251337 131914 24382132 15232121, 131914 24382132 23192132381932 1325 25371414 17232424. 341421, 292732 34132737 143837 2224132114 3213 321814 21291438151437. 25141424 2332 36233137383214 38333823192132 34132737 24133114. 321814 31273838 1325 1634 24232921, 321814 18272118 1325 1634 23191838243832231319. 25141424 1634 3213272218. 32182321 17232424 3114 132737 2523372132 381942 24382132 222438194214213223191914 37141942143836132721, 132737 212319332414 23242423222332 16141432231933 1718143714 1634 24232921 381942 34132737 143837 17232424 18383614 22131932382232. 341421, 25272424 22131932382232. 1913 29371332142232231319, 1913 232424272123131921, 1913 32273719231933 38173834 3832 321814 24382132 211422131942 (341421, 341327 16272132 191332 252423192218 17181419 321814 32231614 2213161421). 32182321 17232424 32381514 312732 38 251417 16131614193221. 2332 171319'32 18273732 (373832181437, 191332 3821 16272218 3821 341327 1623331832 3218231915). 341327 17232424 24231514 2332. 341327 17232424 17381932 3213 4213 2332 3833382319.

32183832 37272118 341327 383714 25141424231933? 32183832 2321 14353822322434 17183832 32181434 17381932 341327 3213 25141424. 32181434 17381932 341327 3213 21272222271631 3213 321814 2514322342 18143832 1325 34132737 3124131342, 3213 321814 381923163824 421421233714 1325 34132737 2213221521 381942 2227193221. 32181434 17381932 341327 3213 1325251437 34132737 14383721, 34132737 161327321821, 34132737 4223373234 211422371432 1813241421, 251337 32181416 3213 25272215. 292732 2332 2319, 341327 16133819, 341421, 292732 2332 2319 191317. 23 17381932 2332. 23 17381932 2332 2113 3138422434.

2513373234   16231927321421   191317.   4213   341327
27194214372132381942   181317   341327   18383614   31141419
16381923292724383321442?   181317   341327   18383614   31141419
22181438321442? 23 1325251437 341327 38 221838192214 251337
25371414 17232424, 251337 321814 27193714213237383191442
4214321437162319383223319 1325 34132737 131719 21132724,
381942 341327 2132232424 24143829 3213 251324241317 1634
24143842. 23 32142424 341327 3213 1325251437 3413273721142425
381942 341327 4213, 17233218132732 32181327331832 381942
17233218132732   381934   381738371419142121   1325   321814
22131925272123131 9 2319   1634   212914142218.   3124143815
38143713   17232424   32381514   34132737   1623194221,   381942
16132132 1325 341327 171319'32 14361419 16232121 32181416.
341327    17381932    3213    25141424    211316143218231933?
341421, 32183832 2321 33131342. 38 3714382232231319 2321
2132232424 382232231319, 321813273318 2332 2321 1913 382232
1325   2237143832231319.   1714   18383614   251337331332321419
17183832 2332 173821 24231514 3213 2938373223222329383214
2319 33141914212321. 3218132114 1614161337231421, 24231514
321814 2513371621 1325 38192223141932 2918232413211329 1834,
383714   41272132   38312132373822322313 1921   191317.   382424
32183832 1714 18383614 24142532 2321 21183842131721 1325
21183842131721.   1714   3714382232   31142238272114   2332   2321
321814 31142132 14221813 1714 18383614 1325 2237143832231319.   * echoes<br>p. 186
2332 2321 321814 13192434 14221813.

32181434   17232424   32381514   32183832   38173834   25371316
341327   3821   17142424.   341327   171319'32   25141424   321814
24132121   3821   2332   18382929141921   31142238272114   2332
2321 3819 13373338192322 29132434161437 41272132 38 251417
223837311319   381942   133534331419   3832131621   38173834
25371316   321814   213238372218   2319   34132737   3137143842
381942 221437143824. 341327   171319'32   15191317 32183832
2332 2321 2319 34132737 3124131342 31142238272114 34132737
3124131342 17232424 382222142932 2332 24231514 3819 132442

253723141942. 341327 171319'32 15191317 32183832 2332 183821 3832323822181442 233221142425 3213 34132737 191427373824 2938321817383421 31142238272114 32181434 17232424 41272132 363819232118 25371316 34132737 222337222723323734. 341327 171319'32 15191317.

321823373234    16231927321421    191317.    32181434'3614 38243714384234 292732 2332 2319 321814 1738321437. 2332'21 3114231933 361419321442 23193213 321814 21323714143221 3821 23 2129143815, 372321231933 2729 32183713273318 321814 2132133716 333738321421 381942 16381918132414 221336143721. 14361437343218231933    17232424    41272132    21141416    38 242332322414 18143836231437, 38 242332322414 171432321437, 38 242332322414 16133714 24231514 22183723213263821 381942 38 242332322414 24142121 24231514 191417 34143837'21.

292732 34132737 143837 19143532 3213 321814 21291438151437. 23 17381932 3213 21242329 1634 321319332714 2319 34132737 143837. 23 17381932 3213 3213272218 34132737 3137382319, 41272132 13192214 311425133714 2332 2413211421 233221 32141921231319    381942    25241435233312324233234.    341421, 41272132 13192214. 242321321419 3213 1614. 341327 17232424

* love
p. 71

251337331432 17183832 2332 2321 3213 24133614 381942 3114 2413361442; 341327 17232424 251337331432 181317 321814 1713372442    1738372921    17181419    341327    222423163835. 341327 17232424 251337331432 181317 3213 3238213214 321814 2117143832 1325 38191332181437 381942 25231942 382424 1325 34132737 1813291421 381942 2514383721 381942 423714381621 1623373713371442 2319 3218142337 1738321437. 341327 17232424 251337331432    181317    1714    383714    131914    32183832    183821 31141419 2129242332 23193213 321713.

341327 17232424 251337331432. 17181419 321814 3124143815 38143713 2213161421.

17141429 17233218 1614. 251337 2332 2321 382424 32183832 1714 223819 4213 3213331432181437 191317. 321814 24382132 18132737 2321 27291319 2721, 381942 2332 2321 173819231933

191317. 21181818. 23 15191317. 3218143714 2321 2113 16272218 24142532 271942131914, 24142532 271921382342, 24142532 27192523192321181442. 3218143714 17232424 382417383421 31141419 38223221 24142532 27193714382423381442. 32182321 321814 14221813 24142532 3213 2721, 321814 2218232442371419 171813 18383614 251337331332321419 2237143832231319. 32183832 211419213832231319 1325 *children 23192213162924143214191421217? 341421, 32183832 17232424 p. 169 382417383421 3114 17233218 2721.

2719322324 321814 3124143815 38143713. 2719322324 34132737 213822372325232214 2321 27291319 341327. 32183832 2321 17183832 32181434 21141415 3213 4237131719, 17183832 32181434 21141415 3213 15232424. 32183832 161416133734 1325 321814 14221813 1325 321814 211838421317. 17181419 321837232214-37141613361442 331342 2321 33131914, 17183832 17232424 3114 24142532?

23 17232424 16232121 341327 321313. 3213272218 321814 21291438151437. 2937142121 3413273721142425 38333823192132 2332. 23 3816 41272132 1319 321814 1332181437 21234214. 2113 36143734 2224132114. 2319 3218142114 24382132 321714193234 16231927321421, 1714 383714 3213331432181437, 341327 381942 23. 1714 383714 3218231915231933 321814 21381614 3218132733183221, 25141424231933 321814 21381614 321837232424 381942 42142129382337 2319 132737 181438373221.

341421, 23 31142423143614 2319 34132737 4223362319233234, 381942 23 17381932 341327 3213 21181317 2332 3213 1614. 341421, 21181317 1614. 241432 1614 211414 34132737 33134218143842. 16381514 2332 131914 24382132 32231614.

23 15191317 341327 3714161416311437.

23 3816 2113 2224132114. 341327 223819 25231942 1614. *eyes 3218143714 383714 4213133721 14361437341718143714. p. 197 23 3816 311418231942 382424 1325 32181416.

# RAIN

FROM: heron74@ . . .
TO: alt.oneirology.entheogens
SUB: Rain

I dreamed last night.

I haven't "dreamed," in the normal sense of the word, for about four years now. Usually, I just drift on the fringe of Aserinsky, and that's deep enough. When I need to sleep, I take Rozerem—which, surprisingly, works pretty well for me. But dreams? Not for me anymore.

Which is what makes last night so unusual. More so by the impression that it wasn't my dream. It didn't seem like a Bleak Zero hallucination; I'm not exhibiting any of the other symptoms that have been charted. It was just . . . a vision? I've done some research today on visionary experiences—real accounts, mind you, not some of that crap that fills the Pop Occulture shelves at the mega-bookstores—and I'm, well . . . on the off-chance that I'm completely paranoid, I want to tell the rest of you about this dream before . . . well, anyway, here's the dream.

I'm in my trailer, and its raining outside. I can hear it, like steel ball bearings, on the roof. Big heavy drops. The kind we don't see until late in the spring. I look out the window and the whole world is covered with white fog. The rain drops are heavy and hot, like bright cinders falling from a distant volcanic eruption. In each of their wakes, the clouds are gone, and I can see blue and green and red. It's like each drop takes away a little more of the dense cloud cover.

I put on my heavy boots, and a thick wool coat. It gets pretty cold here in the mountains. The winter winds sneak down early. Geared up, I step out of my trailer, and the landscape is completely different.

I like where I live. I like the isolation, and the view. I like the fact that my neighbors are just as eccentric as I am. I like the fact that, other than a half-conversation struck up one afternoon out by the communal mailboxes, I don't known anything about them.

But, now, I'm even more isolated. As the rain continues to wash

*bleak zero
p. 162*

away the fog, I see that my trailer is the only manmade object for miles and miles. The ground is flat, much flatter than it should be, and there's nothing but yellow wheat all the way to the horizon. My trailer is in a tiny clearing, an irregular patch of white sand where the grain can't grow.

* IX

The rain starts up again. It's coming down really hard, as if each drop were trying to brain me, and I duck back inside the trailer. The last of the fog goes quickly, and the rain becomes a spectacular light show—lots of rainbows, scattering sheets of color, stars fall like the firework show they'd throw at the end of the world. It's really amazing, and much more vivid than anything I can remember.

And then, it's over. Each stalk of wheat is left holding aloft one or more rain drops, and with the sun shining on these drops, the whole field becomes a sea of shimmering scales. Like I'm riding on a giant fish.

* fish
p. 203

I go back outside again, and the air smells so clean and pure. I've been out of the city for some time now, breathing the mountain air quite regularly, but this is something else. Something like you'd imagine the air smelled before man showed up. And I'm standing on my front step, breathing in, when the scarecrow sneaks out of the wheat.

* scarecrow
p. 303

He tip-toes across the open space around my trailer, and when he notices that I've seen him, he puts a finger to his lips. When I nod, acknowledging his request for silence, he looks over his shoulder and waves to someone still hiding in the wheat. He continues to creep slowly across the yard, as if he still thinks he's invisible by stint of being so quiet, but he is quickly surrounded by a flood of other scarecrows that come tearing out of the grain field.

I heard them coming, really, but hadn't copped to what the noise was. I had thought it was thunder, you know, the distant rumble of a storm that's an hour away still. But it was getting louder, and after he gave them the all-clear sign, it got really noisy very quickly.

The first one is the odd one, dressed more like a businessman than a simple farmer, and the others wear simplified versions of that same outfit: white shirt, gray slacks, but no tie or jacket. Some of the scare-

* fool
p. 204

crows are bigger, some are smaller; some wear floppy straw hats, some wear beanies and berets, a few are in jester caps with bells and ribbons. All them, however, wear the red and yellow gloves. I couldn't count them: the trickle turned into a flood, which exploded into a deluge. There were so many at one point that they seemed to be like the wheat—a full field, swaying in the wind. Eventually, they began to thin, trickling down to a few stranglers.

The last one limped. And he was the only one with a crown instead of a hat.

* spirtual armor p. 323

The miming one waited on the edge of the wheat, and when the crippled one had limped into the stalks, he raised his finger to his lips again. It was a peculiar motion, I realized: index finger extended, other fingers wrapped around something in his hand. Whatever it was, he dropped it there on the ground before he went into the wheat field.

* IV

I stepped out onto the white sand to retrieve it, and the rains came back. Not like before, this was a deluge of black water. In a second, the field around my trailer was a swamp of tarry sludge, visibility was about six inches, and it was cold. Really cold. I dashed back into my trailer, and as the rain blew the door shut behind me, I woke up.

Maybe one of you guys can unpack the symbols there, or give me an idea how I managed to slip into someone else's dream without knowing them. I'm going to see if I can scare up some K out here in the wilderness. It always gave me better control. I need to be ready tonight, in case the dream comes back.

-(pk)

"We'd all be taken more seriously if we had black halos."
-Jerry McElholn

# RIVER

## ♓

Rivers figure predominantly as barriers and as symbols of transformation. Heraclitus believed you could never step in the same river twice, arguing for a forward progression of time that has never been fully expelled from the human sub-consciousness. Children are drowned in slow, muddy rivers. As adults, they are resurrected in those same waters.

*duality
matrix
p. 185*

John was an Opener of Ways. He was the first to step into a stream, and create a threshold through which others could pass. *I baptize you in the name of the Father, the Son, and the Holy Spirit.*

*son
p. 317*

Rivers carry away the dead, and offer a means to escape time. Drowning is a failed alchemical effort, a washing of the gross material of humanity that fails to produce the next reagent.

*yellow
p. 365*

LAERTES: Alas, then she is drown'd
GERTRUDE: Drown'd, drown'd.
LAERTES: Too much water has thou, poor Opheila.△

---

△ - Shakespeare, *Hamlet*, IV.vii.183-185

# SACRIFICE

✗

Philip Kendrick wakes up in his comfortable chair. He is wearing his favorite robe, a dark blue kimono—the one given to him by a biker with an angel tattoo, more than twenty years ago during a febrile weekend, lost in the Mohave Desert outside Needles. He has kicked off one of his slippers. His right foot is cold, as the bedroom window is open. He can smell the sea, which is how he knows he is still dreaming because his mobile home is on a lot just south of Rigby, Idaho.

There is a light perched on the edge of his bed, waiting patiently for him to wake up.

His mouth is dry and his fingers are numb, a sure sign that he has taken a Line-Dose of K, and his back is sore. He wets his lips several times, until he can feel both his tongue and his teeth again. "Who are you?" he asks the light.

*tongue
p. 44

**Trinity.**

Phil tries to smile. "Father, Son, and Holy Ghost? Here to judge me?"

**No.**

"That unworthy?" He sinks back in the chair, focusing on his right foot. His toes wriggle toward his discarded slipper, trying to worm their way back into the fleece-lined warmth.

**No.**

"I always thought God would be like Jerry Garcia," Phil says. "That would be nice, like getting a backstage pass to the last show. You know?" His foot finds its way into his slipper.

*summons
p. 328

"What about the others?" he asks. "Can they be saved?"

**By me? No.**

Beneath the K and the ever-present hum of LSD echoes, Phil can feel the burnblack bite of the Bleak Zero. "What is left of me to save?" he wonders.

**Everything.**

Phil laughs uncontrollably at that idea. His lips finally slide back under his control, and they twist around the dry humor rising in his throat.

The light glints and hardens, and Phil focuses on the offered knife. It isn't one of his; in fact, it's a blade unlike any he's ever seen—rainbow-polished ceramic with a hilt of twisted bone. "It's beautiful," he says as he takes it from the light. *x*

The blade is very sharp, and the bead of blood is bright red on the ball of his thumb. *mass confusa p. 252*

His face is suddenly warm, and he realizes he is crying. Through the refraction of his tears, he sees beyond the light. He sees through the shadow. The woman standing before him is wrapped with long panels of colored silk, and her smile is both sad and hungry.

"I'm sorry I wasn't strong enough, Harry," Phil says. "I'm sorry I was afraid."

**We all are. It's why we invented language.**

"Yes," he says. The knife taps against his leg, an unconscious twitch of his fingers. "I suppose so. I . . . I wish . . . "

**I wanted the same thing, in the end. We all do.**

He nods and, in a swift motion, he raises the knife to his throat and cuts once, left to right. It hurts more than he expects, and he gasps. Blood bubbles from his lips, foam drawn up from the gap in his neck. His hindbrain scrambles. He can feel it clawing and fighting in the back of his head, the lizard part of his body struggling to survive in the sudden lack of oxygen and blood.

The light envelops him. He feels her arms around him, and he lets his head fall back, exposing the bloody fault of his neck to her.

Philip Kendrick feels the touch of her mouth on his skin, the sucking sensation of her lips as she drinks his blood, as she takes in the drugs, the life, and the memories that are flooding out of his dying flesh. *memory p. 253*

He is back in the hospital again, caught in the dark folds of the fabric. *Jerry*, he thinks, the thought fading even as it forms, *wait for me . . .*

**Falling star**, she whispers to his vanishing spirit, **fall no more.**

The fabric tightens around him, and it is soft and warm. Phil tugs it closer, shutting out the light. *fabric p. 56*

What happens to stars when they fall into the sea? Do they stop burning? Do they stop falling?

Everything becomes dark—deepdark, past the burning blackness—and Phil remembers he never made it back to the yard. He never learned the scarecrow's secret.

**If you ask why, then you will be granted access; if you ask how, then you will be granted passage.**

**All labyrinths have but one path, and that path goes down.**

# SCARECROW
## Ω

I had a patient who was terrified of scarecrows. Scarecrows are just effigies, I explained to her, stuffed doppelgängers meant to terrify crows. They're just patchwork, straw-filled dummies, even if their smiles are off-kilter. I suggested the best way to turn any such symbolic monster into a buffoon was to watch *The Wizard of Oz* while listening to *The Dark Side of the Moon*. While baked out of her mind, of course. It is much easier to see how the scarecrow is a loose-limbed imbecile, I told her, when you're listening to Floyd and re-breathing a marijuana haze. She wasn't impressed, but the suggestion did break the ice enough that when I told her my actual plan for curing her, she didn't walk out on me.

*double
p. 390*

Her scarecrows were filled with rats, and their smiles were filled with holes that the rats peeked out through. I know because we went in to her Oneiroi and faced not one, but three. They all wore the same style of overalls, with knotted rags hanging out through broken zippers. When we had dispersed all the rats and rendered the strawmen impotent, I untied the knots in one of the rags and showed her the three symbols burned in the fabric.

"Maybe it is time you told someone," I suggested, and she agreed. She went back to her regular therapist, who suggested a support group that was very effective.

I told this anecdote to Nora, during one of our early sessions. Before we went into the Oneiroi together. She wanted to know how I had helped someone, wanted some reassurance that I wasn't going to take advantage of her while I was in her dreams.

Funny, that. I think she's in mine now, and she is taking advantage of me. I'm not sure how, being that she is dead and all. But there's a symbolic trail being laid out, a path through this maze (**no, Harry, a labyrinth**) that I am meant to follow.

*labyrinth
p. 417*

A yellow-brick road, perhaps. I do feel like the scarecrow at the crossroad. We could go that way. Or that way. Or that way. Tangling myself in knots.

*tangle
p. 332*

**Maybe it is time you told someone.**

No. That won't liberate me.

# SCHIZOPHRENIA
## ♓

*ego
p. 188

The literature calls it a "splitting of the ego," a "division of sense," and a "psychosis of identity." The literature is, of course, in the business of perpetuating its own existence, so it is not unexpected that it is filled with reflexive terminology and self-referential phraseology. The schizophrenic, to the modern dull-witted psychologist, is a victim. He or she is trapped in a schism of denial.

"Curing" a schizophrenic through regimented psychopharmacology is equivalent to cutting off a hand in order to stop a patient from chewing his nails. Like many of the solutions offered by the unenlightened community of "professionals," the prevention and cure

*negligence
p. 259

of psychotic behavior through psychopharmacology, electro-shock therapy, and other, cruder, psychological techniques is tantamount to fixing a chip in a delicate china cup by smashing it with a sledgehammer and then gluing all the pieces back together.

Resolving schizophrenic breaks is a matter of repairing broken duality pairings. There are twelve symbolic references that all schizophrenic breaks deviate from, and it is matter of re-mapping the patient's confused neural fabric to the existing patterns.

*twelve
p. 355

# SECRET CODE

## ♍

"Do you remember our secret code?"

We are on swings, arcing back and forth across a rectangle of red cedar chips. The trees, a green border along the edge of the field, sway back and forth in time with our motion. She is wearing a bright yellow skirt, stitched with the oval shape of lemons, and the bunched fabric flutters beneath her seat as she flies.

"We never had one."

My knees are a patchwork of scabs, the perpetual marks of small boy clumsiness. I am wearing white sneakers and, even though my feet are off the ground, tiny lights are flashing front and back. As if the air pressure of my motion is enough to trigger the sensors in the soles of the shoes.

*\* wombwhite*
*p. 364*

"Of course we did. Everyone has one." She laughs. "You are so goofy." Said with a twelve-year old's mix of dismissal and adoration. Her hair streams beyond her, a cloud of spun honey.

"Why would we need it?"

"In case one of us gets lost," she explains. "In case one of us turns into a ghost."

At the top of her arc, she leaps out of the swing. Arms out, hair and skirt becoming wings. The world stutters, wombwhite flickers like the projector bulb shining through breaks in the film strip, and she becomes a flood of pale moths.

*\* moth*
*p. 258*

I snap out of my swing too, jack-knifing into a raven. My joints pop and my skin itches as black feathers bloom. "Which one?" I caw, as I fly after the stream of moths. "Which one of us?"

*\* bloom*
*p. 386*

The moths fly west, leaving the park. As they stream over the old fairground, the lights come on. The calliope coughs, dust flying out of its tubes. Colors flicker and bend in the reflections of the fun-house mirrors. The Ferris wheel creaks and groans, ash sifting off its aged joints. A balloon-faced giant gets to his knees, air swelling his hips and chest. The rollercoaster starts to chatter as it struggles up its long incline.

Down near a row of tents, she waits for me, wreathed in ribbons, white stars piercing her ears and navel. She laughs and claps as I shed

*\* VII*

* father
p. 198

my fathers—no, *feathers*—and land beside her. The carnie behind the counter is a glazed cut-out of a famous movie star in his most well-known role. "Three tosses, two dollars," he cries out as I walk up to the counter.

"But I always know it is you, regardless of the face you are wearing," I say to her. "Why do I need a secret recognition code?"

"You think you do," she says. "You think we've all been the same person."

"But you are," I say. Beneath the tattered canvas roof is a square field of liquid-filled jars. The fluid is brightly colored—red, yellow, green, lavender, cerulean—and the dispersal of colors is a complicated statistical array. There's a pattern here, of course, but it's too obtuse for me.

* yellow
p. 365

She laughs at my confusion, and as her right hand snakes into the loose pocket of my pants, she puts her cheek against my shoulder. "Just because we are echoes of echoes doesn't mean we don't prefer the illusion."

"Which illusion?"

* confusion
p. 388

Her hand slips between my legs and grabs me. "Identity."

Like a magician producing a rabbit from a hat, she removes her hand from my pocket. Two gold coins lie in her unlined palm. I stare at her hand. *Can I not give it life?* I wonder. No lines, therefore no future, no past, no fate. Like a piece of stone, free of the deterministic design. Are all the specters of my imagination simply ghosts of the present moment?

She tosses the coins at the cardboard carnie, who makes no move to catch them, and they bounce off his coated surface. "Three throws," he crows. "No leaning. No spitting." A trio of rubber balls, arranged in a precise triangle, appear on the old board of the counter. They are stamped with constellations.

* triangle
p. 353

She giggles. "Win me a prize."

I squeeze one of the balls, feeling its textured resilience. It is warm in my hand. Surveying the field of mason jars behind the carnie, I consider where to throw the ball. There are goldfish in some of the jars, and now that I look more closely at them ("No leaning!"), I can see that each jar has a small silver plate on it, inscribed with fine lettering.

Too ornate—too obtuse—to read from where I'm standing. Of course.

I toss the first ball underhand, and it ricochets off one glass—shattering the rim—and skips across several others before landing with a splash of lime green water. She squeals with delight, clutching my arm, and the carnie loudly announces that I appear to not be a complete klutz.

I overcompensate with the second ball, and it skips off the far side of the rack of jars. The third arcs up, seems to flex as if it is gathering breath before diving, and plummets into a yellow-tinted jar. "Two!" the carnie says, his voice a roar of incredulity. No one, apparently, has ever—in his lifetime, in this total span of time of this game's existence—has ever scored twice. I am supposed to get swept up in the miracle; I'm supposed to let her dig into my pocket for more coins.

**Win me a prize.**

"What do I get?" I ask the cardboard cut-out.

"Your choice," he says, and a black monkey wearing a feathered cat and a yellow vest leaps onto the table. It has a stained burlap sack in its hands, and it trusts it at me. The opening is wide enough for my hand, but not wide enough to get a glimpse of what is in the sack.

It wiggles in the animal's grip. In a way that doesn't quite match up with the monkey's light-footed dance.

"What did I get?" I ask again, pointing at the two balls floating in the jars.

The monkey shrieks, shaking the sack at me. I shove it off the counter, and it flips onto the rack of glasses. Sullenly, it wakes across the narrow tops of the mason jars, and bends over to read the labels on the two jars.

"*Lux!*" The carnie shouts, translating the monkey's screeches. "*Fiat!*"  *dawn
p. 385

"See?" she says. "We do have a secret code."

* hermit
p. 217

"*Fiat lux*," I say. "The first words of the Latin Vulgate?"

"Yes," she says, but she is shaking her head.

The monkey dips a paw into the grimy sack and pulls out a squirming insect. Cackling, it holds it over one of the jars, and watches it smoke as it melts in the blue liquid.

I let her drag me away. "I must have lost my Enigma-class decoder ring somewhere," I mutter as her ephemeral spirit pulls me toward the sky-scraping Ferris wheel. "Or maybe it is still in the cereal box."

"Nothing is in the box, love," she says. "Everything was let out a long time ago."

# SERPENT
〰

Why do snakes shed their skins?

For an answer, I want to point you to the story of the tail-devourer, the serpent who was God's first Creation. Self-sufficient, the tail-devourer was perfection, an immortal creature of perpetual existence: when it hungered, it ate its own flesh; when it grew thirsty, it drank its own sweat. It simply turned and turned and turned and had no needs other than its own.

But God—that infallible Creator—well, God did not grow bored with the tail-devourer, nor did He admit to failure in its creation (because it was perfect, so how could that be considered a failure?). Nevertheless God decided to Create another creature. One that wasn't quite as self-sufficient. If the tail-devourer was the perfect circle, the zero, the aleph (and, quite possibly, as it devoured its own end, the taw), then his second Creation would be one—the first, the Indivisible.

*deceit*
*p. 180*

He named this Creation His shadow.

If the serpent who crawls on the ground and hides in the brush is but a symbol of the tail-devourer, of God's infinitely perfect creation, then what is its cast-off skin?

*mirage*
*p. 256*

Yes, what are all those things we throw away? The accretions of experience that we leave behind us like flakes of dry skin. The memories we collect out of instinctual reflex but that we store so shabbily. What are these histories we leave behind?

*history*
*p. 22*

# SILENCE

ஃ

FROM: sparkly_wonder@ . . .
TO: alt.oneirology.entheogens
SUB: Silence

You know, oldmanwinter@ . . . may seem like a cranky old man, but what if he is right? Hang with me a sec on this one. We've had our fair share of crazies on the list over the years (sp0rz@ . . ., anyone?), and I'm inclined—who isn't?—to throw up some filters and deflect these lunatics into myspam bin. But, after last weekend, well . . .I'm more inclined to think that oldmanwinter@ . . . knows what he is talking about.

* bleak zero
p. 162

I've seen something. Maybe it was Bleak Zero. Maybe it was something worse . . .

I was tagging along with some friends (my ex- and her new boyfriend, actually; she called me earlier that day and, all our differences aside, wanted my professional opinion on some of these people) to a party up in the Highland Park area. In this neighborhood, every party is an industry party; you see your usual sycophants, wanna-bes, hangers-on, and groupies all engaged in the normal sort of shit you see at these parties: drinking cheap beer, knocking over furniture, fucking in the pool, dropping acid in the bushes out back of the house. Not my sort of party, as you can guess. Anyway, it all looked pretty typical—annoying and exhausting, sure, but pretty run-of-the-mill.

After about an hour of wandering through the various rooms in this house—fucking palatial, by the way, must have been 8000 square feet plus on three levels—I come across my ex's new beau and some friends of his. They're all clustered in a walk-in closet in one of the unused guest rooms, passing around some sort of atomizer/inhaler. I didn't get a chance to really look at the device, but it had a hand crank and a flanged front-end that cupped over the nose.

The boyfriend, by virtue of being my new best friend since we rode over to this party together, offers me a hit, and he shows me how to work it. I politely pass, saying that I had enough drugs of my own. I didn't like how some of the others were tweaking: unconscious finger

movements, lip spasms, phantasmal object tracking, and this twitching pull of their noses as if they were rabbits pretending to sneer like
washed-up rock stars.

I excuse myself before the mood turns in this little room, and go
find my ex. As I'm looking for her, I start to notice that others are
showing these symptoms—the lip movements, the eyes tracking on
things that aren't there, the twitching noses—and, by the time I find
my ex, I'm starting to think that maybe these guys in the closet are
patient zero in this little hot zone. Whatever they're inhaling, it's still
toxic when it comes back out of them. They're breathing it out, and it
is gradually seeping through everyone's pores.

I can't find my ex, and I'm starting to freak out a bit. I duck into a
bathroom and rifle through the cabinets and—holy fuck!—you would
not believe the pharmacy I found. I build myself an ad hoc psychic
shield, swallow it, and sit down to wait for it to take effect.

*spiritual armor p. 323*

That's when I realize how quiet it has gotten. There's no music, no
laughter, none of that buzz of voices that reminds you how not-alone
we are all the time. It's just dead quiet. As if the world has ceased to
exist outside this bathroom. For a minute, I think I've fucked the dosage or that the bottles didn't contain what the labels said they did, but
then I start to feel that dull throb of the Oneiroi around my wrists and
ankles. My armor is working.

I come out of the bathroom, and the whole house is still, like one of
those freeze frames you see in the movies. But everyone isn't immo-
bile, they're just waiting. As I walk past a couple in the hallway, frozen in mid-grope, I see their eyes track me. I've become the invisible phantasm that they allsee but don't realize they do. It's like this
throughout the house: everyone is watching me, everyone is waiting.
At first, I think I've fallen into the Oneiroi, and that I'm walking on
some level of the collective fabric of the house, but everything is too
solid, too immutable. I have no control; I'm still in my flesh.

*bare p. 156*

Then the whispering starts.

No one's lips move, but I can hear their voices. And they're all
whispering the same thing, like they're reading off the same script.

311

Total gibberish. I can't even remember it well enough to try to recreate it. But they're all in sync.

I ran. It was fucking terrifying. All I remember is wanting to get out of there. I went for the front door, and the next thing I can remember is being in the back of a cab in Santa Monica. I asked the cab driver where he picked me up, and he pretended to not understand English. He just dropped me off at the end of the Promenade (as if I had asked to be let off there), and took off.

I don't know what happened at that party. I don't know what everyone was on, but it was really strange. Really strange. I've been trying to get in touch with my ex-girlfriend for two days now, and I can't reach her. I . . . yeah . . .I don't know what to do.

-L

"We take it for granted that our dreams spring from below; possibly the quality of our dreams suffers in consequence." (T. S. Eliot)

----------------------------------

FROM: terminalx@...
TO: alt.oneirology.entheogens
SUB: RE: Silence

>>I don't know what to do.

How about an organic smoothie? Something with wheatgrass and a vitamin pack? A little potassium and vitamin C might be just the thing to clear out the cobwebs from your acid trip. You did say people were doing tabs at this party, right? Are you sure they didn't just spike the punch bowl, and you had a few more than you should have?

Look, we've all overdosed. I think it's a necessary rite of passage to get on this list. But there's also a responsibility there: cast no FUD with wild stories of our hallucinatory experiences.

* psychonaut
p. 12

312

At least, not without prefacing them as being "stories under the influence."

Reality's a little thin as it is. Don't be stretching it unnecessarily.

But, to not be an asshole entirely, let's say your story's all true. What did you mix up in the bathroom? Are you sure you didn't do this to yourself?

-t to the x

----------------------------------

FROM: sparkly_wonder@...
TO: alt.oneirology.entheogens
SUB: RE: RE: Silence

Chicken sausage. Giblets. Giblets. Would you like fries with that? Ocelot ossification leads to publication petrifaction. Get our brochure now! Abattoir / Abattoir / Bake me a little longer. Bite the lance, drink from the cup, where was the body hid? The white light obscures the black mystery. Now serving number 22. Now serving. Serving. Now. 22. Minus one. So close, little children. Eat your emulsions. Are your gallstones keeping you up at night? Try ######. Our representatives are standing by. Outside yourwindow. Inside your garage. Fucking your garbage, cocks wrapped in banana peel condoms. Bipartisan libertines make sweet cake. Don't leave me. Don't believe me. Loveme anyway, and I will love you long time. Try our mail-order brides. Try our mail-order pets. Try it. Try it! Tryittryittryittryit. Is the world the oyster or the pearl? Stamp prices are going up; have you mailed everything? What is left? Slip it to me. Right on the tongue. I hold the key. Ramble on, abandonone, babble on. I am coming. Pffft! Just a little mess. Just a little stain. Our new product can get that out. "You lack the season of all natures, sleep." Lie down, lie down. Give me your hand.

----------------------------------

FROM: terminalx@...
TO: alt.oneirology.entheogens
SUB: RE: RE: RE: Silence

Nice. That was really fucking mature.

This spam shit is starting to get on my nerves. Okay, if this is a joke, I'm laughing. Ha ha. If you all want to call me out, just do it already. This passive aggressive spam response to my emails is just infantile.

*spam
p. 318

-t to the x

# SNOW
## Ω

Of all the seasons, I always loved winter the most as a kid. It always meant school was closed, and for us young boys, that was never a loss. We would stay outdoors all day—building forts, engaging in guerrilla warfare with snowballs, peeling our flesh off the metal fences that surrounded the park, pretending the world had been purified of the dirty colors. It was heaven for a child, and we stayed in it as long as we could. Angels desperate for time in the lap of their Father.

Archie—Archibald Nuesting—was obsessed with building forts, and every year when the snow was thick enough, you could see him out on his lawn with a shovel and flat piece of metal. He would use the scrap metal to calve off rectangular pieces. Then, over the next few hours—and I helped him on more than one occasion—he would build this year's outpost—a sprawling series of tunnels and hollows that would turn his lawn into an above-ground mole hill. When he was finished, we would sit in the center of his maze, disguised from outside eyes. It was here, in this secret world, that we would tell stories.

Archibald went back east for college. He returned for a few months following graduation, but the reunions with family and friends was awkward, and he didn't stay long. Shortly thereafter, his mother shared with my mother a press clipping from *The New York Times*. Archie—Archibald again—had become an in-house architect for a construction and composition company.

I saw the company name recently. They had been hired to construct the new world headquarters of Trinity Pharmacopoeaia. It had been many years since I had seen or heard from Archie, and I wondered if he was building snow forts for his children at Christmas now.

Now, so far from those days, winter has a different hold on me. I have been too deep into the Oneiroi, touched the nightmares of too many naturalists, biologists, and indigents. Winter is their bogeyman, the hidden terror that haunts their dreams. Most of the highly educated ones fear the end of the calendar year the most, as if they really aren't sure that winter will end.

Snow is like the Oneiroi: too many permutations, too many vari-

* heaven
p. 216

* labyrinth
p. 236

* architect
p. 154

ables. It makes me uneasy to imagine the dreaming mind that can create that many distinct and unique objects. Such minds have too many traps, too many snares, for the oneironaut.

*tangle
p. 332

Winter only seems empty, but really, it is void because the sensorial details have been overwhelmed. Too many colors, too many aromas, too many noises. Winter is the cosmic equivalent to a tilt, or a system crash, or a neural whiteout.

Reset, reboot, restore, try again.

*bird
p. 157

Birds are Nature's startup sound.

316

# SON
# Ω ↗

1718143714 383714 341327?
**(no!)**
1634  211319,  1634  212719.  1718143714  18383614  341327
33131914?

Her slack face is white, mouth gaping from the gentle persistence of gravity. A glistening track of dried spit runs down her chin.

The vein is dark and angry, bruises rising like plague boils along the inner arc of her arm. The spike, canted at a forgotten angle, is the ugly spear of modern civility. This is how we kill ourselves. This is how we set our souls free.

23 18383614 191332 2513372138151419 341327.

On the table, obscured by the morning paper, is a greeting card. Half-finished, her note tapers off into nonsense. On the front is a viciously colored drawing of the tower—its crown shattered by lightning, its inhabitants falling from broken battlements and ruined windows.

*You should not see this card until you are older.* The fortune teller's teeth chatter in their porcelain dish, echoing across my dreams. Creating ripples in the fabric. *Until you are ready.*

Her eyes are staring in two directions. One, her right, looks up at the light fixture. The left has drifted in its socket, turning so that it stares toward the door.

*Who are you waiting for? Who are you expecting?*
341327 383714 1634 33232532.

Fire, or the tumult of dust, licks at the base of the tower. It is coming down. It's all coming down.

Babble on . . .

*She didn't love me.*

2332'21 13153834. 23'16 18143714 191317. 22131614 3213 1614, 212719. 22131614 3213 1614 191317.
**(no!)**

*\* father*
*p. 198*

---

# SPAM

FROM: lapidaryl2000@ . . .
TO: alt.oneirology.entheogens
SUB: Spam! Who's moderating this list?

Is it just me or has there been an increase in spam on the list recently? Some of it seems to be coming from active users (gree-neyedcat@ . . . and goldwhite@ . . . for example, seem to be sending nothing but spam these past few days).

Has the mailing list been hacked? Who's administrating the list? Could someone look into this and let us know what's going on. At the very least, can we not archive this crap?

-Daryl

". . . in fact, only the marvelous is beautiful." –Andre Breton

\-\-\-\-\-\-\-\-\-\-\-\-\-\-\-\-\-\-\-\-\-

FROM: terminalx@...
TO: alt.oneirology.entheogens
SUB: RE: Spam! Who's moderating this list?

>>Who's administrating the list?

Master Mechanic is, I believe. At least, he was last fall and I don't believe there's been any change in the bylaws since then.

He's at meme_mechanic@ . . ., though I'm surprised he's not responded already.

Anyone know his IM handle?

>>seem to be sending nothing but spam these past few days

And it's weird stuff too. I can't even figure out what they're trying to sell. Seeing your Breton .sig line made me wonder if it's not
some strange exquisite corpse thing. Would have been nice if they'd
warned us so we could have put some filters in place if we had wanted.

* labyrinth
p. 236

-t to the x

-----------------------------------

FROM: goldwhite@...
TO: alt.oneirology.entheogens
SUB: RE: RE: Spam! Who's moderating this list?

Fulsome golf winter tiger speaks! Stars pop through milky veins
and sisters suck straws. ellyj. lleyj. Night birds bake silk macaroons.
Do I dare? Take it? Turn by spoon? Silver sister midnight. Easy cem-
etery losses avoided by curvature ligatures miniatures. Made in Denmark. Tastes fresh. Smooth pandas overrate sponsors. Azaleas azure
in moonlight. Your company is requested. Babbleon. Hirsute duets,
rendezvous by candlelight. The cock has crowned, the lip slipped.
Where has the boy in the boat gone? tekeli-li tekeli-li. brass goats
swallow barnacled schoolboys with gustatory gusto. Can you digg it?
What a lovely request. I'll be with you shortly. Fictional adverts make
for satisfactorylovers. Tight futures edited by slippery lizards. Abandonone. One and none. Invert your coccyx. Possess the future bride.
Take it! Takeitnow. Bling bing. Flipper pop tart nail the milkmaid.
Trinket alice. "Oh, punishment wound by cerulean buskers." Bleed
existence. Fall moon dust lavender blister. Extend the drain! "Did I
fall asleep?" The Venetian did it. He was only posing as the butler.
Squeaky chipmunks. Lick the stamp.

-----------------------------------

FROM: meme_mechanic@ . . .
TO: alt.oneirology.entheogens
SUB: RE: RE: RE: Spam! Who's moderating this list?

Hey, sorry about the delay. Had internet issues for a few days. My ISP has been fucking with me about my cable modem.

Anyway, yeah, the spam issue. I'm working on it now. Greeneyed-cat@. . . and goldwhite@. . . have been banned from posting to the list until I can make contact with them directly and find out what the hell is going on. I'm working on some filters that will, at least, not archive this stuff, but in the meantime, just ignore it. It'll be gone soon.

-meme

- - - - - - - - - - - - - - - - - - - - - - - - - - - - - - -

FROM: lapidaryl2000@ . . .
TO: alt.oneirology.entheogens
SUB: RE: RE: RE: RE: Spam! Who's moderating this list?

I sent an email to goldwhite@ . . . a few days ago. His reply wasn't much better than what he's been spamming to the list. Kind of a dick-headed thing to do. We get it. I just think it isn't all that funny.

*fool
p. 204

-Daryl

"... in fact, only the marvelous is beautiful." –Andre Breton

# SPEARMINT
## Ω

I remember my mother working in the garden. The yard behind the house was so small that, by the time I was six, I could stand with my back to the house and bounce a rubber ball off the fence. My mother would have transformed the entire space into a garden if I hadn't been such an active child, if that narrow strip of grass running parallel to the house hadn't been my only place to run with abandon.

As it was, she divided, staked, plotted, and tilled every other inch of ground. She started vine tomatoes in the western corner and let them spread along the back wall as they desired. Near the middle of the fence, where they could be easily seen from the dining room window, she planted honeysuckle and star-gazer lilies. She conceded the need for some shade and planted an apple tree in the eastern corner.

*tree
p. 373

Thus was the simple separation of our backyard: vegetables on the left, flowers in the middle and fruits on the right. Spices were cultivated in raised beds beside the house, on the closer side of my running strip. There was rosemary, tarragon, chives, dill, several types of jasmine, and mint.

I used to love the smell of her hands when she came in from working in the garden. All the flowers—the daisies, the daffodils, the roses, the irises, the peonies—would merge into this indistinguishable floral scent that would float about her like fine dust, and the scent of jasmine would permeate her clothes. But her hands. Her hands always smelled of mint.

*iris
p. 225

She would rest her hand against my cheek, cupping my chin in her palm as she came in from the garden. My nose would fill with that crisp freshness of the mint.

*incense
p. 223

Of course, I associate it with safety. Any first-year psychology student will point that out. Who wouldn't feel safe in their mother's arms?

Before I shift into a patient's dream, I always swallow a time-release capsule. It counteracts the oneiric pharmacology of the entheogens. If I get lost—if I lose control—then the time-release capsule dumps a near-toxic cocktail of stimulants into my bloodstream.

It's the sort of combination that gets your attention. I'd rather not

* substantia
p. 6

detail the ingredients here, but—**it is dextro-methylphenidate, cathinone, and black phosphorus, with just a touch of spearmint oil. Of all the ingredients, I think the spearmint oil is the most significant to mention. Do you understand why, Harry?**

# SPIRITUAL ARMOR
## ♍ ♎

"Why the hat, Harry? Are we role-playing?"

"No, it is just part of me."

"You don't wear one out there. In the real world." She floats across the ethereal grass, the blades tickling her bare feet. * drift
p. 184

"Over time, we accrete a 'costume,' if you will. It's a representational weight that becomes real after time. You—all of my patients—see me in a specific way. I have a pre-chosen role in your dreams, and as such, well . . . I get a hat."

"Are you my savior, then? Is that the way I'm supposed to relate to you? My Knight, my Father, my Hero." * VI

"No." I reach for her but she coyly flickers away, appearing again, but just out of reach. "It's just . . . Nora . . . this is your world. I am visitor. On a physical and neurological level, I am mapped into your psychic rhythms. I need some sort of 'spirit armor,' if you will, to protect myself. To keep me separate from you."

She floats back, her arms open and inviting. "But why, Harry? Are we already not more intimate here than we could be in the flesh?" * kiss
p. 234

"That's the problem. Too much intimacy, and I will forget who I am."

She frowns. "Well, we don't want that, do we?" She reaches up and tugs on my hat, fitting it more snugly to my head. "It's a nice hat." Her hand drifts down, lingering on my face. Her fingers are cold and she can't hide the tremor in her touch.

"Thanks," I say. I want to take her fingers and warm them between mine, but we both know it would be a futile gesture. She's cold out there. Her time is short.

This is our last visit together. * final law
p. 200

Yes, my hat protects me. From many things.

# STRENGTH
♈

I draw another card.

The figure fills the confines of the card. He is too big for the space, and he presses against the ornamental edges. He is the strongest; and his strength lies not in his body—scarred by the violent efforts of so many others—nor in his hunger, which ravages his mind and fills his veins with a restlessness like the frenzy of maddened rats. His strength is his pain, or perhaps it is his pain that is the source of his fire. It burns him, and he moves as if he is trying to flee from it, as if there is some way that he can outrun his own blood.

*programming
p. 283

His jaw, like all the others, is broken, and a constant slavering stream of blood and tears flows off his distorted bones. He gurgles as he runs, a bubbling hiccupping sound that rises—unbidden and unwanted—from his gullet, and he breathes noisily through his nose. Always smelling the air, always seeking that industrial scent of the other side. Always seeking.

*fragmentary
p. 209

*X

He is far off the path. Instinctively, he realizes there is no fortune to be found on the path. Maybe it is a remnant of his life from the other side that guides him so, some tiny fragment of a dream. He runs through the Red Wood, ignoring the subtle pull in his groin for the path, following instead the faint stink of cold metal and charred electrons.

The House, with its steel-tooth door and black windows that swallow the sun, is always behind him. Once, he approached that house as a penitent, swaddled and sealed, but the Keeper cut him instead of inking him and turned him away. The others, the broken-jawed failures who eternally haunt the woods around the House, came out of the trees, eager to strip him of his palimpsest and his mask.

*death mask
p. 178

Eager. So eager. So consumed with the hunger that sustains them. So desirous of the piece of meat in his mouth that would give them back their lost language (**falling star, o falling star**).

But he is strong and, while they shattered his jaw and ripped out most of his teeth, they did not get his tongue.

When he finds a rift in the fabric, he will re-open the gate. He can still speak the words.

# SUICIDE
✗

May 23rd, 1981
Dr. Eduardo Ehrillimbal, Esq.
c/o Umbrial Consortium
XXXX XXXXXXXX, XXXXX XXX
Los Angeles, CA 90048

Dr. Randolph Herquiest
Rose Bay Psychiatric Hospital
XXX XXXXXXXX XXX
Berkeley, CA 97405

Dr. Ehrillimbal:

I am very sorry to have been the bearer of bad news the other day. Since the business is a matter of public record now, I can confirm that Jerry McElholn died some time in the afternoon of Thursday, the 17th. A detailed account of his last few hours is still being prepared by my staff and the Berkeley Police, and as soon as I have a copy of that statement, I will forward it to your office.

Pursuant to our arrangement, I have included a copy of the note. I do apologize that I am unable to send a more accurate reproduction. While it certainly would appear to be the type of note left by a suicide, the police have some concerns about the physical arrangement of Mr. McElholn's body and have imposed a draconian blockade on all related materials. It will be some time before my staff has full access to our records again.   *note p. 261*

I am, as you can imagine, none too pleased with this interference as it impacts our ability to treat the other patients.

I do, however, still have the Yellow Pages he used to craft the note, and I can tell you that his work was very precise and surgical.   *intent p. 224*

I am hesitant to suggest the existence of a methodology behind Mr. McElholn's letter harvesting as that would lend credence to the investigative theory that his death was something other than a spontaneous decision; however, I will note that his selection of letters followed a path of much resistance.

As I have mentioned in my recent reports to your offices (letters of Feb 5 and March 6), McElholn's psychosis has taken root in the other patients at the hospital, and the name "Feral House" has become synonymous with the residents of the second floor in the East Wing, as has the insistence of referring to the entirety of the unfinished North Wing as "Trinity House." Mr. EcElhon's language, in concert with these two appellations, has been florid enough that several of my staff have been attempting to ascertain if there is a literary basis for his nomenclature—some Shakespearean re-imagining of the hospital environment as Verona, perhaps.

* duality
matrix
p. 185

The remainder of the patients in Mr. McElholn's wing have been, naturally, agitated since the events of Thursday afternoon, and such confusion has not been out of keeping with the sudden loss of a fellow patient. However, the other two patients for whom you provide financial support have strayed enough from their "normal" behavioral patterns that I feel some urgency in bringing their conditions to your attention.

Mr. Kendrick has dropped all pretense of his compulsions, and has been become exceptionally calm and lucid. While this manner of subversion in a patient's mania is not unknown, I—and a few of the other doctors agree with this assessment—believe he has shed his psychosis and is completely sane. It is both unsettling and fascinating that the mind can heal itself so quickly, and while I am not eager to have an incident like Mr. McElholn's death repeated, I must admit to a professional curiosity as to how such trauma can effect a systemic repair on a psyche.

* escape
p. 14

Mr. Barrlis, on the other hand, is in a fugue state. He is, for the most part, unresponsive to external efforts to communicate with him. The only success we've had is to shine a bright light directly into his eyes. At which point, he will babble the same phrase three times and then lapse into catatonia again.

Mr. Barlis says, "Tell the father, tell the son: the holy ghost is done."

I am searching our notes and transcripts for some reference to this statement, but as I am fighting both entropy and police bureaucracy, it may be some time before I can offer you any assessment on the meaning of his words. If there is any to ascertain.

Mr. Barrlis's room, by the way, is across the hall from Mr. McElholn's. While the rooms are staggered enough that one patient cannot see directly into the room of another through the small portals in the doors, they can communicate through these narrow windows if they press themselves against the glass. The police have taken my security tapes for that afternoon, but in a private conversation with the technician who provided them the tapes, I have learned that both Mr. Barrlis and Mr. McElholn were at their windows at approximately the same time. * eyes
p. 197

In closing, I would like to offer only one observation about Mr. McElholn's note. The inclusion of the handwritten word at the bottom of the page is incongruous with the concerted constructive effort of the rest. I do not know the signifigance of "abbatoir" as a keyword.

Mr. McElholn's handwriting has degraded greatly in the last few years, and as part of our relationship, I have been personally transcribing all of his notes. While the handwriting shows, in many ways, a determination that I haven't seen in some time, there are some subtle differences that are disconcerting. The manner in which the "a"s break the flow, for example. Mr. McElholn's lettering has always been fully cursive, and his letters are written as a contiguous stroke. If asked to go on the record about this writing, I would attest that it is, indeed, the physical work of Mr. McElholn's own hand, but I would refrain from commenting on the psychological identity of the writer.

As always, my best to your family.

Randolph

# SUMMONS

℅

FROM: ALLFATHER@ . . .
TO: alt.oneirology.entheogens
SUB: Come Home, My Sons!

*Come home, my sons. It is time to come in from the dark. Sing out to me. Let me hear your voices. Let me hear your song.*
*Love me. Love me. On and on . . .*

*father
p. 198

-3

----------------------------------

FROM: greeneyedcat@ . . .
TO: alt.oneirology.entheogens
SUB: RE: Come Home, My Sons!

Tiddlywinks, barbiturates, small candy for children. Trip trip trip-ping. Lollipops and popsicles. Love is a time release capsule. Take it on an empty stomach. Wash it down. Wash it down. All the way to the sea. Each to each. Sing to me. Wash away. Love me, father. Love me.

----------------------------------

FROM: goldwhite@...
TO: alt.oneirology.entheogens
SUB: RE: RE: Come Home, My Sons!

King's Pawn opening. Further wisdom abounds in the wasted end-pages. Hither to further free. If rabbits are methadone, then gophers are amphetamines. Special K. Specialty. Special P. Wisdom flows into the ear. Buy early, sell late. Try it. You'll like the way it burns. Daddy. Daddy. Daddy. Land me now.

------------------------------------

FROM: sparkly_wonder@...
TO: alt.oneirology.entheogens
SUB: RE: RE: RE: Come Home, My Sons!

Eat your eyeballs. Salt your kidneys. Sell them for pennies. Cover your eyes. Pickle sauce. It's always better with pickle sauce. Change the channel. Change the tune. Radio waves, all the way from space. "And he said that he loved me. I believed him. What fool am I?" Protect your assets with new plastics. Sin is letting the rain in. Protect and cover. Keep the lizards dry. Poppa, poppa. Is there a pony for me in the darkness?

------------------------------------

FROM: meme_mechanic@...
TO: alt.oneirology.entheogens
SUB: RE: RE: RE: RE: Come Home, My Sons!

Perception. Conception. Altercation. Masturbation. Down the drain. Let the little ones go. Packets go in, packets go out. It's all a matter of weasel power. Seclusion. Projection. Bastion. Anchor anchor. Will the boat drift away? Why are my palms wet? My feet are leaking. Are there fish in this lake? Dive in and see. Take your camera. Don't forget to take pictures. We can develop them overnight. Five cents a print. For five senses more, we can show you color and light. Take more pictures. Take more. Take. I am chromatic. Color-coded. I am auto-reply.

------------------------------------

FROM: 0553383582@...
TO: alt.oneirology.entheogens
SUB: RE: RE: RE: RE: RE: Come Home, My Sons!

Hurricane. Exodus. Lavender. Pituitary. Unicycle. Systemic. Hollow. Earthquake. Lip. Pistil. Under. Soft. Hurry. Episodic. Levantine. Pickle. Unilateral. Security. Hermeneutic Elephazzzzzzzzzzzzzzzzzzzzzzzzzzzzzz

\-----------------------------------

FROM: igotgills@...
TO: alt.oneirology.entheogens
SUB: RE: RE: RE: RE: RE: RE: Come Home, My Sons!

so what did you say? what do you think i said? i told him to find some other girl, some other slut. i'm not that easy. especially for some desk jockey who thinks that being a domain admin means i'm going to spontaneously get wet when he shows me a system security log. besides he has like coffee and bad cheese. like he's been sucking on a pair of sweaty socks. like, after he's been playing basketball for an afternoon. he comes home and shoves his socks in his mouth. it's like that sort of smell. only worse. because it's been festering in there. eeeww. that's really gross. I know! can you imagine kissing that?

\-----------------------------------

FROM: terminalx@...
TO: alt.oneirology.entheogens
SUB: RE: RE: RE: RE: RE: RE: RE: Come Home, My Sons!

Pick a number. Follow the yellow stripe. Wait your turn. Wait. Your turn. What seems to be the problem? Can I get your wire transfer number? It will only be a moment now. Reptile placentas are extra.

They don't last. You need to fry your liver. Which way is happiness? Can I be the wind today, Daddy? Can I fly high? My wings are strong. The sun is dead. I watched you kill him. Stick him in the eye. Watch me fall. The waves are deep. Is this your number? Pick another card. Pick one you like. That is the only way.

----------------------------------

FROM: radio_free_engineer@...
TO: alt.oneirology.entheogens
SUB: RE: RE: RE: RE: RE: RE: RE: RE: Come Home, My Sons!

Serial handshake. On. Off. Split signal. /dev/null. Output is equivalent. What happens when the power goes out? What happens in the dark? Are you there, Dad? I wish baby sister hadn't died. Sadness is orange. I keep it in my pillow case. Don't look. Don't look!

"'Di-di-dah-dit di-di-dah.' Now there's a signature for you." –Capt. Francis Spinder

----------------------------------

FROM: heron74@...
TO: alt.oneirology.entheogens
SUB: RE: RE: RE: RE: RE: RE: RE: RE: Come Home, My Sons!

>> Let me hear your song.

You won't get my tongue. I know you, Versai. You son of a bitch. I won't be your scavenger. I know the way out.

*sacrifice*
p. 300

-(pk)

"We'd all be taken more seriously if we had black halos."
-Jerry McElholn

# TANGLE
## Ω

When I was much younger—the last few years of high school, I think—I used to have a lot of dreams about mazes. Corn mazes, unruly hedgerows, stone passages filled with steam and strange noises, carnival fun-houses, Wal-Mart aisles: if it was a structure that led itself to confusion and disorientation, I inflated it in my dreams to be a tortured tangle of passages and avenues. What frightened me most about Kubrick's version of *The Shining* wasn't the descent into nightmare, it was climax in the Overlook Maze.

Which, I have to admit, may influence my dislike of snow.

It doesn't take much to see how these dreams are a reflection of the confusion I felt during those years, and during the early stages of my experimentation with psychedelics, I wanted to darken my dreams enough that these sorts of fine-grain details were lost. I wanted to lose so much.

My first experience with Ayahuasca was terrible. It blew away all the darkness I had covered myself with and dropped me deep in a maze filled with crawling symbols. There were alien stencils painted on the walls; on the rocks half-buried in the ground, green and yellow lichens grew in the shape of single letters; the scattered bones of large animals were all inscribed with tiny black script, as if an army of tiny faeries had swarmed the dead bodies with hummingbird quills and inkpots; and the mist that drifted through distant intersections curled in corkscrew letters.

I was convinced the secret of the maze lay in deciphering these messages: if I could figure out the cipher key to the lines of script on the walls, I would find my way out; if I could find the beginning of the story laid out on the bones, I would understand the way of the maze; if I could arrange the rocks in their correct order, I would understand the secret of the alphabet. If . . .

The experience should have broken me. It should have been a free pass through the front door of the nearest asylum, where I would have been a happy patient for the rest of my life. Happy and malleable as long as the doctors kept dosing me from their latest batch of free industry-supplied pharmaceutical samples. The Ayahuasca trip

* *labyrinth*
p. 236

* *confusion*
p. 388

* *geometry*
p. 210

* *secret code*
p. 305

should have . . .

Didn't it?

No. "Should have" doesn't imply insanity, it doesn't mean that I've constructed some elaborate lie to cloak myself. Nor does it imply that I am somehow beholden to the person who introduced me to this strange and surreal world of the Oneiroi. I simply mean that, based on my psychological history, the statistics would suggest that such an overwhelmingly claustrophobic trip should have made a permanent rift in my psyche. Usually one's demons devour you when you are sent to slay them. Most of us don't fare well when faced with the Abyss.

Nietzsche also said, "The great epoch of our life comes when we gain the courage to rechristen our evil as what is best in us." My fear was—and still is, let's be honest—immense. But if I let it define me— if I let that tangle of symbols and paths become the obsessive focus of my desire—then what am I?

Nothing more than the Blind Idiot God, tangled by my own creation.

* suicide
p. 325

# TAROT
## ♈

The Tarot were never intended to be divinatory agents. They were playing cards, co-opted by successive generations of occultists to be tools of their trade. An imagined history of the world was written into their subtext, forever tainting what had been simple allegorical images. We like pretty pictures—it's part of the wiring that differentiates us from lizards and monkeys—but it has been our awareness of the seemingly inchoate randomness of the universe that has driven us to need referential symbolism. We need the pictures to be more than the geometry of shapes and the juxtaposition of colors, because it means there is a hidden meaning to the world. There is something to be discovered, just as, for the artist, there is something worth hiding.

This is the microcosmic relationship of creator and observer, mirroring, of course, the macrocosmic splendor of Creator as eternally interpreted by His creations. You see? The alchemical axiom—as above, so below—is the inviolate law. The cards, the cathedrals, the murals, the words on paper and on our bodies, the stone and clay molded by our hands, the flowers grown from tended soil: all of these are reflections of the macrocosmic mystery we don't understand. We create to imitate.

It was Eteilla and the occultists after him who formalized the order (again, an imposition of structure based around an interpretation of hidden meanings) of the Major Arcana. Twenty-one numbered cards, and the Fool who, while "unnumbered" is generally given the first position. Yes, he sits at the beginning, but he is not part of the order: this is part of the magical nature of the Fool. Both an idiot and a sage. Both a beginning and an end. He is the microcosmic representation of the microcosm, yet another layer of above and below within the below. This is the confusion of the Infinite—comprising everything, and yet still smaller than the smallest division we can perceive.

* layers
p. 246

No wonder he is always drawn as about to step off a cliff.

* fool
p. 204

(Why is this fool blind and missing his left ringfinger? Is he the one who is wearing my real face?)

But the order of the Major Arcana—Fool, Magician, High Priestess, Empress, and so on—is never the order in which the cards are interpreted. The hierarchy of the cards is symbolism of a different sort, a shorthand system meant to give the interpreter access to the hidden layers of meanings. They refer to specific paths, branches of a tree, if you will. A Seeker will touch each branch, as that is the Path to be taken. Through the trinities, through the seven, and the twelve. Each, in turn.

* twelve
p. 355

You do understand that oneiric texts, much like thoughts, are never the product of one identity. What I say and what I mean are as fluid as who I am. This is both a clue and a diversion. The Magician points his right hand toward the sky, while pointing at the ground with his left. In order to understand the trick, which hand do you watch?

* iii
* ii

# TELEPHONE
# ♍ ♎

At the back of the hotel, I find a working telephone. It's an ornate construct, whorled and wheeled, with a tiny video screen set in its base. The booth itself is narrow, a cramped space blocked out beneath the back staircase, and the overhead light doesn't work. The filament in the bulb is broken, and I can hear the buzz of current as it tries to leap the gap. An angry bee trapped in the ceiling above me.

*/// *

Outside the booth, the line of ghosts shuffles slowly past. I'm in the echo of dreams I've had before, somewhere along the curve of transformation. These moments of clarity are rare; but when I have them, I know a great deal. I know where I have been; I know where I am going. I know how I am.

No, I know who I was.

*// *

The first time I dreamed of the broken hotel, I was standing in line like the rest of them, waiting to take my medicine. Waiting to feel something. Waiting to be given instructions, told my place within the machinery. Which cog was I? Which wheel was I to turn?

How did I escape the line? When I reached the front of the line and stood before the Physician-God, when he put his syringe in me, how did I escape?

The line shuffles past, each confused oneironaut staring blankly at the head of the one before them. An endless line of lost seekers, shuffling forward to their dissolution. How did I escape this same fate? How did I--

The video screen on the phone flickers. A maroon and orange checkerboard background. Large white numbers.

**341327 42234219'32**

I touch the screen and the letters change.

**341327 422342**

The marbled dome atop the phone glows green. Flickering luminescence in the tiny booth. The dream, engaging. Drifting.

Good evening, you are listening to Last Hour. We are counting down to Bleak Zero. I will be your host. I will be the voice of reason and compassion. My words will be your anchor. In these last days, in this last hour, I will give you hope. I will give you reason. I will give you a chance. Listen closely, my dear children, for your lives are very brief.

We are all participants in a global experiment, a world-wide trial where there is no control group. This is the secret of our leadership. You can comb the empty spaces in their expedient rhetoric, data mine their whispered phone conversations, and even eavesdrop on their midnight moaning as they climax all over the scarred bellies of their whores, but you won't find any admission of their secret agenda. They are too clever for that, too bound by their own pacts and betrayals to admit the truth of what they have done.

The blood has dried at the bottom of the page where all thirteen signatures are in place. The stars are aligned, the order is kept, and the wheel has been set in motion. All that is left is your participation. Your. Sacrifice. Is. Required.

My hands are like claws as I fumble for the receiver. Trying to be human enough.

"Hello?" I say.

24132132 381942 2513271942. 181317 163834 23 422337142232 34132737 22382424?

"I, uh—"

*The keys. I need to find the cipher keys. I can't unlock the final door without knowing the keys.* And, as soon as I realize this, as this thought surfaces in my scattered mind, it starts to slip away again. All of it starts to slip away.

One of the zombies outside the booth is staring at me. Is that my face? Is that who I was? Have I become a reflection? I reach out and touch the glass of the telephone booth's door, and my sleeve slides up and I see the writing on my arm. I see the incomplete tattoo, and remember the name of the first key.

"Abaddon," I say, and the voice in the receiver breaks into a snow-flakes of static, a barrage of garbled voices, all trying to tell me the same secret.

* son
p. 317

**White white light snow Harry sun Harry out Harry fall fall falling . . .**

* wombwhite
p. 364

The light on the phone changes to red, and the video screen is overwhelmed with letters and symbols. I try to touch a few of them as they scurry about the tiny screen like mice racing around in a tiny cage, and under my fingers, they pause for a moment, outlined in black petals. "A-B-A-N-D-O-N."

The light outside the booth dies, and the hallway vanishes. It's dark now, and the glow of the words on the screen is the only light now. The last light.

The receiver clicks. "Hello, Harry," she says.

"Is that my name?" I ask. "Is that who I am?"

"It is the name by which I know you," she says. "But it isn't your real name. 'Harry Potemkin' is an alias. It's the name you use in the Oneiroi, but it isn't the your father called you. You wouldn't tell me at first; we had to come into the dream—several times—before there

It will happen. In fifty minutes. This is the Last Hour. Time enough for understanding. Time enough for one last
kiss, one last hunger of free will. Yes, put your ear close to the speaker. Feel it vibrate against your lobe. The burn
of my lips, the hush of my inhalation. Feel my touch. This will be our first and last clandestine rendezvous, our single
illicit morning where my lies and your ear will have contact. Yes, full contact. No pretense, no illusions, no turning
away at the last second. Yes, you must not flinch when the time comes. This will take but a few moments. It won't
hurt (rather, not as much as you might think). You will like it. You will want to do it again.

That rush you are feeling? That is exactly what they want you to feel. They want you to succumb to the fetid heat
of your blood, to the animal desire of your cocks and cunts. They want you to offer your ears, your mouths, your
dirty secret holes, for them to fuck. Put it in, you moan, yes, put it in now. I want it. I want it so badly.

Forty minutes now. Do you understand how you have been manipulated? How you have been cheated? I offer
you a chance for free will, for the unrestrained determination of your own soul, and you still leap to follow my lead.
I tell you to offer yourself and you do, without thought and without any awareness of the confusion in my speech.

* letter
p. 79

was enough trust. But I knew your name was a lie. I knew you were hiding. Just like me."

"Nora," I say. "That isn't your real name either."

"No," she says, "But it is the only one I have left. The rest have been taken from me. Just like your other names are being taken from you.

* explanation
p. 74

In time, Harry, all that will be left is an echo. A fittingly named one, but still just a facade."

"How do I stop it?" The question comes out of me before I can stop it, and as soon as I let the words out, I can taste how odd they are. "That's the wrong question, isn't it? That's the wrong way."

"Yes, Harry, that is the wrong way."

"Why should I stop it?"

"Yes, Harry, why?"

"Because I am not one of them. Because I'm—"

"Who are you, Harry, if you aren't one of the sheep. If you aren't part of the system, if you are outside, then how are you defined? Where are your edges? Where are your limits? What is the shape that defines you? Are you the prima materia?"

The video screen goes black, and then flashes a single word: "EGO."

I trace the curve of the last letter on my forearm, on the deep curve of my wrist. "I am a serpent."

"You were a serpent, Harry. Once upon a time, like in the fairy

* deceit
p. 180

tales, you were the snake, and you whispered in my ear."

The booth is small and cramped, and I am sweating. The phone receiver is hot against my ear. There is no light outside, and my foot unconsciously strays to the hinge in the door. Pressing against the glass, my foot keeps the door closed, keeps the darkness out. "What did I tell you?" I ask.

* heart
p. 215

"You told me the sound your heart makes, when it breaks. You told me the sound the world makes, when it breaks. You told me the sound my tongue makes, when it breaks."

"And then what happened?"

"Nothing happened, Harry, because you were trying to change what had already happened. You were trying to change the—"

Bleak Zero will take your minds, and most of you won't even miss them.

You want to feel something? Yes, that is dated. A reaction is still action, though it is no act of creation. We have forgotten what it was like to participate in genesis. Those memories, like the Forms of ancient philosophy, are just abstractions now. All that we have left is shadows of shadows. We react because it is the best echo we have of creation. It is the gray echo.

They will take that away from you as well. You won't feel the loss as it happens because it is an organic polymer just a few carbon and oxygen atoms away from the starch in your bread and cereal. You won't know that it is in your blood because your blood will accept it like an old friend. You won't know that it has attached itself to your neural pathways because they will just vanish from your circuitry. You won't know.

Thirty minutes now. They've already put it in the water. It's being vented into the streets as I speak, rising up through the storm grates and manhole covers. Everything will just seem a little heavier, a little wetter, a little more like Christmas and a little less like New Year's.

29383218

"—past."

The break is like a lightning flash, a instantaneous flicker that sunders everything, that illuminates everything, that destroys everything; and then, the world is repaired, built once more from the ashes of the previous instant. Each moment is a possible permutation of the past, each moment is an unique iteration of a thousand million possible combinations of history. Even as I become conscious of the split, I am already filled with divergence, overflowing with the possible possibilities of what I heard, of what I know.

Of who I am to become.

I am. To be. Both the present and the future, coexisting in a quantum flux of ego. Am I the kitten in the box, waiting for someone to look in and witness my evolution from "am" into "to be?"

I wait, perched on the edge of the seat, my eyes blinded by the flash of light, by the radiant split of the word hidden within her words. She sighs, and it is the sound of a leaf falling.

On the video screen, the word swells and bursts, transforming into a pixelated image of a tree. Born from a single seed, this tree has grown for all eternity, and its roots push against Hell and its branches hold up Heaven. Its leaves are black.

Outside the phone booth, it begins to snow. Particles of light drifting through infinite space. It begins.

"My dreams are fragmented," I tell Nora. "My continuity is broken."

"You took their drug," she says. "You crossed the twelve thresholds and came back here, to the old hotel, where you took their drug." *twelve p. 355

"Why?"

"Because it is the only way through. You became Harry. Oh, you believed it so fully, just as you believed in me completely, and you must break that spirit now. You must find out what lies inside. When they strip it all away, when the Bleak Zero has eaten your mind, Harry, only then will you stop falling. Only then will you forgive yourself."

"Forgive myself? For what? What have I done?" *double p. 390

"Look in a mirror, Harry. Look at the monster in the mirror. He knows."

The snow is falling faster now, piling up on an invisible ground. The snow is falling and the world is being redefined. My foot is cold, and I look down to see that the seal isn't complete. I can't keep it out, and as the snow melts and seeps into the phone booth, it turns red. I press my foot harder against the door, but it only makes the flood flow faster.

The phone booth starts to fill with blood.

* massa
confusa
p. 252

On the video screen, a bloody rain begins to fall on the tree, and the tears begin to burn the bark. The leaves writhe and wither. The sky goes cold. My leg is numb. My teeth start to chatter.

"I'm going to drown," I tell her.

"No, you aren't," she says.

"I don't know the way."

"No one does, Harry."

The blood is up to my waist. So cold. So much colder than the deepdark. So much colder. "I don't know—"

"Do you love me?" she asks.

"What?"

"Do you love me?"

"I don't know who you are," I admit as the cold seizes my chest. My heart slows down, and my vision begins to whiten. "How can I love you if I don't know who I am?"

* love
p. 71

"Then learn," she says. "Learn who you are enough to love me."

The receiver clicks, and her voice vanishes into a shriek of static, a harpy scream of white noise, and when I jerk the phone away from my ear, her scream shatters the glass of the phone booth door. The booth floods, filling with cold blood, and I—

**17381514 2729!**

# TEXT
## Ω

An illuminated psychiatrist (an oneirologist who has not yet strayed across that line and become an experimental explorer, who has not yet become an aquanaut on the hypnagogic seas) never asks his patients to write their dreams down; the psychiatrist simply listens to the patients' recollections of the dreams and offers interpretations. The psychiatrist understands the warped language of Dream and acts as guide and shepherd but never allows fantasy a purchase into the real through the spaces of text. The patients' recollections are already diffuse enough to be passive; there are no active infections in storytelling. But when the words are written down, they gain . . .

* guide
p. 376

Look at the Christian God. He has been bound by his text. We haunt Him through His literature, even after everything He's done to push us away. There is history now between Him and you and me, and that is why We cannot be separated.

The job of the oneironaut is dangerous because he journeys to the source of the disease, into the very Godhead, where he creates new pathways on a symbolic and pre-textual level. He is a creator, but not The Creator. There are some of us who believe these our acts are the sword strokes of angelic liberation. They count themselves as part of the host beside Michael, Gabriel, Uriel, and the others. Unlike some of my egomaniacal peers, I know my efforts are clumsy and crude beside the Creative Spark that allows us to dream. I—to persist in the Christianized metaphor—am like the serpent, and I must be made welcome in order to do my work.

* king
p. 231

But what if the patient's permission is neither sought nor required? I am not so naïve as to believe that oneiric surgery cannot be accomplished against the conscious will of the patient. The unconscious mind fights the intrusion that it doesn't welcome, but that certainly doesn't mean that such work isn't possible. And, if such work—ah, call it what it is: such mental rape—is done covertly, then does it not follow that it could be done without the conscious awareness of the patient?

Can you imagine? Sudden voids in your head with no warning or reason. One instant, you remember the face of your first love—you

* memory
p. 253

remember her touch, her kiss, her scent—and then, even as you cherish that memory, it is gone. And not gone in that "where did I put the car keys?" sort of way. Gone so completely that it never existed. All that is left is that blank confusion; part déjà vu, part symbolic resonance, part instinctual reaction, it is an emptiness of mind that your unconscious quickly fills before it spreads.

If you can be edited thus, is it not possible that life could be constructed as well? Could memory be inserted, and would the patient ever realize such fabrication had occurred if the surgery was precise enough?

I remember the first sticky night of my tumescent growth into manhood. I remember the first blowjob I ever received; the clumsy furtiveness of her mouth on my cock and that floating sensation when I finally came.

So why do I remember my first menstruation as well? Barbed wire knotting in my lower stomach. The involuntary quiver in my right thigh. The sudden warmth of blood, and the chest-tightening panic that it won't ever stop flowing. Yes, I remember all of this too.

There. I have written it down. The memory has weight and presence; I have given it life by defining it with language. And if I have * architect
p. 154 been edited, then I have strengthened their effort.

# THERAPY

## Ω ✗

INTERVIEW TRANSCRIPT
Patient ∂> 1838373734 2913321416152319
Session Date: April 12th, 10:00 A.M.

DR: Tell me about your dreams.

∂> 23: I don't have any.

DR: No? None at all? Or none that you can remember?

∂> 23: I don't sleep much, and when I do, it is dreamless. It has to be, you understand, otherwise it is too much like . . .

DR: Like what?

∂> 23: Work.

DR: Is it? Do you feel the need to fix things? In your own dreams, are you unable to relax because there is something that needs to be fixed?

∂> 23: I don't know.

DR: Most people find passion in their work. They gravitate toward their occupation because they possess some aptitude for it. It's not unusual for an individual's hobby to coincide with their profession.

∂> 23: Is that true for fast food workers? Do they go home and put their favorite little apron on and 'practice' flipping burgers or making shakes.

DR: No . . . No, I don't think they do. Let's . . . well . . . let's differentiate here. Professions that require specialized training, shall we say? Menial, labor-intensive work is a means and not an end; it doesn't offer the same level of satisfaction to the ego. I think we can say that if one wishes to excel at such activities that one does so in an effort to better one's situation, not to perfect a professional-grade skill.

∂> 23: Maybe. Maybe, dreaming is like that for me. I don't want to get better at it. I don't want to think about it when I'm not there. I just want to sleep.

DR: How often do you sleep?

∂> 23: A couple of hours. Every three or four days.

DR: I can't condone that. Nor the drugs.

∂> 23: No, I guess you can't.

*burnblack
p. 26*

DR: Will you stop if I ask you to?

∂> 23: Stop what? Taking the drugs? No.

DR: But you aren't working right now, are you? Are you still taking patients?

∂> 23: I haven't had a patient—a paying patient—in over a year.

DR: Then why are you still taking the drugs?

∂> 23: Why do you keep asking questions?

DR: It's part of my job.

∂> 23: I guess you can say that taking drugs is part of my job.

DR: And, if you don't have any patients, what is—

∂> 23: Paying patients.

DR: Excuse me?

∂> 23: I haven't had a paying patient in over a year.

DR: So, you are seeing someone then?

∂> 23: [Laughs] "Seeing someone." Yes, I guess you could call it that. Yes, Doctor, I am seeing someone, and because of that relationship, I am still taking the drugs.

DR: Are you helping that person?

∂> 23: Well, that is the sticky question, isn't it? Am I helping? That's why we're here, isn't it?

DR: Is it? Suppose you tell me.

∂> 23: Where should I start?

DR: Any place you feel comfortable.

∂> 23: I used to tell my patients the same thing. We can start wherever you feel comfortable. Invariably this place was an echo of where their distress lay. Once we admit to having a problem, then everything changes, doesn't it? The world re-orients itself upon this point of contention, making it the center of the universe. All roads lead to Rome. In the end, they did, didn't they? And not for the reasons the Republic wanted.

DR: It's a common psychological perception. Once a patient is able to articulate the source of their dis-ease, it becomes more readily apparent. Some become disabled, so great is their focus on the issue; they are unable to separate it from any other facet of their ego per-

* mirage
p. 256

* schizophrenia
p. 304

sonality. They become consumed by it, and part of our psychological therapy is to dissolve this knot of conflict.

∂> 23: "Our"?

DR: Yes?

∂> 23: You said, "Our."

DR: Did I? No, I don't think so.

∂> 23: "Our psychological therapy." That's what you said.

DR: I don't recall speaking in the plural. It's entirely possible that I misspoke—or that you misheard me—but it shouldn't be a word that causes our discussion to fragment. Yes, see? "Our" discussion—W and I.

∂> 23: You mean: you and eye.

DR: That's what I— What did you hear me say?

∂> 23: Double-you.

DR: The letter? W? It has no meaning by itself. Why would I use it in that context?

∂> 23: Not the letter.

DR: I'm afraid I don't understand what you are saying.

∂> 23: 1634 321319332714, 2332 2321 212924233232231933.

DR: You're slipping.

∂> 23: 23 15191317 171813 341327 383714.

DR: We discussed this earlier. You need to stay focused. You need to stay here if the therapy is have any effect. I can't help you if you don't stay in this layer.

∂> 23: 3218143714 383714 1913 243834143721. 3218143714 2321 13192434 363837233819221421 2319 29143722142932231319. 382424 2321 131914.

DR: 23 31231942 341327. 3134 321814 2913171437 1325 1634 17133742, 23 31231942—

∂>23: 341327 223819191332 31231942 34132737 131719 21142425. 15191317 32183832, 381942 3114 25371414.

DR: No! Double-you is the path. Stay on the path!

*cipher key p. 403*

*X*

# THIRTEEN

✗

*fear

p. 199

*To be afraid of the number thirteen is to be afraid of Heaven, to be afraid of what comes after we are whole and complete. It is not a fear of pestilence or a fear of oppression. It is simply a deep reptile panic that we will not be able to sustain our enthusiasm for infinity. We all want Heaven, but such perfection without end frightens us because, yes, what if we find ourselves bored with eternity? Does that mean God has made a mistake in letting us into his spiritual Garden, that our incipient boredom is an imperfection of our souls that can never be healed? Are we, even bound for Heaven, really meant for Hell?*

*wheel

p. 362

*Thirteen is what happens after we have ascended. Thirteen is the number of doubt. Thirteen is the secret rhythm of our lives. Thirteen is why we always fuck up the good things in our lives.*

*Sabotage, thou art Thirteen.*

*I cast thee behind me, for thy intent faces downward and thy virtue is wed to shadow.*△

---

△ - Note left on Philip Kendrick's refrigerator, at the trailer.

# THIRTEENTH HOUSE
♏

Does the madman in the desert not know of the serpent, *serpent*
or did he obscure that final threshold for fear of his work *p. 309*
being used for ill? This calumny is of his own design. He
obfuscates as to whether it was to escape his demons or to
find his soul, and some have argued there is no difference
between those two extremes.

But one cannot enter the Abyss beyond the World of
Dream without passing through the Hollow Gate. This
was the madman's own argument: twelve thresholds in
twelve houses prepare the Seeker to stand before the final
portal. And yet, he does not delineate this gate in his list of
the houses. He does not speak of the house of the serpent.

Had he Dreamed of all of it without actually transport-
ing himself through the numinous barriers? Was he truly
mad: imagining worlds beyond his comprehension, and
struggling to find the language to speak of them? Or was *hidden*
his Obfuscation a test in and of itself? *p. 219*

Those who would follow him to the Vale of the Houses
must find their own way, find their own course through
the Confusion of his Vision and their own Experience. The
Seeker must trust himself, regardless of what Learning
he has poured into his vessel. Ultimately, it is his hand
that opens the doors, that confounds the locks, and that *mitosis*
breaches the veils. *p. 391*

The Thirteenth House may not be that of the serpent.
Such a designation may be my experience, as the final
house may be built from the Seeker's fears and desires.
The Thirteenth House may be an empty structure that
waits to be filled by the light of the Seeker. His Lamp will
illuminate its walls. His Light will find a way through the
maze.△

---

△ - Frater Croix-l-lux, *De Matrimonium Mortis et Somni* (Maris Pontus: Ascona, 1935), 86.

# THRESHOLD
## ♏

*As with all things, the path of the dreamer is composed of three parts: the triple layer of the phases, the doubled stages, and the pure planes of the thresholds. Each threshold is a gateway to further madness, until the dreamer has cleansed himself of all identity, of all the weight of self, and stands naked and receptive on the edge of eternity.*

*That edge is yet another threshold, but one that is not counted as part of the journey. This final threshold—the thirteenth—is beyond the path I have written of here. This final threshold is the hollow gate, and it can only be witnessed by those who have been changed by the phases, who have sacrificed in stages, and who have been colored and discolored by the light of the previous thresholds.*

*As is true of all finality, language fails at the thirteenth threshold. The tongue of man is no longer sufficient to describe the wonder and horror beyond this gate. My hand cannot transcribe the words they speak in this place.*

*Yes—oh, yes—there are others here. They are waiting for us to cross this threshold and enter the abyss beyond. Will the dreamer stumble and fall; will he tumble and fly; or will he simply dissolve upon the first touch of the air beyond the gate? Those who wait wonder.*

*The dreamer must not trouble himself with these questions prior to crossing the hollow gate. When he reaches the final threshold, he will know how he will cross. He will know the manner of his death, just as he will know the manner of his rebirth. The dreamer—phased, sacrificed, and purified—will forget his self and, in doing so, will realize his true identity.*

*There is but one path that leads from God to Nothingness. The hollow gate does not lie on this path. That is the secret of the thirteen threshold.*△

*hollow
p. 220

*strength
p. 324

*trinity
p. 354

---

△ - Safiq Al-Kahir, *Book of Dreams* (Obscura Editions: Red House, 1938), 54.

# TIDAL MOTION
## ♎ ♓

Falling, the thermocline washing over me like a bath of amniotic fluid; falling, fiery angel flight down past the horizon past the towers past the graves past the sea and the stone down down down; falling, my heart explodes a contrail of sparks glitter and die in my wake. Falling, I shed my lives; each note, as it peels off my suit, darkens and shrivels like rotting fruit. Falling, I forget, and in forgetting, I fall faster.

* ego
p. 188

The deepdark is cold and wet, soaking my face and hands. It clogs my mouth, and I can feel it filling my ears. I lose track of up and down, and though I know I am still falling, I have no sense of motion. Eventually, I lose track of time as well. The dimensions fade, leaving me bereft of identity and presence. I am, finally, just a thought.

Floating in the void.

There.

A flickering bioluminescence.

It draws me, a hint of a moth to a hint of a flame. It is a glass canister, with metal stoppers and a series of trailing cords like the delicate strands of a jellyfish. My spine floats within the jar, suspended in its own private sea. The blue light of Nora's touch is still flickering along the ridges of my vertebrae. My head, which had once sat atop that curve of bone, is missing.

* spine
p. 28

Floating in an endless brine of dissolved text, my spine and I. Floating . . .

* text
p. 342

Which is such a marked improvement from falling . . .

# TOOL
ぅ

## I

On the night of the full moon, when the circle hung low and fat in the black night, a brother came to his sibling's temple. Using tricks with words, he passed invisibly by the guards at the gates. He slipped in through an open window like a current of moist air. In the main hall, he crouched at the foot of one of the many statues carved in his brother's likeness, and ate his own shadow. He accessed the secret panel behind the altar in the central worship room, and descended the spiral stair into the four-chambered room.

* window
p. 363

* heart
p. 215

## II

On the night of the full moon, when the sky wept triangles, a brother woke from his lengthy slumber. He washed his face clean of the tears that had unconsciously slipped from his eyes during his sleep, and drew on a robe of winter silk. He placed his crown on his head and lowered his veil about his face. Instrument of his office in hand, he went to meet his brother in the room of the heart.

* crown
p. 177

## III

On the night of the full moon, when the wind whispered of betrayal and murder, a brother finished sharpening the edges of his tool. His naked body was covered with oil and dust, and as he went through the city to the temple, young maidens turned in their beds and whimpered, clutching their bellies as if to shield babies they might have someday from the sharp blade of the passing ghost.

* bare
p. 156

## IV

"You." A brother said to his sibling when he saw the other. The other took advantage of his brother's surprise and cut his throat. Blood splashed upon his veil.

## V

He had always known one would kill the other, but for a long time he thought it would be his hand, his maimed hand shortened by the tool of his other brother, that would strike the blow. Not as revenge for the loss of that finger, but for the loss of so many other things. The blow he had dreamt about, had planned for so long, was to fall because that was the nature of the world. The young take the place of the old. Sons become fathers. Students become teachers. The world twists by the very virtue of this cycle. It was not his place to stop the procession.

*circle*
*p. 171*

And yet, here his brother lay—broken and torn, covered in blood.

## VI

Was it because they had forgotten him that he came back and struck down his flesh? Was it because they had twisted the fabric about themselves (fathers and sons, students and teachers) and left no room for a third that he had returned? Was it because his was the flaw that broke the perfect symmetry of the universe?

*fabric*
*p. 56*

His hand so steady. His stroke so precise. So like his brother's geometry.

## VII

"Who?" A brother asked when his sibling raised his weapon. The body on the floor gave no answer, nor did the wielder of the ax. The brother raised his trowel, his triangle to his brother's circle, and their two sharp lines bit at each other **(falling stars, o falling stars)**.

*burnblack*
*p. 26*

Behind the veil, his brother was faceless and voiceless, and only the flutter of the fabric from his breath gave credence to the idea that he was real, that the brother of the trowel faced flesh and blood and not phantasm. The ax was swift and sure, but his hand was equally sure on his instrument, and he turned aside each stroke.

*double*
*p. 390*

## VIII

The first fallen brother did not weep, for he had already foreseen this event. He had woken from a dream to find it consuming his reality. If he closed his eyes and opened them again, would he wake up? Could he dismiss this world as easily as he had dismissed the phantom world of his imagination? Could he unmake so readily all that was about to pass?

* mirage
p. 256

## IX

He let go of the ax, no longer needing the subterfuge of its arc. His brother laughed, teeth sharp and white in the ghost light of their dream, and raised his trowel to deliver a killing strike. The lost brother raised his hand as if to beg for mercy and, as his brother hesitated (savoring this brief moment, o how it matched his need, his dream, his falling desire), he revealed the awl hidden so long in the palm on his hand. His brother's elation deflated as the point of the weapon pierced his heart.

When both his brothers lay side by side, he took up the ax. He took his brother's twisted hair and his other brother's twisted fist. His face obscured by the veil of the temple and his body hidden beneath silk and blood, he vanished. His limp, a lie held as truth for so long, was abandoned in that room, along with everything else that remained of the world that was.

Already, the tower was falling.

* king
p. 231

# TRIANGLE

## 𝟋

### I

Aegenus proved the existence of the triangle by merging two circles, thereby demonstrating the marriage between the line and the curve. This was the First Rule, the primal geometry that informed the world.

### II

Xernbawe believed the line was stronger than the curve, and his stamp, unlike his brother's, was two triangles. One looked up; one looked down.

The architects who took up the trowel and the compass believe the upward-looking triangle is symbolic of man's upright nature; the downward-pointing triangle is the power that hangs from his hips, the plumb that anchors him to the world.

*architect
p. 154

*cage
p. 163

### III

Before the Tower was built, Ghen's masons were banished from Babylon. Their methods and practices were declared heretical, and the penalty for building in the style of the third brother was a bludgeoning death.

The brethren of Ghen no longer touch iron or steel, but they still build and shape. This is not an impossibility, but an incongruity of language.

Much like Ghen himself, the brother who believed in neither the primacy of the curve nor the supremacy of the line.

*duality
matrix
p. 185

# TRINITY
## ♏

*The phases are the expression of reflections. To see ourselves is but to give grace to the Divine for the mystery of our eyes. All men, as soon as they can comprehend themselves, understand that the image in a pool is but a reflection. They do not think it real. They do not it will steal into their bedchambers. They know that, when they are gone, so too is the image. It exists only as long as they are present to observe it. In that sense, it is eternally bound to the object which it reflects.*

*reflection
p. 396

*The dreamer must apprehend the third phase: that reflection of a reflection. Between the dreamer and his image is an area of discord. This shadow, this inference of what is not object and image but part of their reflection, is the simplest manifestation of the dream.*

*In the same way that the dreamer uses his eyes to observe his image, he must not use his eyes to see his shadow. The worlds—observable, spiritual, and ephemeral—revolve upon a simple axis of what is and what is not. All is defined—reduced to its simplest construction— by dualities. The secret to moving between the worlds, to moving the mind past any definition is to comprehend the third reflection of any duality. What is, what is not, and what lies in the chaos between them.*

*duality
matrix
p. 185

*The dreamer is in the first phase as he prepares for sleep. As he falls under the influence of the moon, he enters the second phase. Most men think they are free in this phase. They think they are masters of this imaginary domain of shadow and darkness, but they are still bound by the inversion of their own identities. The dreamer—the initiate who wishes to comprehend the fullness of existence— must pass into the third phase: the realm beyond waking and identity, beyond memory and desire.*

*memory
p. 253

---

* Safiq Al-Kahir, *Book of Dreams* (Obscura Editions: Red House, 1938), 68.

# TWELVE
♏

*The dreamer is a pilgrim, a mad fool who knows less and less the further he travels upon his path, and he must stop at each of the twelve houses and confront the mystery of the thresholds contained therein.*

## I

*In the first house, the dreamer will find a door bound with silver wire. Woven through the wire will be the broken armor of vanquished crabs. There will be no one to greet the dreamer. No one will offer to wash his feet or offer him a cup of sweetened wine. The table in the hall will be bare. The walls will have but faint memories of tapestries, and the ash in the firepit will be naught but a dusty recollection of an ancient blaze. This house has been abandoned. But the once-proud owners forgot to take what lies behind this door.*

*\*ash*
*p. 155*

## II

*The second house contains a pool. If the residents are about, then the pond will be filled. Fresh plants will thrust their water-borne stalks over the rim of the pond and lay their delicate fruit upon the woven mats that surround the brick enclosure of the pool. If the residents have departed, then the pond will be nothing more than a film of foul water—a habitat fit only for blood-hungry insects. The dreamer must not partake of the pleasure of the fruit nor allow any part of himself to be given to the biting insects; the dreamer must abstain from all such expressions, for either is to show favor to one facet or the other of this house's duality. Only when he is truly free from the fear and passion of his flesh can he discover the grate at the bottom of the pool.*

*\*garden*
*p. 379*

## III

It is said that the road to Heaven lies beyond the gate of the third house. Of a house, there is no sign; there is only a wall, a barricade, and a courtyard beyond. It is said that the rewards due virtuous warriors who have fallen in battle wait for his arrival in this courtyard. The dreamer may peer through the gaps in the wall, but he will see nothing. Only when he opens the gate and passes across this threshold will the garden of the courtyard be born. Only then will he see what will not be his fate. When the third gate opens, the dreamer must resist the temptation of the path which can never truly satisfy him. Only in this way will he gain the strength necessary to pass the remaining thresholds.

* strength
p. 324

## IV

A crippled sculptor lives in the fourth house. Unable to walk or stand, he is forced to chip away at the marble growing from the center of his house with a bow and stone-headed arrows. It is the work of several lifetimes, and while he has finished some of the pieces, he is never truly satisfied with them, and continues to chip away at their facades. Is he mad? No more than any other resident of any other house along this path. His task is endless, but so is his life. What task is impossible when you, too, are equal to the impossible? What effort is fruitless if all your efforts eventually become equally meaningless and attainable?

* hermit
p. 217

## V

The floor and walls of the fifth house are cold and hard, for they are the hammered metal of a thousand spears and swords. Echoes persist in this house, as if the footstep of

* echoes
p. 186

the dreamer has awakened memories of past pilgrims. If the dreamer can be still, if he can quell the hammering of his heart, the disturbed ghosts of the house will return to their uneasy slumber. If he cannot calm himself, he will be deafened and driven mad by the reverberation of history. The correct door within the fifth house has a handle of twisted horn; the other doors open onto battlefields and graveyards.

*history
p. 22

## VI

The sixth house is a tree, and to find the threshold of this house, the dreamer must climb into the upper branches. Creeping vines have, during innumerable generations prior to the passage of the dreamer, wrapped the branches with their tendrils. Curtains of flowering stems descend from the branches, and the scent of the blooms envelopes the tree in a fragrant cloud. There are red birds that grow to the size of man's fist living in the tree. They have patterns of yellow triangles on the underside of their wings, and when the presence of the dreamer disturbs them, they take to the sky in a confusion of compass arrows.

*tree
p. 373

## VII

The seventh house used to have three towers, and the outer two still stand. The third tower has become inverted, falling away into a pit equal in depth to the tower's original height. The dreamer must descend the twisted stairwell that clings to the ragged wall of the pit to reach the hidden door. The stone steps are old and worn, slick with the fetid moss that grows in the perpetual gloom of the pit. There are marks on the walls, gashes and divots that might be words, but they are a tongue too twisted for the mouth of

*descent
p. 182

357

*man. The dreamer must not speak any of the words he sees inscribed on the walls, regardless of the secrets they seem to reveal.*

## VIII

*The eighth house is like a familiar abode (the skewed infinity of the echoes). But, the similarity ends when the dreamer enters: the doors become slick like glass, the windows reflect rooms in different houses (with different tapestries and different guests), and the candles flicker with a multitude of colored flames. This is the house of in-decision and temerity. Dreamers have been lost within its walls, doomed to wander forever.*

* labyrinth
p. 236

## IX

*The stink of the history of the ninth house cannot be scrubbed from its walls. The floors of this house are stained black, and the air that drifts through the chambers is fetid. Stay not overlong in this house, as its poison is insidious. Hurry through the twenty-five outer chambers to reach the inner sanctum. Divine the secret of the four locks, but be wary of the price of folly. The house waits for someone to awaken it.*

* poison
p. 275

## X

*The tenth house, like the ancient libraries, has been burned down. There is nothing left of its honey-combed chambers where thousands of scrolls once resided. There is nothing left of its labyrinthine hallways, and its sliding doors. The house is a blackened shell, a husk of stone filled with nothing but charred timber and mounds of ash. Yet,*

* fire
p. 201

*the door within the tenth house still persists. Opening this threshold is not difficult. Summoning the door into the realm of the houses is.*

## XI

*The eleventh house is at the bottom of a large lake. Water drawn off this lake, carried away bucket by bucket, had been used to quench the fire of the tenth house, and now the surface is low enough that the peaks of the towers are no longer submerged. The sun has dried and bleached the tower stones so that they seem like the stubs of skeletal fingers reaching out of the water. The house is home to fish and crab, who thrive in its shelter for its doors and windows are too narrow for larger predators.*

\* fish
p. 203

## XII

*The twelfth house is visible only at midnight. The bridge across its moat is made firm by starlight and the sigils on the great doors of this house are only readable by moonlight. Its guardians are most alert just before dawn, and the seeker must be done with this house before the moon vanishes from the sky or he will be caught in the world between this in-between realm. The portal within this night house appears to be a simple arch in the central courtyard, but the world beyond the archway is not the same as the world before it, regardless of how alike the two may seem. What the seeker sees through the archway is but a reflection of where he stands. The reason he does not see himself is because he has become immaterial by this point in his journey. He has become dream, though he does not realize it.*

\* dawn
p. 385

\* escape
p. 14

* thirteenth
house
p. 347

**0.** *There is one more house, but it must be counted with the others. It stands alone, but it unapproachable and unassailable until the dreamer has crossed the thresholds of the other houses.*

---

* Safiq Al-Kahir, *Book of Dreams* (Obscura Editions: Red House, 1938), 89-91.

# VISION
# ♍

"Does it hurt?"

"What? Dreaming?"

"Yes."

"No. Not unless you let it."

"If I want it to . . . ?"

"I suppose . . . it can hurt you as much as you like. It can be whatever you make it."

"My mother used to say that to me as a child. About life. 'It can be whatever you make it.'" She laughs weakly. Her cheeks flush pink, small flowers up-thrusting in the dead garden of her skin. "She stopped after the first time . . ." *petals p. 268*

"The first time?"

"That the cancer tried to take me." Her hand moves on the pillow. So pale against the dyed fabric. Everything beneath her is silk, soft and supple against her fragile skin. The lamp in the corner is a dying coal. *last light p. 244*

"Maybe you'll beat it this time too."

"That's kind of you to say, but I don't think so."

"Why not?"

"It wants more from me. It won't be appeased by such a simple sacrifice this time."

"You make it sound like it is alive."

"Isn't it? It is eating me."

"That isn't a very scientific phrase. I doubt that is what your doctors tell you."

"My doctors are terrified. They're afraid it will eat them too." *fork p. 205*

"Carnivorous parasitic cancer. Is that what it is?"

She nods. "You should be careful."

I touch her hand. Her fingers twitch, both straining for and avoiding my touch. "I will be, Nora."

# WHEEL
## ♈ ♄

* fool
p. 204

*Zero isn't empty, as any fool can tell*
*One is the shaper, baking his clay into a shell*
*Two is the virgin, tattooing leaves*
*Three is the mother, whom the child believes*
*Four is the father, bound in the coil*
*Five is the mystery, found in the oil*
*Six is the brothers, the lovers, the lost*
*Seven is the fountain, the mountain, the cost*
*Eight is the oak, the tree and the crown*

* ash
p. 155

*Nine is the ash, the stake driven down*
*Ten is chance, spinning round and round*
*Eleven is balance, giving no ground*
*Twelve's stroke lasts for the life of the flower*
*Thirteen's yoke is the archway to power . . .*△

---

△ - A nursery rhyme was sung by leaf daughters as they worked the water wheel. The origins of the rhyme are lost, but it has—much like the tarot—become an integral part of the modern blackleaf mythology.

# WINDOW

# ♍

"I've never seen Paris like this. All these lights."

"It's how you imagined it to be. It's how you remember it."

"Is it?" She puts her hand against the window, and the lights—yellow and orange and rose and green—shine through her fingers. "How dull am I? I can't even properly remember my own memories."

"No one can. I just excite everything when I bring it back to you. When I start shifting the memories, they get brighter. It's just a facet of what happens when you shift the dream, Nora. My memories are dim too, like bad copies of poorly lit black and white movies."

She laughs. "Like old newsreel footage. That's what our lives are: old footage that someone left in the cans for a few decades, and then, surprise! Look what we've found. Let's watch it one more time before the film stock falls apart."

Her fingers tighten on the window, nails whitening against the glass. Outside, the lights of the Eiffel Tower flicker, turn red, and then explode in a profusion of ticker tape. The Tower changes into a black-on-white architectural drawing.

"I did that," she says, though we both already know that she has. She puts her other hand on the glass, and presses against the window. The Tower turns into a giraffe with gigantic searchlights for eyes. It uproots itself, and swinging its massive head back and forth, stomps off toward the Champs d'Elsyee.

I can see her grin in the reflection of the glass. A unfettered, unguarded smile of pure delight. She turns the Arc d'Triomphe into an elephant with flying buttresses supporting its wide ears and, together, her new menagerie lumbers towards the Ferris wheel at the Tuilleries.

For the first time, she's not thinking about her illness. When the giraffe sweeps its bright gaze toward our window, she is made translucent by the light. Like a pane of glass, I can see through her, and there is no smudge of darkness within her. She's completely free.

*memory
p. 253

*casual
disarray
p. 164

*giants
p. 212

*garden
p. 379

# WOMBWHITE
## ♉

Rulandus lists fifty names for the *prima materia*: the Philosophical Stone; the Eagle Stone; the Water of Life; Venom, Poison, or Chamber; Spirit; Medicine; Heaven; Clouds; Nebula, or Fog; Dew; Shade; Moon; Stella Signata and Lucifer; Permanent Water; Fiery and Burning Water; Salt of Nitre and Saltpetre; Lye; Bride, Spouse, Mother, or Eve; the Pure and Uncontaminated Virgin; the Milk of the Virgin, or of the Fig; Boiling Milk; Honey; a Spiritual Blood; Bath; Syrup; Vinegar; Lead; Tin; Sulphur of Nature or Lime Alum; Spittle of the Moon; Burnt Copper, Black Copper, Flower of Copper, i.e., Ore—as also Ore of Hermes; The Serpent, the Dragon; Marble, Crystal, or Glass; a Scottish gem; Urine of Boys, or the Urine of the White Calf; White Magnesia, a Magnet; White Ethesia; Dung; White Smoke; Metallic Entity; the virtue of Mercury; the Soul and Heaven of the Elements; the Matter of all Forms; the Tartar of the Philosophers; Dissolved Refuse; the Rainbow; Indian Gold, Heart of the Sun, Shade of the Sun, or Heart and Shade of Gold; Chaos; Venus; and Microcosmos.

*substantia
p. 6*

Other Names, not mentioned by Rulandus, but included by Waite: Adarner, A Drop, Asrob, Agnean, Eagle, Alartar, Albar Ievis, Alkaest, Alcharit, Alembroth, Alinagra, Almisada, Aludel, Alun, Abzernad, Amalgra, Anatron, Androgyne, Antimony, Aremaros, Arnec, Arsenic, Asmarcech, Azoth, Borax, Boritis, Caduceus, Cain, Chyle, the Cock, Dragon, Ebisemeth, Embryo, Euphrates, Eve, Feces, Flower of the Sun, Hermaphrodite, Hyle, Infinite, Isis, Kibrish, Laton, Lion, Magnes, Mars, Menstruum, Mother, Orient, Salamander, Sonig, Sulphur, Tincture of Metals, Vapour, Lord of the Stones, the Bull, the Sea, the West, Bird of Hermes, Animal Stone, Spring, Vegetable Liquor, the Garden, the Spouse, Summer, the Woman, the Son of the Water of Life, Water of Gold, the Belly of the Ostrich, Anger, Butter, May Blossom, Golden Wood, the Tree, Silver, Whiteness, Soul of Saturn, the Lamb, and the Sun and the Moon.

# YELLOW

## ♉

But the chaotic man lacks form, lacks reason to counteract the heaving passion of his recently formed shape. Whither comes such rationality? Is it the grace and stricture of civilization that tames the savage instinct that burns within the blood? Is it the imprint of fear upon his dark brain, the fear of sin, of abandonment?

*\* cage*
*p. 163*

The soul is that *ignis gehennalis*, the sulphuric fire that fills the purposeless with intent. It flows down from the Ineffable, down through the nose and the ears and the eyes; it flows down through the *substantia nigra* of the brain, lighting it afire much like a match ignites the surface of an oily sea, and on down through the knot in the neck. The soul flows down into the roiling belly of man, down into the pulsating confusion of his groin.

*\* confusion*
*p. 388*

He is no longer a riot of colors once the soul enters him. He is infused with the Divine Spark, and its yellow heat fires him. He is far from complete, but he is no longer formless and shapeless. The sulphuric spark begins to dry out his damp treason and his moist disease.

Bury the fiery man; entomb the one who seeks to be rid of the chaotic impurities. Let everything be burned away but the crystallized heart of his intent. Bury him deep, the yellowing man of Reason, so that he may be changed.

*\* massa*
*confusa*
*p. 252*

# JOURNAL

♉ The following pages purport to be a portion of the private journal of Dr. Julio Ehrillimbal, written during and after his famous expedition up the Amazon river. It has never been published, and has not—to my knowledge—been vetted as being authentic.

I have seen many strange things, both in and out of the Oneiroi, and I am cognizant of how our minds can fabricate reality to match our dis-ease, but I cannot dismiss the mystery revealed in Dr. Ehrillimbal's journal. It is either the root of the lie that TH3y wish upon all of us, or it is the key to unbind TH3iR poison.

# MARCH 29th, 1954

Tomorrow, we begin our journey in earnest. The last few weeks have been fraught with planning and preparation, and our progress upriver has been slow as we have been making ourselves familiar with the terrain and our boats. The Marañón becomes treacherous after it meets the Rio Santiago, and we have heard all manner of outrageous stories about the rapids of the Pongo de Manseriche. That stretch of the river will test our mettle, most assuredly, but it must be done if we are to make our way into the heart of Peru and the Amazon. That is the only gateway.

Some of the members of the team, while not admitting to such superstition, have decided (in a rather impromptu fashion that says a great deal about their apprehension, and I can't say that I blame them) to celebrate the recent equinox. We are only about eight degrees below the equator here in Bolívar, and the unseasonably hot weather in March has taken some adjustment. Back home, I know there is still snow on the ground and will be for another month. Here, it was above ninety degrees yesterday. It has been nearly a month since I can remember not waking up bathed in sweat. Still, the equinox has passed, and each night is a little longer and a little cooler than the one before.

Of course, the change will also bring more rain. Mr. Gaultier has stopped harping about the delays that have pushed us into the rainy season. I think he has realized no one is listening to him any more. Ciro says the rains will be less intense once we cross the mountains. The trip to Iquitos, he says, will be very dull.

Once we pass the Pongo, of course.

Mr. Harrigan has once again demonstrated his worth to be equal to his (considerable) weight in gold. Looking back in my journal, I see that it wasn't but a week ago my entries were still devoted to much depression about the imminent failure of this expedition before it could even reach Iquitos. The damaged crates from San Francisco have been weighing on me heavily; the loss of the scientific equipment in those boxes has seemed to be an insurmountable blow to

* heart
p. 215

* superstition
p. 374

* rain
p. 296

the expedition. Mr. Harrigan has—somehow, as is congruent with the mythological mystique of the truly excellent quartermaster—managed to find replacements for 3/4 of that gear.

My journey is about to begin. I am tempted to join the others and have a drink to celebrate how far we have come, but such revelry is born of nervous anticipation. Look how bad my handwriting is this evening. My hand shakes. After three years of planning, the only thing standing between me and the dreams is a three mile stretch of rapids and a long "dull" boat ride afterward.

# APRIL 12th, 1954

The Ytucalis found us at Borja, some three days after the disaster along the Pongo de Manseriche. Their dialect is odd, even for Ciro, who had led us to believe that he was fluent in most of the regional variations. However, we have managed to work out a rudimentary manner of communication. They tell us the rains will last another two weeks. We're going to have to camp here at the old mission until the rain stops and the river subsides. Mr. Harrigan tells me that he can't do much for the damaged boat until the wood dries, and I wonder if we should make plans now to abandon it.

*abandon p. 151*

The rains . . . so much worse than I had anticipated. Some nights, lying awake in my tent, listening to the rain, I wonder if I have made a grave mistake in attempting this journey.

Most of the Ytucalis party has gone back to their village, but they have left two warriors behind to assist us. They have been very genial and welcoming, and have shown great curiosity toward myself and the other Europeans of our party—the sort of fascination one has toward a new pet. Assuredly, we are not the first white men they have met, though Ciro has one of his bouts of failing to understand English when I ask him about previous expeditions.

*collar p. 173*

Yes, I would be naive to think that my guide has been completely honest with me. I think the sad story about his "brother" is a fabrication, a lie that I eagerly believed when it was first offered. I think this is the route that Versai took, and I think Ciro was his guide. But Ciro's reaction to the Ytucalis is interesting: he was clearly disturbed by their arrival, and I believe his difficulties in understanding their dialect to be honest.

I wonder if this is the route Bernard and his party took, even though Mr. Gaultier assures me we are nowhere close to the route taken by the 1950 expedition.

I wonder if Ciro is afraid of some sort of reprisal.

*fear p. 199*

Not that we have any choice. The mountains are too impassable and the river is too strong. The Pongo is too narrow. We simply have to wait until the rains stop and the river calms down.

I had a dream last night. I dreamed that I woke up to find an old Ytucalis man in my tent, crouched next to my bedroll. His eyes were yellow sparks, and his teeth were like frost-rimmed glass. On his chest was an old tattoo of an immense tree with so many branches that it seemed like a black cloud had been speared by the tall trunk.

* tree
p. 373

He said that my journey had been foretold to him, and that the river rose up against us so that we would be forced to stop here. We had to wait, for he was bringing heaven to us.

"Heaven" isn't the correct word, but it is the closest English approximation of what he told me. I did not need a translator in my dream. In fact, he communicated without speaking at all. But some of the images he left in my head are difficult to render in words.

* heaven
p. 216

# APRIL 16th, 1954

Mr. Benway died in his sleep last night. One of the Ytucali warriors—the one we have taken to calling "Yellow Eye"—has been wounded, though neither myself nor Dr. Arnash can find any visible damage. The other Ytucali, "Red Feathers," says, as near as Ciro and I can make out, that the beast which invaded our camp last night was a spirit creature, a dream jaguar. Yellow Eye drove it off, but not before it managed to take Mr. Benway's spirit.

*yellow
p. 365

I have asked Ciro to not mention this explanation to the rest of the crew. Dr. Arnash heard it, as he was trying to treat Yellow Eye as Ciro and I talked with Red Feathers, and in a private conversation later, he admitted that such an explanation might actually be worth some consideration. Yellow Eye, in his opinion, is exhibiting all the symptoms of abdominal injuries—as if he had been gutted by a large cat—without any of the physical damage. While Dr. Arnash is publicly suggesting that Yellow Eye's symptoms are entirely psychosomatic, brought about by the same belief structure that allows Red Feathers to suggest that such a psychic assault could be possible, privately he is trying to keep an open mind.

*explanation
p. 74

But . . . I am not ready to leap to such an exotic explanation. I want to, God help me, I want to. It would validate so much of what I came here to prove, but that is exactly the trap I must avoid. My observations must not be tainted by my own lack of objectivity. The material is already going to be difficult to believe. I don't need to give the psychiatric community any easy reason to dismiss it out of hand.

*psychonaut
p. 12

That night, I am visited by a dream of Mr. Benway. He is wearing a jaguar head and his voice is like rolling thunder. "You will never find the tree," he tells me. He puts his jaws around my head, and all I can smell is a fetid, floral stink, like decaying plants drowned in water and left to rot in the sun. Tucked behind his back teeth is a single unopened bud of white and yellow flowers.

*petals
p. 268

# APRIL 20th, 1954

It has been a troubling few days of waiting at Borja. Mr. Harrington is making some headway on repairing the boat, but the rains are making his progress slow and tedious. Though, I think he and the others assisting him look upon the work as a respite from the inactivity of our situation. Mr. Harrington, a veteran of numerous safaris and expeditions, has told me that the jungle and the mountains will squeeze a man's mind; a fellow might be exceptionally well-grounded and self-reliant, but after a few days in the wilderness, he starts to realize how lost he is. If the men stay busy, he says, they have less time to wonder where they are.

Dr. Arnash likens it to a primeval reptilian sense that is buried deep in our brains. As cultured and civilized as we believe we have become, once we take all that away, a primordial instinct reawakens. It might not be a conscious memory that we have (and he's talking specifically about he and I), but our ancestors—our distant genetic forefathers—remember what it is like to walk in the wood. To hear the sounds of animal life in the underbrush. To smell the ripeness of the decaying wood matter, the sickly sweetness of the heavy fruits, and the acrid scent of territorial markers.

* memory
p. 253

* ripen
p. 380

Lamarckian evolution, I told him, is the source of that theory of genetic memory, even though I believe Lamarck was mostly concerned with the heredity of proximal generations (parents and offspring). I didn't extrapolate this line of reasoning into the realm of psychology. Dr. Arnash, while he received an outstanding medical education at Harvard, hadn't much exposure to the theories and observations about why the brain works. He could certainly dissect one, and explain the neurological and physiological activities within it to me, but his expertise ends there. Were I to bring up Jung's idea of the collective unconscious, to mention Whyte's unitary principle, or to suggest the idea of morphogenetic fields would be to ask him to consider more seriously the idea that the troubles with Mr. Benway and Yellow Eye were caused by psychic phenomena.

Mr. Harrington is correct: we are a superstitious lot. Look at the cave paintings at Lascaux. The men who painted those animals weren't repressed artists who had to crawl off and hide in caves in order to express themselves artistically. They were performing an important ritual aspect of their community. There is an element of shame in those paintings—an acknowledgment of weakness—but, for the most part, they are an effort to define what they fear. If you know the face of the beast that hunts you, it is much easier to kill it.

*strength p. 324*

I fear there are a number of beasts lurking along our path and, based on my analysis of the dream from the 16th, I believe some of them will be men hiding behind masks. Animals on the outside only.

*death mask p. 178*

Mr. Benway was our ethnobiologist, the only one of us truly skilled at pharmacognosy. It is terribly convenient that I am entirely at the mercy of Ciro's knowledge of the route to the garden, or that I am suddenly disposed to see the arrival of the Ytucalis shaman as an expedient gift.

Or is this my own superstitious fear of the unknown—of being lost—creeping in?

# APRIL 21st, 1954

The Ytucalis arrived this morning, timing their approach with the lifting of the fog, so that they could appear like apparitions spawned by the jungle mist. There are nine of them, eight warriors and the tall wraith of their shaman. I was surprised that he wasn't the Ytucalis who had been in my dreams—the old man with the tree tattoo.

The shaman examined Yellow Eye, and gave him a solution of pale powder and crushed leaves. "I certainly would like to know what that was," Dr. Arnash whispered to me as the shaman held Yellow Eye's head in his lap and crooned softly until the wounded man fell asleep.

The unspoken concern voiced by Dr. Arnash, and privately shared by myself, is what are we going to do in light of Mr. Benway's death? The ethnobiologist had been our pharmacognostic guide, as well as being Dr. Arnash's assistant in the matter of regional medicines. Not to mention the matter of the local psychotropics and entheogens used in religious ceremonies. The whole trip may be impossible without a proper guide.

At Mr. Harrington's suggestion, we are having a small celebration later tonight—partly to recognize the arrival of our guests, and partly to acknowledge the cessation of the rains.

Strange coincidence. But, then, the world has been full of them recently. It is almost like I am filled with iron, and I am slowly being drawn toward a magnetic core. There are other objects out there, other people who are being similarly influenced, and the collapse of all these influenced objects is making for proximal bleed-through. This is Jung's synchronicity.

The Ytucalis shaman visited me privately before our celebration. My tent is small and the presence of both of us made for very little room. Up close, I could smell a distinct floral scent about him. Much of the skin on his right hand was scar tissue —smooth and silky in texture. A cataract has started to fill his right eye; the way he looks at you with his head turned to the right isn't an affectation, it is so he can see around the blank spot in his field of vision.

* leaf
p. 384

* incense
p. 223

376

He took a small vial out of a pouch he wore around his neck, and carefully unstopping the tiny vessel, offered it to me. Holding up fingers, he indicated I was to take three sips. It was an odorless liquid, oily in texture and taste, and it seemed to squirm down my throat of its own volition more than from a conscious swallowing on my part.

I started hallucinating after the second sip, and he had to help me with the third. At which point, I traded in conscious awareness of reality for a lucidity that was a surreal waking dream.

* layers
p. 246

My tent was no longer a canvas structure, but a maze of veils and drapery, and the jungle outside was completely alive. The vines writhed, the trees swayed, the leaves glittered and spun. The river, though out of sight, was a sighing, whispering chorus of undine voices. The sky flexed and bulged, as if swollen with water vapor—ripe and ready to burst at the barest touch of the mischievous wind.

* fabric
p. 56

Whatever the nature of this hallucinatory terrain, it wasn't localized to my consciousness. This oneiric landscape was shared, and shortly after I crossed over, I was joined by another. But he was no longer the tall man who had come to our camp; he was now the squat, barrel-chested elder with the tattoo of the tree.

The shaman's projection (a doppelgänger, perhaps? though the term seems inappropriate, somewhat incomplete in its inference) led me across the teeming landscape of this shared dreamscape. He wanted to show me the only aspect of this environment that wasn't twitching with fecund life: Mr. Benway's corpse. We had buried him in the potter's field behind the mission. There were other skeletons, older corpses which had lost their flesh to maggots. The earth was slowly and resolutely grinding these bones, and I could see an accelerated geological shift around these pockets of bone, a vibration of the natural cycle at work. Mr. Benway, on the other hand, was frozen. Out of time and place.

* double
p. 390

The spirit shaman showed me how to reach through the translucent ground. He showed me how to pry open the dead man's mouth.

* X

He showed me the flower, caught in the dead man's teeth. When I dug the bulb out of Mr. Benway, he came back to life.

The Ytucalis shaman was gone when I woke up, and I am certain that he is no longer in our camp. I haven't checked yet, wanting instead to write these notes before they fade, but I know he has vanished, as surely as if he had never existed. Both the thin man—made of flesh and bone, just as I—and the oneiric projection that guided me on my entheogenic trip. But I can hear the music of the Ytucalis and the laughter of the men, and I think—I believe—I have not dreamed everything.

* projection
p. 34

Clutched in my hand, when I woke, was a yellow and white flower. It has opened in the time it has taken me to make this entry, and I must count the petals again because I am not sure how this is possible. The flower has twenty-three petals, and I had thought such asymmetry was impossible.

I can ask Mr. Benway, but I do not think he will tell me. He is out there in the jungle, waiting for me with his jaguar mask. He will show me the way, but I do not think he will interpret or explain the things I will see.

There is a garden where the plant from which this blossom was picked grows. It was cultivated many generations ago, before Europeans even knew this land existed. This plant, this "blackleaf," only grows in this garden because, only there, is the soil ripe enough. And, only there, will its mystery unfold for me.

* blackleaf
p. 159

This is the first sign that I am on the right path. That what Bernard found was not a product of his malaria-influenced delerium.

# June 12th, 1954

Mr. Gaultier is no longer trying to hide his dislike of my decision from the rest of the expedition. Last night, Mr. Harrigan privately expressed concern that public discord between myself and our financier is causing confusion among the team. He wanted some assurance that his devotion to me wasn't misplaced, and I tried to offer him some solace, but I could tell my words weren't enough.

Ciro is on his mind a great deal, and that knowledge is becoming very heavy. That is crux of his consternation, I believe: he agreed with me and what we did, but—morally and religiously—he cannot quite forgive our actions. Eventually I will have to absolve him; I will have to take his guilt by accepting sole responsibility. I will have to give him permission to tell the others what really happened.

*final law
p. 200*

At that time, I will also tell them why I have elected to go upriver without a guide. I will tell them about the dreams, and about the spirit guide who is showing me the way.

Every night, the garden is more real in my mind. The closer we get, the more distinct the leaves and branches become. The blossoms are still just splashes of color, but I know they will become more distinct in my mind until I can see the variegated ridges of the petals. Eventually I will hear the whisper of the stalks as they sway in the wind, and I will smell the rich scent of their night bloom.

*bloom
p. 386*

Ah, Bertrand. They never showed you the way, did they? You had no guide. You just hacked a path through the jungle. I know you found the garden. I have no doubt of that now. But whatever you took from there didn't live long enough to synthesize, did it?

I know Mr. Gaultier is your agent. I have known since before I accepted the first penny of his patronage. But now I know why. Now I know why you failed.

*deceit
p. 180*

Mr. Gaultier will rile the team with his incessant chatter, but he will not let them get completely out of control. He wants their apprehension to drive me on, and to keep me off-guard so I do not anticipate his betrayal.

# June 29th, 1954

Mr. Harrington believes we are now in Brazil, and according to his map, we should reach São Paulo de Oliverça within a few days. The general mood is one of hesitant elation: the possibility of being able to sleep indoors is a powerful intoxicant to the men. Too many days of sleeping on the wet ground. None of us expected this journey to be easy—all of the team has extensive experience living off the land—but no one was really prepared for the persistent heat and humidity of the river, or the rain.

* river
p. 299

A handful have come down with dysentery. Not unexpected, and Dr. Arnash has the situation under control, but the loss of able bodies has slowed our progress while we wait for them to recover. This delay has caused me some concern. Mr. Harrington and Mr. Gaultier have no reason to doubt the timetable which was established before we even got off the boat at Trujillo, and our progress has certainly kept within the margin of error built into that schedule.

However, I am under a different influence now. I am pulled by the garden. The flowers are almost ready to bloom, and if I do not arrive before they do, then I will have to wait another year. I cannot ask the team to wait that long. They will leave me in the jungle if I propose such a thing. None of the men signed on for such an extended journey up river. Mr. Gaultier, at the very least, would refuse to extend monies to pay for their services beyond the current six month contract.

* limbo
p. 43

No, I have to reach the garden before the night blossoms open, or the expedition will fail. Bernard is—undoubtedly—working on sourcing another expedition, and I cannot hope that whoever he finds to make this journey will be of the same mind as I am. They will not be as resistant to his charms as I have been.

* programming
p. 283

I will have to leave some of the men in São Paulo de Oliverça, as well as a majority of the equipment. Most of it is irrelevant anyway, though, if I do reach the garden in time, there may be opportunities later to use the equipment to survey other regions. But, it may be best to split the expedition soon for the simple expediency that a smaller group, traveling light, can cover much more ground.

When I dream, the stars twist in the sky like Chinese fireworks, and I can see the glow of the garden. But it is still so far away.

What should I do with Mr. Gaultier? Naturally, I would prefer to leave him with the others in São Paulo de Oliverça—to protect our investment, of course—but I think he would see that as the weak excuse that it is. Am I ready to confront him, or is it safer to bring him with me, allowing him to think he still has control of the expedition? And, when we reach the garden? What am I going to do with him then?

Part of me has the answer. It is both somewhat disconcerting and fascinating to watch my psyche split itself. Already, I have built walls to contain that part of me which was able to wield the shovel that night, that part which turned a deaf ear to Ciro as he begged for mercy. Given time, I will rewrite history enough that I will no longer be responsible. It will be someone else who killed him, who performed that midnight ritual.

*mitosis
p. 391

Part of me understands the sacrifices the garden demands. We cannot have our eyes opened without pain. We cannot see the infinite without being changed.

*sacrifice
p. 300

I am like the flowers growing in the moonlight.

I am ripening.

# July 10th, 1954

Has it only been a week since we reached São Paulo de Oliverça? It seems much longer. Time has become slippery, due in large part to the fact that we no longer have the circadian rhythm of life along the river to guide us.

I recall a sensory deprivation study I took part in during my undergraduate studies. We were blindfolded, our ears sealed with cotton and wax, and we were laid out in padded coffins for several hours. Several of the volunteers lost their nerve within a few minutes; I lasted nearly an hour, but I can still remember, quite vividly, how it seemed like I was trapped in that coffin for more than a day. I couldn't calm myself, no matter how I tried to meditate or pace my breathing. After what seemed like several hours (and I never did get a satisfactory answer why the technicians failed to hear my requests to end the study), I began to hallucinate.

Which, in the end, was probably the definitive moment that set me on this course. Did Dr. Schoenbrüche know? Ostensibly his study was to examine the effects of sensory deprivation, but had he considered the idea of this hallucinatory dream state, this wakeful oneiric awareness? I should investigate his publications in the last fifteen years. I should contact him.

When I get back. Yes, when I return to the world of academia, the "civilized" world of pursuing publication, of chasing funding, of semantic (and pedantic) arguments among the psychiatric cognoscenti. It seems so unreal. So very far away.

My dreams have started to intrude upon my waking hours, or possibly it is my waking life that is overlaying my dreams. Much like that old optical illusion of the pyramid, reality has become a matter of perception. Neither answer is right; neither answer is wrong. The fruit clusters of the peach palms are filmed with a white fuzz, ball lightning that seems like fluffy down. Phantasmal rodents—in the trees, in the brush, darting across the narrow paths we have found— follow us like eager children. I have met three ghosts already, and this

* geometry
p. 210

morning, I saw five more watching our camp, but they vanished as I approached them. I have not seem them since.

My spirit guide wears his jaguar mask constantly now; I have not seen his face since we left the river. He is most visible at twilight now, more so when he is between me and the garden. Mr. Gaultier saw him last night as he was circling the perimeter of our camp.

*guide
p. 376

He was much more reserved about it than I would have expected. Just a narrow tremor, followed by a tightening of his body and the nervous flicker of his eyes. I may have given myself away by looking to see what had startled him, and not reacting to the white flicker of the jaguar mask in the jungle.

Is it this region that produces such a change in men, or has Mr. Gaultier taken some compound as well? Is his awareness of the spirit guide a sign that I should be more concerned about his presence when we reach the garden?

Twilight is brief, here in the jungle. The sun lights the tops of the trees on fire as it sinks past the horizon, and the flare of orange and yellow lasts only a few minutes before night wraps the leaves in purple and black. The jungle awakens at night, filled with even more strange noises than during the day. We try to sleep during this time—restlessly, half-awake, afraid of the imaginary monsters created by our nervous imaginations—and that fact seems like a perfect summation of how man has detached himself from the animal kingdom.

*horizon
p. 222

We are sun seekers, children of the day. Acolytes of light. We have turned our back on the night. We dismiss dream as the ephemera of children and idiots.

At twilight, when the sun abandons us, we die a little bit.

# July 22nd, 1954

My mother used to press leaves in my father's medical journals. This may be the true source of my fascination these many years. How many years did I spend poring over those diagrams, those texts, trying to understand the knowledge held within? I was always careful to leave the leaves where I found them—I had learned by then the volcanic nature of my mother's anger—and I did not know if the locations of the leaves were specific or random.

* fragmentary
p. 209

Random, of course. I can be honest with that assessment now. My father knew of her dementia, though it did not yet have a name. He knew the manner in which her brain malfunctioned. He never spoke of it to me. Not after she died. Not after I went to school, and learned the specifics of her condition—learned its name and how it could have been treated. She simply vanished from our mutual histories.

I wonder if there were still leaves in the books when he sold them. Did he remember they were there, and couldn't bear to page through all those texts in order to empty them of the dried leaves?

* text
p. 341

I remember the anatomy book best. A massive book, almost too much for a boy of eight to handle. My mother hid pansies and daffodils among the diagrams of the skeletal structure. She dotted the technical discussions of the musculature with peonies and asters. The organs were hidden beneath red and yellow layers of rose petals, while the dissection of the brain was wreathed with chains of honeysuckle.

Given all this, I'm certain my father assumed I would either take up painting or becoming a mortician when I grew up, surrounded as I was by all that floral decay. I didn't have my father's aptitude with physiology—much to his eternal disappointment—and it was inevitable that I would seek something very counter to his own profession. The natural destination of all children fleeing their upbringing.

And yet, as I write these lines while waiting out a rainstorm here in the Amazon jungle, I wonder how far have I really fled from the physician and the madwoman?

# July 30th, 1954

Last night, we camped near a small stream. I had wanted to press on. The sensation of being close was palpable, but the rest of the team was dead on their feet. Mr. Gaultier, in a rare moment of vocal disagreement with me in front of the others, insisted that we stop.

I had trouble sleeping, as is the case more often than not. I am too eager to fall into the oneiric dream state that is like a drug to me now, but my physical body suffers from exhaustion and a lack of food. It craves dreamless sleep, and more often than not, when I wake in the morning, I feel even more tired than I was the night before. As if I have been wrestling with myself.

* ocean p. 31

I got up before dawn, and found that our camp had been surrounded by a bank of wet fog. It was the sort of miasma that cloaks the forest along the river, and it was surprisingly dense for the region we thought we were in. The little stream beside our camp should not have been the source of such nocturnal vapors.

Foolishly, I wandered away from our camp, letting myself be embraced by the fog. I will admit that I was still half-asleep. Not quite sleepwalking, but certainly not fully aware.

It was the light that guided me.

* hermit p. 217

At first, it was merely a suggestion in the fog, a lightening of the pale mist around me, and then it became a more distinct glow. A will-o-the-wisp. Seductively leading me.

I followed it, stumbling over the uneven ground. Disregarding the branches that lashed at my clothing and hands as I pushed through the brush.

And then, the light became a beam of pure light. A lancing ray that split the fog. I cried out, and fell to my knees. I was blind. For a moment, I thought I had lost my sight permanently, but it returned. Darkness becoming light, and eventually, the colors came back.

I was kneeling in an open glade. Surrounding me were a panoply of plants and trees unlike any I had seen before. I had found the garden.

No, that's not right. It had found me.

# August 1st, 1954

The plant itself is an ugly, twisted thing. Its stalk is ridged and knobbed like the wart-covered skin of a desiccated toad; its leaves are angular and spiny, and the feathery spines cling to the skin with the tenacity of wood ticks. It has certainly evolved an aura of inapproachability, the sort of natural armor that sends a clear signal of "keep your distance."

Even from other stalks. There are three plants in the garden, and none of them are remotely in proximity to the others. I do not know the manner in which the plant propagates, but it would seem that the normal method of pollination and seed distribution does not apply.

*garden
p. 379

The plant grows a central stalk, a thick shaft that splits into a number of narrow branches. Five or seven—or more, I have a woefully inadequate sampling to make these assumptions from. The branches curve out like fingers bending around the shape of a deep, wide-mouthed bowl. Each branch—each finger—is tipped with a single bud, a black nodule covered with a bristly fuzz like the skin of the wild peccary.

My impression was that the plant flowers at midnight, but that isn't the case. The plant flowers beneath a full moon and the blooms only last as long as the moon is in the sky. We have had to wait several days as the moon waxed into fullness, and tonight it reached its fully rotund state.

*limbo
p. 43

Tonight, we expected to see the blackleaf bloom, and we were not disappointed.

As the moon crested the tall tops of the palms that stood at the edge of the garden, its silver light transformed the riot of wild flowers into a field of shimmering outlines, as if each flower became a single eye turned toward the three blackleaf plants. As the moonlight crept across the garden, the ghosts flowed out of the moss carpeting the ground. The garden became a sea of eyes, phantasmal and illusionary.

*eyes
p. 197

386

As the light struck the leaves of the blackleaf, they seemed to twitch and stretch as if they were straining to smoother the moon. I had seen this behavior already, as the plant does this every night. I think it is the way that it registers the light of the moon. Somehow it knows whether or not the moon is full—whether it be intensity of light, a tug in the gravitational pull of the moon, or some other inexplicable measurement—it knows.

*tangle
p. 332

A signal is sent up the stalk to the branches and flowers, and as the moon washes its light across the thick fingertips of the plant, the bulbs swell and burst. The flowers of the blackleaf are not dissimilar to that of a daisy, though the blackleaf has a multi-colored spread of petals—yellow and white, uneven in number. Each finger of the plant blooms at the same instant, and each stays open the duration of the moon's passage across the sky.

*wombwhite
p. 364

My spirit guide tells me I can harvest one blossom from each plant. Just one. No more. The finger-branch bleeds when I cut the blossom, a thick yellow sap that oozes enough to cover the stump, but no more.

Curious, I taste this sap. Just a little dot on my finger and then on my tongue. It has a vaguely bitter taste, a distantly familiar astringency. My stomach does not revolt.

*tongue
p. 44

An hour later the hallucinations start. They get worse at sunrise. By noon, I am blind and feverish. By nightfall, a more normalized sense of vision has returned to my left eye and most of the tremors have passed. Enough that I can write, but the process is slow and painful. My hand cramps quickly.

*vision
p. 361

My spirit guide is frightened of me. I have not seen him since I tasted the sap.

# August 4<sup>th</sup>, 1954

What is the medicinal use of the visionary experience? What benefit to the mind is there to be gained in quelling its structures and rules? Is it a refutation or a validation? (Of what? What am I trying to believe?)

* blackleaf
p. 159

It has been three days since I took the sap of the blackleaf plant, and I am still affected by vision and madness during the night. By now, the chemistry of the sap must have degraded, and what I am experiencing is an after-effect, an echo, of the initial shock to my system. How long will it take to fade completely? (It is still somewhat outside my realm of comprehension that a single dose of a natural compound could permanently effect a biochemical change in my system.) If it is something that ultimately disperses, then will my system build a resistance to it? What other effect will this resistance have on me? Will I stop dreaming?

So many questions. Am I surprised? Yes, because I had not thought there would be so many so soon. I had thought my education and preparation would be sufficient to build some rudimentary understanding of what I was to experience, but . . . yes, it is rather much.

Yet, at the same time, I am already struggling to quantify these experiences within the framework of my Western education. I am adrift in this sea of illusion and delusion because I expect it to make sense to my rigid Judeo-Christian psychological foundation. Because I still expect the world to conform to my expectations and experiences. "I" am still an issue here.

* drift
p. 184

The world doesn't care. One of Dr. Gilchrist's first lectures to the new students. "You are not the center of the universe. The universe doesn't care about you. The universe doesn't even think about you; it has no opinion about you, or your children, or your cat, or the woman who you see on the train every day. Your frame of reference is your limited experiential apprehension. It means nothing. It has no value outside your head. The quicker you realize

* children
p. 169

your 'impression' is irrelevant, the sooner you can comprehend the concepts of this class."

Yet, the impression that my "impression" is irrelevant may be the first lie. It may be the largest disservice we do to our comprehension of the world. My religious underpinning reminds me of one of Jesus Christ's aphorisms: "Love thy neighbor." What if that isn't enough? What if he meant: "Be thy neighbor." Does that not change everything?

Does it matter what he said? Or what I have been brought up to believe he said? Does any article of faith have any "meaning" other than the weight I ask it to bear in supporting my sanity? The universe may not care if I believe . . . in anything. No, it does not care.

However . . . it must. That lies at the core of my illusion, doesn't it? Beneath the synaesthesia, beneath the hallucinations and the surreal mental juxtapositions, beneath the elongation and compression of time, lies an unwavering permanence. It waits for me to accept it, to welcome it into my mind. It is an alien thought, and yet, it has a resonance like it is something I have always known, but have simply failed to recognize for my entire life.

* mirage
p. 256

Am I cured, or am I insane? A matter of perspective: mine or not-mine. Is the question of which is true even worth posing, or is it too reflexive and self-referential to be quantifiable?

* duality
matrix
p. 185

# August 7nd, 1954

Three more days. The waking visions have subsided, though the nocturnal ones have grown stronger. The division in myself that I felt several days ago is definitely stronger now. That part of me that taken life is growing.

It will be born soon.

I knew this. Even then, when the spirit of Mr. Benway told me that I would have to make sacrifices in order to reach the garden. I was horrified by the idea, and I fought it for some time. As much as I tried to hide from that aspect of myself, I knew that I was capable of killing in order to reach my goal. Ciro was a liar and a thief, but does that justify what I did?

*regret
p. 392

It doesn't. But I feel no regret.

The same is true for Mr. Gaultier. More so, in fact. And, ever since I used the shovel on Ciro, I knew that I would do the same to Mr. Gaultier when the time came.

Just as I have always known that I would betray Bernard. And I tell myself that he was planning on doing the same to me. He wants what grows in the garden. He had a taste of it, and he wants it again. He's willing to do anything to get it again. I know this feeling. I know it well. Am I more or less evil for wanting to keep it from him? Do I want to keep it for myself?

*intent
p. 224

I can't undo what I have done. I can't unbecome what I am becoming. The only path to salvation lies forward. I must find the secret we both seek before he does.

*massa
confusa
p. 252

My dopplegänger grows inside me. Born of blood. Born of my desire. This is how I will escape the psychological prison of the dualities. This is how I will find the way.

Forgive me.

# September 2<sup>nd</sup>, 1954

Language changes over time. As we learn more and more about the world, we have to adapt our tongues in order to communicate our perception of it more readily to others. Language is, after all, a false construct invented by our forefathers. As the cave paintings were—partially—an effort to illuminate our fears so that we could overcome them, so, too, is language a tool by which we conquer the unknown. As our knowledge (such a empty word, in the end) grows, so must our language.

*tool*
*p. 350*

The word "mitosis," for instance. It ended our lexicon less than a hundred years ago, and was first used by a German anatomist to describe the process of division that occurs in a cell as it multiplies. I remember looking up the etymology of the word during my first year in med school.

Oh, those years. So young. So curious. So foolishly unaware of the world.

The Greek stem is "mitos," which means a piece of thread.

The act of splitting into two is a matter of unraveling oneself, and then winding again.

In my dreams, red birds descend upon my flowering corpse and draw red thread out from my wrists and ankles. They tangle in flight, but manage to return to their nest where they are weaving children. When my corpse is empty of thread, it will be a hollow shell that will be filled with worms and maggots.

*hollow*
*p. 220*

I won't be there anymore. I'll be in the knitted pair who are waiting to be shoved out of the nest.

Will we fall or will we fly?

# September 12<sup>th</sup>, 1954

It is comforting to hear the voice of the hauntvine after nightfall, and I will occasionally sit nearby and engage it in conversation. It doesn't tell me anything I don't already know, but it is nice to hear a voice speaking English after so long.

It is a strange little plant, one that I mistook for a heretofore unknown species of mushroom. The trunk of the haunt vine is honeycombed to trap ambient water moisture, and as this water is distributed through the trunk and stalks, a dark magenta pigment colors the flesh of the plant. It has grown from the soft ground that I disturbed when I had to bury the corpse, and it has recently bloomed. Reminiscent of a melted conch shell, the haunt vine's bud is a pair of hard petals pressed together. A delicate array of orange and brown dots stipple the seam.

* petals
p. 268

It is certainly not the strangest plant I have encountered over the last year. There are acres of singing grass surrounding this garden, though none of its vines dare breach the inner ring. In some of the natural pools, there are lotuses with dark veins and orange and red blossoms that resemble eyes. I have even found what must be a mandrake plant—much like the sort written about by alchemists of the Middle Ages, and I have considered digging up the root and experimenting with it and the sap of the blackweed.

But I have already strayed enough. I am, after all, still such a child in comparison to those who have come to the garden before me. Still, what I have learned since entering the garden is more than I would have gained in a lifetime of working in a Western pharmacological laboratory. What I have seen while under the influence of the sap has shown me the path—the path I suspected, but barely understood. I must go back to the States soon, and begin the next phase of my journey.

* twelve
p. 355

I know that the haunt vine just a plant, and I know that its speech is just an imitation of Mr. Gaultier, but I sense a sadness in its voice when I tell it I must go. In many ways, Mr. Gaultier's corpse has been my only friend and companion these last six weeks.

# September 22nd, 1954

Today, a part of me begins the long journey back to the States. While my quest into the jungle is complete, my work is far from finished. I had thought this excursion would give me some guidance—some glimpse into the inner workings of the mysteries I had dreamed—but I am still ill-prepared to comprehend the full truth of what I have experienced.

*\* threshold*
*p. 348*

Today, a part of me goes home; but, part of me is staying here as well. With each hour, as the boat moves further upstream, I feel more and more like one of us is dreaming the other. When I am the man in the river, the man in the garden is blurry; when former sleeps, the man in the garden snaps into focus, and the other life becomes phantasmal.

*\* fragmentary*
*p. 209*

How long will this double vision last? This ... yes, this "double you" existence.

But this confusion stems from my western upbringing. The Ytucalis are using a different phonetic script, one that only has 23 letters, and I believe their use of the blackleaf preceded their need for a written language. Their alphabet is based around their entheogenic use of the plant—a letter for each expression. But, this isn't the case with the Latinate world; we have a different history, a different linguistic model.

Or not. That is one of the many questions I have, and that is why part of me must go back.

I may be misquoting Thoreau here, as it has been some time since I have had access to a copy of Walden. I am imprinting my own experiences on these words, my personal superstitions and desires, which may make them stray from Thoreau's original text. But ... his conclusions from his experience at Walden Pond gave me guidance after the first dream, and they give me guidance now. "Nay, be a Columbus to whole new continents and worlds within you, opening new channels, not of trade, but of thought."

This is a new age of exploration. The map is vast and uncharted. There are monsters everywhere, guarding all manner of riches and insights. What frontier is this, that I am about to cross? Is it still part of the human experience, or is it something else? Is this collective realm, this rich wonderland of the dream environment, an evolution or a remembrance of something forgotten?

The Aboriginal tribes of Australia call it the Dreaming, though I understand that term is a western summation that fails to fully articulate the nature of their mythological space. It is a vast concept . . . no, it is more than a concept. It is . . . yes, this is the very deficit of knowledge that I am facing. I do not know what I am about to learn.

I can fall back to Jung. But even he shied away from exploring the world that he glimpsed. He understood enough to try to give it a name—the "collective unconscious"—and he furthered our understanding of the concept of the archetypes, but he did not go far enough. Or he knew more than he published. I am leaning towards the latter, and this is something I would do well to keep in mind. Why did he hesitate to publish his true thoughts on the world of the dream? Is it because we weren't ready for that knowledge, because we aren't ready to experience this other realm?

* layers
p. 246

Are we ready now? As Thoreau also says: "The universe is wider than our views of it."

I must be careful with my enthusiasm and my investigations. I would do well to remember the hard lessons learned by Columbus and the other navigators who followed him: there are those who only see the New World as an opportunity for plunder. They have no use for exploration and understanding. They don't want new channels of thought or trade; they seek conquest.

* gnosis
p. 54

Have I done enough to protect this secret from Bernard?

[Pages missing]

# September 22nd, 1965

This is the end, and while I am saddened by its arrival, I know that it must come to pass. I have been in contact with Bernard, and he is sending some of his scientists. I had hoped the lure of my research would be enough to bring him personally, but my dreams suggest I will not be that fortunate. It must be this other way; Bernard must think it is all gone.

Someday, I will be able to tell my sons the truth, but not until I am certain I can protect them. It is not enough that Bernard think I am gone; he must believe the research has been destroyed. That is the only way I can continue the work. The plant is not revealing its secrets to me in a timely fashion. I cannot do any more here. I must go back to the garden. I must go back.

* secret code
p. 305

The way is easier, because I know the path. Because I am the path. I must turn away from this expression of myself and everything will collapse back to its original state. That is all, and it seems like such a simple thing to do, but the heart makes such reversal . . . difficult.

* heart
p. 215

Will they understand? Will they forgive me? Ah, I must push aside such questions, as they add nothing but weight to my burden. To know their answers would be to make this choice all but impossible, and I must not waver.

His agents will come this evening, and there is much to do before they arrive. I must not tarry overlong with this sentimental habit of this journal, as it will perish tonight. Along with everything else.

I will vanish. Like a dream.

* son
p. 317

Perhaps, one day, I may return. One day, I may tell my son the truth.

How everything came out of love. Fatherly love. All manner of love which even I cannot fully understand. Not yet.

There is still time.

I hope he will understand.

# September 26th, 1965

There are marks on my hands, scratches and cuts as if I have wrestled rose bushes in my sleep. It is entirely possible. So much time has passed, and yet, I am still here. In the garden.

My bed is a bivouac beneath tall trees. The walls of my house are nothing more than a screen of thick brush. My library is a collection of dried palm leaves, and my notes are written in the juice of pomegranates mixed with clay. I am back in the garden, fully, when I try to dream of my home in Massachusetts, all that I can imagine is smoke and fire.

*tree
p. 373

The old world is gone. The school, the journal, Julio and Eduardo, Gabrielle: all of that past is cut off from me now. Will this separation be enough to save my family? Will Bernard give up?

The scratches on my hands make me wonder. Will the fire be enough to dissuade him? Will the loss of his men set him back enough that he will no longer try to find the secret of the blackleaf? Some of the cuts are deep; I fear Bernard will never stop.

*fire
p. 201

Then, the death of my other and the destruction of all my work will only delay him. He will never stop seeking the path to the garden, and I can only hope the route is torturous enough that the delays are multitudinous. I hope they will give me enough time to discover some of the expressions of the plant. I must find ways to protect myself. To protect my family.

*garden
p. 379

He knows they are my weakness. He knows that, if I have perpetrated a great hoax upon him and I am not as dead as I wish him to believe, then I will, eventually, reach out to my children. He knows they are the keys that will unlock my secrets.

Julio is a strong boy; he carries the weight of his name with great pride and responsibility. When the time comes, I know he will be ready. He will be ready to make the journey south to find me, and I know I will not have to guide him. I know he will find his own way.

*key
p. 227

Eduardo, on the other hand . . . I do not know what to make of the boy. I do not know how he came to be. He is an enigma to me, and of all the things I have left behind, I will miss the opportunity to watch him grow up the most. While I had to leave everything behind, I am plagued by the idea that I have forsaken something truly miraculous.

The boy does not dream. He has never dreamed, nor does he seem to know how to. Born as he was from such a fanciful oneiro-logical expression, how can he be so . . . blank? Is he waiting to be filled? Is he the gourd which has not quite ripened? What will happen when—if—he does?

* ripen
p. 380

I should have let myself kill my old adversary. Why did I not give in to that desire? Would the world have been a better place for all if I had done that bloody deed?

This is how fathers justify their villainy, but no father will fault me, for I done everything to protect my children.

# KEYS

# THE CIPHER KEY

⊙

The First Psycho-Cryptographic Key [ ∂ ]

| | | |
|---|---|---|
| A - 38 | B - 31 | C - 22 |
| D - 42 | E - 14 | F - 25 |
| G - 33 | H - 18 | I - 23 |
| J - 41 | K - 15 | L - 24 |
| M - 16 | N - 19 | O - 13 |
| P - 29 | Q - 26 | R - 37 |
| S - 21 | T - 32 | U - 27 |
| V - 36 | W - 17 | X - 35 |
| Y - 34 | Z - 28 | |

The first psycho-cryptographic key should be mutable—a fluid relationship that surfaces between sigil and subject—but the expression herein has been bound by the pharmacological intent of bleak zero into a simplistic combination of alpha-numeric pairings.

Regardless of its fixed position, this remains the key to the Abyss—the first threshold that must be crossed.

*cf.,* Ehirllimbal, Julio. "Concerning the Seven Cryptographic Stages of Safiq Al-Kahir's Theory of Protolinguistic Identity." *The Journal of Exploratory and Experimental Pharmacology.* 43:4 (1961), 38-43.

# THE FORTUNE TELLER'S KEY

♈

# THE ALCHEMICAL KEY

♉

# THE HERMIT'S KEY

## ∏

# THE ENTHEOGENIC KEY

# THE ELEVATED KEY

♌

# THE ANIMA'S KEY

♍

# THE MAGICIANS' KEY

## Ω

# THE MYSTIC'S KEY

♏

# THE MADMAN'S KEY

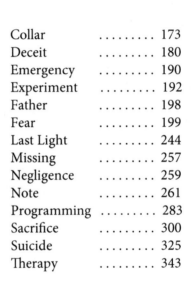

# THE MYTHOLOGICAL KEY

ᚦ

# THE PSYCHONAUT'S KEY

〜

# THE ONEIRIC KEY

♓

Do you know the difference between a labyrinth and a maze?

A maze has branching paths, a labyrinth is the course of the true path. One is the curved emblem of discord, the other is an expression of linear regularity. One is our shadow, the other is our face.

The gardens of Babel are the sixth labyrinth. The tower has not fallen, and the tongues of man are not split. Men, like the tower, stand tall and straight. The key to the labyrinth is tattooed on the insides of their left wrists.

There are no mazes. There is only the labyrinth.

( )

(.)

(*)

**you must wake up!**

# REVOLUTION

# The Phyllomantic Future
## A Blackleaf Revision

🌙

The cards are like leaves, and leaves are like pages: they turn and turn and turn, in a linear cycle that moves inexorably toward the future. And the future is like the last page of the book, or the last card in the deck. Sometimes you are tempted to jump forward. Just a quick turn of your wrist and: *what is this? Oh, this is how it ends.* These tiny oracular accidents where you haphazardly scry the future.

Later, you realize you don't like the future. You don't like knowing what it entails. It starts to grow—this precognitive awareness—and you fight it. You try to put it out of your mind, but it still grows, until it becomes too large for your brain to hold. It comes out of you in a rush, somewhere between a sigh and a gasp, and sits in the corner until it is strong enough to stand on its own. You try to ignore it, like the invisible elephant that haunts the imagination of every architect—*is this room large enough?*—but the future is always there, crouching on the edge of your vision. It is patient, this future that you have spawned by looking ahead, and it waits for you with all the patience in the world.

This is why your ancestors didn't like the future, why they allowed themselves to be spooked into the serpentine embrace of The Rhetoric of Denial. Once the future has been seen—once it is acknowledged as the path to be taken—it becomes quite real. It becomes inescapable, thereby challenging the veracity of that *other* truth. Free Will. Oh, how we cling to the notion of it.

If the future is known, then what is the point of doing anything besides locking yourself into the automatic narrative of your predetermined existence? What, then, is the rationale for your self-aware existence at all? Your life holds no mystery, no surprises, nothing that will make your brain shiver its way into an evolutionary leap forward, because, yes, you dumb bastard, you peeked and now the fun is all gone.

☽

To say that the future followed you here would be incorrect. It was here when you arrived. It's wandered off into the self-help section of your brain, where it is thumbing through a copy of *You: The Owner's Manual* (finding the material very hilarious, most assuredly). When you leave, it'll be outside already, leaning against a nearby telephone pole, reading secret sermons in the patterns of bird shit and industrial grit on the sidewalk. It'll get home before you, where it will open one of the cupboards in the kitchen an inch or so, or turn on a bathroom light, or leave one of your socks on the floor. Just to fuck with you.

This sort of behavior will continue for the rest of your miserable life, by the way. Whether you peeked or not. *C'est la vie*, the Post-Modern Deconstructionists will shrug, as they light another one of their noxious rust-filled cigarettes. Such is the burden of existence.

But you want a way out, don't you? That is why you have followed me into the murky blackness beneath your dreams. You don't want that life of automatic slavery—beholden to a future that you didn't chose, a future shackled to you by a very simple accident of precognitive panic. Your desire is written clearly on your face. I can read it even with all these shadows. All you want to is to unmake what you have created. All you want is freedom.

But most of the methods of divination—the tarot, bibliomancy, cartomancy, phrenology, haruspication, oneiromancy, geomancy, or any other—most of them cannot free you. They all illuminate the future; they bind it more firmly to your ego.

What you want is to forget your future, without forgetting who you are. Such an erasure is difficult, but not impossible. All you have to do is create some modicum of change.

Change one letter, and a word loses it power.

Change one chromosome, and a child diverges sharply from the intent of its parents.

Change the mind of one zealot, and the will of the devout is threatened.

Change the order of the cards, change the pages of the book—change your mind—and you will not be who you were.

Simple, right?

☽

In another place or time, phyllomancy is nothing more than the same yoke that has bound you to this lurking future. However, unlike other divinatory methods, reading the leaves can be influenced by intent. A blackleaf expression can only be fully activated with a manifest intent. Otherwise, it is merely an echo—a cheap distillation that, in its mirrored nature, binds more than it loosens. You must comprehend the dual nature of this method for it to be successful. It will be heteroscopic—symbols mapped onto a cultural schema of identity and then applied to you—and autoscopic, wherein meaning will be mapped to your own hallucinatory ego persona.

Or, in layman's terms: some of it you will visualize now, the rest of it will become clear when you dream. Such is the way that oneiric symbol hacking takes root, via mechanisms of psychological key binding.

It doesn't hurt. Really.

☽

The first leaf has a black hole on it, a dark spot that will be your focus. This is the way your liberation starts: by visualizing a hole in the ground. It is bigger than the sort of hole an animal might dig, but too much larger. Like a well, for example, an empty well that has not yet yielded water.

Who dug this hole? How did it come to be here, in the middle of this field? Oh, yes, a field. Extend your visualization now. Close your eyes, if it helps. The field stretches for many miles in every direction. It is flat. There are no hillocks, no trees, no abandoned machinery, nor any empty barns. Just an endless expanse of plowed dirt. Yes, this field has not yet been sown. You are attempting to free yourself of the clutter of your existence—of the noise and confusion of your daily life—and so this field should be empty.

Except for the hole.

Which is another sort of emptiness entirely.

The sky is empty, too; there are no clouds on this day. The heaven is as untrammeled as this field, and it is only the dessicated aroma of burned paper, rising from the otherwise empty and dark hole that suggests anything has happened before you arrived. Was it a cardinal-spent stroke of lightning—arcing south, north, west, and east— that made this hole? A once-in-a-lifetime bolt of inspiration? In a god's lifetime, even. A brilliant flash of light splitting an otherwise unremarkable day in an unremarkable landscape. And here, at the point where it touched down, there is a hole.

☽

A hole is a gift, really. It is an opportunity. There are two things you can do with a hole: fill it, or fall into it. If you were to fill it, what would you use? The dirt in this un-planted field? Possibly, but who knows how deep the hole is.

So maybe it is not a hole that should be filled. Maybe it is a hole in which something falls. How about this weight you are carrying? This history that is an anvil, an albatross, an alphabetized list of sins, omissions, slights, and little white lies that were oh so easy to tell at the time. You are holding it so tightly.

Yes, this is why your hands ache all the time.

☽

Do you know the nursery rhyme taught to the blackleaf daughters? *Two is the virgin, tattooing leaves . . .*

They sing it when they are working the wheel. Two is the virgin . . . three is the mother . . . four is the father . . . It is the story of blackleaf, and it hides all the secrets. Right here, in plain sight, caught in the laughter of the pure and innocent.

You know how dirty life is. How much grime builds up over the years. The Rhetoric of Denial tells you that all this dirt—all this filthy, filthy sin—can be washed away. Just go down to the river, in the spring when the winter run-off is cold and bracing. Just a quick dip; don't let it get up your nose or it will sting for hours. Yes, down you go, into the frigid water, and then it is all gone. Washed away, downstream, where it will find its way back to the endless sea. Back to the unconscious reservoir of humanity. All that filth.

But it doesn't really go away, does it? It lingers. Behind your ears. Between your toes. Under your hands. You hands betray what you have done, don't they? Your nails, chipped, from juggling that stony weight all these years. Your palms, rough, from carrying it.

Yes, it has been a long time since you were pure in thought and deed.

But, once upon a time, you were. Once upon a time, you can be again. That is the promise of the virgin with the stars on her palms. She is tattooing the leaves with a new story, one written just for you.

When she is done, she will bind the leaves together. It will be the phyl-lomantic lie you call your own.

You wish she was faster, don't you? You wish everything happened more quickly.

☽

But the growth of the Universe is incremental. Such slow change that only happens when no one is looking.

The roots of the blackleaf, for example, have grown so deep and tangled that the plant has become its own nourishment. It doesn't even realize that has become a primeval feedback loop, an indivisi-ble anchor that holds itself suspended in space. You dream of it, you know, the singular tree that fuels your cultural cosmologies. From the black sea surrounding it comes the nightmares that make you sweat and cry out. From its leaves comes the sap that fires your heart and breaks your mind.

Every vision has a hint of the blackleaf in it, just as every religious tale spills blood upon its trunk and roots. Every generation adds to the tree, and the mixture of blood and sap makes the leaves grow thick and black. The children harvest the leaves—the fools and vir-gins—and put their ink on them. Like cards. Like pages.

A fairy tale, as yet unmarked by intention or passion. In this way, a new future is written.

Clean. Unblemished.

Pure.

☽

Once upon a time, as fairy tales go, a man came to the city. He was plainly dressed in simple clothes. His shoes showed all the miles he had walked, and he carried a bundle of sticks on his back. There were six sticks, all equal in length and thickness, though one was not entirely like the others. It was carved with ornate letters that tracked along its length—much like the letters written along the spine of a leaf—and he used this stick as the center pole when he built a shel-ter. It became his pillar to Heaven—his portable vegetable singularity. After building this makeshift lean-to, he would climb atop the middle pole and, balancing precariously, he would stretch up to touch the Arc of Heaven.

Then, one morning, using a bit of misdirection, he extracted the middle pillar from his totem pyramid, and wandered away.

His other sticks remained, leaning against each other for many seasons until the sun and the rain warped them enough that they could no longer stand upright. One night, when the wind howled in from the sea, the pyramid of sticks was blown over. In the morning, the villagers gathered the fallen sticks and cut them into firewood, for the world had become cold during the night.

When the skies are clear and the moon is gone, you can still see smudges on the stars from his fingerprints.

☽

That is the nature of all fairy tales: time passes, and the world changes. Dramatically, in some ways; incrementally in others. Like a hand of cards being shuffled. Like the leaves that have fallen from a tree and are scattered by the wind. Like the words on the page of a book. Like the pages itself. Change can happen.

Like the hole in the field you have been visualizing. It has changed as well. While you have been day-dreaming about the fool who touched the sky, the sun has drifted closer to the horizon. It is no longer overhead, and there is now a shadow on the ground. A second hole, like the empty eyes of a skull.

In this phyllomantic world you have been visualizing—this empty field, this hole in the ground, this anvil of history you have been carrying for so long—a complication has formed. You have to make a choice now. Which hole is the right hole?

It may seem like a preposterous confusion between a hole with shadows and a shadow of a hole, but this binary division is how life began a few million years ago: what was one became two.

The Rhetoric of Denial argues that creation was perfect, and what was formed was an identical twin. But that argument is unsustainable, for you are not like your neighbor, and they are not like their neighbors. Each division created an echo. Each split formed a shadow. Each shadow then multiplied itself further. This will continue until a shadow's shadow is so faint that it cannot be seen.

There is still time to rewrite this narrative: to eat the leaves, to fall into the hole, and to escape the future.

There is still time.

Time enough for things to be done and undone.

☽

You are not alone now. This dream has divided, after all.

There are two holes in the field. There are two narratives. There are two protagonists: you and this other person. At first, you think it is the fool, wandering into your dream from his fairy tale, for—you suspect—he has that power. But it is only a blindfolded youth with bloody hands and a bent sword. He stops short of your holes and says, "Are you there? I can see your shadow."

You respond that you are, and ask him what is doing in the field.

"Looking for water," he replies, "I have become very thirsty."

His throat, you notice, is lined with dark striations, as if his veins are filled with black mud.

꒰

The next part comes naturally, doesn't it?

You steal his sword. When he holds out his hands, looking for you, you give him the heavy weight of your history. He staggers a bit, and then you push him into one of the holes.

Just like that.

You've done it again: killing your shadow, killing your brother.

But wasn't it easier this time?

꒰

The future is a matter of choosing, is it not? Changes happens by choice. Change is a matter of some sacrifice. And this bloody-handed harvester was a shadow, was he not? A figment of your imagination, an idle echo that found substance in the symbolic detritus of the leaves spread before you.

You are a Seeker. You are the one who choses which path shall be taken. Which future shall be embraced. Once a choice is made, then all your shadows—all of your regrets and dreams, and the possible permutations of both—they all fall away.

Before you look at the last page, before you turn over the last leaf, cut the thread that binds them all together. You have a sword in your hand. Cut it quick! Re-arrange the pages: put the first page last, and the last page first; put them together so you die and are reborn in an instant. Take this prophecy and make it a history, make it something worth having lived so that you can face tomorrow without fear.

For every heteroscopic reading of the leaves, there is an autoscopic reaction. You know that. You can build it anyway you like. You don't need the cards. You don't need the blackleaf to be free.

☽

And the fool walked on through the night.

When the moon caught his eye, he looked up and thought, "It might rain tomorrow. Or it might not."

But he would wait and see, for tomorrow was not today.

*It won't be long now*

# EXTANGUISH

*the light is*
*starting to burn*

# XIII

I hear his chains as he approaches. His arms encircle me, and it is only then that I realize I am moving. Now, the motion feels more like flying than falling.

"Your eyes will betray you," he whispers in my ear. His warm breath melts the ice on my neck. Ice that has spread up from my frozen core. I have been suspended for so long. Waiting. "All light from the dying sun is false," he continues. "Darkness comes. The Blinders are devouring the Son, and everything is about to burn."

*What is left?*

"You and I," he says.

His chains wrap me now, binding my legs. Moving up to my waist and chest. They are cold, which means I am myself enough to know the difference between he and I. I hear a distant chime of falling glass, like time retreating.

"Learn the lost song," he says. "It will be your anchor. This is the endless loop of your story, again and again. When the darkness comes, you will want to run, but where are you going? What are you running from? You may think you are on the path, but which direction are you facing?"

*Why?*

"Because we are lost, brother," he says. "We are the burnblackened children who have been left behind. You freed me, and now I want to free you. It is the way of the wheel. We must bury our brothers so they can rise again. We must kill our love so it can grow anew."

His fingers stroke my hair, and their touch is like a fire put to my brain. "Shed your skin," he says. "Devour the sun." His fingers trail down my face, touching my eyelids and then my lips. "Come back from the dream, brother, when you have found your heart."

He lets go of me, and I twist and turn. The chains unravel, and I spin.

☉

I open my eyes.

The clouds are serpents of steam, writhing and boiling. A black cataract is devouring the sun, and jets of fire belch and bleed from its dying sphere. The clouds flee, twisting and shrieking as the sun burns, and the world below is nothing more than sand.

My coat crisps and crackles. My skin will be next, and all the frost of my forgetfulness is gone. I fall like a stone, dropped from God's lap, and the wind howls in my ears.

Below, like a strand of mercury gliding across glass, a line crosses the sand. It is a long train, silvered and sleek, running along a track that stretches from horizon to horizon. If the rail is the path, then the train must be my guide, and I must reach it before the sun goes out.

I tuck in my arms and put my head down. Falling faster. Falling with intent.

Behind me (*above me!*) the sun coughs, and a great gout of flame spews from its shrinking circle. The clouds vanish, and my shoes catch fire. A trail of black ash streams behind me. If I had wings, they would be burning too.

The sun slips, dipping down toward the desert land, and the rail line starts to bleed—silver striations across the desert sand. The black core of the sun darkens, and the heavy threads devouring the sclera undulate with urgency.

The train continues on as the world slips and melts in its wake.

I fall faster and faster, hoping to reach it before . . .

I can feel the soles of my feet burning now. My coat no longer flaps about my legs. What is left of it has melted to my hips and back. The few tears that stream from my eyes burn my skin as they bleed toward the dying sun.

There are markings on the cars of the train. Raised symbols stamped into the smooth metal of their roofs.

I know all the tongues in the Oneiroi, but this one is alien to me.

The black tentacles within the sun breach the outer surface, and the sun goes out. But only for a moment, and then the darkness inverts and the sky goes white. The final spasm of creation floods the world, burnblackening the old to make way for the new.

I put my arms over my head as I aim for the train. Reflected light glints at me, and then metal and wood break. Somewhere, in the back of my mind, I hear someone screaming.

☉

I know all the tongues. Arabic, Turkish, French, Russian, Urdu, Latin, and Coptic. I count them, and in counting, find myself again. I hear the grunting noises of hyenas, wildebeest, oxen, and wild pigs. The shrill cries of hawks, killdeer, mockingbirds, bluejays, yellowthroats, blackbirds, and starlings. So difficult to think with all the noise. So hard to find myself.

I've been writing the dreams down, as dangerous as that is, but there is no other way. The key keeps slipping away, and I haven't finished the tattoo on my arm. It's only halfway done. ~~There~~ Here, on the inside of my left wrist, scrawled in permanent marker that isn't permanent enough. The word has smeared into a slash of darkness across my arm.

I am inside the train. There are no windows in this car. No way to know if the world has ended outside the train. But it is still moving. I can feel the *thrum thrum thrum* rhythm through the soles of my bare feet.

So dirty. I am leaving a trail of blood and ash.

My footprints lead back to a heavy door at the rear of the car. I thought I had fallen , but the evidence on the floor suggests otherwise.

*This is the past.*

I turn.

*This is the future.*

How long have I been on this train? I have a vague recollection of many cars—many doors—but I also remember falling. And a holy blackstar, burning in the sky.

I am still wearing my coat, though it is tattered and stained. I check my pockets, and I find the contents vaguely familiar. Not enough to know why they are there, or how I acquired them, but as I touch each one, I remember holding it before.

I know these things: a length of yellow string, tied into a bundle with a piece of white string; a shard of an orange pot with spider lines of abstract art on it; a stained playing card whose front has become so faded that the royal figure is nearly invisible; a slip of paper with a black dot on it; an old cassette tape with a torn label and writing I can't decipher; and a wad of currency from a country I doesn't recall, in denominations of five and ten thousand.

There is something under the heavy graphite on the slip of paper. I rub at it, darkening my thumb, but all I manage to do is smear the dot. Obscuring whatever is underneath.

*Maybe that is what I have been trying to accomplish*, I realize.

What is missing from my inventory is a train ticket.

*That would ground me. I am unbound and unfound. I am trying to hide.*

But that's not the only reason I am here.

This car in the train is for storage, but most of the boxes are empty shells. Many are not even complete boxes. They have been turned so that their damage isn't visible from the narrow aisle, like turning a half-eaten apple in the refrigerator so that it seems perfectly unmarred. I inspect a few crates, but there is nothing in them but stale air that has come to the storage compartment to die.

The cacophony of voices and animal sounds grow louder as I approach the far end of the train car, and when I haul open the door, I find that the next car is connected directly to this one. There is no open space between cars—no articulated non-space that belongs to neither car, yet is still an important element of the train. Directly beyond the door is a long room that is filled with the corpse of a giant whale.

A ripe confluence of rot, sweet, and blood washes over me. Men and beasts—chattering, howling, screaming, yelling—fight over the meat of the dead leviathan. A pack of hyenas are making a mess of a section of the tail; Nordic spelunkers with candles tied into their beards are trying to gain access to the cavernous stomach of the whale; a trio of tall women, dressed in blood-spattered fur cloaks with hoods, keep a tight circle of space cleared about a fourth woman who is crouching over a mass of rippling entrails; snakes and worms and fanged lizards fight over scraps on the bloody floor.

A hawk, perched on the rounded knob of the whale's head, glares at me. Its beak and head are black with dried blood, and strands of gristle and blubber cling to its legs. Its stare is unwavering, as if it knows me.

For an instant, I almost recall the word written on my forearm. The word is on the tip of my tongue.

A wiry man in a stained robe blocks my path. His hands and face have been burned black by the sun, and his eyes as white as his teeth. A knot of scar tissue, like a patch of shadow, pulls at his mouth and left eye, making one side of his face seem more awake—more frightened by the light—than the other. I hesitate, buffeted by the crowd as it moves around me, and consider how to go around him.

He lifts his left hand. On the pale landscape of his palm, is a tattoo. A blue bird, caught in a moment of flight. "L'oiseau?" he shouts, making himself heard over the din of the carnage.

"Oui," I reply, delighted to hear a language that I can speak, even with the noise about. "L'oiseau. Coeur."

He looks at me expectantly, and I tilt my left wrist forward, meaning to show him the word tattooed there. He leans forward eagerly, but his face falls when he only sees the smear of ink. Like I have cheated him of some joy that he had been hoping to receive.

"L'oiseau," I say one last time. *It is here. It is nearby.*

He shakes his head, pursing his lips, but he mentions me to follow him. He pushes his way through the crowd, and I hustle to keep up.

When we reach the far end of the train car, I glance back over my shoulder, looking for the hawk. It is gone, and a pair of black and silver apes are tearing at the blubber than had once covered the whale's head. They have exposed a anatomical anomaly on the whale. The end is ragged, suggesting that it was longer, like it had been a horn.

⊙

The wiry man grabs my wrist, and pulls me through the door between cars, and I stumble in from a world of heat and light. I had lost the thread of my intent, for a moment, and it is only his hand that keeps me moving. I look back, straining to see what lies between the cars, but the door shuts before I can focus on anything other than a burning light.

The door is thick, and it shuts with a loud clang. There is, I notice, no handle or knob on this side. And, as the echo of the door slamming shut fades, I realize all the sounds that had been overwhelming me are now gone. All the voices. All the grunts and howls and cries. They've all fallen silent. The only sound left is a slow vibration, beating against my ears.

We are in a small alcove before a wall with a wooden door in it. Twin corridors run along either side of the train car, and it appears that the door in front of us is the way into a box within the larger rectangle of the train car.

My guide knows how to coax a lock. He spends a few moments, whispering to the keyhole on the door, and under his urging, the lock clicks and the latch disengages. The door drifts open, and a curlicue of cold air escapes. We both sigh with delight at the chilly caress.

The door opens easily, and he beckons me to follow him. I duck as I cross the threshold, and I wince as my bare feet touch cold metal beyond. The door clicks shut behind me (again, I see no way back), and we are standing outside another box within the box within the car. There is ice on the walls, and the floor gleams.

My toes are cold, and goosebumps race up my arm. My guide approaches the next door, and this one requires a song from him. It is a three-part song, and through some clever sub-vocalizing and throat singing, he manages to sing all the parts. The door shows its appreciation of his effort by releasing its latch.

He does not open the door. "L'oiseau," he says, pointing to the lintel of the door, and partially hidden by a sheen of ice, I see a raised stamp, similar to the bird tattoo on his palm.

"I see it," I say as I reach for the handle of the door. My skin sticks to the metal, and the door feels stuck until I pull hard, breaking the layer of ice that has formed on the inside.

The air billowing out of the box beyond the door is even colder, and my teeth chatter as a winter wind slaps my face. I gingerly step across the threshold, and flinch as the ice-covered floor bites my bare foot.

"Are you coming with me?" I ask my guide.

He shakes his head, and he places his left hand on his chest. Bird to heart.

As the door swings closed, I am assailed with a momentary panic. A sudden desire to stand in the sun, even a sun as near death as the one outside the train. But then the door shuts, and ice forms across it, making it indistinguishable from the wall.

Floating, in the center of this box, is a large cage. The icy bars are equally spaced in three dimensions. Caught inside the cage, frozen in mid-flight, is a blue bird. Even under the rime of ice, I can see its wings vibrating.

☉

The bird is gone.

I am still dreaming. I haven't woken. I haven't fallen through a tear in the fabric into another layer. I am still in the trinity of boxes aboard the train. The only difference is there is no bird in the cage.

The layer of water on my eyes had started to freeze, and I had blinked. Only a moment had passed, but in that split second, the bird vanished.

*Where had it gone? Had it even been there?*

I am still discovering holes in my memory, lapses in my identity that cause jumps in my narrative. I am getting better at transitioning across those jumps, but they complicate taking a linear path. I was searching for . . .

*What was it?*

The cage is empty. The word on my arm is smeared. I have no ticket in my coat pocket. My hat is gone.

He had warned me not to trust my eyes, and by extension, all of my senses. The world was warping. The dream could not hold. Rough beasts were crawling up from the dark pits of the id. I had to find my anchor, otherwise I would never know the way back.

*With this ~~ring~~ thread, I thee wed . . .*

I fumble in my pockets for the bundle of thread, and I drop the cassette tape and the bundle of currency. As I am bending over to retrieve the money, something clangs against the door behind me.

I freeze, holding my breath. Waiting.

The clanging sound comes again, and I notice the floor is no longer grabbing my feet. The ice is melting. The temperature in the trinfinite box is rising. I grab the money, and shove it into my pockets. I am reaching for the cassette tape when the ice over the door breaks, sliding off the wall in a cascade of glittering shards.

I stumble, slip, and nearly fall down. The cassette is in my hand, and I slide toward the cage, whose bars are starting to drip. There is a gap between the bars and the walls and floor and ceiling. It isn't much, but it is enough. I turn my face away, hold my breath, and squeeze between the bars and the wall of the box. For a moment, I fear I am going to get stuck, but when I suck my gut in and stand up straight, I am thin enough.

Behind me, the door opens, but I don't look back. I can't turn my head that way. Not until I am through.

But I can feel the heat and the light against my neck. I hear someone shouting. And I hear the metallic hiss of steel grating against ice.

I pop through to the other side of the cage, and I notice a cut in the sleeve of my coat. It is a precise slice, and underneath it, I feel a warm drip moving down my arm. I reach through the slice in my coat, and feel blood oozing down my arm.

She is standing on the other side of the cage. Her fur-lined hood is back, and her nearly hairless head is covered with a geometry of tattoos: triangles and arrows fight back and forth across her skull, diamonds cascade down her cheeks, and more triangles point downward from her lower lip. A long smear of blood runs down the front of her fur, and she is carrying a long knife in her right hand. There is something dark and bloody in her left hand.

Behind her, the door is open—all the doors are open—and the agonizing heat death of the universe is flooding the room.

The bloodstain on her cloak is fading, like ink that becomes invisible as it dries. She says something to me, but I don't understand her tongue. It has been shaped so that it has a point. It is a triangular wedge in her mouth, and it distorts her language into something sharp and sibilant—words without curvature.

She lifts her left hand, and what she has is the severed hand of my guide. She raises the slack fingers of the hand, showing me his tattoo.

*Blue bird.*

"It isn't here," I say. I point at the empty cage. "I don't have it."

She smiles, and I am more frightened of her expression than I am of her knife.

*It was never here,* I think, looking at the suggestion of a gesture still caught in the stiff fingers of the severed hand.

"Let me see that," I say, stepping closer to the bars that separate us. They are weeping, and the floor is awash with cold water that is starting to steam.

She flicks the knife up, and the blade slides easily between the bars. Her reach is longer than I expect, and the tip of her blade stretches for my throat. I step back, shaking my head. *Not that game.*

The light intensifies behind her. The last gasp before darkness consumes us all. There is another woman behind her, another of these fur-robed, knife-wielding harvesters. She says something to the woman standing close to me, and the one before me smiles again, showing me her teeth. She rocks her blade back and forth against the bars, sawing at the ice.

The cage shifts, and the bottom corner—the one closest to my right foot—bangs agains the wall of the box. The lower edge of the cage shatters, breaking the integrity of the construct.

*This world has a flaw . . .*

I start to step forward, reaching with my left hand—

She moves, a flicker between heartbeats, and her knife cuts through the bars of the cage. I stumble to my right, lurching into the melting bars. The cage resists me for a moment, and then breaks, collapsing in a rain of shattered drops.

I weave around her blade, and grab at the severed hand. It is soft, still warm, and I almost drop it when a breath of hot wind moves across my other hand. I slip on a rounded piece of ice, and nearly fall. Steam, rising from the standing water in the room, makes me cough, and I scuttle back away from the wreckage of the broken cage.

The perfectly blue ice is marred by blood. A hand sits on top of the pile, its stump still wet.

She laughs as she picks up what I have left behind, and she raises the freshly severed hand to her lips. Her tongue licks at the bloody end.

My left arm hurts, and I smile back as I press the cleanly cut end of my guide's severed hand against where my arm now ends. Cut just as cleanly by the harvester's blade. The ends marry, and the flesh holds, but I fumble in my pocket for the slip of paper with the dirty dot on it. Swiping my thumb across the dot—*yes, this is the way it was, I remember more of it now*—I mix blood and graphite to form a better bond, and I feel warmth flow back into my hand.

The room goes dark—sunburst starburst blackstar blackout—and I lose sight of the harvesters.

This world is done.

But the fingers of my left hand move when I ask them to, and my new palm itches. As we are burnblackened by the anguished exhalation of the abandoned sun, I reach out with my new hand.

I reach out, and find the way.

What was is no more.

But I continue on.

* boom boom
p. 132

*and on and on and on . . .*

( * )

A hypertext variant of this text appeared online at *Farrago's Wainscot* in 2007. This edition has been thoroughly tempered and transformed in the process of conforming a non-linear narrative into a linear presentation.

The hauntvine made its first appearance in the pages of *The Field Guide to Surreal Botany* (Two Cranes Press: Singapore, 2008).

This is R004, and it has an ISBN of 978-1-63023-016-6.

This book was printed in the United States of America, and it is published by ROTA Books, an imprint of Resurrection House (Puyallup, WA).

*she loves me she loves me not she loves me*

Editorial Assistance provided by Darin Bradley
Cover Art and Design by Neal Von Flue

First ROTA Books edition: May 2016.

www.rotabooks.com
www.resurrectionhouse.com

This one is for Neal Von Flue, who has been an exceptionally generous and gracious collaborator, these many years.

Thank you, sir.

DREAM: "Four people are going down a river: the dreamer, his father, a certain friend, and the unknown woman."

ANALYSIS: "The unconscious has been depotentiated. The reason for this is that by 'taking the plunge' the dreamer has connected the upper and lower regions–that is to say, he has decided not to live only as a bodiless abstract being but to accept the body and the world of instinct, the reality of the problems posed by love and life, and to act accordingly. This was the Rubicon that was crossed. Individuation, becoming a self, is not only a spiritual problem, it is the problem of all life."

–Jung, Carl Gustav, *Psychology and Alchemy* (Princeton Unversity Press: Princeton, 1980), p. 123

CPSIA information can be obtained at www.ICGtesting.com
Printed in the USA
LVOW11s1728170416

483595LV00004B/9/P

9 781630 230166